Daughter of the Sunset Isles

DINAH DEAN

Daughter of the Sunset Isles

BARRIE & JENKINS
LONDON

First published in 1991 by Barrie & Jenkins Ltd,
Random Century House, 20 Vauxhall Bridge Road
London SW1V 2SA

This book is a work of fiction. Any resemblance between the
characters portrayed and real persons, living or dead, is purely
coincidental.

The right of Dinah Dean to be identified as author of this work
has been asserted by her in accordance with the Copyright,
Designs and Patents Act, 1988.

British Library Cataloguing in Publication Data
Dean, Dinah
Daughter of the sunset isles
I. Title
823.914 [F]

ISBN 0-7126-3458-4

Phototypeset in Linotronic Baskerville by
SX Composing Ltd, Rayleigh, Essex

Printed and bound in Great Britain by
Mackays of Chatham PLC, Chatham, Kent

*In grateful remembrance of all the priests and deacons
who have served Waltham Holy Cross in Essex
in the past ten centuries*

CONTENTS

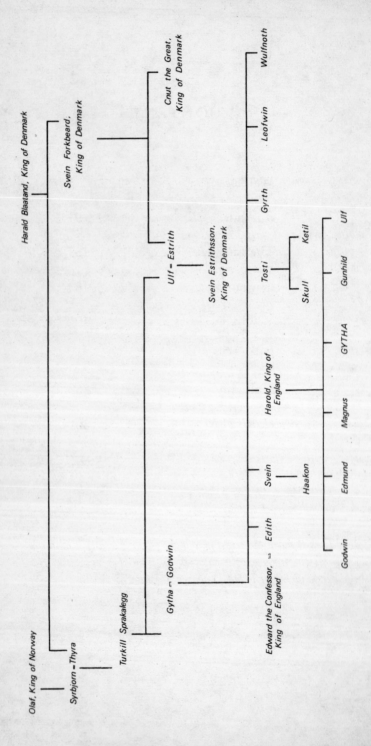

GYTHA'S FAMILY

'Six of them,' said Father Turkill quietly. 'Two to serve the Lord, two to serve a king, and two to travel far beyond the sunrise.'

Father Osgod, who was polishing a silver almsdish with his thumb, looked up in surprise. It was quite half an hour since either priest had last spoken, for Turkill had been counting his stock of candles.

'Another of your seeings?' he asked, his harsh northern accent sounding overloud in the sacristy of the great church.

'I don't always see, exactly,' Turkill replied. 'Usually it just enters my head, rather like a memory of someone saying it.'

'You can't have a memory of something that hasn't happened yet,' Osgod objected.

'That's the nearest I can come to describing it,' Turkill said apologetically.

'What does it mean this time, any road?'

'I don't know. All I can say is that it's to do with King Harold's children.'

'Well, they are six, to be sure – Godwin, Edmund, Magnus, Gytha, Gunhild and little Ulf.'

Turkill nodded. 'And their fates will be as I said.'

Osgod crossed himself, twitched his nose and resumed polishing, frowning uneasily.

Turkill noted the crossing and the frown ruefully, and began counting his current box of candles again from the beginning. He did not understand his gift, but he was not afraid of it.

Waltham

Chapter One

The great willow stood by the bend in the mill-stream, where it turned to border the garth of Earl Harold's hall at Waltham. Audrey stood by it and looked about her anxiously. The child had been here playing among the roots of the tree, not a quarter-hour before, but now she had vanished.

'Gytha!' she called. 'Gytha, where are you? Your father is here!'

'My father can't come. He's busy,' replied a solemn little voice, apparently from beneath the grass at Audrey's feet. The nursemaid crossed herself as she looked down and gave a gasp, partly of relief and partly annoyance, as she met the clear eyes, each sky-blue iris ringed with a darker circle, which were gazing up at her over the edge of the bank of the stream.

'Oh, you naughty girl! You gave me a fright! Whatever are you doing down there?'

'Making mud pies,' Gytha replied, taking the question literally.

'Just mind you don't fall in!' Audrey exclaimed, starting forward to the edge of the bank.

'I won't,' the child said calmly. 'It's not deep here.' Looking down, Audrey saw that the stream was low, for the two mills had been grinding all morning and the water barely lapped the little beach where Gytha had made a neat row of mud-pies decorated with pebbles.

'Now come home at once!' Audrey scolded. 'You've to put on your best gown and have your face and hands washed and your hair brushed, and your father's waiting!' She seized Gytha's wrist and hurried her across the garth, dodging between the various huts which stood round it, heading towards the great turf-walled longhouse, which was older than anyone living in Waltham could remember.

Gytha, trotting along to keep up, looked sharply about her for signs of new arrivals, and saw strange horses being led to the stables and unfamiliar figures among the scurrying servants. 'Where's Father?' she asked. 'In the hall? Let's go straight there.'

'With mud all over you, and your old gown on and your hair in tangles?' Audrey sniffed. 'A fine sight you'd be for Earl Harold to see! To the bower first, and then to the hall when you're fit to be seen.'

A quick scrub with a damp linen towel removed the mud from the child's face and hands, and she had the sense to stand still while Audrey dressed her in her best blue woollen with the pretty red and white braid trimming, and combed out her long hair, which was as yellow as new butter.

'Will I do?' she asked solemnly as Audrey stepped back to inspect the finished picture. She was tall for a six-year-old and had lost her baby plumpness, so that she looked like an elfin princess, Audrey thought, with her wiry body, pale golden hair, and those wide blue eyes huge in her little pointed face.

'Yes, you'll do well enough,' Audrey replied consideringly. 'Mind your manners, now! You call your father *my lord*, and don't speak until you're spoken to. Your brothers have come as well, and some of your father's important friends, so you're to be very good and quiet.'

'Yes,' Gytha said, looking a little anxious. 'Shall I say *my lord* in Latin, French or English?'

'English, of course, and don't show off!' Audrey replied sharply. 'Come along now, and don't keep him waiting any longer, or he'll be angry!'

'He hasn't been here for a long time,' Gytha said very quietly during the short walk from the bower to the ceremonial entrance at the far end of the hall. 'I don't know if I can remember him.'

'Of course you can!' Audrey said scornfully. 'It's not half a year since he was last here.'

The hall doors stood open, for it was a warm, sunny spring day. Coming in from the bright sunshine, Gytha could hardly see anything at first, for the windows were few and small, mere shuttered openings in the thick turf walls, but as she walked forward in a dignified manner as she had been taught, her sight gradually adjusted, and she saw that her father's great chair had been moved from the dais at the far end to stand by the hearth in the middle of the hall, where the fire was laid but not yet lit. Her father sat there, with two-year-old Gunhild on his knee and eight-year-old Magnus standing before him. Lady Edith sat on a stool beside the chair, and two strange boys stood behind her, watching Magnus, who was reciting Latin.

Earl Harold's eyes moved from his youngest son's face to look beyond him at the newcomer, and he said, 'Very good, Magnus. You're working hard at your lessons, I can tell. And here is Gytha.'

He rose to his feet, gently transferring Gunhild to her mother's waiting arms, and advanced to meet Gytha, dropping down on one knee as they met, which brought his face on a level with hers. His hair was a darker gold than his daughter's, and his eyes a darker blue, but there was a strong resemblance between the two faces which gazed seriously at each other for a few seconds.

'Well, Gytha, do you remember me?' he asked quietly.

'You've been busy a long time,' she replied, then, remembering Audrey's instructions, added 'my lord'. She frowned a little, studying his weathered face and the thick moustache which framed a firm mouth and chin. 'I do remember you,' she said at last, with some relief, and a surge of affection which made her stroke his cheek with her fingertips.

He smiled. 'Will you kiss me, then?'

'Yes, my lord.'

'You usually call me Father.'

'Audrey said I was to say "my lord", but I like "Father" better.' She stepped forward and kissed the moustache, which tickled pleasantly, for it was soft and silky, then put her arms round his neck in a strangling embrace.

5

He hugged her slight body tightly, and said, his voice muffled in her hair, 'You're thinner than you were last year!'

'That's because I've stopped being a baby and turned into a girl,' she explained. 'You're not thin. You're solid and hard, like a tree trunk.'

Earl Harold laughed and stood up, lifting the child in his arms, and turned to Lady Edith, looking from her still-lovely face to Gytha's and back again.

'Our elder daughter promises to be as beautiful as her mother,' he said. 'Now, Gytha – do you remember Godwin and Edmund?'

Gytha regarded her elder brothers thoughtfully, and then said, 'They've grown a lot, and Godwin looks quite old.'

'I'm sixteen,' Godwin admitted, amused. 'I'm a man now, so of course I look old!'

'You haven't got a moustache yet,' Gytha replied, peering to see if there was any sign of that requisite badge of manhood.

'I soon will have,' Godwin assured her. 'You've grown a lot, too. So has Edmund.'

Edmund, who was fourteen, said nothing, for he found children difficult to talk to now he was poised on the uncomfortable line between childhood and manhood, but he nodded and forced a wooden-looking smile, then, feeling his father's eyes upon him, he made a great effort and managed a gruff, 'You were a pudgy little thing last time I saw you. I suppose you must be five by now.'

'Six!' Gytha corrected sharply, and her mouth and chin firmed suddenly in her indignation, strengthening her resemblance to her father. Lady Edith laughed to see the two loved faces close together and so much alike.

'Where have you been?' asked Magnus, looking enviously at the jewelled daggers which his brothers wore hanging from their belts. 'Have you been learning to be soldiers like Father?'

'We've been at the King's court with Aunt Edith – the Lady,' Edmund replied, adding his father's sister's title as the king's wife for greater clarity, for it was confusing having mother and aunt with the same name. 'We've learned all sorts of things. Godwin can wield a battle-axe, and I shall learn too, when I'm bigger and stronger.'

'A *real* battle-axe?' Magnus asked, wide-eyed. 'I can't even lift one!'

'You're still quite little,' Godwin said kindly. 'You'll be able to when you're as old as I am.'

'No, I won't!' Magnus said, suddenly confident and no longer overawed by his elders. 'I'm going to be a priest, so I shan't need to learn about swords and battle-axes.'

'A priest?' Earl Harold asked questioningly, sitting down again in his great chair and setting Gytha on her feet beside him, but still keeping an arm about her shoulders. 'Have you told Master Athelard?'

'Yes. He says I'll have to work hard at my studies,' Magnus replied. 'He thinks I can learn enough, though. He knows all about everything, so he can teach me all I need to know.'

'It would be good to have a priest in the family,' said Earl Harold. 'Perhaps you'll be a bishop one day.'

'An *arch*bishop!' said Gytha firmly, for she had learned of this superior variety of bishop during the past week. 'An *arch*bishop's more important. We only have two of them at a time!'

'Two in England,' her father said absently. 'Other countries have them as well. Have you ever seen one?'

'No. What do they look like?' Gytha asked, hoping for a description of something strange and wonderful, like the man with an eye in the middle of his forehead in Father Wulfwin's bestiary, or even the man with one huge foot, which he used to shelter himself from the rain.

'You'll see later today,' Earl Harold said, smiling. 'Archbishop Kinsey of York is coming here to consecrate the new church. And someone even more important! Can you guess whom that might be?'

'Nobody's more important than an archbishop,' said Magnus positively, 'except the Pope! Is the Pope coming?'

'No, but the King is! He'll attend the consecration, and he hopes for a few days' hunting while he's here. He'll have to

7

leave after the octave, for he must wear his crown in Winchester at Pentecost.'

'Doesn't he wear his crown all the time?' asked Gytha, for she had always assumed that he did, underneath the hat which he had been wearing on the two or three occasions when she had seen him.

Edmund laughed scornfully, and exclaimed, 'Silly goose! Of course not! He wears it three times a year. Fancy you not knowing that!'

Earl Harold turned an icy blue gaze on his second son, and said coldly, 'You may feel yourself entitled to laugh at your sister when you achieve perfection yourself, *child*! I gather from Master Athelard that Gytha's Latin is much superior to yours at the age of six, and her manners are better than yours at your present age!'

Edmund flushed, stood on one leg, busied himself in making sure that his belt was properly buckled and murmured a gruff apology, and there followed an awkward silence. The children had been well disciplined all their lives, and their father had so rarely had cause to reprove any one of them that the present occasion was an awesome event. Gytha felt sorry for Edmund, and presently, when Lady Edith had hurriedly started to tell of Gunhild's latest achievement, she edged over to him and slipped one of her greatest treasures into his hand. It was a pretty shiny blue bead flecked with gold, which she carried in her purse.

'Why, what's this?' Edmund exclaimed, looking at it from various angles.

'It's a present for you,' Gytha whispered. 'Father Turkill gave it to me. He found it in his garden.'

'What's that?' asked Earl Harold. Edmund showed him the bead, and he said, 'It's a lapis lazuli! I expect it came from Egypt. Turkill found it in his garden, you say? I wonder how it came there.'

'He said an old Roman lady lost it when her necklace broke,' Gytha explained.

'That would explain it,' Earl Harold replied gravely, handing it back to Edmund. Everyone was satisfied, for they all knew that Father Turkill, the Sacristan, had the gift of sight beyond normal limits, and would often look vaguely at nothing for a few moments, then speak briefly about something which had happened long ago, or would happen in the future. Edmund looked at the bead again, wondering what to do with it, and then said, 'Thank you, Gytha. It's very pretty, but I might lose it. Will you look after it for me?'

The slightest flicker of a smile passed between his parents at this unexpected diplomacy, and Gytha received back her treasure with great satisfaction, and put it carefully into her purse.

'This won't do!' Earl Harold exclaimed. 'The King will be here in an hour or so. He'll sup with us, of course, but his own people will tend the rest of his needs, and I must see that they have all they need. I've told them to put up his pavilions in the north mead, just across the mill-stream. The hay will have time to recover before mowing time, if it doesn't rain too much while he's here.' He strode purposefully down the hall, calling his steward as he went.

King Edward arrived later that afternoon, with his wife, Earl Harold's sister Edith, Kinsey of York, the Bishops of Sherborne, Wilton, Exeter, London, Elmham, Lichfield, Dorchester, Durham, Selsey, Hereford and Wells, eleven abbots, Earl Harold's three brothers, Tosti, Gyrth and Leofwin, Earl Alfgar of Mercia and what seemed to Gytha to be an enormous number of other important men and their servants.

She watched the procession arrive with her mother, Magnus and Gunhild from a vantage point behind the mill, and saw her father, with Godwin and Edmund behind him, greet the King and all the others in an easy, friendly fashion, which made her think that he must be very important in that unknown world away from Waltham to be able to smile and talk so readily to such great folk.

It was only as the procession passed on, with her father walking beside the King's horse and talking to him, with one hand on the fine beast's bridle, that it occurred to her that something was missing. Usually, when guests arrived at Waltham, her mother greeted them . . .

'Mother,' she said, tugging at Lady Edith's sleeve, 'why aren't you with Father?'

'Because . . .' Edith began, looking down into her daughter's puzzled face. Then she hesitated, biting her lip, and presently said casually, 'Magnus, would you please take Gunhild back to Audrey for me, and then you may go to see the King's horses, if you don't get in the way.'

Magnus, willingly enough, took his little sister's hand in a firm grip and walked slowly away, matching his pace to her still uncertain steps. Edith watched them out of sight, then sat down on the low wall which edged the mill-stream at this point, drew Gytha closer to her, and said, 'The King doesn't like to see me with your father. You see, your father and I are married in the Danish fashion, not in church, and the King doesn't approve of it.'

'I thought people always got married in church,' Gytha said, her brow creased in puzzlement.

'Not always. In law, it's enough for a man and a woman to say in the hearing of other people that they take one another as husband and wife, and their children have the same rights as if they had been married by a priest.'

'Then why don't they have a priest?'

'Because then it would be almost impossible to end the marriage later, if – if it became necessary.'

'Why would they want to end it?'

'Perhaps they might find that they don't like each other after all . . .' Edith paused, thinking, then made up her mind to tell the whole truth, hoping the child would understand. 'You see, your father is a very important man. He stands next to the King all over England, as his chief adviser and the commander of his army. I'm not important. I'm just the daughter of the steward of one of his many estates. I'm very lucky that he chose to marry me at all, even in the Danish fashion, but he did because he loves me and he wants our children to have a rightful place in the world. One day, though, he'll probably have to marry someone else, a lady of his own rank, and he must be free to do so when the time comes.'

'Why? He can't do that! How could he want to marry someone else?' Gytha was bewildered and anxious, her eyes filling with tears.

'Can you keep a secret?'

'Of course I can!' she replied, moving closer and blinking back her tears.

'Well, the King and the Lady have no children.'

'I know.'

'One day the King will die, and there must be someone to follow him, or goodness knows what will happen! You see, King Edward has no brothers now. He had seven brothers once, but they've all died, over the years, and only one of them had a son.'

'Then the son can be the next king!' Gytha said. 'Where is he?'

'He was sent a long way away, to a far country, when Cnut came to be King of England. Three years ago, the King asked him to come back to England, and he came, with his children, but he died soon after he arrived. He had a son, Edgar the Atheling, but he's only a little boy, much the same age as Magnus. He couldn't rule England, or lead the army, until he's much older.'

'Won't he be old enough when the King dies?'

'The King is very old – past fifty-five – and few men live to be as old as sixty. He would have to live to be more than seventy for Edgar to be old enough to rule. There must be someone else for the Witan to choose.'

'The Witan? That's the King's council, isn't it? Master Athelard told me about it. Father belongs to it.'

'All the great men of the land belong to it. They are the wise men who help the King to govern. When a king dies, it's their right and duty to choose someone to take his place. They must choose a man who will be able to govern well and protect the country from our enemies. Sometimes in the past they've chosen a boy because there wasn't anyone else, but it's always led to great trouble, and I don't think they'll ever do it again. It says in the Bible, *Woe to the kingdom whose king is a child!*'

Gytha pondered for some time, while her mother waited, hoping she would not have to say anything more. She watched the little changes of expression in the child's face as gradually her thoughts sorted themselves into order. 'You mean that Father might have to marry someone who could be . . . the Lady?' she said.

Edith was amazed at the sharpness of the child's understanding, for she had not only grasped that her father might one day be king, but had connected that with the earlier part of the conversation. She nodded, slowly and significantly.

'I shall pray that the King lives to be a hundred, so that Lord Edgar will be quite old enough when the time comes,' Gytha said firmly. 'Then Father won't have to leave us and marry someone else.'

'He wouldn't leave you or the others,' Edith said quickly. 'Only me.'

'But he can't – he mustn't!' The child's eyes filled again. 'What would you do? I won't let him leave you!'

Edith sighed. 'We can't, any of us, do as we please all the time. Your father is a very important man, and he has to pay for that sometimes by doing things that are hard for him. I've always known that I wouldn't have him for long, that some day he would have to marry someone else. I've been very lucky that I've had twenty years of happiness with him, but I'm ready to let him go when the time comes, and I've told you now so that you'll be ready, too. He won't ever leave you – you need have no fear of that! As for me – I shall go to a nunnery. The Lady Edith has said that I may go to Wilton if – if I ever need or wish to be a nun. She's refounded the house there, but it's very old, and many great ladies – even the daughters and widows of kings have been nuns there, so it's a great honour to be admitted. We'll say no more about this, Gytha, and we'll keep it a secret, just between the two of us, for it may never happen, and it wouldn't do to talk about it. The King's well and strong, and some men do live to be very, very old. He doesn't lead the army, so it's not likely that he will be killed in battle.'

She spoke cheerfully and with confidence, and failed to notice that Gytha gave her a sudden sharp, shocked glance. It did not occur to her then, or after, that her words, meant to reassure, had in fact conveyed to her daughter that the man who did lead the army might be killed, and that was her father.

Gytha had much to think about, so, when her mother gave her leave to go, she went to the church, which she thought, with so many guests about, would probably be the only quiet place in Waltham. The new building was just finished and not yet consecrated, but the preparations for that great event were almost completed, and only Turkill was there, spreading the dozen new altar cloths on the new altar, one after another, trying to decide which should adorn it after the Archbishop had blessed it. He was too absorbed in the problem to notice Gytha as she slipped in through the wicket of the great west door and went to sit on the wall bench in one corner, which was her favourite thinking-place.

She had understood most of what Edith had told her, but it was a shock to her to know that her father was so important that he might one day be king, and, if that happened, he would have to take another wife. It was something to cry over, and she did cry, her body shaking with almost silent sobs. Then she prayed about it, as she had been taught, but she was too young to understand all the implications, or to realise that her own life might be greatly changed if her father became king.

During the building of the church, a temporary wooden chapel had been erected in the churchyard for services and to enable each of the priests to say his daily Mass, and Turkill, who never forgot the important things, however absorbed he might be in his Sacristan's duties or his visions, had his turn to use one of the altars in the chapel an hour before supper. In good time, he put away the altar cloths and walked silently down the nave to lock the west door before he went to robe for Mass. He saw Gytha in her corner and went to stand beside her.

'You're troubled, child?' he asked softly.

'Yes, Father.' She sniffed and scrubbed her eyes with her fists.

He waited in sympathetic silence, but she said only, 'It will all come out right, won't it?'

'It will go as God wills,' he replied, 'and God's will is always for the best in the end. We may not like it at the time, but we must be patient and brave.'

Gytha did not like the sound of that at all, and *in the end* could be a very long time. Turkill read her face easily enough, and rested a gentle, kindly hand on her head in blessing for a moment.

'You mustn't be late for supper,' he said. 'Your father wants you to do something special for him, so perhaps you should go now.'

Gytha accepted that Turkill *knew* about her father's wishes, so she hurried out of the church and picked her way through the throng of scurrying servants who were still unloading their various masters' belongings from the wagons and taking them to the pavilions. Savoury smells issued from the kitchen buildings, and, through the open doors of the hall, she could see the trestle tables set up and the household servants putting out the trenchers and drinking cups for a great many people.

She rarely ate supper in the hall, and never when guests were here, for even Magnus was considered too young for that, so she went to the bower, where a single table had been set for Gunhild, Magnus and herself, Audrey, and, to her surprise, her mother. She remembered in time to stop herself from asking why Edith would not be welcome to sit at a table with King Edward, but then she noticed a sixth place, and exclaimed, 'Is someone else going to eat with us?'

'Your aunt, the Lady, has asked if she may join us,' Edith replied quietly. She flushed a little as she spoke, for the King's attitude to her was a matter of some secret bitterness to her, and the Lady Edith's kindness a solace. 'Gytha, do you remember that at Christmas you carried the cup to Bishop William when he came to look at the new church?'

'Yes.' Gytha did indeed remember, for it had been a great occasion for her. It was the duty of the senior lady of the house to serve a ceremonial cup of wine to an honoured guest at the start of a feast, and she had been carefully coached and re-hearsed for the task at the time, wondering all the while why she was doing it instead of her mother. Now she knew the reason.

'Your father would like you to do it again, but only if you feel that you could manage it.'

'To Bishop William?'

'No. It will be the King this time.'

One of Harold's clerks came to fetch Gytha as the guests went into the hall for the feast. He stood outside the door with her, holding her hand with the idea of comforting and steadying her, but she was too excited by the honour ahead to be nervous. She jigged up and down a little as she waited for all the great men and the not quite so great to take their places.

There was a hubbub of voices, which suddenly changed to a reverent silence, and the old Archbishop's slightly quavering voice rang out in a long Latin grace, which, thanks to Master Athelard's good teaching, she understood better than many of the adults within the hall. Then there was a scraping of benches, stools and chairs, and talking, more muted now, began again. Harold's household steward peered round the doorpost, beckoned to her, and gave her the golden goblet with its jewelled cover that was used only for really important guests.

'The King is next to your father, in the middle of the table, with the silver beard,' he said hastily. 'Walk slowly, mind, and don't trip on your skirt going up the step, or coming down!'

Gytha nodded, took a good grip on the stem of the goblet with one hand, and put the other on top of the lid, which did not fit quite perfectly, for she remembered that it had given her a fright by wobbling last time.

'Now?' she asked.

'Just a moment . . .' The steward flicked a long strand of hair back over her shoulder, and straightened her gold circlet. 'Now!'

It seemed a very long way up the hall, and there was the hearth in the middle to negotiate, but once she was safely past it, she looked towards the dais and was comforted by the sight of several familiar faces. Bishop William was there, of course, looking as calm and absent-minded as ever, and Archbishop Kinsey, smiling encouragingly. Her uncles Gyrth and Leofwin sat one at either end of the table, also smiling at her, and her father was watching with a faint frown of anxiety, so that she could not help smiling at him to tell him that all would be well.

Then she turned her attention to the man on his right, who was tall, with long silver hair and beard framing a placid, rather expressionless face with such clear, transparent skin that the blood seemed to shine through it, and pale, sad blue eyes. She fixed her gaze firmly on his face, and forgot about everyone else as she advanced, quite slowly, towards him.

There were two steps up to the dais, and she could not lift her long skirt, for both hands were needed for the heavy goblet, but she remembered the trick of kicking forward which her mother had taught her, and successfully walked up the steps, not the inside of her skirt. Biting her lip with concentration, she gave a stiff little bow, and then stared severely into the King's face, waiting for his response. A faint smile appeared on the bearded face, and he bowed his head in response. Bishop William had given her only a little nod last time, she recalled.

Her own ready smile lit her face, and she carefully deposited the cup on the table, as close to King Edward as she could reach, and piped up clearly, 'Welcome to our home, my Lord King!'

'I thank you for your welcome, my niece,' he replied gravely.

They bowed to each other again, and Gytha, greatly relieved that she had not dropped the cup or forgotten what to say, turned and skipped down the steps, recollected herself, and walked sedately back down the long hall. For some reason, everyone clapped or banged on the tables, but it did not occur to her that they were applauding her, for all her attention was on reaching the door without tripping over anything.

As soon as she did reach it, she ran back to the bower, feeling suddenly very hungry and ready for her supper, but there was another ceremony to go through before she could eat. The Lady Edith was in the bower, and Gytha had to make her reverence to her, of course, and, inflated by her success in the hall, she added, 'Welcome to our home, Lady Edith,' for good measure.

'Aunt Edith, sweetheart, in the privacy of this bower!' the Lady replied, hugging and kissing her. The King's wife was much younger than her husband, and dearly loved children, but had none of her own, for it was well known that King Edward had taken a vow of chastity before his marriage. What the Lady Edith felt about it, no one knew or cared to speculate, but her affection for her brothers' children, both Harold's brood and Tosti's two sons, was deeply and freely indulged when she had the opportunity to be with them. Although her husband disapproved of Harold's irregular liaison, she always treated her namesake at Waltham with consideration and friendship.

Supper consisted of fish and vegetable dishes, as it was Friday, but the cooks had prepared a variety of herb stuffings for the carp and trout, and there was a serving of smoked herring to vary the taste. The children ate in silence, as they had been taught, but the two Ediths talked freely and in friendly ease about household matters and other topics.

The Lady had recently visited the abbey she had refounded at Wilton to inspect the rebuilding, and had brought her brother's wife a beautiful linen smock which the nuns had embroidered.

'They do a little secular work to help earn their keep,' she said, 'but I've brought some of their altar linen as well, for the new church. How quickly Harold's masons have worked! The King's new church on Thorney Island is far from being finished. They talk of five or six years more of work.'

'But the King's minster is a deal bigger than ours,' Edith pointed out, 'and we had the advantage of the old church also being of stone, so the same foundations could be used. Digging the trenches and making a strong foundation takes much time and labour. How grand the King's minster will be! Does he mean to make it a college of secular priests, like Waltham?'

'No. It will be a Benedictine abbey, as was the old church which it replaces. The King has great respect for the Order. Now, Gytha,' turning unexpectedly to her niece, 'how did your little task go? Did you do it well?'

'I – I think so, Aunt Edith,' Gytha replied, stammering a little because she could not recall ever before having been invited to speak while at table. 'Uncle – the King – smiled at me.'

The children did not venture to speak again, and they were not invited to do so, but they were allowed to play a noisy game of spillikins with their aunt before they went to bed, and the Lady heard them say their prayers and kissed them as she tucked them into their little truckles. Then she and her namesake went out of the bower and found a quiet corner in the orchard to continue their conversation.

The men intended to go hunting in the morning, after Mass, so the feast did not continue to a late hour. Harold escorted his royal brother-in-law to his pavilion, and stayed talking to him about Monday's ceremony for a while before walking through the warm spring night, threading his way between the pavilions in the meadow, to visit the horse-lines to see that the grooms had all they needed. He then went to the new church to pray before the great crucifix which hung in the chancel arch of the crossing.

The Cross had been covered with silver many years before, and now gleamed softly in the light of the candles which were kept burning beneath it day and night. Harold knelt on the new stone-flagged floor, praying, his eyes on the Figure of Christ in Glory, carved in black stone, crowned with golden thorns, with a great ruby glowing in the subpedaneum which supported His feet. Turkill, who slept in the sacristy, crept out to see who was there, paused to say a silent blessing on the Earl, and stood transfixed with joy as his gift allowed him a glimpse of the heights to which the Earl would ascend. Then he crept back to his pallet, murmuring the *Te Deum* under his breath.

Presently Harold arose, at peace within himself, left the building, and went towards the small house which he shared with Edith when he was at home. At the door, he checked, thought for a moment, and then went to the bower. A guard stood outside the door, but he only nodded in greeting, recognising his lord in the moonlight, and Harold quietly entered.

A tallow dip burned dimly by the hearth for a nightlight, and by its faint gleam Harold went to his elder daughter's bed and knelt beside it. She was still awake, her mind grappling with the new knowledge she had acquired that afternoon. She stirred and sat up.

'Father?' she whispered.

'I wanted to tell you that I was proud of you tonight,' he said quietly. 'You're a good girl, Gytha, and a credit to your mother and to me. Your royal blood showed in every movement you made in the hall.'

'Royal?' she queried, puzzled.

'Your grandmother, my mother, is descended from the kings of Denmark. Her great-grandfather was King Harald Bluetooth, and King Svein of Denmark is her brother's son. Never forget that, Gytha. Your cousin is a king, and your descent is royal. Goodnight, my little princess.'

He kissed her, his moustache tickling her face, and he touched her cheek gently with one finger as he murmured a blessing.

'Father?' she said as he turned to leave.

'Yes?'

'You won't go away from me, will you?'

'What do you mean, sweetheart? I have to go away, but I always come back when I can.'

'I mean – you won't stop coming back?'

'Of course not. This is my home, and you're my dearest daughter. I'll always want to be here with you, and I'll come as often as I possibly can.'

'Yes. God bless you, Father.'

'And you, my sweet. Goodnight.'

The ceremony three days later was the greatest occasion Waltham had ever seen, with so many great and splendid figures taking part, all magnificently dressed. The bishops, of course, were all in fine embroidered capes with a great deal of goldwork, and the congregation in their best clothes, with much gold and silver jewellery in evidence. Earl Harold wore a jewelled gold circlet on his head, like a small crown, and King

Edward, a magnificent sight in a purple robe with heavy gold embroidery, wore the real crown, the actual Crown of England, on his silver hair.

After the Archbishop had gone round with a procession of bishops, blessing the crosses cut in the stone of the building, both outside and inside, he blessed the threshold, then returned to the high altar and consecrated it to the honour of the Holy Cross. After that, there were the altars of the side-chapels in the transepts and aisles to be consecrated, each bishop going to pronounce the proper words and prayers over one, so that all could be done at the same time.

Mass followed, and then a lengthy ceremony during which the office-holders of the new minster were officially appointed, and charters presented by the King and Earl Harold to the new Dean, Father Wulfwin. Finally, a great iron-bound chest was brought in by six of Harold's strongest soldiers, and was presented to the new church. It contained many relics of saints, as well as more altar vessels and crucifixes of gold and silver, which Harold had obtained some time before, during his pilgrimage to Rome, and kept for this day. Dean Wulfwin received the treasures with great delight and amazement, for he had not known that such precious things as the relics were to be entrusted to the new college. He touched the linen-wrapped bundles of bones with awed reverence, obviously considering the gold and silver ornaments to be comparatively trivial things beside them.

By now, Gunhild was asleep in Edith's arms, Magnus was fidgeting and looking about for some way to escape unnoticed in order to relieve himself and Gytha was wondering what had happened about dinner, which was usually eaten an hour before noon, for it must be well past time.

At last the final blessings were spoken, and the clergy processed out of the church with solemn dignity, followed by King Edward and the Lady Edith. When they had passed, Harold turned to gesture to his sons and daughter to follow him and their mother as they led out the earls and the other great men. Gytha stumbled as she set off, for her right foot had gone to sleep and gave way under her, but Godwin shot out a hand and steadied her in time to preserve her dignity.

Dinner awaited Harold and all his guests in the hall, and in a couple of pavilions for the lesser folk, including the representative townsmen. To judge by the red faces and anguished expressions of the cooks, scullions and servitors, who had been on their feet since before dawn, the strain of feeding so many was wearing them out. Edith and the children ate in peace in the bower, and after dinner Magnus and Gytha were given leave to go out into the town to see how the folk were celebrating.

Everyone had been given (or had taken) a day's holiday from all but the most essential tasks, although cows, sheep and goats had still to be milked, and Harold had given two fine bucks to be roasted over a fire-pit on the open ground outside the churchyard gate. The townsfolk hoped that one day they might be allowed to have a fair there, or even a market, and were careful to see that nobody presumed to build on the ground, which was useful, in any case, for celebrations of the present kind. Harold had also given two great barrels of good Rhenish wine, one of which was set up by the roasting-pit, and the other at the crossroads just outside the town, and anyone was free to drink from them.

The two children were, of course, recognised by the people, who cheered them and gave them cups of wine and thick, juicy slices of venison on bread trenchers. Magnus, with a boy's appetite, munched happily, with gravy running down his chin, but Gytha wished she had taken less dinner, as she did not wish to offend the people by not eating the food, and succeeded in smuggling most of it unnoticed into the ready jaws of the blacksmith's dog.

The feasting and celebrating continued all day until quite late in the evening, but the morrow was an ordinary working-day for the townsfolk, and many of the guests were to depart in the morning, so the merrymaking subsided at sunset. The King and his immediate companions stayed on, for they meant to keep the whole octave of the feast of the Invention of the Holy Cross at Waltham, not so much in feasting and celebration as in quiet prayer and meditation, interspersed with a fair amount of hunting.

During the week there were two wet days when, instead of hunting, the King, Harold and the other great men sat in the hall, talking. Gytha, playing quietly with her dolls at the back of the dais, listened and watched. Most of what they said was beyond her understanding, but she found the differences in character and manner of these important men strangely fascinating.

Her favourite, after her father, was Lord Ansgar, who was the leader of the King's military élite, the housecarls. He was tall, fair and lean, with a quiet, watchful manner, and seldom had much to say, but when he did speak, the others listened attentively. Her uncles Gyrth and Leofwin were as well built and handsome as her father, but Gyrth was a forceful man with plenty to say, not all of it to the point or well thought out, and Leofwin was very quiet and thoughtful, slow-spoken, and inclined to pause frequently, when he did speak, to consider every word, but what little he did say was sensible.

Earl Tosti, although he was also her uncle and next in age to her father, Gytha disliked. He was very handsome and charming, with a ready smile and a smooth, persuasive voice, but Gytha instinctively distrusted the way he looked from one speaker to another, weighing every word, watching expressions, yet avoiding meeting anyone's eyes in direct and open gaze. He was on very good terms with her father, so she supposed he must be a good man, but later, when she was older, she remembered her first, unfavourable, impression of him, and realised that it had been right.

The only earl who was not a Godwinsson, Alfgar, she thought a very strange man. He was a Mercian, dark, fiery and intense, spoke volubly and over-energetically, but seemed to change his mind a great deal, arguing against whatever one of the others had said one moment, but going on to propose exactly the same thing himself a few moments later. The others often glanced uneasily at one another while he was talking, and avoided contradicting him directly, but to little avail, as even the most tactful disagreement seemed to throw him into a passion, when he thumped on the table and shouted.

After one of these conversations, when the others had gone, Harold turned in his great chair and said, 'Gytha, are you still here?'

'Yes, Father,' she replied, going to stand in front of him, a wooden doll in each hand.

'What did you think of all that?' he asked, smiling.

'My dolls don't like the black man,' she said firmly. 'He shouted at Uncle Gyrth.'

'That was Earl Alfgar of Mercia. He loses his temper,' Harold said, as if that explained everything.

'I don't like people who shout,' she said.

'Shouting certainly doesn't help to solve any problems, but it sometimes makes an angry person feel better,' Harold observed with a slight smile. 'You lose your temper sometimes, and no doubt you shout, too.'

'He didn't look as if he felt better. Anyway, I don't like him. He's bad and cross, not good like you.'

'Good?' Harold was taken aback. 'I'm not good, Gytha!'

'Yes, you are. Everyone in the town after the big service on Monday said how good you are, and Father Turkill said this morning that you were good to give the church all those lovely things. He was polishing the new silver, and he said you've made our church the finest in England!'

'That doesn't make me a good man, my dear! I'm a rich man – it's easy for me to give things to the church, or the poor, but giving other people a little of what you have doesn't make you good. It's the sort of person you are that counts. I have many, many faults. I'm very ambitious, for one thing. Do you know what *ambitious* means?'

Gytha considered the word, looking at the expressionless faces of her dolls for inspiration, then admitted, 'I don't think I've heard that word before.'

'It means that I know what I can do well, and I want the chance to do it, even if it might hurt other people.'

Gytha mulled that over for a few moments, then said,

'Master Athelard says that we should try to do everything as well as we possibly can, whether we're good at it or not, because that's what God wants us to do.'

Harold sighed. 'Yes, but what if we only think we can do it well, and push out someone else who might do it better?'

He could see from the expression on the child's face that this was becoming too difficult for her, so he shook his head and said, 'Never mind, sweetheart! I wish you were older, so that I could discuss these things with you. You're easier to talk to than the others. Godwin and Edmund seem to be interested only in learning to be soldiers, and Magnus wants to be doing things, not talking about them!'

'I shall get older,' Gytha said gravely, making it sound more like a promise than a statement of fact.

For nearly two years, apart from a Scottish raid into Northumbria, England enjoyed a period of peace and prosperity such as the country had hardly known for longer than most people still living could remember.

Archbishop Kinsey died not long after he had dedicated the new minster at Waltham, and Aldred, Bishop of Worcester, was appointed in his place. He set out early the following year for Rome to receive his pallium from the Holy Father, and, because the land was peaceful and settled, Gytha's uncles Tosti and Gyrth went with him on an embassy from King Edward, and to make their pilgrimage. It was probably Tosti's absence from his earldom of Northumbria which emboldened the Scots to make their raid, but he soon restored order when he returned.

Earl Harold was able to make more frequent visits to Waltham during this time of peace, spending some time praying in his church and talking to Dean Wulfwin and Master Athelard, but he was glad to be able to see more of his family, playing with Gunhild, taking Magnus hunting and hawking, and talking to Gytha, with whom he seemed more at ease even than with Edith.

He told her, one summer afternoon as they strolled through the pastures looking at the beasts, about her uncles' journey, and she asked if he wished he might have gone with them.

'Yes and no,' he replied. 'I'm glad I had the chance to go to Rome a few years ago, but I feel uneasy out of England, wondering what might be happening here in my absence. The King seems less and less interested in governing as he grows older. He wants to spend all his time either praying or hunting, and there are men about him who encourage him in that, so that they can do as they please without his noticing.'

'Is that black man one of them?' asked Gytha, remembering how dark Earl Alfgar's black hair and brown face had seemed beside her fair Godwinsson father and uncles, and how much she had disliked him, although she could not remember his name.

'Earl Alfgar? Yes, I suppose so. He's jealous of your uncles and me, and thinks the King should have made him Earl of Northumbria as well as Mercia, instead of your Uncle Tosti. The King wouldn't, because he doesn't trust him, but Alfgar doesn't seem to realise that fighting with the Welsh against his own King and countrymen isn't a good way of winning the King's friendship.'

'Did he do that?' Gytha was shocked, for the Welsh were the great bogeymen to English children. Audrey often threatened that 'the Welsh would get them' if she or Magnus misbehaved.

'Yes, and I wouldn't be surprised if he does it again, for he married his daughter to Gruffydd, the Prince of Wales.'

'Married her to a *Welshman*!' Gytha exclaimed.

Harold smiled at the expression of horror on her face, and said, 'He's quite a civilised man, not a dragon! I believe she's grown fond of him, although he's much older than she is.'

'You won't marry me to a Welshman, will you, Father?' Gytha asked anxiously.

'Not unless you want to marry him,' Harold assured her. 'I wonder whom you will marry? Perhaps a great prince or even a king.'

'Like Aunt Edith,' Gytha said thoughtfully. 'I'd like to have some babies, though. A lot of babies.'

Her father laid a gentle hand on her head, then gave her long

25

plait a playful tug. 'I'll remember that,' he promised light-heartedly. 'Talking of your Aunt Edith – she would like me to take Magnus to the King's Court when I go back, so that he can study with the other children she's gathered about her. Would you like to go, too? You'd have other children to play with – Uncle Tosti's two boys are there, and Edwin and Morcar, Earl Alfgar's sons, and young Edgar, the King's nephew.'

'No girls?' asked Gytha pointedly.

'Yes, there are some, but I'm not sure whom they belong to. Various relations of the King, I think. He has a few distant cousins who all expect places at court. The Lady likes to have children about her, even if they're not her own. Would you like to join them?'

Gytha thought for a few moments.

'No, thank you,' she said at last. 'I'd rather stay here with Mother and Gunhild and Master Athelard and Father Turkill.'

'Father Turkill?' her father queried. 'Is he a friend of yours? Don't you find him rather strange?'

'Sometimes,' she replied thoughtfully. 'He goes vague and dreamy and says funny things about what's going to happen, with his eyes all cloudy, but most of the time he's very sensible. He explains things when they're hard to understand.'

'So you don't want to leave Waltham? You're sure?'

'Quite sure, thank you.'

'If you change your mind, you can send a letter to tell me.'

'How does a person send a letter?' she asked, interested.

'You ask Father Wulfwin to send it to me. He writes quite often to tell me how things are going here, and a messenger brings the letter to me, wherever I am.'

Gytha stored this item of information away, thinking that it might be useful one day, and pointed out that one of the cows was limping. By the time it had been caught and inspected, and a sharp piece of flint dislodged from between its two toes, the matter of Gytha leaving Waltham had apparently been forgotten.

Magnus, eagerly looking forward to his entry into the great

world, left with his father, and Edith saw him off with encouraging smiles, saving her tears for after he had gone, when she went to the church to pray for him and weep in private. She was a gentle, quiet woman, and deferred to her husband's wishes in all things, but sometimes found them hard to accept cheerfully.

Chapter Two

Gytha saw her father at intervals during the next four years, for he came to Waltham whenever he could, if only for a day or two, and always found time to talk to her about his life away from home, but the time between his visits seemed very long.

There was, of course, plenty to occupy her at home as she grew older. She continued her lessons, and learned to spin, to weave and to do fine embroidery, and more and more became her mother's companion, particularly after Gunhild's sight was found to be very poor and she was sent to Wilton. There the skilled sister infirmarian could look after her and try to find some means of saving her from blindness.

Edith was very sad for a time after losing yet another of her children, particularly as she had counted on keeping both her daughters until they were old enough to marry, but Earl Harold came himself to take Gunhild to Wilton, and, a few weeks later, Edith confided to Gytha that she was expecting another baby.

Ulf was born while his father was in Wales, fighting Gruffydd, but the Prince of Wales was killed, and his followers were glad to make peace on reasonable terms. Harold returned to England, escorting Gruffydd's widow, Aldyth, to the care of her brothers on his way.

Once again there was a period of peace, and Harold decided to undertake a task which had long been in his mind. He told Gytha that he was going to Normandy to try to persuade Duke William to release his youngest brother, Wulfnoth, and his nephew, Haakon.

'Why? Are they prisoners?' Gytha asked.

'Hostages. William took them as sureties for my father's good faith in an old quarrel, years ago. There's no reason now why he should keep them, so I mean to ask him for their freedom.'

Gytha shivered. 'I wish you wouldn't go,' she said. 'I don't like Duke William.'

Harold laughed. 'There's nothing to fear! He's a hard man, and thinks of nothing but soldiers and castles, but he's honest, and it's important that I should meet him and get to know him. I'll only be away a few weeks.'

He did not, in fact, return to England until the late summer of the following year. Before going to join the King at Winchester, he called at Waltham to see Ulf and to reassure Edith and Gytha that he was, indeed, safely home.

'I wrote to you frequently,' he assured them, 'but I suspected, rightly, it seems, that my letters never left the Duke's hands, despite his promises.'

'You were gone so long!' Edith exclaimed. 'I thought you expected to be away no more than a month?'

'Indeed; but as soon as we landed a local baron took us prisoner, and kept us locked up until William came to "release" us, as he put it. Then he wouldn't discuss my business until after I'd accompanied him on a short campaign into Brittany. Oh, he was *friendly* – insisted on treating me as his brother, and piled honours and favours on me! That's the trouble – one of his honours proved to be more than I realised. He insisted on knighting me!'

Gytha had read something about knighthood in her studies of the French language but had little idea of what it involved, and Edith knew nothing of it at all, so Harold explained.

'It's considered a great honour for a man of high rank to give the accolade of knighthood to a comrade, and it's accompanied by the gift of a warhorse and its accoutrements, a suit of mail, a sword and spurs. In exchange, the new knight swears an oath – of friendship, William said. I thought it was all just a ceremony of honour, with no great significance beyond that, and it seemed simple enough. I knelt before William, and he gave me a great buffet on the side of my head – nearly knocked me over – and then slapped me on the shoulders with the flat of his sword. It turned out, in fact, to have far greater significance. I didn't hear

the words of the oath until I had to repeat them at the ceremony, in the present of William's entire Court, and it turned
out to be an oath of loyalty. I couldn't back out without in-
sulting him in public, and he made it very clear that I'd not
leave Normandy until the ceremony was completed in every respect! I had to lay my hands on two covered tables – he said it
was just an old custom – while I swore; afterwards the covers
were thrown aside to reveal two altars full of relics! Then he
blandly informed me that my oath, in his belief and that of
every man present, including the clergy, made me his man, and
he would require my support in his claim to the English crown,
which he said Edward had promised him.'

'What did you say?' Gytha asked, appalled.

'That no king of England had ever had the power to nom-
inate his successor, for the crown of England passes by election.
His answer to that was that all the members of the Witan – the
Curia, he called it – were known to be in my pay. I came near to
striking him for that insult!'

He scowled, looking more angry than either Gytha or Edith
had ever seen him before, and the latter said anxiously, 'But it
was a forced oath, obtained by trickery. He can't keep you to it!'

Harold gave a bitter laugh. 'Who says it was forced? All the
witnesses were Normans. He made sure that all my companions
were kept out of the hall for the ceremony!'

'What will you do?' Gytha asked, her eyes huge in her solemn
face.

'I'll never trust William again, that's for sure! As for the oath
– I'll make confession that I was a fool who let himself be
tricked, and hope my confessor will absolve me from it. I can't
keep it – I haven't the power to order the Witan to do anything,
and I'm convinced that the King changed his mind long ago
about recommending William as his heir – indeed, I doubt if he
ever made such a promise, for he knew he had neither the right
nor the power. I tell you I'd rather risk eternal damnation as an
oath-breaker than let that Norman bastard take England! His
rule is harsh and oppressive. I love this land with its green fields
and forests, its flowers and meadows and its peaceful villages.

The English folk are free, governing themselves under the King, and they love learning and honour good craftsmanship. Everything they make has beauty and rightness, from a great poem to a simple tool. If William comes, he'll turn them into near-slaves. He'll tax them to starvation to build his ugly castles and fight his foreign wars. He cares nothing for England, save for its wealth and the additional power it will give him to be its king. He's a savage, in love with war and power! He can barely write his own name, and considers learning only of value in serving him for his tax records and keeping his chronicles. He wants the title of king, but not the love and care for the people that make the other side of the coin. If he comes, he'll have to fight me for every inch of this land, until one or other of us is dead.'

Edith and Gytha exchanged a half-frightened, half-proud look, and in that moment, Gytha, at eleven years of age, felt that her childhood had ended. Harold, his elbows propped on the table, covered his face with his hands and was silent for a time. When he looked up, he was calm again.

'What of your news?' he asked. 'Ulf seems well and growing.'

'He's a good baby, so contented. And see, he has teeth, and he can almost stand by himself!'

Harold played with his small son for a while, watched smilingly by Edith and Gytha, but then he gave the child back to Audrey to take back to his cot, and said gravely, 'You know what I must do now?'

'Yes,' Edith replied calmly. 'I know, and I've always accepted that it must be so. I've had you for more than twenty years, my dearest – far longer than I ever expected. I've been very lucky. Marry her, with my blessing.'

'We've both been very lucky,' he replied, and Gytha, seeing the expressions on both their faces, silently rose and crept out of the bower, beckoning Audrey to follow her. Outside, she asked the nursemaid to stay away until morning, and, to her surprise, the girl went without argument.

Gytha went to the orchard, where nobody could overhear her, and there gave way to the storm of tears which was threatening to choke her. 'Why?' she demanded of the silent trees. 'Why must he do it when he obviously doesn't want to? Why can't he be king without having to leave Mother? It's not fair!' With a rare spurt of rage, she pummelled one of the trees and kicked it, bruising her toes in their soft leather slippers. 'Why do people have to do things just because they were born to be important?' she demanded.

'If we knew that,' said Turkill quietly, coming between the trees to her side, 'we'd understand a great deal more than we do now. You know that your father loves you and all his family, but there are two things he loves more – more even than your mother – and those are God and England. He understands that God wants him to do something important for England, and it matters more that he tries to do it than anything else in his life. One day you'll feel the same about something you will have to do, and then you'll understand, for you'll have to make a choice nearly as hard as his.'

'I?' Gytha swallowed her anger and misery, and looked at him with bitterness. 'I'm only a female, and a woman has no choices. What chance will I ever have to choose my own path!'

'Many chances; and when you do, you'll remember your father, and understand why he chooses to marry Lady Aldyth now. Come to the church, and we'll pray together.'

Gytha hesitated and stood thinking. 'He doesn't love her, does he?' she asked.

'He's sorry for her, if you mean Lady Aldyth, and he'll be kind to her, but he loves your mother and all his children. Come to the church and lay your troubles before the Holy Cross.'

Reluctantly, Gytha went with him. They prayed together until, gradually, her anger and misery abated and were replaced by a sad resignation, an acceptance that she could not change her father's decision, and so must endure it.

Harold reached Winchester in time to join the expedition to Wilton for the dedication of his sister's church, and married Aldyth, with her brothers' blessing and her own calm acceptance, a few days later.

32

Earl Tosti had come from Northumbria for the dedication and the wedding, and Harold, who knew that he found the Northumbrians difficult to govern, expected that he would go back to the north again at once, but he lingered on, hunting with the King, and then accompanied Edward when the Court returned to Westminster at the end of October.

Harold had invited Gytha to join him at Westminster, thinking that she should learn to take her place at Court as his daughter and that, once she had met Aldyth, she might accept her more readily. It was soon after her arrival that a group of Northumbrian thanes came to the King to complain against Earl Tosti.

The charges that they laid were very grave, and Tosti was unable to refute them. Instead, he lost his temper and turned on Harold, shouting that he had stirred up the Northumbrians against him. This, the thanes denied so vehemently that there was no doubt that Tosti was lying, and the King, despite his great affection for Tosti, was greatly angered and sent him into exile.

Gytha was very upset for her father's sake. She had witnessed the scene and, to her surprise, it was Aldyth who sought to comfort her, seeking her out to offer sympathy and understanding in a shy and hesitant manner.

'I know you've no reason to like me,' she said. 'I didn't want to marry your father and he didn't want to marry me, but neither of us had any real choice so we have to make the best of it. I know what brothers can be like – my two are always squabbling – but this was a dreadful business! Your father is safer with Earl Tosti gone, you know. Tosti was always jealous of him, and my brothers say that he's taken every possible opportunity to try to turn the King against him for years. It says a lot for the King's good sense that he never succeeded! The enemies closest to you are always the worst.'

It had not occurred to Gytha that Tosti might have been jealous of his elder brother. She found the information enlightening, and even comforting, for at least it explained why Tosti had acted so strangely. It was also a surprise to her to learn that

Aldyth had not wanted to marry her father, and, once she had digested the idea, she ceased to dislike her, and even admitted to her father that she was quite a pleasant person.

King Edward's great church at Westminster was finished at last in the autumn of 1065, and he ordered its consecration to be on Holy Innocents' Day, three days after Christmas. A great feast was planned to last for all twelve days of Christmas, and Harold hoped that Gytha would stay for it, but she said that she would prefer to go home to Waltham.

'Mother will be all alone, save for Ulf, and I should be with her,' she explained. 'This is the first Christmas since – since you married . . . There'll be other times when I can be here.'

Harold accepted her decision without demur, and she left him a week before Christmas, as the guests were beginning to arrive at Westminster. The weather was fair, and presented no difficulties for the travellers from long distances, and every man who was entitled to attend the King's Witan was able to get there, as well as all the others who had been invited. Both feast and consecration took place with every guest present. Only the King was unable to attend.

At first, it seemed that he had a chill or some such slight indisposition, but the revelations about Tosti, whom Edward had loved and trusted, had been a greater shock to the old man than anyone had realised, and it soon became clear that he was sinking, with no will or desire to recover. He listened while his wife, Harold and Archbishop Aldred told him about the consecration, describing every detail between them, and he smiled with obvious pleasure, but as if it were already some pleasant, half-forgotten dream, and even fell asleep several times during the telling of it.

He lingered through the turn of the year, sleeping or lying still, speaking rarely, and then only in a whisper, until two days before Epiphany, when he seemed to sleep, but so restlessly that the watchers roused him, thinking he was more troubled by his dreams than was good in his weak state. There were four of them there: the Lady, warming his feet in her lap, Harold kneeling by his side, Stigand praying, and Robert FitzWimarc, his cousin and chaplain, anxiously watching every breath. When Edward woke, he asked for all his household to be summoned. Once they had crowded into his chamber, he recounted, in a weak and rambling voice, a dream he had just had, which seemed to be a prophecy, but no one could understand it.

He was silent for a while after that, then roused himself and said in a strong voice, 'Don't weep, but pray to God and Our Lady for me, and give me leave to go to Them,' and then he gave them his blessing, and whispered words of comfort to his wife. After a while he held out his hand to Harold, who took it in both his own, finding it very cold. Then he raised his voice again, and said to Harold, slowly and distinctly, so that all present heard him clearly: 'I give this woman, your sister, and all the kingdom into your keeping. Keep my Norman servants in your service, for my sake, or let them go home, as they wish. Bury me in my great church, and send out the news of my death without delay or concealment, that all my people may pray to God for me.'

Stigand gave him the wayfaring bread and prayed over him, and presently he fell asleep and his soul slipped away in the night. He was buried on the Feast of Epiphany in the tomb he had ordered to be prepared for him as part of the building of his minster, beneath the crossing and before the altar of St Peter.

Harold sent Lord Ansgar to tell it all exactly to Edith, Gytha and the canons of Waltham, gathered together in the hall after supper, for he had witnessed almost all of it. Ansgar paused at this point in his narrative, looking consideringly at the two women (for he, like Harold, already thought of Gytha as a woman), and then continued, choosing his words with care.

'On the day between the King's dying and his burial, the Witan met in the church to decide who should rule England. I think all expected that there would be a long discussion, for there seemed at least five claims to be considered, but, in the event, there was no need. Archbishop Aldred pointed out that one man, whose claim was as good as any and who had already proved himself a wise, just and strong ruler, had been recommended to them by the saintly Edward on his deathbed, and he proposed that he should be our new king. Everyone agreed . . .'

He paused again, seemingly for a long time, for everyone was hanging on his words, and almost guessed what he was about to say. His eyes sought Gytha's face again, and, for some reason which he could not explain, he spoke directly to her. She could hardly breathe, waiting for what she knew was coming.

'*Everyone* agreed, without exception or hesitation, and, re-member, the whole Witan was present. After the King was laid in his tomb, your father was anointed and crowned by Arch-bishop Aldred before the high altar, with the consent and accla-mation of all present.'

Gytha closed her eyes, her first feeling one of relief that Duke William would not, after all, come to bring his harsh rule to England, as her father had feared. It was a few moments before it really penetrated her understanding that her own father was now king – her beloved father, who would be such a great and good king, as good as any England had ever known – and a wave of golden happiness flooded through her. By then, the canons, faces wreathed in smiles, had already begun to sing a *Te Deum* and Edith had dropped to her knees, her hands over her face and tears of an emotion stronger than mere joy or relief trickling between her fingers as she prayed for the man who had always been a king to her.

Only Ansgar remained calm, and rather more serious than the occasion seemed to warrant, and, when the outburst of re-joicing had died down a little, he said, 'My lord the King asks your prayers for the kingdom and for him. The Witan was in agreement, but there are others who will object. Tosti God-winsson is gathering men and ships in Flanders, and this news will make him the more determined to return; by force if his brother refuses to restore his earldom, which he certainly will. He's sworn brother to Malcolm of Scotland, who would enjoy any chance to add to his territory on our borders, and both the heirs of Cnut consider they have a right to this part of his former empire. There's also the Norman . . .'

He said no more, for no one seemed inclined to take much notice, but Gytha quietly left her place and slipped out of the hall, unnoticed in the flickering shadows, into the January night. It was bitterly cold outside, but dry and cloudless, and the dark sky was set with a myriad of stars, bright and twinkling in the frosty air. She stood looking up at them, and wondered if one of them was the little hole in the heavens through which King Edward was watching to see what would happen to England.

'If you can hear me,' she said quietly, addressing the man whom many people believed might be a saint, 'ask Our Lord to bless England and keep her safe! Ask His blessing on my father, for you wanted him to be king in the end, whatever you may have said to your Norman cousin in the past! You know of how much he is capable, and how great a king he can be. Ask the Lord to let him prove you were right to choose him.'

The silent stars continued their slow procession across the turning sphere above her, and Gytha had no feeling of having been heard, let alone answered. So, after waiting until she was shivering, she turned abruptly and went to the church, expecting that all the canons would still be in the hall and she would have the great building to herself.

One canon was there, however. Father Turkill was trimming the candles below the Great Cross, singing quietly in a thin, nasal voice perhaps to himself, perhaps to the Cross or the Figure on it. He turned as Gytha walked up the nave towards him, her long skirts whispering on the stone floor.

'So now you're the daughter of a king,' he said quietly. 'Never forget that, whatever befalls. A king of England must be chosen by the Witan. The crown is given, by God and the people. It may not rightfully be taken by force or trickery, or given by one man alone.'

'But men will try to take it by force,' Gytha said, her eyes huge and shadowed in the candlelight. 'As soon as the spring comes, they'll gather like wolves! What will happen, Father Turkill?'

'Whatever God wills,' he replied. 'I cannot see to order, my child. Whatever it is, even a king's daughter must accept it.'

'I'm afraid, Father!'

37

Turkill nodded serenely. 'Then pray for courage. Any man or woman may be afraid, but you must learn to master your fear and trust in God to turn all to good. Do you think your father is never afraid?'

'He must be, very often, but he can be *doing* something – preparing, training his men, planning . . . What can *I* do?'

'Pray. Praying is the most important of all the things to be done, and your father will have too many calls on his time to pray enough, so you must do it for him.'

Turkill's advice was sound, and Gytha took it. She continued to pray, and to hope, despite the strange portent which appeared in the heavens as spring began to yield to summer.

It was a star, but such a star as nobody in Waltham could recall ever having seen before. It was faint at first, but grew steadily brighter and bigger on each successive night until it blazed in the sky, brighter than the moon, with a long tail of light streaming out behind it. Naturally it amazed everyone, and, human nature tending towards pessimism, most people considered it a very unlucky omen – but for whom? Master Athelard said that he had read of such stars appearing in times past, and, as everyone in the world could see it, there was no way of telling who was to suffer the ill fortune – if it was an ill omen, which he doubted.

'What do you think it is, then?' Gytha asked.

Master Athelard shrugged and shook his head. 'Something beautiful to see. Perhaps a gift from God to remind us that we're not forgotten. It's very beautiful, and why should such a lovely thing portend evil to anyone? Perhaps it's the Star of Bethlehem come again.'

Gytha took comfort from his opinion, but everyone else continued to shake mournful heads and look gloomy, except Father Turkill, who said vaguely that bad luck for one might be good luck for another, and he didn't really believe in luck, in any case.

'But what does it mean?' Gytha asked.

'Mean? Who knows? It's beautiful. What does a snowdrop

mean, or a bird? Why should it mean anything? It's a lovely thing, and will go away all too soon.'

In that, at least, he was right. The strange star faded as it had come, and was gone by Midsummer Day, but everything ill which happened that twelvemonth was ascribed to its influence, from a calf born dead, to the greater ill that befell England during that evil year.

The waiting went on all summer, for the wind blew foul for ships from Normandy, although it was well known that William had gathered a great army and a fleet to transport men and horses across the narrow seas. Of Tosti's whereabouts there was no news, and nothing from the north, from Norway or Denmark. King Harold summoned the fyrd, the force of one-third of the able men from every shire which he was entitled to call upon for the defence of the kingdom, but the law allowed him to keep them for only a limited time, and he had to let them go home to bring in the harvest.

Still the wind blew the wrong way for William but it was the right way for the Norwegians, and when the invasion came in September, it was from the north, not from Normandy. Earl Edwin sent an urgent message that Harald Hardrada and Tosti had landed near York, intending to take England and share it between them, and he was hastening to the support of his brother Morcar with every man he could gather.

The speed of King Harold's march to York was talked of with awe and admiration for years after. The experienced Norwegian king defeated Edwin and Morcar, the two young earls, with little difficulty, but mistakenly let them escape into the city of York, and waited for them to sue for peace. Instead, Harold and his housecarls came on him out of the morning mists like a swarm of angry hornets, and Hardrada found an enemy more worthy of his men. At the end of a hard-fought day, he and Tosti lay dead in the meadow beside Stamford Bridge, and Harold had captured his young son and all his ships. He sent the boy home with a seemly escort of Norwegians in some of the ships, bidding him rule his own land well and leave other countries to manage their own affairs.

But, meanwhile, the wind had changed. William had already landed in Sussex. If Harold's march north to York had been remarkable, his return was hardly less rapid, and he was back in London, his men weary and wounded, but determined, before William had done more than establish a foothold south of the Weald.

Harold allowed his men little time to rest and recover, and he had bidden Edwin and Morcar to follow hard on his heels, but there must be a brief interval to gather more men, call out the fyrd again and rest the horses, so he took the opportunity to go again to Waltham, to thank God for one victory and pray for another.

It was so brief a visit. Both Edith and Gytha yearned to keep him longer, but they knew they must not. They welcomed him with brave smiles, prayed with him in the minster, and left him there when he asked them and all his followers to leave him to pray alone for a while.

Only Turkill remained, unnoticed in his usual quiet, self-effacing way, moving silently about the church, putting away the gifts Harold had brought and the vessels used in the Mass of thanksgiving. Only he saw the King lie prostrate below the Cross, praying with all his heart and soul, then rise and go quietly out, and only Turkill saw the Figure on the Cross bow His head in sorrow. Whether the stone head bowed in fact, or only in Turkill's strangely gifted sight, he had no means of knowing, but he guessed what the sign meant, and went weeping to Father Wulfwin.

In the morning Harold embraced Edith in silence, for they had no need of further words. He kissed Ulf and blessed him, then held Gytha to him for a few seconds, and whispered to her, 'Take care of your mother, sweetheart. You're both more precious to me than anything in this world. Remember that Svein of Denmark is your kinsman.' He then held her at arm's length, his hands on her shoulders, looking deeply into her eyes, nodded once or twice, smiled, blessed her, and turned to mount the horse which Ansgar held ready for him.

They all watched him ride away with his men, the October

sun shining on his golden hair and straight broad-shouldered back, until the little group dwindled out of sight across the long causeway over the valley. There was a last flash of light in the far distance, as if someone had briefly raised something bright, perhaps a sword-blade, to catch the sun, and then they were gone.

'Lady Edith,' Father Wulfwin said quietly, 'I and my fellows would like to talk with you, if we may.'

'By all means,' Edith replied, almost absently. 'Come to the hall and take a cup of spiced wine. It's a chill morning.'

There were eight canons in residence at the time, including Master Athelard, the rest being at work in the outlying parishes. They gathered round the high table and sat down at Edith's invitation, gratefully sipping the warming wine, and then Wulfwin said gently, 'My lady, we feel great concern for the King's safety in the days to come. We think that two of our number should follow him to the battle, to pray for the slain and to tend the wounded.' He deliberately said nothing of Turkill's disturbing vision, but Edith, looking at him in silence for a few moments, seemed to know that there was more in his mind than his words indicated.

'I shall go too,' she said. 'Your good fathers can leave me in some safe place nearby, where I'll be at hand if I'm needed. I leave my son and daughter in your care.'

Gytha opened her mouth to protest that she must go too, but caught the eye of Father Osgod, and something in the look he gave her made her close it again without speaking. She eyed him curiously, for she had never taken much notice of him before. He was a very big man, tall above average, with powerful shoulders and a deep chest, and he was usually called Osgod Knop, for he had a large wen by his right nostril. She knew he was of Danish blood, for he came from somewhere in the north and spoke in a strange, harsh accent, clipping his vowels, and using many words unknown here in the south.

'Ailric and I'll tak t'mules,' he said, 'but Lady Edith'd best hev a norse. We'll need food and drink and blankets . . .' He gestured with a pair of very large hands which were strangely delicate in their movements. 'Happen we mun sleep on t'ground.'

Ailric said nothing, but looked apprehensive. He was a Welshman, despite his English name, and looked apprehensive about most things, but his doubts never deterred him from volunteering for any task which arose, or from carrying it out.

The two priests and Edith set out two days later, early in the morning. She said little to Gytha, save, 'Take care of Ulf and be brave. Pray for us all.'

Gytha said only 'Yes, Mother,' for there seemed to be no words for all that she wanted to say. She knelt in the church for hours at a time during the next week, her eyes on the face of the Figure on the Cross, oblivious of anything save the need to keep open a channel between herself and Heaven through which the formless, wordless prayers could flow.

Turkill, too, spent much time in prayer, but in the comparative privacy of the sacristy, for he was tormented by visions. Unusually, they were not pictures of the past or 'memories' of the future, but fleeting glimpses of the present. For one whole, dreadful, day he saw glimpses of something which seemed to him like a vision of Armageddon, although what remained of his consciousness told him that it was an ordinary battle taking place only a couple of days' journey away.

Master Athelard and Dean Wulfwin, realising that their fellow-priest was in the grip of his strange gift, looked in on him from time to time, and were greatly relieved when, at the end of that long day, they found him sleeping.

'It must be over now,' Wulfwin whispered.

'Pray God it is! At least, it seems to be over for him,' Athelard replied, and they tiptoed away not knowing that, for Turkill, worse was yet to come.

In his mind, it was suddenly afternoon, a bright October afternoon, with the sun declining in a blue sky marred only by a few streaks of cloud – a clear, beautiful sight.

The earth below was hideous, the steep slope trampled to mud by the feet of men and horses, the good soil stained and ugly with an alien redness. Everywhere bodies were sprawled, heaped high where the worst of the battle had been, lying solitary elsewhere. Some lay as if they slept, but most sprawled obscenely, lacking limbs, even heads. Some lay face down, others stared unseeingly at that perfect sky, their faces distorted with anger, or fear, or amazement. A few stirred, groaning, then presently were as still as the rest, save for one or two who managed to drag themselves away, crawling, bleeding and sobbing with effort and pain.

Among the dead, living people moved, some stripping the bodies, others searching. Turkill's vision centred on a group of four – two priests, a soldier and a woman. The soldier was a Norman, to judge by his long horseman's hauberk. The others were known to Turkill, who groaned aloud as he realised what they were doing. Presently the woman fell to her knees by one body, so hacked about that it was barely recognisable as a man. She gently turned him over, helped by the bigger of the two priests, and then the group was still, seemingly frozen, for a long time. The kneeling woman broke the stillness at last by lifting her arms and flinging back her head, her face distorted with grief and her mouth wide open in a soundless scream.

Turkill, also on his knees, gave a strangled cry and fell senseless on the stone floor. Master Athelard, who was waiting nearby, came running to his aid; although he soon recovered consciousness, he could not speak of what he had seen, except to say, 'She found him! God be thanked that He granted her that small mercy, at least!'

The canons brought Edith home safely, but she was changed almost out of recognition. Her once beautiful face was grey and haggard, her hair ashen, and her eyes were shadowed and vacant. She seemed to be in a dream, unaware of anything about her, and simply went where she was led, sat when she was pressed into a chair, and stood when she was lifted. She did not speak at all.

Father Ailric looked white and sick, and could only shake his head when the canons and townsfolk crowded round, anxious to

43

hear what had happened, and it was Osgod Knop who said briefly, 'T'Norman won. T'King and's brothers are dead. Best say no more.'

'And the King's – body?' Wulfwin asked unable to think of a euphemism.

Osgod shook his head. 'Lady Edith found him – eventually. We pleaded with t'Norman – offered him gold, but he wouldn't let us bring him away. He said . . .' He broke off, seeing that Gytha was standing there, listening, with an expression of stunned disbelief.

'What did he say?' she demanded, for she could hardly believe that anyone would be so vindictive as to refuse a dead man decent burial.

Osgod was too blunt a man to choose his words carefully. 'He says that a leader should share t'fate of his followers. They'll not have Christian burial, so neither should he.'

'Were many . . .?' Wulfwin began, but could not finish the question.

Osgod nodded soberly. 'Almost all, as well as t'King and his brothers Gyrth and Leofwin. Lord Ansgar was left to guard t'baggage and t'rear of t'army, much against his will. He gathered together the few who survived t'battle with his rearguard, and ambushed t'Norman horsemen who pursued them, and did enough damage to get a couple hundred away safe to London, but that's all.'

'I knew it!' Turkill said, his eyes filling with tears. 'Our Lord bowed his head in sorrow over the King as he prayed for victory! Did I not tell you? I knew what it portended!'

'Indeed you told us, and we heeded you,' Wulfwin said soothingly. He surveyed the crowd about him, seeing shock, sorrow, horror, but chiefly fear in their faces. 'A requiem!' he said in a firm, clear voice. 'Now, everyone to the church! Father Ailric, assist Father Turkill to prepare the high altar. The King and his men may be beyond mortal aid, but we can and will pray for them.'

'I'm filthy, unshaven . . .' Ailric faltered.

'Wash your hands. God will forgive you the rest,' Father

44

Wulfwin told him with a nicely balanced mixture of kindness and command, and Ailric went obediently to do as he was told, and, despite his bone-weariness, felt the better for doing something positive to counteract the misery of his and Osgod's failure to bring the dead King home for burial.

Gytha hesitated, then put her arm about her mother and gently led her away to the bower. Her women followed, but seeing their tears and hearing the note of hysteria in their voices, Gytha sent them to the church instead, except for Mildyth, Edith's tiring-woman, who remained calm and dry-eyed, although she was clearly deeply moved by the news and the state of her mistress.

Edith was undressed, bathed, fed and put to bed like a helpless baby, and apparently slept. Master Athelard came to see her after the service, and advised Gytha in a whisper not to worry her mother, but to talk to her when she was awake about ordinary or everyday things in a quiet, calm voice, and make no attempt to persuade her to speak.

'Master, what will happen now?' Gytha asked.

Athelard shook his head. 'God alone knows! It appears that your father had only his housecarls and the fyrd from the shires about London, but his force nearly equalled the Norman's. The men of the fyrd were brave but lacked discipline . . . There are still all the Northumbrians and Mercians under their two earls, and your grandmother has raised all Wessex and beyond, but who can lead them? We're left with only young Edgar, Edwin and Morcar.'

'Ansgar?' Gytha offered uncertainly.

'Osgod says he's sorely wounded and, in any case, he's but a minister. Would the young earls follow him? He might command in your brother Godwin's name, with him as ostensible leader, but Godwin's young and inexperienced. . . .'

And not the man my father was, even at the same young age! Gytha thought to herself, recognising for the first time something which she had long known, but not admitted to herself.

There seemed nothing more to be said. Gytha bowed her head for a more than usually fervent blessing from Athelard, and walked slowly out of the bower, hardly noticing where she was going. Her feet took her to the stream, and along its bank until she was some distance from the garth.

The contented quacking of ducks caught her attention, reminding her poignantly of the many times she had come here with her father to feed them and to talk. She sank down on the grass, covered her face with her hands, and wept until she had no tears left to shed.

She sat there for a long time, remembering, while the ducks squabbled and dived for food, indifferent to the troubles of mankind. Presently, she made herself think of what she must do now, and knew that her father would expect her to be true to his teaching, to take charge of things until her mother recovered. She sighed, wiped her eyes on a corner of her head-rail, and walked wearily back to the garth to give instructions to the servants about supper.

Chapter Three

The weeks after the battle passed slowly. Gytha wept and prayed when she could, but she had little time to herself. Her mother's strange withdrawal continued unchanged, her little brother Ulf, suddenly deprived of his mother's care and bewildered by the atmosphere of grief and fear, needed constant attention, and the household had to be managed. The servants were heartbroken at the loss of their much-loved master, and too apprehensive to give his daughter the support she needed.

What little news reached Waltham was all bad, but that was to be expected. The shadow of fear hanging over the community was caused less by the great changes taking place in the country as a whole than by the knowledge that, sooner or later, the Normans would come seeking King Harold's family.

Meanwhile, time passed, however slowly, and spring eventually arrived, with its seasonal task of cleaning hall and bowers. For two days there was such a beating and cleaning and boiling of linen as the garth had not seen for a long time, and everyone seemed to feel the better for it. It was while Gytha was hanging out the sheets on the lavender bushes to dry, however, wearing an old gown and with her head-rail blown askew as she wrestled with the flapping wet linen, that a boy from the choir school came running to her.

'Lady Gytha!' he gasped. 'Father Ailric says there are twelve men riding over the causeway! He thinks they're coming here! What shall we do?'

Gytha's mind raced through the possibilities, and quickly picked out the most likely. 'I suppose Duke William has remembered our existence at last,' she said, sounding a deal calmer than she felt. 'Ask Master Athelard to receive them in the church. I'll come as soon as I'm fit to be seen.'

The boy looked at her nervously, then bobbed a bow and ran off, while Gytha abandoned the sheets to the servants and went to the bower to change into her best gown, put on her amber beads, tidy her hair and pin a fresh head-rail to the plaits wound round her head.

'It seems we have visitors,' she said to her silent mother. 'I wonder what they want.'

She walked slowly to the church, composing herself by praying that she might be able to deal with whatever was about to happen. She found a group of men in Norman hauberks standing outside the west door, their horses tethered to the church-yard fence. They stared at her as she approached, and she nodded to them in as regal a manner as she could manage, as she had seen her aunt, the Lady, do to bystanders. She was heartened when they shuffled their feet and bowed respectfully as she passed.

She paused just inside the church door, partly to allow her eyes to adjust to the shadowed interior after the bright sun outside, and partly to take stock. Master Athelard was standing under the nearer arch of the crossing, talking to two men. They wore mailshirts, and each had a helm with a nasal bar under his arm. Both were tall and well built, one fair, the other slightly shorter and dark. They turned as she approached, both looking at her with some surprise, but she ignored them until she had made her reverence to the Holy Cross, to the altar and to Master Athelard. Only then did she give them her attention.

'Our errand is to the Lady Edith,' the fair man said to Master Athelard in slightly accented English.

'To the best of my knowledge, *the* Lady Edith, King Edward's widow and my aunt, is at Winchester, or maybe at Wilton,' Gytha said. 'Do you, perhaps, mean my mother Lady Edith?'

'By God,' exclaimed the dark man in French, with a quick, merry smile, 'there's no doubt whose daughter this is! You've only to look at her face and hear the tone of her voice.'

'May I know who it is that recognises my resemblance to my father!' Gytha asked coldly in her best French.

48

A faint smile of appreciation flitted across Master Athelard's face and vanished as he said gravely, also in French, 'This,' indicating the fair man, 'is William Malet, who speaks English. The other is William de Warenne, Lord of Lewes in Sussex. Gentlemen, Lady Gytha, elder daughter of our late lord and patron.'

The two Normans bowed, and Gytha inclined her head slightly in acknowledgment.

'And what is your purpose in coming here?' she asked.

'We bring a letter from our master to the – to Lady Edith,' William Malet replied. He, too, now spoke French, and seemed relieved that he would not have to translate everything for his companion's benefit.

'My mother is too ill to receive visitors or deal with letters. You may give it to me.'

The two Normans looked at one another, and Malet nodded. Warenne produced the letter, a rolled piece of parchment with a dangling seal, from the long cuff of his gauntlet, and said, 'Perhaps your chaplain will read it to you. It's in Latin.'

'This is Master Athelard of Liège, the famous scholar from the University of Utrecht, of whom no doubt you have heard. You may give me the letter, and I will read it for myself.' Gytha held out her hand somewhat imperiously.

Warenne's eyebrows rose, but he hastily gained control of his expression and handed her the letter, trying to look as if he was use to encountering young ladies who could read at all, let alone Latin!

It was a brief letter, beginning with a formal greeting to *The Lady Edith, concubine of the late Earl of Wessex*, and continued with two short statements: that the daughter of the said Earl was to join her sister Gunhild in the nunnery of Wilton, and that the said Edith might accompany her daughter or remain at Waltham, as she chose. In the latter case, two hides of the manor of Waltham which had been granted to William de Warenne would be administered by him for her upkeep. It ended with William's name and titles, and the information that it was given under his hand at Rouen in Normandy, his seal appended in confirmation.

Gytha, who had been trembling inside, for all her brave face, at this first encounter with Normans, felt sick with fear. So William thought she and her family were his property, to go where he ordered and do as he required! A spurt of controlled anger gave her fresh courage, and she opened her mouth to make a sharp remark on the subject, then closed it again and tried to think calmly. These were orders from the *de facto* King of England. She had no choice but to obey them – or had she? It would be hard – perhaps dangerous – to refuse, but her father had chosen the hard way when it led to what he wanted, and so must she.

Resolved, she swung round to face the Normans, and said, 'I have no desire whatever to enter a nunnery, and no power on earth can force me to take vows against my will. My mother is too ill to travel, or to be left before she is fully recovered. She has estates of her own in Norfolk and Kent, and has no need to take land here from the canons for her upkeep. In any case, almost all the lands in this place belong to the college of the Holy Cross, so I do not understand why your master thinks he can give them to someone else.'

She glared defiantly at Warenne, and was surprised to see that his dark eyes were looking at her with what seemed to be admiration, and he was smiling faintly.

'All the land in England belongs to the King,' Malet said stiffly. 'He will grant it to whomever he chooses. No one else may own land in his kingdom but only hold it from him by charter. Women do not hold land under our laws, so your mother cannot have any manors elsewhere. When will she be fit to travel?'

'You must ask Master Athelard,' Gytha snapped, biting back an angry retort about land-thieves. 'He is responsible for her treatment.'

Malet looked at Master Athelard, who shrugged and said, 'Her recovery is in the hands of God, and beyond the skill of any physician. She may recover in time, or perhaps only in the next world. Lady Gytha is right, however. She cannot possibly be taken to Wilton, or anywhere else nor can her daughter be

50

taken from her without endangering her life. If your master attempts to separate them, it is more than likely that he will be responsible for her death.'

'May we enquire the nature of her illness?' Warenne asked in a neutral tone.

'She followed our lord to the battlefield, and sought for his body afterwards. The shock was too much for her. Her body lives, but her mind seems dead,' Athelard replied briefly.

The two Normans were nonplussed, and glanced uneasily at one another. Warenne recovered first, and said, 'If you would be so kind, Master Athelard, to write a letter to the – to our master to that effect, I should be grateful. We had intended to escort Lady Gytha to Wilton, but must accept that we cannot do so for the moment.'

He paused, and seemed undecided whether to say more, but made up his mind and went on slowly, picking his words with care, 'I learned to know your father well in Normandy, Lady Gytha. I found him a fine, good man.'

Gytha's lips trembled slightly at this unexpected tribute, but she clamped them together tightly and said nothing for fear of bursting into tears.

'I'm sorry that – that things turned out as they did,' Warenne went on doggedly. 'I hope you may find it possible to look on Malet and myself as – well, perhaps not as friends, but at least men who wish to help you. We have no wish to hurt you and your family in any way.'

Gytha thought he sounded sincere, but how could she believe him? He was a Norman. He might even be the man who had killed her father. The thought, once defined in her mind, passed out of her control, and she asked abruptly, 'Who slew my father?'

Warenne, to her surprise, winced as if she had struck him. 'I don't know. There was such a mêlée at the last that nobody is sure. Several men claimed . . . I know it was neither me nor Malet, for we were further along the ridge. I give you my word to that, on my faith and on my honour as a knight!'

Gytha's eyes darted from his face to Malet's, then to Master

Athelard, who nodded, as if to confirm what she had read in their expressions. She thought for a few moments, her eyes on the ground, considering all that Warenne had said and the manner in which he had said it. Perhaps he really did wish to help. Her father had said that he had made friends in Normandy, and she vaguely remembered that William Malet had been here before, many years ago, in her father's company, and had been on good terms with him. It was possible, she supposed, that these men could serve William while not agreeing with everything he did.

'Thank you,' she said stiffly. 'I hope that your – your master will not be angry with you for not being able to carry out your orders.'

'I trust he will understand,' Warenne replied with a glimmer of a smile in his dark eyes. He suddenly reminded Gytha of a robin, and she felt an unexpected touch of liking for him. He was not at all as she had expected a Norman to be, remembering her father's condemnation of their roughness and uncivilised way of life.

'May we see your brother?' Malet asked, sounding strained and abrupt in contrast to Warenne's more relaxed manner.

Gytha bit back a sharp, reflexive 'No!' and substituted a smoother, 'I regret that will not be possible. Lord Ulf is out riding with his groom and will not be back for some time. Then, he must go straight to his lessons.'

Malet looked for a moment as if he might be about to insist, but Warenne made a slight movement with one hand, and he said instead, 'May we at least assure our master that you will go to Wilton as soon as your mother is better?'

'No!' Gytha snapped. 'You may assure him that I shall not go to any place or do anything else he *commands* me, until I have seen my father receive Christian burial in this church which he founded. And by no means will I ever take vows as a nun!'

She surprised herself by her own vehemence, but was aware that it stemmed from a great deep-seated longing to be a wife and a mother, to breed sons worthy of her family, grandsons her father would have been proud to own. Even if William succeeded in having her shut up in a nunnery, she determined, she would not take the vows, and she knew that the whole power of the Church would be allied with her against anyone who tried to force them on her. Equally, how could she rest easy or feel that the chapter of her father's life was closed while he remained unburied?

Malet looked alarmed and anxious at her defiance, but Warenne gave her a nod of approval, although he said warningly, 'You'll anger our master if you say things like that!'

'No more than he angers me by ordering me to do something which Holy Church specifies must be done willingly,' she said coldly, secure in the knowledge that this was true, and the more often she stated her objection before witnesses of such standing as Master Athelard, and perhaps even these two Normans, the better. 'And my cousin, the King of Denmark, will also be angry when he hears of your master's attempts to force me to take the veil against my will! I have no doubt, also, that he will have much to say when he hears that a close member of his family has been refused Christian burial by your master. If that is all you have to say, I'll leave you with Master Athelard. I regret that my mother's illness and its cause make it impossible for me to offer you the customary hospitality of our hall, but no doubt the good fathers will provide you with refreshment before you go.'

With that she made a stiff little inclination of her head, emulating her aunt again, and walked away in a slow and dignified fashion, despite a certain unsteadiness in her knees and a strong desire to run away and hide before she dissolved into tears. She was startled to hear Warenne exclaim '*Magnifique!*' behind her, but she did not hesitate or look back.

Later, Master Athelard came to see her, and told her that the Normans had insisted that they must take Ulf away with them. 'They refrained from telling you themselves, for fear of harming you with the shock. I fear we'll have to let him go, for they'll seize him otherwise, and that will frighten him. I'll tell him, and make it sound as if it's something good while you collect his belongings together. You must be brave and cheerful for his

53

sake – no tears, mind! He's back from his riding-lesson now.'

Gytha drew breath to protest, but she knew and trusted Master Athelard, and the stern gaze of his grey eyes prevented her from resisting. If he said it must be so, then it must be. She nodded dumbly and went to make a neat bundle of Ulf's clothes and his favourite toys, particularly a disreputable stuffed cloth animal called Horsey, blinking and sniffing all the while, and managed a dry-eyed farewell, helped by the boy's determined jerk away from anything so shaming as a kiss. He seemed far more interested in the horses and equipment of his escort than concerned about his destination. He took an immediate liking to William Malet, and rode off in the crook of the Norman's arm, chattering so busily in his rudimentary French that he hardly gave more than a perfunctory wave to his sister at Malet's prompting.

Gytha watched as the small cavalcade set out towards the causeway, glad of Master Athelard's firm hand on her shoulder. Warenne lingered for a moment, stepping his horse close to them, and said, 'I'll bring you news of him next time I come here. Try not to worry. All will be well in the end. He's to go to Queen Matilda in Rouen and be brought up with her own children. She'll be kind to him, and see he has the upbringing proper to his rank. For your safety here, I'll be sending some of my people soon to take charge and see that your family and the minster are unmolested.'

Gytha made no reply and turned her face away from him, too bitter and close to tears even to take in what he said, although it came back to her later, and was, surprisingly, comforting.

'I shall inform His Holiness in Rome that your master has taken the boy into safe-keeping,' Master Athelard said, with a stress on *safe*.

Warenne nodded. 'I shall tell my master,' he said, and made it sound like a promise. He wheeled his horse and set off after the others, glancing back and bowing an acknowledgment when he saw that Master Athelard had raised his hand in benediction.

As soon as he was out of earshot, Gytha turned and ran to the

54

church, where she fell on her knees under the chancel arch and wept bitterly, praying incoherently between bouts of sobbing. Father Turkill peeped out of his sacristy from time to time, and when at last she wiped her eyes and climbed wearily to her feet, he came out and said, 'Denmark's in the east, isn't it? Not far enough, though. He'll be a – what do the Normans call it? – a knight. Jerusalem, no doubt of it!' His vague, half-focused gaze wandered up to the Figure on the Cross shining in the candle-light, and he smiled radiantly. 'You'll watch over him, won't You? As You watch over all of us!'

Father Turkill's odd statements usually filled Gytha with a mixture of comfort and alarm, and this time was no exception. The thought of little Ulf one day becoming anything so Norman as a knight was decidedly alarming, but the comfort came from the mention of Jerusalem, for everyone knew that people who died on pilgrimage there were bound to go straight to Heaven. She bowed her head for Turkill's blessing, then walked slowly out of the church.

Father Osgod met her in the doorway, and looked sympath-etically down at her. 'What did they want?' he asked, with a jerk of his head towards the causeway where the Normans had long disappeared.

'Ulf. They've taken him,' Gytha gulped, near to tears again. 'And their Duke says that I'm to go to Wilton and be a nun. I don't want to go.'

'Why?' asked Osgod, staring keenly into her face.

'I don't want to be a nun,' she confessed, afraid that, as a priest, he would think her wrong to reject what he must see as the ideal life for a woman.

'Then you mustn't go. You'd make a bad nun if you did. That life must be accepted joyfully, or not at all. God has a pur-pose for you, and if it's not in t'nunnery, it must be in t'world. He'll call you to it when the time comes. Does your mother know about Ulf?'

Gytha sighed, bracing her shoulders at the reminder that she had not yet attempted to tell Edith. 'No, not unless her women have told her.'

55

Osgod gave a bark of laughter. 'Not they! They're on their knees on t'drying-ground, praying for deliverance from t'Normans! I'll tell her.'

He probably thought that the news would cut through Edith's unnatural detachment, but it did not. He told her what had happened in a surprisingly gentle manner, and she turned her eyes a little in his direction, but made no other response.

'Perhaps she can't hear you,' Gytha said.

'She hears, but t'words have no meaning.' He closed his eyes in silent prayer for a few moments, then left the bower, after signing Edith and Gytha with the Cross in blessing.

Gytha went slowly to her own small chamber to take off her best gown and resume her ordinary one, her mind wandering restlessly over the events of the morning and the frightening possibilities of the future. What hope was there that Duke William – she would never call him King! – would accept her refusal to obey him? None at all, she knew very well, but somehow she must find the courage and determination to go on refusing, and trust in God and Holy Church to protect her.

Warenne came again a few weeks later bringing a dozen of his men, who were lodged in the minster guesthouse while they built themselves a dwelling. One of them was obviously a steward, for he set to work to sort out the precise location of the two hides of land Duke William had allocated for Edith's support. The others were soldiers, although they were prepared to work on the land most of the time. Their leader was a grizzled, grim-faced veteran named Robert.

'I've picked them carefully, and you'll find them trustworthy,' Warenne told Gytha, but the words were intended as much for Master Athelard and Father Wulfwin, who were both present. Master Athelard spoke pleasantly to Warenne, but Wulfwin maintained an aloof silence.

'They won't harm any of your people unless someone is silly enough to start trouble,' Warenne continued. They were standing outside the church at the time, and he surveyed the scene about them with the practised eye of a land-holder, noting the unusually large area of meadow, the two well-kept mills on the nearby stream, the long, low hall, and the cluster of thatched cottages which formed the town. Then he turned and looked past the church towards the great black bulk of the Forest, which filled the whole of the eastward view.

'Much game there?' he asked.

'Very much,' Master Athelard answered. 'Many deer.'

'Coneys?'

Gytha and Master Athelard looked puzzled, and then the scholar remembered his youth in the country around Liège, and the small furry animals from which pies were made. 'No coneys,' he replied.

'A pity. We must introduce some. Wolves?' Warenne sounded hopeful.

'No wolves.' Gytha answered this time. 'A few boar,' she offered in compensation, determined to be civil to the man, as she needed information from him.

Warenne nodded absently, looked up at the sky, surveyed the massive walls of the church, and gave a general impression of a man who is not quite sure what to say next but does not wish to terminate the conversation.

'Have you any news?' Gytha asked abruptly, thinking it time to ask her questions.

Warenne's sharp dark eyes were instantly on her face. He had a quick, jerky way of moving, and seemed very alert. She had noticed that his eyes missed very little, whether he was talking or listening, studying the face of the speaker, yet seeing most of whatever else was going on about him. He even walked quickly, apparently unconscious of the weight of his hauberk, which must have been considerable, for it covered him from neck to knees and was made of interlocking iron rings.

'Your brother Ulf is in Normandy with Queen Matilda,' he said. 'She's taken a liking to him, and he to her, it seems. He has that deplorable stuffed animal, and his uncle Wulfnoth, who supervises his lessons, and he seems very happy. He was seasick on the way over the Narrow Seas, all over poor Malet, but soon recovered when he was on shore again. Your other brothers

57

seem to have disappeared, but I expect your grandmother knows where they are – a very formidable old lady, I understand. She's in – er – what is it called?'

'Exeter,' Gytha supplied without thinking, and then wondered if she had been trapped into letting something slip but he gave no sign of interest.

'My master is still at home, in Normandy, and has a number of guests with him – young Prince Edgar, Earl Edwin, the Archbishop of Canterbury and a few others. The country is reasonably quiet, for the moment, at least.'

'My father . . .' Gytha heard herself say, and shivered, unable to go on.

Warenne met her gaze steadily, but he looked ill at ease, and said nothing for a few moments, then spoke in a hurried, low voice. 'Soon, but not yet. And his brothers.'

'When?' Gytha felt a surge of relief, almost lifting the dead weight of her grief for a moment.

'I can't say, but soon. Malet is arranging it. He and I together concealed him, at the – our master's order. I knew it was Exeter, by the way, but not how to pronounce it!'

Gytha gave him a startled, wide-eyed look, and found there was a smile in his eyes. She almost smiled back, and thought that she might have liked him, had he not been a Norman.

When William of Warenne came again after haymaking, he found his men well settled and content. He had sent word of his coming to Father Wulfwin this time, for he was bringing Harold, Gyrth and Leofwin for burial. He and Malet arrived with a strong escort and three stout carts drawn by oxen, carrying the lead-lined oak coffins which, surprisingly, William of Normandy had provided.

A silent crowd awaited them as the cortège came along the road from the causeway and splashed through the mill-stream ford. Everyone in the town was there, filling the space between the stream and the minster, save for the actual roadway and the gravelled area before the west door. Robert and his men stood

58

among the others, and Warenne's quick glance noted this with some surprise.

Gytha, in her best gown, waited at the church door to receive them, standing very stiff and straight, her pale face set in an unconsciously tragic expression as she prayed very hard that she might not break down and cry in front of all these people. Luckily she had nothing to say, as Father Wulfwin welcomed the Normans in a courteous, subdued tone, speaking in formal Latin as befitted the occasion.

He was a very tall, austere-looking man, who looked even taller and very dignified in the gleaming folds of the great cope which had been one of Harold's gifts to the minster. It was made of cloth of gold and embroidered with words from the scriptures in coloured silks, and decorated with jewels. Gytha wondered why he was wearing it, for it was usually only brought out for the Great Feasts.

'This is a day of both sorrow and happiness for us,' Wulfwin said when he had finished his greeting. 'We are glad that our Founder is restored to us, and mourn that he comes to be entombed, yet, even so, we must rejoice, for surely he is with the saints.'

Malet looked distinctly taken aback at this confident claim, for the Pope had declared an anathema on Harold, and even Warenne, in better control of his face, raised his eyebrows a fraction. Neither made any comment, but stood to either side as the three coffins were carried into the minster. They followed after as Gytha and Father Wulfwin walked behind them and stood to see them laid before the high altar, and then knelt to pray beside them.

As neither of the Normans seemed to know quite what to do next, Master Athelard beckoned them away, out of the church, and invited them to his small house for refreshment, while their men were settling into the guesthouse. Later, he came to the bower to talk to Gytha. 'There are – conditions,' he said.

'Conditions?'

'Yes. There will be no public acknowledgment on either side that William has gone back on his sworn oath. As long as he lives, it must not be said by anyone that he allowed your father Christian burial. Consequently, the service will be secret. Four priests, your mother and yourself may attend, and the same number of Normans. No other witnesses. Others may talk afterwards, but cannot swear to being witnesses if they were not there. There will be no tomb or memorial erected while William lives, not so much as a name carved on a stone. I'm afraid it's for you to agree or refuse, my dear child, under the circumstances . . .' He glanced at Edith, who sat silent and oblivious.

'Considering that he swore he'd never allow it, it seems a generous offer.' Gytha stumbled a little over *generous*, which stuck in her throat, but she managed to speak reasonably calmly, despite her continuing helpless anger at William the Bastard's far from generous oath. 'Will it be tonight?'

'Yes. Which priests do you wish to attend?'

Gytha considered carefully. 'You, of course, and Father Wulfwin, and I think Father Osgod and Father Ailric, for they went to – to find him when . . .' Her eyes filled with tears, which she brushed away quickly. 'The – c-coffins looked very heavy . . .'

'Yes, I discussed that with our friends – for, like it or not, dear child, they are our friends indeed. This would not be happening without their aid! They propose that the Normans, including themselves, should carry each one in turn the short distance necessary, but, as it takes eight men to lift each one, they ask that two canons should help. Osgod and Ailric should be able to manage that, and will certainly be willing.'

'*Normans* to carry my father and uncles to their graves!' Gytha exclaimed, horrified.

'Why not? Warenne has chosen men who knew your father in Normandy, and admired him. Two of them owe him their lives, for he saved them from drowning in quicksand, at great risk to himself. I see nothing wrong with the idea.'

Gytha was silent, thinking, and then said slowly, 'Yes, I suppose it's reasonable, and there'll be no one else to do it if only four canons may be there. Very well, I agree to that.'

Athelard nodded approvingly. 'Our Lord told us we must

love our enemies, and bless those who curse us. How much more should we love an enemy who makes a gesture towards friendship.'

Gytha sighed, but had the sense to realise that he was right. She sat thinking for some time, while Athelard also seemed to sink into a reverie. If she had looked at him she might have seen that he was studying her face, but her eyes were fixed unseeingly on the rush-strewn floor.

'It all seems very stupid,' she said at last. 'Even Duke William liked Father, and Father liked him in some ways. Why can't people be content with what they have, and not keep wanting more? Duke William already had Normandy – why did he want England as well?'

'Your father already had Wessex and the highest place in the land, next the King. Why did he want to be King of the English as well?'

'The Witan chose him . . .' Gytha began defensively, then gave a little shrug, and admitted, 'but he wanted it too, or he'd have spoken for Edgar Atheling. I suppose he really wanted to marry the Lady Aldyth as well.'

Master Athelard noted that she allowed her father's wife the definite article due to the wife of the king as he nodded in reply. 'But not for love of her, poor lady, only for her blood and the support of her brothers.'

'What has happened to her?' Gytha asked, realising that there had been no mention of her since . . .

'I heard that she went to Chester after the battle, with her son.'

'Son!' Gytha was startled.

'Your half-brother, born after your father's death, God protect him, poor orphan! His name is Harold. I heard – only a rumour, mind – that the child is now in Norway. King Olaf owed his life to your father's mercy after Harald Hardrada was killed in Yorkshire, so no doubt he will care for the boy.'

'But my father *killed* his father!'

'The chance of battle. After the battle was over and won, the victor should make peace. Your father thought so, and spared young Olaf to go home and rule Norway. Clearly, he was set a good example.'

Gytha thought hard about that, then said, 'I suppose it's a great honour for a man to be carried to his rest by his enemies, by their own wish. I don't think Father Ailric should help carry those heavy . . . those heavy burdens. He's too small and slight. Would you please ask William of Warenne to find two more Normans, if any are willing?'

So it was that King Harold II Godwinsson and his brothers were carried on their last short journey to their places about the high altar of his minster by eight stalwart members of the army which had defeated and killed them. Two graves had been prepared before the altar, and the third, for the Founder, behind it. After each coffin had been lowered into its last resting-place, the two extra men left the church and Warenne and his companions drew back tactfully into the shadows while Father Wulfwin proceeded with the service.

Only the candles about the altar lit the scene. They flickered gently in the draughts, casting strange shadows on the pale stone of the apse pillars, gleaming softly on the vessels and gold frame of the altar and the bronze strips inlaid into the great columns of the nave arcade. Above the chancel arch, the silver covering of the great, mysterious Cross gleamed softly, and the ruby in the subpedaneum glowed crimson.

Gytha, who had been in the church in the middle of the night only when it was crowded for the Easter and Christmas services, shivered from time to time, not from cold or fear, but with a sense of strangeness, of a brooding Presence somewhere high above in the darkness. It was difficult to make any association between her memories of her father and uncles and what now lay in the bottom of those black pits. They were only coffins, each containing a body, one of them her father's, which even those who knew him well had not been able to recognise after the battle. Only Edith had known him. Her father was not really there, of course. Not in that box. Not the living soul of him. That was – surely it must be – *up there*, with the Presence she could feel hovering over them in the dark shadows beyond the reach of the candle-flames.

A sudden movement beside her turned her attention to her mother.

Edith had shown no sign of awareness when Gytha and Mildyth got her out of bed at midnight, when she had not appeared to be asleep. She had stood unmoving while they dressed her warmly, and Gytha had quietly explained to her what was about to happen. She had followed like a sleepwalker when Gytha took her hand and led her to the church, lighting their way with a little lantern. She had stood where Gytha put her, moved when Gytha led her, and still showed no awareness of anything, but now she had suddenly sunk to her knees and lifted her hands in the attitude of prayer. Her face was in the shadow, and she made no sound, but remained kneeling while the final prayers were said and the ritual handfuls of earth dropped on to the coffins by Gytha and the canons. Gytha then turned towards the shadows, where the light gleaming faintly on the rings of hauberks showed where the Normans stood, and extended her hand in an unconsciously graceful gesture of invitation. After a slight hesitation, the Normans came forward, led by Malet and Warenne, and each bent to take a few crumbs of earth and cast them into the black rectangles at their feet.

Then Edith moved. Still kneeling, she leaned forward and took a handful of the dry, crumbly soil, held it before her for a moment, then rose slowly, walked to her husband's graveside, and let it fall, little by little, on to his coffin. When her hands were empty, she took the gold crucifix from about her neck, kissed it, and dropped that in too. Then she crossed herself and stood like a statue.

There was silence for several seconds. Edith did not move, until Master Athelard went to her and gently drew her away down the church. Wulfwin took one of the candlesticks and led the way towards the west door, holding it out to the side to light the way for the others. Gytha followed, finding Warenne at her elbow, turning his conical helmet round and round in his hands as he walked beside her, while the others came behind, two by two, in silence. Osgod and Ailric alone remained behind, to fill the graves and replace the stone paving slabs.

Chapter Four

Life went on as usual for a few more weeks. The harvest looked promising, and somehow the tax money was found and paid when the sheriff's men came for it. Edith seemed no different, save that she would sometimes rise abruptly from her chair and go to the church to stand silently by the chancel arch for an hour or more at a time, until someone took her by the hand and led her back to the bower. Gytha felt it was an advance, however small, when the women tried to dress her in a gown which she had never liked, and she pushed it away repeatedly until they brought another. Master Athelard said it showed that she was not as unaware of her surroundings as she seemed, but she showed no other signs of awareness.

With the threat of being carried-off, willy-nilly, to Wilton hanging over her, Gytha began to try to work out how she might escape, and decided that she must go to Denmark, for King Svein was her father's cousin, and no friend to William. She could think of nowhere else that would offer a safe haven. It was the obvious solution to her dilemma, but she had no idea how to set about such a journey, and taking her mother would be difficult while Edith remained in this strange half-life, yet she could not leave her. There was no reason now for remaining in England, and many good arguments in favour of leaving while she could, before William returned from Normandy and thought to enquire if she had gone to Wilton. She had a little money, but not nearly enough, she thought, to buy a passage in a ship – and how could she find such a ship? Presumably ships did sail between England and Denmark, but from where? Who might know? Whom could she ask?

It would be easier to give in and go to Wilton. She could not be forced to take vows, and she would be safe there. Safe, but unfree . . .

'What do I want?' she asked herself during one of her sessions of thought and prayer in the church. 'To be safe or free? Free, yes, but why? There's something I must do, something for Father. He meant to do so much for England, but he's been denied the chance. He'd have been such a glorious king if he'd been given time, but William robbed him of his chance of glory, and now he'll be forgotten, or just remembered as an ambitious man who failed. . .

'That's what I must do! I must find a husband, a *royal* husband, and bear sons, fine sons, so that men will see their glory and remember who was their grandfather! William's determined to shut me up at Wilton and never let me marry, so I must make sure that I don't let him succeed. Somehow I must get to Denmark and appeal to King Svein for help. Please, dear Lord, show me the way. It would be easier to give in and be a safe, cloistered nun, but that's not what You or my father expect of me, is it? Very well – I make my choice. I choose the hard path. I will go to Denmark, and I trust in You to show me how.'

Her answer was not overlong in coming. Warenne returned shortly after barley-harvest, arriving unexpectedly through the Forest and entering the town from the east, leading his usual escort and sounding the horn as he approached the town palisade, in the proper manner required by the old English law. Ostensibly he had called at Waltham to bait and water the horses, but while this was being done he sent a courteous message to ask Gytha to grant him a few minutes' conversation in the church.

She changed quickly into a new gown which Mildyth had finished making her a few days before, for her former best gown had become too tight over her growing breasts. Her figure was now far more womanly than it had been when the Norman first came and she felt confident that he could no longer think her a child – if, indeed, he ever had, for he had never treated her otherwise than as a grown woman. She went to the church with a curious mixture of pleasure and apprehension, for she had to admit privately that she was coming to like William of Warenne a great deal, but he was a Norman, and it was likely that he had unpleasant news for her.

He was alone in the cool shadows of the great stone building, standing looking at a wall-painting near the south door. A ray of sunshine made a bright path, full of dancing motes, from one of the windows to a spot near where he stood, and set the rings of his hauberk shining like silver. It passed between him and Gytha as she approached, so that, when he turned towards the sound of her light footsteps, it dazzled him and made him fling up a hand to shield his eyes, then start towards her in his usual quick, jerky way of moving.

Gytha, vaguely aware of Master Athelard's voice reciting his office at one of the altars in the north transept, looked searchingly into the Norman's face.

'I had to see you, but I can only stay a few minutes,' Warenne said, without any preliminaries. 'I'm bound into Norfolk in a hurry, but I turned aside to call here.'

'Is something wrong?' she asked apprehensively.

'No – nothing immediate. Young Ulf is well and happy, and can read easily now, and I've no news, good or bad, of anyone else belonging to you.'

'Then what . . . ?'

'I'll be in Norfolk for two or three weeks – a month, at the most. When I return, I'm instructed to take you and your mother to Wilton.'

'And if I refuse to go?'

'I'm to take you, whether you will or no. They can't force you to take the veil. You'll be safe there, and well looked after.'

'And a prisoner! You don't understand that I'll be shut up in that place, I'll never get out, and they'll keep on and on at me, trying to wear me down! Why must I go? I'll not cause any trouble here. I'll promise anything he wants if only he'll let me stay free and marry some good man and bear children. He can say whom it's to be, and I'll even marry a Norman, if he

66

chooses. I'll marry you . . .' The words poured out in her distress and agitation, until she suddenly realised what she had just said and stopped dead, staring into his face as her cheeks turned first white, then crimson. There was a pause, and then she said, quite calmly, 'Yes, why not? If I marry you, someone he trusts, will he not be content that I can do him no harm?'

'My dear girl!' he breathed, and then they were silent as the little sanctus bell chimed to signal that Master Athelard was about to elevate the Host. They crossed themselves almost automatically, then Warenne closed his eyes for a moment and shook his head.

'I'm sorry. I already have a wife, and my elder son must be as old as you. I'm twice your age, I suppose. I'm very honoured that you should think of me, but I don't believe for one moment that he would ever let you marry even one of his own men. He doesn't trust anyone to the length of giving them the least chance of laying claim to his crown. He'll not wed you to one of his sons, either, for that would be an admission that you're something more than . . .' He broke off suddenly. *The bastard daughter of a dead and dishonoured usurper,*' he finished. 'I'm sorry, but that's what he called you.'

Gytha winced and turned away blinking back tears of anger and chagrin. Warenne looked at her stiffly-held back, biting his lip.

There was a pause, and then he untied a small leather purse from his belt and pressed it into her hand. It was surprisingly heavy, and clinked. 'This is yours, or, rather, your mother's – from the land I administer for her, you remember? I expect you'll want to buy some things for her and yourself, for your journey to Wilton, and – er – various other expenses . . .' He made a typically Gallic gesture to cover those other things, raising his hands and shrugging.

'Thank you.' Gytha could find no more words for a few moments, and then she said thoughtfully, 'You said your elder son – you have two, then?'

'Yes, and another child on the way.'

'What are their names?'

'William and Reynald.'

'I'll remember them in my prayers. I wish your wife a safe delivery.'

One of Warenne's men appeared in the west doorway, his sword clattering against his long hauberk, and cleared his throat loudly, not wishing to enter the building armed, or to interrupt his master. Warenne turned towards him, and called, 'Everyone ready, Ralf?'

'They're just mounting,' the man replied.

He stood waiting as Warenne turned back to Gytha to say, loudly enough for the man to hear, 'I expect to be back in about three weeks. I trust you'll be ready to set out for Wilton.'

'It shouldn't take long to prepare for our departure,' she replied, holding out her hand. 'I wish you a pleasant journey into Norfolk, and a safe return.'

He clasped her hand briefly and bowed, then made his reverence to the altar and strode away down the nave, putting on his helmet as he passed through the door. Gytha stood where he had left her, listening to the sounds outside as his cavalcade departed.

She felt a strange sensation inside her body, which seemed to be located in her stomach. It was a mixture of fear and excitement, and she paused to consider it for a few moments, then decided that it was mostly excitement, and went round the corner into the crossing to wait until Master Athelard had finished his Mass.

He saw her as he moved away from the side-altar, and said anxiously, 'What is it, Gytha? You look as if something important has happened.'

'Warenne was here again. He's going into Norfolk, and is to take Mother and me to Wilton when he returns.'

Master Athelard frowned, but preferred to remain silent while he considered what best to say.

'I shall have to go away, and take Mother with me,' Gytha said hurriedly. 'The King of Denmark is my father's cousin. How can I get to Denmark, Master Athelard? There must be some way.'

'By sea, of course.' Master Athelard did not waste time exclaiming or raising objections. 'Father Osgod mentioned yesterday that there are two Danish ships lying at Barking Creek – he was wishing he might go there to talk to the sailors. He's half Danish, you know. You'll need money to pay your passage.'

'I have some money. Look!' Gytha opened the purse and tipped its contents out into her hand, giving a little gasp of surprise at the number of silver pennies she found herself holding.

Master Athelard raised his eyebrows. 'Did Warenne give you these?' he asked.

'Yes. He said it was from the land he holds on Mother's behalf, but surely two hides can't bring in as much as that in less than a year!'

'It certainly seems a large amount,' Master Athelard said absently, 'but I expect it included rent from your mother's properties in Canterbury.' He walked slowly across to stand under the great Cross, looking up at it, while he either prayed or thought, and then he turned back to Gytha. 'You can't go alone,' he said. 'You need at least one woman with you, quite apart from the problem of looking after your mother unassisted. Mildyth is the most sensible of her women. Ask her if she'll accompany you, but don't let the others know about it. They'll gossip, and the news will get to Robert, who will stop you from going. You must have a man with you as well, for protection, and to bargain with the shipmaster.'

Gytha was silent. It was all very well planning to run away to Denmark herself, but how could she ask anyone else to go with her? Master Athelard was right, though. She could hardly undertake so long a journey without another woman and someone to protect them . . . Her eyes filled with tears as she realised that this wonderful doorway of escape which had opened for her was already closing, and she turned towards the Cross with a wordless surge of misery, fear and beseeching.

'That Norman was here again!' Father Osgod exclaimed sharply as he stalked into the transept by the north door. 'What did he want this time?'

'To warn Lady Gytha to be ready to leave for Wilton when he

returns in a few weeks,' Master Athelard replied, looking at him thoughtfully.

'Wilton! She'll never make a nun!' Osgod said bluntly, turning to Gytha. 'Why don't you go before he comes back?'

Gytha looked up into his dark, shrewd face, and remembered how he had gone into Sussex, to the battlefield, with her mother and Father Ailric. She found herself saying in a rapid, breathless voice, 'You told Master Athelard that there are Danish ships at Barking Creek and you wanted to go to see them. I have some money. If I could get there with Mother, and someone would go with us, we could pay the shipmen to take us with them . . .'

Osgod's face lit up with a happy smile. 'I've always wanted to go to Denmark!' he said. 'My father was a Dane, you know – we always spoke Danish at home. I've kin over there . . . How soon can you be ready?'

Gytha wondered inconsequentially what race his mother could have been to produce so dark-haired a son by a Danish father, but then it wasn't necessarily true that all Danes were fair-haired and blue-eyed.

'You'd go with them?' Master Athelard asked, his face and voice giving away nothing of his opinion of the idea.

'If Father Wulfwin gives me leave.'

'And come back again?'

'Of course. My place is here.'

'But you'd leave your duty to travel overseas?'

'Would you see a wild bird shut up in a cage, or a deer penned in a hen-house?' Osgod's eyes blazed, and his skin seemed to be drawn tightly across the bones of his face as he rounded on Master Athelard. 'Can my brothers not manage a little extra work for a few weeks while I see our King's daughter safely to her cousin's charge? Do you expect a sick woman and a young maid to travel alone because no one here is man enough to go with them?'

'Indeed no,' Master Athelard replied mildly. 'I was merely enquiring whether you realised the difficulties and dangers of a sea-voyage to a strange and half-heathen country, and the possibility of returning to a warm welcome from an angry William of Normandy.'

'T'Lord protects His servants,' Osgod replied confidently. 'I sinned against you, Master Athelard, and I humbly beg your forgiveness.' Master Athelard bowed his acknowledgment, but Osgod was already continuing, 'I'll go seek Father Wulfwin straight away. We'd best go tonight.'

'Tonight!' gasped Gytha with a mixed feeling of fear and excitement.

'Aye! T'sooner, t'better. If we go at night, nobody need see us go, and tonight's best before anyone can wonder and talk.'

'We'll be ready.' Gytha made up her mind without further hesitation in response to Osgod's decisiveness. 'You'd best take charge of this,' and she gave him the bag of money. His eyebrows rose as he weighed it in his hand. 'And thank you!'

'I'll come to t'bower when I've see Father Wulfwin,' he said, and strode off.

Gytha turned towards Master Athelard, who seemed to have withdrawn a little into the background, and hesitated, unsure of his opinon.

'It all seems to be coming together very satisfactorily,' he observed. 'The Lord bless you and keep you, dear child.' Gytha dropped to her knees and felt his hand rest lightly on her head for a few seconds, and then he helped her to her feet, and said, 'You have much to do, and I must hear no more. The less I know, the fewer half-truths I must tell in the future!'

Gytha found Mildyth alone in the bower with Edith when she returned there. She said nothing of her plans for the moment, but picked up her spindle and worked with it for a while, until Osgod suddenly appeared in the doorway. He caught her eye, nodded once, then went away again. She turned at once to Mildyth and hurriedly explained what she intended to do, then asked hesitantly if the woman would consider going with them.

'I must do whatever you say,' Mildyth replied evasively, looking frightened.

'I ask you as a free woman, not a slave!' Gytha said earnestly. 'I know it's a great deal to ask of anyone – to leave home and everything you know, and go into a strange land. I'll not blame you if you refuse, but for me, it's Denmark or a nunnery, so I must go, and take Mother with me.'

'You think King Svein will help you?' Mildyth said doubtfully.

'His father was my grandmother's brother. He's the only one of my kin who can help me now, and I trust he'll not refuse,' Gytha said, answering her own doubts as well as Mildyth's.

'My husband and children are long dead. I've served Lady Edith since before you were born,' Mildyth said reflectively. 'With both of you gone, there'll be nothing left to keep me here. My grandfather was a Dane, from Hedeby, so it won't really be a strange country . . . Yes, I'll come, and willingly!'

'Oh, God bless you!' Gytha hugged her impulsively, at which Mildyth sniffed and bustled away to sort out what clothing they would need to wear and to take with them, while Gytha sat by her mother and quietly explained to her what she was planning to do. Edith showed no sign of understanding, but, when Gytha finished by saying desperately, 'I have to go before Warenne comes back, but I can't leave you. Will you come?' she nodded her head. It was only a slight movement, but quite unmistakable. Gytha closed her eyes and offered a brief prayer of thanks before going to help Mildyth select the few things they would be able to take with them.

Obviously, all they had of value must be taken. Gytha had very little jewellery – a pair of gilt and enamel brooches, the small silver cross given to her at her baptism by King Edward, her amber beads – but Edith had several gold and silver chains, pins, brooches, and a long rope of freshwater pearls. All these were carefully sewn into the hems of the garments which Gytha and Mildyth would wear for the journey. For each of them, there would be a change of clothing, rolled into neat bundles. Gytha was tempted to take her favourite garments, but had the sense to choose warm and serviceable things and put all the rest back in the clothing-chests, except for her best silk overtunic. She spread that out on her bed and stroked its shimmering folds sadly, then carefully folded it and set it aside. When the bundles had been wrapped and tied securely, she carried them and the overtunic to the church, and sought out Turkill in the sacristy.

'May I leave these bundles here for a while,' she asked him, 'and I wonder if you could find a use for this?' holding out the silk.

Turkill accepted it gratefully, and bade her leave her bundles by the door. 'We'll find them there easily when it's time to go,' he said. 'I'm to come with you to Barking. I know the way, and then I'll go on with the mules to our church at South Weald. I was going there anyway, for a few weeks. The Normans will think Osgod's with me, and he can join me there when he gets back. I said you would go beyond the sunset, and Denmark's a good start on the way. You'll be late for your supper.'

It took Gytha a second to realise that the last was not foreknowledge, but a practical observation, for the church bells were chiming to call the townsmen home to their evening meal. She thanked Turkill again and hurried to the hall to take her seat at the high table. She was careful to see that everything she did was as usual, for fear of arousing any curiosity in anyone, but it was difficult to make a good show of eating with her normal healthy appetite when her stomach was churning with that odd mixture of fear and excitement, or to keep tears from her eyes when she realised that this was the last meal she would eat in the place which had been her home all her life.

After supper, there were still nearly two hours of daylight left, so, as she often did in the long summer evenings, she strolled round the little town, where the folk were making the most of the light to work in their gardens, tend their bees and all the other jobs that needed doing when their work in the fields was over for the day. She stopped to speak to Robert and his men, who were mending the town's picket fence, more a defence against deer and wild pigs with a liking for cabbages than against human enemies, and several other people who looked up from their work to greet her, just as she always did.

There was time to walk a little way by the mill-stream, thinking about her father and the many times they had come this way, remembering some of the things he had told her, and praying for him in the place he had loved so much.

'I'm going away because I have to, Father,' she said to him inside her head. 'I don't want to leave, any more than you did, but I want to do something with my life to make people remember that I'm your daughter, and leave children to follow me who'll be proud to say that they are your grandchildren.'

When it was almost dark, she went to the church and slipped inside. Father Wulfwin was conducting Vespers, with the other canons in residence and the choirboys assisting. A few townsfolk stood about in the nave, but Gytha moved quietly up the north aisle and into the transept, where she would be alone, and stood listening.

The boys' voices were clear and well tuned, and roused echoes in the high roof of the great building, as if another, unseen, choir was joining with them. The incense and the candle-flames rose with the voices, and looking up into the darkness overhead, she could almost imagine that she saw the gleam of the pale golden stone in the triforium and clerestory. It would be easy to fancy that she could also hear the sound of golden wings up there, but perhaps that was only the flitter-mice in the wooden roof.

When the service was over, the choir filed out, two by two, through the south transept to their own lodging, and the canons to their homes. The townsfolk left by the west door, and only Turkill was left, pinching out all but two of the candles, and taking the rest into the sacristy. Wulfwin walked slowly down from the chancel into the crossing, and stopped briefly beside her.

'You will wish to pray by your father's grave,' he said. 'You may enter the Sanctuary.'

'Thank you,' she replied. 'Will you give me your blessing, Father?'

'Of course. I think you are wise to go, for the cloistered life is not for you. Don't be afraid, my daughter, but trust in God and our Holy Cross, and be sure that we shall pray for you here every day. The Holy Spirit will go with you, for, remember, He is not only here, but everywhere.'

Gytha's eyes filled with tears as Father Wulfwin's hand rested firmly on her head while he pronounced a long Latin blessing, then he gave her a little pat, said, 'Go with God,' and went away.

She went hesitantly into the Sanctuary, for it was a rare privilege to be allowed within the sacred enclosure, and knelt by the plain stone slab behind the altar which marked Harold's grave. Presently Osgod and Turkill joined her, and they prayed silently on either side of her until she felt that she had nothing more to say in her silent communication, and rose stiffly to her feet.

Osgod crossed himself and stood up, then put a hand on her arm and drew her away, back to the nave, where he said quietly, 'Go and lie down for a couple of hours, and sleep, if you can. I'll come for you when it's time to go.'

She nodded, and walked softly towards the door, turned to make one last reverence and take one last look, then slipped out into the summer night.

Chapter Five

There was a sharp crack in the darkness, as if something heavy had trodden on a dead branch, and a sudden rustling in the undergrowth somewhere to Gytha's right. She instinctively reined in her mule and almost held her breath, but Mildyth gave a startled squeak of fright, and Turkill said 'Shh!' soothingly from his place in the lead of the party.

'If you're going to make that silly noise every time we disturb an animal, we'd be better off without you!' Osgod remarked from behind them.

'What was it?' Mildyth whispered in an unsteady voice.

'A pig, probably, or an oliphaunt,' Osgod replied. 'What have we stopped for?'

'What's an oliphaunt?' Gytha asked, kicking her reluctant mule into action again.

'A grey animal, big as a haystack, with a tail at each end,' Osgod replied tersely, and Gytha was uncertain whether to believe him or not.

They had been riding for over half an hour, but had not travelled very far. For the first mile, they had walked the mules on the grass at the side of the road to avoid being heard by anyone wakeful in the town, and almost as soon as they entered the Forest, Turkill had led them off the road and struck diagonally up the steep side of the ridge, heading south-eastwards. Although the moon had just risen, it was dark among the thick trees, and there were marshy areas and gullies to negotiate as they climbed the narrow track which seemed no more than a deerpath.

The ground now started to rise very steeply as they drew near to the top of the ridge, and the mules were blowing heavily. It seemed to Gytha that the sound must carry for miles, and there appeared to be a continuous series of cracks and loud rustles, as if a whole army was crashing about in the undergrowth. She had not thought that the Forest by night would be so noisy.

An occasional break in the leafy cover allowed the odd moonbeam to illumine a tree-bole, the dark figures ahead of her, a ghostly silver birch, a running squirrel, a white owl gliding between the trees, which brought another frightened squeak from Mildyth, who knew very well that owls were evil and unlucky, an exasperated sigh from Osgod and the sudden twitter of an indignant, sleepy bird.

They were riding in single file, with Turkill first, leading Edith's mule behind his own, then Gytha, followed by Mildyth, with Osgod in the rear. They were all riding astride five of the best mules in the college's stables, and were wrapped in the black hooded cloaks that were the canons' normal travelling-wear. A neat bundle was tied behind each saddle, holding all that the three women now possessed, and food for the journey.

The pace of the mules grew slower and slower as the ground reared up more steeply, but suddenly, in a particularly dark area, Gytha's mount gave a heave of its hindquarters and quickened its pace as it reached the more level ground at the top and emerged on an open stretch of grass.

'We'll stop here awhile and let the poor creatures get their breath,' said Turkill, dismounting. He lifted Edith down and then Mildyth, while Gytha dismounted unaided and went to her mother. Turkill sat down on the grass, keeping hold of the mules' bridles, and the women followed suit, Mildyth hesitantly, first peering at the ground in the moonlight as if she suspected mud or insects, and Edith only when Gytha said, 'Will you sit, Mother?'

Osgod took the bridles, one by one, and drew them forward over the mules' heads, so that they hung down in front of their feet, and this seemed to discourage the animals from walking about, for they stood still, heads down in a dejected, weary fashion, breathing heavily and obviously inviting sympathy, which they did not get. After a few minutes, they began to eat grass with good appetites.

Meanwhile, Osgod walked a few yards away to a place where a break in the trees gave a clear view of the town, and Gytha joined him. The minster gleamed white in the moonlight, with the narrow silver bands of the seven streams of the river shining beyond it. The thatched and tiled roofs of the houses huddled about the church, and somewhere among them a dog barked half a dozen times, then was silent. The sound carried, faint but recognisable, in the still night air.

'It looks so small and defenceless down there,' Osgod said, half to himself. 'Just a score of houses and a rickety fence.'

'Like chickens round a mother hen,' Gytha replied. If she half-closed her eyes, the minster did look like a brooding hen. There was a faint yellow gleam in the windows of the eastern apse. The shutters must have been left open, which was unusual at night, and that was the light of the candles round the high altar, she thought, surprisingly bright for only two of them. Then she saw the light increase, growing brighter and brighter.

'What's happening?' she asked. 'Is it on fire?'

'No,' Osgod replied calmly. 'Father Wulfwin's lit more candles. That's a signal that nobody's stirring in t'town. We weren't heard to leave, or, rather, no one's raised t'alarm.'

They watched in silence as the light shone out bravely, picking out each of the windows along the south aisle as Wulfwin flung open the shutters and set a lighted candle on each window-sill in turn. The church glowed like a lantern for a few minutes, then, one by one, the lights went out until there remained only the faint gleam at the east end which they had first seen. Then that, too, went out as the shutters were closed.

'That was beautiful!' Gytha sighed.

'Ay. Something to remember,' Osgod agreed. 'Time to go on, I think. T'mules seem to be rested.'

The animals were fidgeting about now, no longer eating or drooping. Turkill and Osgod helped the women to mount, and they set off, plunging among thick trees again, still heading south of east, but on fairly level ground for a short while.

The weird cry of an owl sounded near at hand, setting the

mules tossing their heads and snorting, and making Gytha shiver. Another answered in the distance, and then the ground suddenly began to slope down as they reached the eastern side of the ridge-top. A moonlit ride ran in the right direction, and Turkill turned into it with a murmured '*Deo gratias!*', then suddenly halted, flinging up a hand to warn the others and jerking it sharply to signal for silence.

For a moment Gytha caught her breath in fear, thinking that they were discovered, that some Normans were come upon them . . . Then she let it out in a sigh of wonder as a group of roe deer crossed the ride in front of them, stepping so lightly that they made no sound, the silver light dappling their smooth coats and glistening here and there on a lustrous eye. They were moving quite slowly and hardly seemed aware of the human presence, although one or two glanced inquisitively towards the five mules as they passed. The last of the group gave a skittish little jump, apparently out of sheer high spirits, before disappearing between the trees.

'Little faery creatures,' said Turkill contentedly as he started his mule forward again. 'Pretty to see.'

'And good to eat,' added Osgod prosaically from the rear.

They rode on through the Forest without any further cause for alarm, and, some two hours later, reached the broad water-meadows of the Roding valley.

'Let's rest here awhile and eat,' Turkill suggested, and then, as Osgod hesitated, 'There'll not be another chance for a long time. We don't want to be sitting about in the open, munching our bread and cheese outside Barking Abbey!'

'Very well,' Osgod agreed reluctantly swinging his long leg over his mule's back and sliding off. He tethered the animals in the shadow of a tree while Turkill helped the women down and unwrapped the bundle of food.

The bread was fresh and crusty, and the cheese some of the best, which was usually kept for the more important pilgrims, and there was a flask of wine as well, which was passed round and gave everyone a good swallow. Despite its being very early for breakfast, they were all hungry. They had almost finished before Gytha realised that her mother had been breaking the bread and eating without any help or prompting.

'How are you, Mother?' she asked hopefully, but Edith made no reply, and did not look at her.

The rest of the journey was made more quickly, for the mules could trot across the level grassland almost without a sound. There was an occasional check when they had to negotiate a ditch or a little tributary, and once they had to wait in the shadow of a clump of willows while Turkill made sure it was safe to cross the grass-grown Roman road which ran from Bow to Dunmow, but was hardly ever used now. There were only three villages to pass and they lay well back from the river, on the rising ground above the winter flood-level.

When the stars had faded and the sky was growing light, Turkill turned to say, 'The banners are out to welcome us!' in a cheerful voice, waving his arm in an expansive gesture. Gytha, who had been watching the ground before her mount's feet, looked up and saw that the eastern sky was streaked with red, which turned to gold as she watched, and the sun suddenly rose behind a group of black trees.

It was full morning when they reached the main highway from London into Essex. Turkill did not slow down, let alone stop, but blew a single low toot on the horn he carried tied to his saddle before leading them to the ford, turning left across it on to the road and trotting steadily between the cottages clustered around the crossing. People going about their work glanced up with little interest as the party passed them. Many travellers used this road, and there was nothing odd about a group of canons riding by, even this early in the morning.

'There's no concealment now, so behave as naturally as you can,' Turkill said. 'Put up your hoods, and most folk will think we're all clerics. If anyone shows more interest, you're three Danish ladies who've been visiting kin in England, and are now going home again.'

'I suppose that's possible,' Osgod said doubtfully. 'Danish women have more freedom than most, and do some odd things, and that's no odder than some tales I've heard.'

'Think of a better story, then,' said Turkill good-humouredly. 'If you can't, pray.'

Gytha tried for half a mile to manufacture a more likely story, and, as they turned right off the highway into the narrow lane to Barking, said, 'Would it be better to say that we've been on pilgrimage to the Holy Cross at Waltham to pray for healing for my mother?'

'Excellent!' said Turkill, and Osgod grunted agreement.

A group of men were coming towards them, trudging from the town to one or the other of the great fields which lay on either side of the lane. They drew to the verge to let the mules go by, and snatched off their hoods and bowed their heads as Turkill gave them a beaming smile and a cheerful blessing, which Osgod echoed in more restrained tones.

Turkill blew his horn again, for ahead they could see the central tower of Barking Abbey church rising above the red roofs of the conventual buildings, and, beyond, the tiled or thatched roofs of houses running down to and along the sides of the creek. Smoke was rising from a couple of score of hearths, and there was a bustle of activity in the street.

As they approached the gate of the abbey, the bells chimed, and it was only then Gytha recollected, with horror, that Duke William had made Barking Abbey his headquarters until a strong castle could be built for him in London. He might still be in Normandy, but surely many of his followers would still be here! She pulled her hood more closely about her face and tried not to look towards the convent, but her eyes were drawn irresistibly towards the wall that surrounded it. If she failed to escape, in a few weeks she would be shut up inside such a wall, with no hope of escape and no sight of the open country all around. It seemed as if hundreds of eyes must be looking out from these walls, all scrutinising the little party, piercing the flimsy disguise of their dark cloaks and hoods, and, in a few moments a horde of Normans must come bursting out of the gateway to seize her and drag her inside.

She hastily turned her thoughts to something else. How strange that William should have chosen an abbey of nuns for his headquarters! Why had he not used the old palace by King Edward's new church at Westminster? Was it because he feared the Londoners? Barking Creek was a good harbour, and ships from Normandy could anchor here without risking the passage under London Bridge, so that must be his reason, but what a disruption for the poor nuns!

Her fears and disjointed thoughts had carried her almost to the abbey gatehouse, and she could not help looking at the gate as she approached it. To her horror, the wicket opened and a man stepped out, ducking his head through the low opening. Like most of the Normans she had seen, he was dressed in a mail hauberk and leggings and a conical helmet, with a heavy sword at his side, but something familiar about him made her go on looking at him instead of turning her head away. He pulled off his helmet and looked up at the sky, and as she saw his face, she gave a start and the hood slipped back off her head. It was William Malet!

Having looked at the sky, he glanced idly at the passing travellers, even as Gytha made a grab at the hood and pulled it back over her head. His eyes narrowed as they reached her face, just before she could conceal it, and he flung up a hand. She held her breath, but he turned away, his hand dropping to his side, and put his head back in through the open wicket to shout to someone inside, 'Can't you wake that horse? We should have been away half an hour ago!'

Gytha glanced back once, and saw that he was still talking to someone inside the gate, his hands gripping either side of the opening and the light dazzling on the hundreds of metal rings on his hauberk. Then she realised that the sun must have been shining straight into his face when he looked up at her, so that was why his eyes had narrowed and he had flung up his hand. She must have been no more than a dark shape against the glare.

'We're certainly under the shadow of His wing,' Osgod said quietly, just loud enough for her to hear. 'I've never seen such a clear sign – to meet t'one man in this place who could recognise you, and to pass him unseen!'

Gytha crossed herself under her cloak and murmured a prayer of thanks, pulling her hood close round her face again as they picked their way along the main street of the town through pigs and chickens and people.

It was a busy place, particularly along the quay, where a dozen fishing-boats were unloading their catches and shrill-voiced housewives were bargaining for the fish. There were two or three larger vessels anchored out in the creek, but none of them looked like Gytha's idea of a Danish ship.

Turkill's mule went on steadily, moving slowly through the crowd of women who were coming or going with their baskets. Most of them were too busy talking to take more than a cursory glance at the travellers, who probably looked like a group of monks to an unobservant eye. In a few minutes they had passed the fish quay, and then the cottages grew more sparse, straggling along towards the mouth of the creek.

Turkill stopped by an old man who was sitting on a barrel in the sun watching the bustle on the quay, and asked him if he knew where the Danish ships might be.

'In the river, down there,' he replied, waving vaguely towards the way they were going. 'The reeve won't let them into the creek.'

Turkill thanked him and gave him a blessing, which he acknowledged with a jerky bow, and they rode on.

The track they were following rose above rough salt-marshes as the cottages petered out, the causeway acting as a low barrier to the high tides which sometimes surged up the creek. In another mile, they came to a few more cottages on the point where the creek widened out into the great river. Gytha had once been to London and seen the Thames there, but here it was much wider. There were many vessels in sight, all moving purposefully about their business. All but two. They were larger than any ships she had ever seen before, quite fifty feet long, broad-beamed, low in the water, with great swelling curves at bow and stern. A long tent-like structure of the weather-faded striped woollen cloth called wadmal ran along the length of each.

Gytha guessed that they must be the ships they sought, but she exclaimed, 'I though Danish ships were long and lean, not fat things like this!'

'You're thinking of t'warships t'Vikings used,' said Osgod. 'These are trading ships. Well, at least they've not sailed yet.'

Gytha ignored Osgod's remark, and concentrated on more important matters. 'How can we get to them?' she asked, for they were anchored several yards out into the river. Then she saw four small boats drawn up on the stony beach.

'There's an alehouse,' Turkill said. 'We'd best wait there while Father Osgod finds the shipmaster.'

They walked along the shore to the alehouse, where Turkill tied the mules to the rail outside, unloaded the bundles and led the way in. They entered a fairly large room with a few benches and trestle tables standing about. Some hens wandered among them, pecking at the earth floor, and a dozen more still roosted in the rafters. A fire was burning on the central hearth and an appetising smell drifted through the smoke from something sizzling in a pan, watched over by a stout woman. A man sprawled on one of the benches, his back against a table and his elbows on the edge of it. He had a woollen cap pulled on at a jaunty angle over a mass of greying fair hair, and that part of his face which was not hidden by a reddish-blond beard was brown and weatherbeaten. He surveyed the newcomers with very bright blue eyes.

'You'd best cut some more bacon,' he advised the woman, who took no notice. 'These folk have been travelling all night.'

Osgod pronounced the customary blessing, at which the man snatched off his cap and sat up straight, but the woman still took no notice, and then the priest said courteously, 'Do you know where I may find the master of the Danish ships?'

'What do you want with him? asked the man, pulling on his cap and relaxing into his former attitude.

'A passage to Denmark,' Osgod answered.

'For all of you?'

'For four of us. You are the shipmaster?'

'I don't carry passengers,' the man replied obliquely.

'We can pay,' Osgod said.

Gytha bit her lips and clasped her hands together. If he refused, her last hope would be gone, and then what could she do?

The man was silent. He looked at Osgod carefully, then at Gytha, then at Edith and Mildyth, who were by the door with Turkill. After a few moments, he looked at Gytha again. She pushed back her hood and returned his stare with as much dignity as she could muster.

'We don't carry women. The men don't like it,' he said curtly, and turned away.

'We'll pay well,' Gytha said desperately.

'Money's nothing to do with it. We don't carry women,' the man repeated.

'Why not?'

'It's unlucky. Everyone knows that.'

Gytha's head suddenly jerked up, and the muscles about her mouth tightened in a way which reminded Osgod sharply of her father.

'And would it bring you good luck, do you think,' she asked in a cold, quiet voice, 'to leave three women and a priest to be done to death by William of Normandy, which will surely happen if you refuse to take us to Roskilde?'

The shipmaster gave her an uneasy look, but made no reply.

'And what will your luck be,' Gytha continued, 'when your king learns that you left his cousin to be murdered by the Normans because you were afraid to carry a woman in your ship?'

The shipmaster stared at her, his jaw dropping. 'King Svein?' he exclaimed. 'His cousin?' His surprise turned to disbelief. 'How do you reckon to be his cousin?'

'The King's father was Jarl Ulf, who had a sister named Gytha. That Gytha was my father's mother, and I am named for her.'

The shipmaster digested this, frowning with concentration as he traced the pedigree in his mind – no difficult feat for a man of his time, used to reciting his own for many generations whenever he met fellow-countrymen who were strangers.

'Lord save us!' he said at last. 'You're King Harold's . . . Oh, saints preserve me! I don't want no trouble, lady!'

'We'll give you no trouble,' Gytha replied calmly. 'We need to go to Denmark and the captain who takes us will earn the favour of my cousin King Svein – and we'll pay.'

'I'm not bound for Roskilde, lady, but I can take you to Ribe. It's easy enough from there, overland and by ferry.' He scratched his head. 'Two silver pennies each, if you have it, and that includes your food. Nothing for the priest – he can come free.'

Gytha looked at Osgod, who said, 'That's a very fair price, and I thank you for your courtesy.'

'One apiece now, and the rest when I set you ashore in Ribe.'

Osgod nodded, and fished out the three coins from the bag which Gytha had put in his charge. The shipmaster looked at them, bit them, spat on them, and put them safely away somewhere inside his clothing.

'Is anyone after you at the moment?' he asked conversationally.

'I hope not!' Gytha exclaimed.

'We can't sail until the slack water between tides, you see,' he said briskly. 'We'd best eat.' He nudged the stout woman in the back, and she turned, starting with surprise when she saw the others standing there. The shipmaster mouthed at her and made signs with his hands, at which she smiled, nodding vigorously, and hurried to fetch more bacon and some eggs and bread.

Soon they were all sitting at the table with a platter before each of them piled with bacon and eggs and good fresh bread. Osgod said grace and they set to with good appetites, despite the bread and cheese they had eaten at dawn. Even Mildyth began to look less worried.

'I'm called Olaf Eriksson,' the shipmaster said expectantly.

'Edith Magnussdaughter,' Gytha replied, indicating her mother. I'm Gytha Haroldsdaughter, and this is Mildyth . . . er . . .'

'Edwardsdaughter,' supplied Mildyth, glancing towards the stout woman, who had just arrived with a jug of ale and some

86

wooden cups.

Osgod took up the tale. 'Father Turkill isn't coming with us. I'm Osgod Bjornsson. Mass-priest,' he added, in case there was any doubt.

'She's called *Wavequeen*,' Olaf said, indicating one of the two ships that were visible through the open door. 'The inshore one. Some of my crew are packing the cargo, and the rest will be back by noon. They've gone to the villages hereabouts to buy honey.'

'Honey?' queried Gytha. It seemed an odd cargo for a Dane to carry.

'There's a good market for it in the north, where they don't get a long enough summer to make much themselves. We'll take it to Nidaros on the Norway coast.'

'What else are you carrying?' asked Turkill.

'Cloth and barley. We brought wine from the Rhine to sell. We come three or four times a year, but we used to go right up to London. This new king put a stop to that – doesn't trust Danes, apparently!'

'He's probably heard how our great-grandfathers towed away London Bridge!' said Osgod.

This caused the shipmaster a great deal of amusement, but, even while he was laughing, he observed that Turkill was eyeing the stout woman uneasily, and said, 'Don't worry about Bertha! She's deaf as a post – has been since birth! I've known her more years than I care to remember.' He rambled on for a time, recalling earlier visits to England, until they had all finished eating and drinking, and then said, 'You stay here, and I'll go and have some sort of a shelter fixed up for you in the ship. You're safe enough inside, but best not go wandering about on the shore. The Normans don't usually come down here, but no point in taking risks.'

The rest of the morning seemed to pass very slowly. Osgod and Turkill had their Office to say, and Edith, as usual, sat still and silent, but Mildyth kept going to the door to peer out at the river and the ships, wondering aloud if the sea would be very rough, and if the ship was seaworthy. Gytha felt more and more depressed and anxious with every minute that passed. She worried about the dangers of the voyage ahead, about what might happen at Waltham when William found she was gone, about whether Olaf might cheat them by sailing without them, about King Svein's reaction when they arrived in Roskilde – if they ever did, which started her off again on the same circle, like a wild creature in a cage.

'There's someone coming!' Mildyth suddenly hissed.

Osgod, who had been sitting contemplating his own feet for the last half-hour, shot across to the door and looked out. The sun was almost overhead, and a group of men had come down the track from Barking and were piling small casks and clay pots into one of the rowing-boats. As he watched, they pushed it out, and two of them began to row out towards *Wavequeen*. The rest turned and came towards the alehouse.

By the time they arrived, Osgod had his party sitting round the table nearest the door, and he stood in front of them, his hood down and his cloak thrown back so that they could see he was a priest. As the men came in, laughing and talking good-humouredly about their experiences buying honey, they each made a little bow when they saw him, and glanced without much curiosity at his companions.

The stout woman was soon serving ale and dishing out great bowls of a savoury mixture of vegetables and meat, and the men sat down to eat in something of a hurry, still talking between mouthfuls, until Olaf came in and uttered a sharp order which brought silence.

'The wind's fair and it's slack water. We'll sail as soon as you're all aboard. We've a few passengers, but they'll not be any concern of yours.'

This brought a stir of interest, but nobody questioned Olaf's obliquely-worded order. The men gulped down the rest of their food and their ale and filed out, wiping their mouths on the backs of their hands. Olaf held another conversation of mouthing gestures with the stout woman and gave her some money and a hearty kiss, which made her bridle and toss her head, grinning broadly. Osgod asked Olaf to find out what he owed for his party's food, but the shipmaster said, 'It's paid. That's part of our bargain,' and ushered them out through the door.

Olaf called three brawny sailors to lift the women into one of the boats as it was pushed out, and Gytha had only time for a swift handclasp and a blessing from Turkill, who stood watching as the sailors and Osgod scrambled into the boats and rowed out to the ship. He saw how neatly and carefully the women were got aboard and taken to a shelter of wood and canvas in the stern, and marvelled how quickly the ship was ready to leave.

The canvas structure was not very substantial, but it was enough to make a sleeping-place for the three women, and somewhere to keep their small amount of baggage. Mildyth disappeared inside with Edith, but Gytha stood beside it and watched as the wadmal awning was rolled up, and the beam which supported it was turned into a yard and hoisted up the mast, the awning being unrolled again to become the sail. This was broached round to catch the wind, and then, suddenly, they were moving.

She turned and looked towards the shore, where already Turkill was no more than a small dark figure standing at the water's edge, waving. She waved back, and brushed away the tears which blurred her vision, regretting all the things (including thanks) which there had been no time to say to him in the hurry of their departure. She strained to see him until he was only a dot in the distance, moving away towards the tethered mules. She supposed she would never see him again, but at least she would be able to send him a message with Father Osgod when he returned to Waltham. For the rest – all the other people and things she was leaving behind – there was nothing more. They were gone now, for ever – her childhood, her home, her father's grave and his church, her little sister, her brothers, and she would probably never see any of them again.

For a long time she stared unseeingly at the shore as it slipped past, receding further and further as the ship sped on its way, her eyes full of tears which spilled over and trickled down her cheeks.

When her vision cleared at last, the coast had fallen away until, in the twilight, it was no more than a grey blur on the horizon. The sky behind them blazed with a fine sunset for a while, and then gradually faded to streaks of crimson, which were finally swallowed in grey dusk, and stars appeared overhead. By then, there was nothing to see but the endless waves. England was left behind.

A lump rose in Gytha's throat and her eyes filled with tears again as she wondered if she would ever see it again. The words of an old poem echoed in her mind:

> *Coldness of heart for the gay countryside,*
> *Wake up and see instead the yellow waves,*
> *The seabirds bathing, stretching their wings,*
> *While snow and hail and frost fall all together.*

It was only the practical thought that at least it was summer, and things could be very much worse, that saved her from sobbing her heart out, and then she thought, 'But I've done it! I've escaped! Thank You, Lord God, for setting my feet on the path I've chosen – the whale's path, over the sea.'

Roskilde

Chapter Six

'My lady,' Mildyth exclaimed, hurrying into the house so quickly that she was almost running, 'do you know who she is? Oh, saints preserve us! Whatever shall we do? Just when I thought we were settled.'

Gytha looked up from her spinning, startled. For Mildyth to forget her dignity enough to indulge in unseemly haste was surprising enough, but her agitation was quite astonishing. During the past year, she had become a remarkably calm and steady woman, her character blossoming in her important new role as principal waiting-woman to the Princess of England.

'Whatever is it?' Gytha asked anxiously. 'Oh, do sit down, Mildyth, and get your breath, and then tell me it all from the beginning.'

Mildyth plumped down on a stool, one hand clasped to her bosom, and took a few gasping breaths, and then said, in something more like her usual practical tones, 'King Svein's new wife's arrived! I've just been talking to one of her women. Oh, my dear lady, didn't the King tell you who she is?'

'Why, yes. He said that her name is Elisev, and she's the daughter of a great prince who lives far to the east, in Rusland, wherever that is, I've never heard of it. Is she beautiful? Does the King like her?'

'Oh, I don't know – I haven't seen her yet – but didn't he tell you where she's been these past twenty years, since she left her father's house?'

'No.'

'Well, she's been in Norway. You remember King Harald Hardrada, whom your father, rest his soul, killed at Stamford Bridge – rest his soul too –? Well, when he was on his travels to

Constantinople, he stayed at her father's court, and when he was on his way back, he stopped there again and married her. She's his widow! Oh, how could the King do this to you! Why didn't he warn you?'

Gytha felt a cold finger of apprehension, and bent her head over her spinning, pretending that the thread had broken, while she tried to sort out her thoughts and emotions. Why, indeed, had the King not warned her? He had been so kind and considerate to her and her mother ever since they arrived in Roskilde a year ago. He had given them this house to live in, near the royal hall, treated her as if she were one of his own daughters, giving her servants, clothes, and lands providing sufficient rents for her to support her little household and live in comfort. He had even given her a place at his table with his own family for supper every night. Did he not understand that Hardrada's widow would be bound to hate her, because her father . . . ?

'Perhaps he didn't realise,' she said uncertainly. 'But he can't have forgotten. He's always so interested in the affairs of other lands, and he's asked me so often about what happened in England during those last two years . . . What am I to do, Mildyth?'

'Pray she's not a vengeful woman!' Mildyth said grimly. 'Well, you'll find out soon enough. You'll meet her when you go to supper in the hall tonight. We must be sure you look your best. She mustn't think you're just a poor pensioner here, who can be slighted and treated like a servant. King Svein calls you the English Princess, and don't you forget it for one moment, my lady! That's just what you are, and that's what she must understand. Your father was a king, and hers only a prince.'

Mildyth, who had put on weight in the past year, looked so much like a belligerent cow defending her calf that Gytha could not help smiling, which made her feel a little less apprehensive, but she was inwardly nervous when she entered the hall that evening, wearing her best gown and her amber beads, with her head-rail held in place by the narrow gold circlet King Svein had given her to wear on special occasions.

94

Svein, who had a great liking for women, particularly pretty ones, eyed her appreciatively and greeted her as usual with a kiss which was rather more than cousinly, but Gytha was used to that by now, and knew that he meant no harm by it.

'Here she is!' he said, his sharp, shrewd face wreathed in smiles. 'The loveliest of my family, to meet my beautiful new wife! Gytha of England, my dear cousin, this is Elisev of . . . Where is it, my dear?'

'Kiev,' said a cool voice, clipping the word to one syllable, and Gytha found herself face to face with a tall, slim woman, perhaps thrice her own age, yet still looking remarkably beautiful, with not a thread of grey in her glossy black hair. She had high cheekbones, giving her eyes an attractive slant and making her look a little like a beautiful cat, for her face tapered from the wide cheeks to a small pointed chin, and her mouth, shapely and upcurving, had the permanent smile in repose of a contented feline.

'So this is the daughter of Harold Godwinsson,' she said, looking Gytha over with a languid, faintly amused expression. 'How interesting!' She had a slight and very attractive foreign accent.

'Elisev was the wife of my old rival and long-standing enemy, you know,' Svein said chattily, as if there was nothing surprising about it. 'He was forever trying to take Denmark from me, raiding and skirmishing like a pestilential hornet. Why, he even burnt Hedeby, the greatest trading town in the north. That was in – let me see – in 1049, I think. Quite pointless, of course, because it ruined trade for everyone, and did him no good at all. The more he burned and pillaged, the more my Danes were sure they didn't want him for their king. Why, even when he beat me in that great sea-battle off Nissa, in '60, they still wouldn't let me give in to him. I take it you managed to talk some sense into his thick head in time, my dear Elisev, for he was quite reasonable when we finally met in '64 and came to an agreement.'

While he was prattling away, Gytha and Elisev observed one another like a pair of cats, neither looking too directly at the other, nor allowing their eyes to meet. Gytha was wondering what Elisev felt on meeting the daughter of the man who had killed her first husband. She was not afraid of her, but could not help feeling apprehensive. So far, Svein had been good to her, but it was impossible to forecast how much influence this beautiful newcomer might come to have on him. Would she persuade him to withdraw his support? What would her attitude be – actively hostile, cold, unfriendly . . . ? She was so very beautiful and self-possessed.

Elisev's black eyes dwelt sidelong and consideringly on Gytha's outwardly calm expression, clear, unlined complexion, watchful blue eyes, and the single corn-gold curl which had escaped from under her head-rail, but her own face remained unreadable, and the faint smile which curved her lips, unchanged. It became clear that she had been listening to her new husband's chatter, despite her interest in Gytha, when she spoke.

'He was ever an old Viking!' She sounded faintly amused. 'He should have been born two hundred years ago. He'd have been happy spending summers raping and pillaging all round the coasts of France and England, and his winters boasting and drinking in his hall. He loved fighting, and he didn't want to stop – his greatest fear was that he might die in bed, like poor Siward of Northumbria! He wouldn't go to Valhalla then, you see.'

'I thought he was a Christian,' Gytha heard herself say in what sounded to her like a disapproving tone. She found Elisev both fascinating and puzzling. How could she talk about her former husband in such a detached way? They'd been married for a long time – more than twenty years – and, from what Mildyth had gleaned from her maid, it had been a love-match.

'Oh, he was,' Elisev replied with a silvery tinkle of laughter, 'but he still preferred to think of going to Valhalla rather than plucking a harp in eternal peace! Oh, the man who fired the arrow which pierced his throat did him a great favour. He was growing too old to fight, and he feared a peaceful old age and a quiet death above all things.'

Gytha looked her steadily in the eyes, her own face grave and questioning, and Elisev, her smile unchanged, said, 'How solemn you are, child! Like a beautiful owl. Perhaps you think I joke in an unseemly fashion? But I do not joke at all! They say he was the last Viking, and certainly my dear son Olaf shows none of his ferocious temper. I suppose he takes after my father, who was a wise and peaceful ruler. Olaf's greatest ambition since he became king has been to make peace with you, my dear new husband, and the agreement between you last year has filled him with content. Now here I am, to seal it with our marriage.'

'Well, now. Let's sit down to our supper and we can drink to that in good Rhenish,' Svein said, spreading his arms and ushering Elisev and Gytha to their seats. 'You here, my dear, on my right . . . I won't trouble you now with the names of all these great tall sons of mine – you'll get to know them only too well in time. This is the eldest, Harald, sitting on the other side of you, with his wife next to him, and Cnut, my second son, on this side, next to . . . Gytha, my dear, you sit on my left – you're the only real princess among my family, after all.'

'Are your daughters and the wives of your sons not princesses, then?' enquired Elisev, raising thin, elegantly arched eyebrows.

'Bastards, the lot of them!' Svein said cheerfully, surveying the dishes on the table with lively interest – he had a good appetite. 'Not the wives, of course, but all the rest. Fifteen sons and four daughters. I've had – how many? – three wives, and not one of them gave me a child that lived. It's obviously not my fault, so I hope you'll bring me a change of luck, my dear!' He leered at Elisev, who looked mildly amused and said, 'Perhaps!' in a faintly bored voice as she began to pick delicately at the food before her, wiping her fingers from time to time on a fine linen napkin.

Gytha ate without noticing what was set before her, for she could not help speculating with considerable anxiety about Elisev's *So this is the daughter of Harold Godwinsson. How interesting!* and the implications thereof. Would Elisev bear a grudge against herself and her mother? She ventured a sidelong glance

97

along the table, and caught a glimpse of Elisev's face, apparently absorbed in something Svein was telling her, with that enigmatic, feline smile revealing a glimpse of even white teeth, and she shivered, remembering how a cat plays with a mouse before it eventually kills its victim.

'How's the Lady Edith today?' Svein suddenly asked.

Gytha was grateful that he always accorded her mother the title she would have had as her father's wife had they been married in church, and wished she could have given him a more cheerful reply, but she could only say, 'Much the same.'

Indeed, there had been no change for the better in Edith's condition. If anything, she had deteriorated in the past year, for on the journey from Waltham she had fed herself and occasionally shown a slight awareness of her surroundings, but within a few days of their arrival in Roskilde she had lapsed into her former state. Her women washed and dressed her each morning, and she sat staring unseeingly before her all day long, moving only when she was fed, or when Gytha took her hand and led her out for a short walk for exercise and air. Every evening, Gytha talked to her, telling her of the trivial events of the day, and sometimes reminiscing about the old times, but Edith showed no sign that she could hear, even when Gytha talked of her father, or her brothers and sister. During the winter, a letter had come, sent on from Ribe by Olaf Eriksson, with the news that *Gytha's friend, the priest, had arrived home safely and all was well.* She had read it aloud to Edith and talked about it, pointing out that it bore no signature or heading to indicate who had sent it, although Gytha recognised Master Athelard's spiky handwriting, but Edith did not respond.

On this particular evening, Gytha talked about Elisev, explaining carefully that she was Harald Hardrada's widow, reminding her mother, how Harold had fought him at Stamford Bridge and he had been killed in the battle. She even expressed some of her own fears about Elisev's possibly enmity to herself, but all to no effect, and eventually she gave up and let Edith's women put her to bed, while she herself went to church for her evening devotions.

Roskilde was a small town, considering its importance as the seat of a king. Its wooden houses, built of whole tree-trunks set upright on heavy sill-beams, clustered within a stout wooden palisade at the innermost recess of a long fjord facing north. It had no pretensions to scenic interest, but was not unattractive at this time of year, with the low hills behind it glowing richly green in the long northern twilight and the sunset throwing crimson banners across the grey waters of the fjord. Svein's 'palace' was no more than a long wooden hall, like the one described in *Beowulf* hundreds of years before, with various private chambers built on to it, without plan or order, wherever they might be convenient.

The town was never quiet. Svein's fifteen sons and their followers brawled and shouted about the streets during the day and half the night, vying with each other in trials of strength or rowdy horseplay. Svein's seemingly casual attitude to his offspring, however, was deceptive, for he seemed to know exactly what each of them had been doing, and his housecarls always appeared in time to prevent serious fighting, rape or murder, usually by knocking the rowdies on the head and carting them off to the town lock-up for a few days, whether they were princes or commoners. Sometimes he sent them out to hunt, or to visit their estates, to give the townsfolk a little peace.

Svein also had the town kept clean. There were raised boardwalks along the streets for pedestrians, and corduroy tracks for carts. Throwing rubbish into the streets was forbidden, and anyone offending was set to empty cesspits for a week as a punishment. Kites and pigs were encouraged, as they kept the backyard middens from becoming too noisome, and the rotted remains of those middens were carted out to manure the fields every spring.

Gytha, attended by Mildyth, walked along the street without fear, knowing that even Cnut – who tended to pester her – however drunk, would not dare to lay a finger on her. She met a pair of the King's housecarls on her way and acknowledged their respectful salutes with a smiling 'Goodnight,' then turned into the church of St Lucius.

It was the larger of Roskilde's two churches, but not the nearer to Gytha's house. She attended it because it comforted her by confirming her right to claim that she had a family connection with Roskilde and its king. The church had been founded by her grandmother's great-grandfather, Harald Blaatand, and her grandmother's brother Ulf, King Svein's father, had been murdered within its walls. Both were buried in it, so she had two family tombs to pray by, although her prayers were mostly for the soul of her father, buried far away in Waltham. She liked to come here every night, before she slept, to pray for him, for her mother, and for her brothers, of whom she had received no news since she left England.

'They'll have gone to Ireland,' Mildyth always said whenever she wondered aloud what had become of them. 'Your father made a good friend of the King of Dublin, and he'll have taken them in and kept them safe.'

She spoke as if they were still young children, like Ulf, but Godwin was now – what? – twenty-five, and must surely have made some attempt to recover his father's lost crown. She could not believe that he, Edmund and Magnus would be content to sit idly in Ireland, leaving England in the hands of the Norman.

Svein married Elisev during the following week, in St Lucius', with no great ceremony. It was his fourth marriage, and he made no bones about the fact that it was a political matter. That Elisev was still a beautiful woman who might possibly give him a son was an added but minor advantage. What Elisev thought, she kept to herself, her enigmatic smile betraying nothing of her opinion on any matter at all.

A few days later, she arrived unannounced and with only two female attendants to call on Edith, catching Gytha in an old gown, supervising the thorough cleaning of the sleeping-chamber. 'How charming!' she exclaimed, appearing suddenly in the doorway of the room. 'Do all English princesses do their own housework? It's amazing how customs differ from one country to another.'

'I have but a small household,' Gytha replied, endeavouring to appear unruffled. 'I'm dependent on my cousin's charity, being an exile, and must make shift to be my own chancellor and housekeeper. Pray, come into the hall and meet my mother. May I offer you some refreshment?'

Elisev disposed herself gracefully in one of the household's two chairs, across the hearth from Edith, who was sitting in the other, a piece of sewing in her lap, although she had never touched it, and what work was done was that of one of her ladies. Gytha drew up a stool midway between them, and signalled to Mildyth to bring some wine.

'So this is your mother,' Elisev remarked, looking at Edith with mild interest, as though she were an unusual piece of furniture. 'Can she hear me, do you think?'

'I don't know,' Gytha replied warily. 'Sometimes she seems to hear things, but she doesn't respond.'

'And she has been like this since . . . Since when?'

'She went to the battlefield to help to find my father's body. She was like this when they brought her back.'

'A battlefield is no place for a woman. She must have had great courage,' Elisev said thoughtfully. 'Perhaps she didn't realise what it would be like. *Now vanish the heroes, time-vanquished* . . . I think there are no men left in the world like our two husbands. The Norman let my son seek his father's body and take him home – to Nidaros – for burial. Where is your father buried?'

'In his church at Waltham,' Gytha replied, puzzled by the turn the conversation had taken. 'The Norman refused to allow it at first, but then changed his mind.'

'For a price, no doubt?'

'He took my youngest brother as a hostage, and ordered me to enter a nunnery.'

'But you ran away to Denmark?'

'Yes.'

Elisev nodded, but whether with approval or not, Gytha could not tell. 'I can hardly imagine you in the cloister. You are, I think, like your father?'

'Yes, I believe so. I hope so.'

Elisev looked consideringly at Edith for a few moments, and

then said, 'We all have to choose which course to take when life becomes unbearable – to give up and die, or to fight on and live through it. Your mother chose one way, you the other. One might theorise about the effect of royal blood in one's veins. Why did you choose to go on?'

'There was no choice,' Gytha said flatly. 'I had to look after my mother and my small brother, because we lost touch with the rest of the family. I still don't know what has happened to my grandmother, my aunt and my other brothers. My sister Gunhild has been in a nunnery for some years, so I assume she's still there.'

'King Edward's widow is your aunt? She's retired to a nunnery, and I believe your grandmother's in Flanders.' Elisev seemed to be speaking absent-mindedly, as if she were really pursuing another train of thought altogether. 'How old are you?'

'Fourteen.'

'Indeed? I thought you might be older. Time you were beginning to think of marriage. I suppose you feel obliged to stay with your mother? Understandable, of course, but it does add to the difficulties of finding you a husband.'

'I realise that,' Gytha replied quietly. 'I feel I ought to try to marry someone who will help me to restore my father's honour. I don't mean reconquer his kingdom – that's for my brothers to do.' She did not say *if they can*, but the thought was there. 'Duke William told lies about my father, so I must do something. If I had a son . . . '

Her voice tailed off into a frustrated silence. The compulsion to do *something* to salvage her father's reputation had been growing ever stronger, but what could she do? She felt so helpless, so alone. Nobody else seemed to care about the Norman's false picture of his defeated enemy, and she longed to find someone who would understand her feelings and, perhaps, advise her. She could not imagine why she had told Elisev so much. She was surely the most likely person in the world, after the Norman, to wish Harold to remain disgraced. She looked curiously, and a little anxiously, at the beautiful face of Hardrada's widow, and saw only a faint trace of interest and a touch of amusement, and cringed inwardly with embarrassment, thinking that she had made a fool of herself.

'Was your father a perfect saint, then?' Elisev asked, a trifle sarcastically.

'No. He was an ambitious and capable man. He knew that he could rule England wisely and well, and he wanted a chance to do it, to prove himself. He was given that chance by King Edward and the Witan, in accordance with English laws and custom, but Duke William robbed him of it, and tried to justify what he'd done by calling my father an usurper and an oathbreaker! It's not fair!' Gytha replied, her voice breaking on the last words.

'Life is never fair!' Elisev retorted. 'Only children complain of unfairness – adults expect nothing else. Grow up, English princess! Fight for what you want, but don't *expect* anyone to help, or to sympathise, or to treat you fairly. If you find someone who does those things, be grateful and thank God, but don't *expect* anything of the sort. Your mother looks frail and old. I think she will be glad to join your father before long.'

Gytha's attention was distracted from the earlier part of what Elisev had said by these last comments. She looked with alarm at her mother, and saw that she had, indeed, changed considerably. She wondered if this had come about so gently that she had not realised until Elisev mentioned it, or if it had happened in the past few days, while Gytha had been preoccupied with her fears about Elisev. Edith looked shrunken, grey and very old, although she was not much past forty.

'You won't have noticed, seeing her every day,' Elisev remarked coolly. 'I must go – my dear husband will wonder where I am. Age seems to have little effect on him, thank God! I'd not bear to be married to a senile man! Which reminds me, my dear – Svein has no legitimate son, you know, and I'm too old to provide him with one. If he should ever suggest that you might like to give him his heir, pray don't encourage him while I still live. If you do, I assure you that you'll soon meet with a most unpleasant and fatal accident. I intend to remain Svein's consort while we both live, and not be sent to moulder in some damp and draughty convent so that he can marry a younger woman.'

Gytha was irritated rather than intimidated by the threat, and replied stiffly, 'I had not even considered such a move! In any case, my cousin the king and I are too closely related for the Church to allow us to marry.'

Elisev smiled, and said, 'I'm so glad that you are aware of the fact, and don't forget that the same applies to all his sons. Don't grieve for your mother, child – she'll be happier dead and re-united with your father. Her present state is neither life nor death, after all.' She spoke calmly and in a matter-of-fact tone which precluded any suspicion that she might have meant to be kind, then stood up and glided out of the house, her attendants, caught unawares, scuttling after her.

'Well,' Mildyth exclaimed indignantly, 'she's a cold one, if you like! She meant that threat of an accident. Don't you trust her, my lady! She's a serpent, mark my words. All that non-sense about having to fight for things! Fine talk for a Christian, if she is one, which I wonder, seeing as half the folk in these parts seem more heathen than not, and she comes from some outlandish place where they don't even honour the Holy Father, by what one of her women was telling me. Can't think what the King wants with marrying her, save the obvious!'

'She brings the friendship of Norway,' Gytha answered absently, her mind more occupied with all that Elisev had said. 'Denmark and Norway have been at war for years. The mar-riage seals the peace. She's right about Mother looking frail. I hadn't realised just how much ... She seems to be fading away.'

'Nonsense!' Mildyth replied sharply, being in a mood to con-tradict everything which agreed with what Elisev had said, but her denial lacked conviction. 'It was a hard winter. She'll pick up again when full summer comes, mark my words.'

But Mildyth was wrong. A few weeks later, while Gytha was sitting sewing in the evening sun by the house door, and Edith was apparently dozing by the fire, the latter suddenly rose to her feet and said, quite in her old fashion, 'I think I'll go to sleep now, Gytha. I shall tell your father, when I see him, what a good girl you are.'

'Mother!' Gytha started up, dropping her sewing, but Edith had already reached the door to the sleeping-chamber, and, by the time Gytha followed her, she was standing still and expressionless, waiting for her women to undress her and put her to bed.

'Mother?' Gytha repeated uncertainly, seeking a response, but there was none, and she wondered if she had imagined that Edith had spoken to her.

'She did speak. I heard her,' one of the women volunteered. 'Perhaps she's getting better?'

'Perhaps,' Gytha replied, but without conviction, knowing in her heart that it was not so.

When Edith was in bed and apparently asleep, she went to St Lucius' and was still there, praying, when Mildyth came early the next morning to tell her that Edith had died in the night.

Svein was kind, in his abrupt way, said he was sorry, but it was for the best, patted her shoulder, and said no more about Gytha's loss, but he ordered that Edith should be buried in St Lucius' church, as befitted his cousin Harold's widow. It was an honour which Gytha appreciated, finding comfort in the knowledge that Svein was prepared to accord public recognition to her parents' marriage and let Edith be entombed among the Danish royal dead.

She mourned for her mother, and missed her, but realised that Edith's mind and spirit had been gone from her body for a long time, and she was, indeed, better off now. Once the first grief had passed, she was conscious of relief that she no longer had to be responsible for her and worry about her, but could now begin to consider her own future.

The prospects did not seem very bright. Svein had made a few half-hearted suggestions about marriage from time to time, but it was clear that he was not at all surprised or disappointed when she politely declined the one or two Danish nobles, the Norwegian lordling, and even one of Svein's young bastards.

'Quite right, my dear!' he said approvingly when she refused the latter. 'With the Norman casting doubts on your own standing in the world, you want a husband of undoubted legitimacy. If one or other of my wives had provided me with a few sons . . . Never mind – we'll find you someone eventually . . .'

His 'eventually' seemed a very long time. Another year passed, and Svein seemed to be more interested in gaining another kingdom for himself than in finding a husband for Gytha. He sent three of his sons – one of them Cnut – with a great fleet of ships to invade England in alliance with Edgar the Atheling and the Earl of Northumbria.

There were mutterings in Roskilde that Svein should have gone himself – what kind of a king sent someone else to conquer another kingdom for him? Svein heard, as he was intended to, smiled slily, and told the mutterers that *he* knew what he was about and *they* did not, which, to Gytha's surprise, silenced them.

'Your cousin Svein is a clever, wily man,' Elisev observed to Gytha with her feline smile. 'He has some profitable plan in mind, and I doubt if it's conquest!'

Despite William's efforts to drive out the Danes, they showed the same reluctance to leave which had distinguished their ancestors, and were still there the following spring, when Svein joined them. Everyone left behind in Roskilde waited anxiously for news, speculating about what would happen if Svein defeated William, or what would happen to Denmark if Svein were killed, with no legitimate heir . . . Gytha was interested to note how Harald, Svein's eldest son who had been left in charge of Denmark, turned to Elisev for advice without seeming to be aware that he was doing so, and how readily and sensibly she gave it, and Gytha realised that Elisev was using Svein's absence to establish her influence on his probable successor.

Svein returned at the end of June, looking remarkably pleased with himself, and not at all put out to learn that his fleet had been scattered by a great storm, and most of his precious ships had disappeared.

'They'll turn up, sooner or later,' he said dismissively over supper on the day of his return. 'I'll admit that I considered conquering the country and recovering that half of my uncle Cnut's empire, but it would have been hard work getting it, and harder keeping it! William offered a good price, and gold in the hand is worth more than an unconquered kingdom.'

'True,' said Elisev, smiling to herself. 'What did he want for his gold?'

'My army out of his lands, my fleet away from his shores, my word – for what it's worth – to give up my claim to England, and not to support that of anyone else.' He gave Gytha an oblique look. 'It appears that our English cousins last year gave him some trouble in the west, even as my men were annoying him in the north. He seemed to think the two were in some way connected. Your brothers, of course, my dear.'

'I knew they must be doing something!' Gytha exclaimed. 'Are they well?'

Svein sniffed. 'William didn't show any concern for their health – indeed, he didn't mention them directly – only as *Earl Harold's – er – offspring*!'

Bastards, he meant! thought Gytha. He probably said it, too! And she was grateful to Svein for avoiding the word.

'I heard of their activities from others. It seems that they've twice landed in the west of England, in successive years, with Irish support, and William's not found it easy to drive them off. They even managed to destroy one of his castles and kill one of his sheriffs. The English, however, seem to be too dispirited to rise against him, after the slaughter and devastation he's spread through the parts of England which have resisted. To be honest, my dear, I don't think your brothers have inherited their father's gifts of leadership, and I doubt if they'll try again. I'm sorry.'

Gytha bowed her head and made no reply, unwilling to admit that she had known for a long time that Godwin and Edmund lacked whatever it was that had made their father and grandfather great men. About Magnus, she was less sure, but she knew that he had never abandoned his determination to be a priest, and she could not imagine that fighting for an earthly kingdom would tempt him from his chosen path.

'And what have you gained worth the loss of more than two hundred ships and their crews?' asked Elisev conversationally.

Gytha glanced at her, thinking that the question sounded decidedly barbed, and then looked to see how Svein had taken it. Elisev was smiling like a svelte and elegant cat, and Svein, hunched over his platter, his strong nose and high receding forehead harshly lit by the candles on the table, had a sly, twisted grin which made him look like one of the carved devils in the church.

'Not lost, as I said, dear wife! Merely mislaid for a while,' he said. 'All good, seaworthy vessels – and men, for that matter. They'll come home, as wind and weather allow, in a week or so.'

He was almost right. Alone or in pairs, the ships came home to the great fjord of Roskilde from the wild coasts of Norway and Scotland, from Flanders and Normandy, even from England. The last arrived nearly two months later, when even Svein had given her up, from distant Ireland. Her captain did not explain how he had managed to be storm-blown from the eastern coast of England to Ireland, and neither did Svein ask him, but merely said that he was glad to see him back, ship and crew undamaged, and with two passengers aboard.

Gytha was at home when that last ship came in, reading a book lent to her by the Bishop of Lund, who evinced both surprise and amusement when she asked him for something to read, as most of the men in Roskilde, let alone the women, were happily illiterate. He could hardly believe that she could not only read, but was anxious to keep up her knowledge of Latin.

The book was an account of the dedication of a church in Lombardy, written in ornate Latin and not in the least entertaining, but Gytha, living in a small house, with four women attendants and two serving-men appointed (and paid) by Svein, as well as Mildyth, had little, other than spinning and sewing, to occupy her, and any book was better than none. She was, however, pleased when Svein's servant arrived, breathless with haste, to bid her attend the King in his hall.

'Has something happened?' she asked, swiftly locking the precious book away in the safety of a heavy wooden chest.

'The last of the lost ships is back,' the man replied, looking a little puzzled, for he had been wondering why the event made the English Princess's presence so urgently required.

'Oh,' Gytha said a trifle blankly, eyebrows arching in surprise. 'Oh, well . . . I suppose the King's pleased about it,' and she called Mildyth to attend her as she set out for the hall.

When Svein dispensed justice or held council, the high table was cleared from the dais and replaced by his great carved oak chair of state, in which he sat apparently cradled among the coils of several intertwined dragons. As he was not normally particularly formal in his mode of kingship, Gytha was surprised to find that the chair had been brought out and Svein was seated in it to receive a mere shipmaster, not realising that the man had already made his report to the King. She assumed that he was in some way culpable for his long-delayed return, and was to be judged.

She took her usual seat, next to Elisev on one of the stools set below the dais to Svein's left, opposite the assorted half-dozen of his sons who happened to be in Roskilde, not in the lock-up, and sober enough to attend their father. Mildyth went to sit among Elisev's women and a number of Svein's housecarls who stood or sat along the walls, leaving the centre of the hall empty, save for two carved stools set midway between the hearth and the dais. Gytha had seen these only once before, when Svein received ambassadors from Norway.

Apart from some subdued whispering among the lesser folk, there was silence until the doors at the far end of the hall opened and a squad of armed housecarls marched in and formed up in a double rank, facing inwards, from the doorway to the hearth, apparently as a guard of honour. A few moments later a man entered – the shipmaster, to judge by his clothing and his rolling gait. He was followed, a few paces behind, by two fair-haired young men dressed alike in blue tunics and bright plaid cloaks, each fastened at the shoulder by a great gold brooch. As if they were indeed ambassadors, neither was armed, although each had an empty scabbard hanging from his belt.

They marched side by side up the hall, separated to pass the hearth, then came together by the stools, where they stopped and bowed to Svein. The shipmaster, by now, had quietly drifted over to one side and faded into the audience against the wall.

'Welcome to Roskilde, Cousins!' Svein said benignly, nodding in acknowledgment of his guests' bows. 'Cousin Godwin – Cousin Edmund – pray be seated!'

Gytha hardly recognised her brothers. It was four years since she had last seen them, and they had changed considerably. Godwin had filled out, and was now as big, broad-shouldered and deep-chested as their uncle Tosti. His hair was a deeper colour than she remembered, and a long scar seamed the left side of his face from the corner of his eye to his chin. Edmund was as tall, but still slender and boyish-looking. As a boy, he had often had a hangdog look, and this had been replaced by a truculent expression and a restless, shifty way of constantly moving his eyes, as if avoiding a direct look at anyone or anything. Gytha's immediate reaction to his appearance was a certainty that, had he not been her brother, she would not have trusted him with any matter of consequence.

Svein made the two young men welcome, and listened when Godwin proposed that he should help them to recover their father's kingdom. He refused, however, pointing out that his own claim was better than theirs, and he, in any case, already accepted William's compensation for that. Instead, he offered them positions at his own Court, and that, perforce, they accepted, with less reluctance than might have been expected.

They were surprised and pleased to see Gytha, and there was a great deal of news to be exchanged once the three siblings were alone together.

'Where is Magnus?' Gytha asked anxiously. 'Why is he not with you?'

'The poor lad lost his right hand in one of our battles,' Godwin said sadly. 'He could no longer fight, and, of course, the injury debarred him from ever becoming a priest as he had hoped.

He sought William's permission to be a hermit somewhere in England, and William sent him to Lewes, to be under the eye of the castellan. He's allowed to assist the parish priest, and he's happy.'

Gytha recollected that William of Warenne was the castellan of Lewes, and she felt pleased and relieved that Magnus was in his charge.

Godwin slipped easily into a place as commander of a section of Svein's housecarls, earning the respect of his men and his fellow-commanders by his good sense and open manner. He had learned a great deal in his brief campaigns in England, not least his own limitations, and put the lessons to good use in training his men, but without mentioning his past experience. The men knew all about it, in any case, in the mysterious way professionals in any field have of learning about each other. Svein's sons tried to get him drunk, and failed, tried to quarrel with him, and failed, and eventually accepted him as a dull dog, but someone to turn to for advice or a loan – so long as it was re-paid on time!

Edmund was unsettled and discontented at first, but Svein granted the brothers some land, and he went to inspect it, be-came interested in the farming of it, and remained there. Soon he married a neighbour's daughter and thereafter seldom visited Roskilde.

Chapter Seven

Nearly two more years crawled by for Gytha. There was a great deal to do in one sense – a household to manage, servants to be supervised, the unending tasks of spinning, weaving and sewing – but she felt that she was wasting her time, for these things occupied her hands, but only a small part of her mind.

There were few learned men in Denmark, and very few books. Conversation among women was all children, food, housewifery and scandal, and among men, battle, seafaring and crops. Only with Elisev could she ever have a real discussion about anything, for Svein's wife was educated, and came from a strange country where everything seemed to be different. Gytha could rarely get her to talk about her homeland, and was not even sure where it was – somewhere to the south, she thought – and it was intriguing that, when they were working together – perhaps spinning – Elisev might say, 'We didn't do this in quite this way at home,' but could not be persuaded to enlarge on the matter. About one thing, however, she was prepared to talk – religion. It appeared that the people in her country were Christian, but differed in many particulars of custom and belief from the Church in England and Denmark.

'I wish you wouldn't spend so much time talking to Elisev,' Godwin said to her. 'I don't trust her. You know who she is?'

'Yes, Harald Hardrada's widow. As if I could ever forget that! I don't exactly trust her either, for I always have an uneasy feeling that she might just be biding her time to do something in revenge. However, she's someone to talk to. There isn't anyone else,' Gytha replied sadly.

'There are dozens of others! There are Svein's daughters, and Harald's wife seems a pleasant woman.'

'But they don't talk about anything interesting,' Gytha protested. 'They can't even read.'

Godwin thought privately that there was no need for a woman to be able to read – in fact, education only made a woman dissatisfied and difficult – Gytha was an example of that. However, he had the sense to keep the thought to himself, and merely repeated his warning to his sister not to trust Elisev.

Not that she needed the warning. Elisev intrigued and puzzled her. Sometimes she seemed friendly and open, and then Gytha would look up suddenly and find Elisev regarding her with a cold stare or that enigmatic smile, and a little *frisson* would pass through her body like a thread of fear.

Svein seemed happy enough with his strange wife, although he continued to indulge in sly remarks aimed at her, as he did with most people. He was ageing rapidly now, his thin hair turned white, his shrewd, clean-shaven face wrinkled. His body, which had always looked slight and small among his big muscular sons, seemed to shrink and wizen almost from day to day, and a slight leg injury, which would once have been forgotten in a week, lingered, and made him lame in damp or cold weather. He had ruled Denmark for thirty difficult years, and Gytha knew he must be past fifty. She began to be haunted by a vague fear for the future, when he would no longer be there to protect her.

One chill, damp day in the early spring of her sixth year in Denmark, when the thaw had begun and the cartways, even in the town, were thick with mud and slushy snow, she went as usual to take her supper at Svein's table and was surprised to find that Edmund was there. He seemed equally surprised that she did not know that Svein had sent for him, but there was no time to discuss his arrival, for Svein summoned everyone to his or her place at the table with his usual lack of ceremony, saying that there was no point in letting the food get cold while they stood about gossiping.

After the meal, he signalled to Gytha and her brothers to follow him to Elisev's bower, where he usually spent his evenings if he had no important guests.

'Sit down, sit down!' he said, subsiding into his big carved chair. 'Put more logs on the fire, Harald!' to his eldest son, who had also been told to come. 'This damp cold chills the bones!' He stretched out his lame leg with caution, wincing as the knee straightened, and rested it on the back of a large, adoring hound.

Elisev was already seated in her own chair, slightly smaller than Svein's, and had picked up a little braid-loom on which she was weaving silk and gold threads into a rich adornment for a gown. Harald took a stool opposite his father across the hearth, and stared gloomily into the flames, sucking a tooth which was giving him trouble. Godwin and Edmund sat on either side of him, and Gytha found herself between Godwin and Svein, and opposite Elisev, who looked at her, and asked conversationally, 'How old are you now, Gytha?'

'Just nineteen,' she replied cautiously, wondering why Elisev should ask something she already knew.

'You said a child wouldn't do,' Svein said irritably. 'Nineteen's not exactly ancient!'

'I didn't say it was,' Elisev replied urbanely. 'A suitable age, I would say. Old enough to have learned sense, but with plenty of time left.'

'Left for what?' Edmund asked bluntly, having listened to the exchange with a puzzled frown.

Elisev and Svein both looked at him, then at each other, and exchanged a smile, Svein's gap-toothed and sardonic, Elisev's, as usual, slightly feline, but they did not reply to the question. Instead, Svein turned to Gytha and said, 'I take it you still have no desire to be a nun?'

'None at all,' she replied more sharply than she intended, having been made uneasy by a sense of something being planned which concerned her.

'Then we'd better find you a husband,' Svein said, as if this was an entirely new idea.

'Had you anyone in mind?' Godwin asked cautiously, after a few moments' silence in which Svein appeared to have fallen into a doze.

Svein opened his eyes and gave Godwin a sidelong look, twitched his beaky nose, and said, 'First, let us consider the problems. I must ask you all to look at this from a point of view other than your own, in order that you may understand why my cousin has remain unmarried so long past the – er – usual age. This you are not going to like very much,' with a meaningful stare at Edmund and Godwin, who were already beginning to look anxious. 'Let's inspect your position from the viewpoint of, say, a French prince of suitable age who is looking for a wife.'

He paused, staring over the fire at a point midway between Gytha's brothers, but infinitely beyond them.

'Yes,' he resumed suddenly, 'a French prince. To start with, your father had only a modicum of royal blood, by descent from Harald Blaatand. He had no claim to the crown of England, save those of election and suitability in other respects – he knew how to govern, how to lead an army, and no one can dispute that! In the matter of the oath which he is said to have sworn to support William of Normandy, we have no independent version of that story. William's given his side of it loudly enough, and made the Pope believe it, at any rate, to your father's detriment. Also, William is alive and king, and your father is – not. That would appear to be God's judgment on the matter.'

He paused again as Edmund shifted on his stool and muttered a protest.

'This is as it would appear to a Frenchman,' Svein reminded him. 'It's not necessarily the truth, and certainly not as I see it, but there's no proposal to marry your sister to me. Unfortunately,' he added, his insatiable liking for women intruding even at this time. Elisev gave him a strange, veiled glance under her long eyelashes, but said nothing.

'So, to resume,' he went on. 'From some angles, she would seem to be the daughter of a disgraced, over-ambitious man – certainly a man whose glory is tarnished, and, in the end, his glory is all a man leaves behind him. Then there is the difficult question of your parents' – er – marriage.'

Both Godwin and Edmund jerked up their heads at this and frowned, looking, for once, very much alike.

'It was a marriage in law,' Harald said suddenly. He was a silent, unassertive man, with something of Svein's looks and manner, but none of his personality and humour.

'Danish law – pagan law!' Svein said dismissively. 'In the eyes of the Church it was no marriage, which means that, to our hypothetical French prince, she is no more than the illegitimate daughter of an over-ambitious commoner. And she has no lands or dowry, apart from her holding in Denmark.'

In these few words, he neatly summed up all the fears and doubts which Gytha had tried not to think about during the past few years, and presented the hopelessness of her position with stark clarity before her face, inescapable, impossible to be put aside any longer.

'I have fifteen sons and four daughters to provide for,' Svein added with a rueful grin. 'Otherwise I'd buy her a husband!'

'You're telling me that I have no hope of marrying,' Gytha said quietly, her voice trembling in spite of her efforts to be calm. 'What am I to do, then?'

'Look further afield,' he replied promptly. 'No prince in France, or the Empire, or Italy, or Spain, Norway or Sweden will take you. We must look for someone who's too far away to have heard about the misfortunes of your family.'

'But you've dismissed all of Christendom!' Edward burst out, scowling, then realised that he was shouting and subsided with a muttered apology.

'Not quite.' Svein looked remarkably like a fox as he grinned at Edmund.

'You have sons . . .' Godwin began tentatively.

'And I've made a promise to William of Normandy,' Svein retorted. 'At a good price, too! I promised not to join any claim your family might be thought to have to my own family's un-doubted claim to England. In any case, no son of mine is suit-able . . .'

Harald scowled at that, but Svein, who missed nothing, added, '. . . being either married or betrothed. So we've been looking at other parts of the world for you, my dear.' He turned to Gytha as he spoke, giving her a kindly, encouraging smile.

Gytha sat silent for a moment, and then a memory stirred in the back of her mind, and she asked tentatively, 'Eastwards?'

'The girl is no fool,' Elisev remarked, suddenly taking the centre of the stage. 'As she knows, although others may be less well informed, I come from a land far to the east. The Norwegians call it Garthariki, or the River Road, but we, its natives, call it Rusland. My brother is now its ruler.'

'I've never heard of such a country,' Edmund said suspiciously. 'Where is it? Is it a Christian land? Is your brother a king?'

'Yes to both questions,' Elisev replied crisply, a small frown marring her smooth brow. 'We do not use the title *king*, but that of *Grand Prince*, and my brother is Grand Prince of the land. He rules from the city of Kiev, which is considerably larger than Roskilde – or Winchester, for that matter. My nephew requires a wife of royal blood and sufficient age to have learned sense and discretion, yet still young enough to bear children. Having failed to find such a paragon among his neighbours, he has appealed to me for assistance, and it seems to me that Gytha fills the requirements admirably.'

'We'll have to consider this carefully, Godwin and I,' Edmund said, frowning portentously. 'I'm not at all sure that we should allow our sister to be packed off to some unknown . . .'

'Allow?' Gytha interrupted, coldly angry. 'What right have you to allow or disallow? It is *my* future, and I shall decide it for myself!'

'Come now,' Godwin said placatingly. 'Of course we shall discuss it with you and take notice of your wishes, but you, a woman, can't decide anything so important by yourself.'

'And, pray, what do you think I've been doing these past seven years?' Gytha asked icily. 'Where were you when I had to decide whether or not to give in to William's order to go to a nunnery? Who do you think decided that I should demand Christian burial for our father? Who decided that Mother and I should come to Roskilde? I've made my own decisions well enough since Father was killed, and this, the most important of all, I shall certainly make for myself!'

With her stiff upright posture, blazing blue eyes and determined chin, she looked so much like their father that both Godwin and Edmund were disconcerted, and Svein's enthusiastic, 'Quite right. Certainly you shall choose for yourself, Gytha, and no one shall contradict you,' completed their rout.

'As the King pleases,' Godwin said diplomatically. Edmund muttered something incoherent and sat scowling and red-faced.

Her rights established, Gytha turned her attention to Elisev and stared at her, unable to find words for the questions she must ask, and experienced an upsurge of a strange feeling of mingled hope and fear within her. Could this be the answer? Turkill had said she would go far to the east, and her father's – what was the word he had used? – glory, that was it! His glory would be avenged in the east!

'Have you no questions, Gytha?' asked Elisev, sounding amused.

'How – How old is he?' she heard herself ask.

'About your own age, not old and doddering,' Elisev replied lightly.

'Grand Prince,' muttered Edward. 'That doesn't sound to me much like a king!'

'My brother's wife, the mother of Gytha's proposed husband, was a Greek princess, the daughter of the Emperor of Constantinople – Miklagarth, I believe you call it in this part of the world,' Elisev replied tartly, the last scrap of information aside to her husband.

'Constantinople!' exclaimed Godwin, sounding bemused. 'Gracious Heavens! Constantinople!'

Elisev looked at him with amusement. 'Ah, so our English cousins have heard of some places in the east!' she said. 'Don't you want to know his name, so that you can savour it in your dreams?' she asked Gytha teasingly.

'Please!'

'I think Waldemar is the nearest to it in this part of the world,' Elisev said consideringly. 'It's more difficult for your tongue in our own language, but no doubt he'll teach you to say it.'

'Why are you going to so much trouble?' Godwin asked her, frowning and sounding suspicious, despite an obvious effort not to do so. 'You've no reason to wish well to any member of our family . . .'

Elisev's smile vanished, her dark eyes suddenly seemed to grow larger and her voice deeper as she replied, 'I do not believe in feuding. Your father fought to protect his country, as he had every right to do, from an invader who happened to be my husband, and it was my Harald who lost.' She shrugged. 'What point in hating your father? He spared my son's life, when he might, with some justifcation, have killed him too. I like Gytha. I like her quiet courage, her intelligence, her good sense, her patience. I would have liked a daughter like her. I think she'll make my nephew an admirable wife, and that is important to me, just as it is important to you that your sister should have an admirable husband.'

'What is all this going to cost?' Harald murmured, loudly enough to be heard in the silence that followed Elisev's surprising declaration, but quietly enough to be passed off as thinking aloud. 'The expense of the journey, assuming she's to travel in the manner expected of a princess, and I suppose this nephew of yours wants a dowry . . .'

'This nephew of mine,' said Elisev coldly, 'wants a wife of sensible age, but younger than himself, whose appearance is not repulsive. He also requires a female of healthy and reasonably prolific stock, with some royal blood in her veins. In view of the length and expense of the journey and the misfortunes our dear cousin has suffered, he does not ask for a dowry. I think, husband, that your eldest son shows a surprisingly miserly attitude for the offspring of a man as generous as yourself. I hope you have made sufficient provision for me if I should outlive you! Are you sure he really *is* your son?'

Harald scowled and flushed, and Gytha felt sorry for him, guessing how frustrated and humiliated he must feel under the lash of his stepmother's scorn, for he had no gift for words. She was thankful that Elisev had never turned that acid tongue on herself. Svein's lined, clever face assumed a satisfied smirk, as if he enjoyed seeing Harald made to look foolish, but he replied to his son's question.

'Prince Waldemar suggests an adequate supply of clothing and a little jewellery instead of a dowry. I think the journey should be made without pomp, or we'll have all the pirates in the East Sea swarming round our poor cousin! If you think it too costly, perhaps you have an alternative suggestion?'

'Well, all the things you said earlier are true enough,' Harald said sulkily, 'and that drop of royal blood is well diluted, isn't it? Why can't she marry one of our jarls, or perhaps a house-carl? I know a few fellows who would take her, and think themselves honoured to wed the King's cousin, with no dowry at all!'

'My sister is not going to marry a commoner!' Edmund snarled, rising to his feet. 'She's the daughter of a king, and I'll not hear you say otherwise!' His handsome face was set in an expression of murderous ferocity and his hand was already where his sword-hilt should have been.

'Sit!' Svein's voice cut in with impressive authority as Harald sprang to his feet, knocking over his stool, and also reached for a sword which had, of course, been left outside the King's hall. The fastest obedience to the command came from Svein's hound, which jerked up from its somnolent position supporting Svein's injured leg, and sat, gazing alertly into his face. Svein was nearly overset by its action, but he retained his balance and his air of command, and the two young men obeyed him, although not without some angry glaring at one another.

'That will do, the pair of you!' Svein continued. 'Certainly our cousin has royal blood, even if there is not much of it. Naturally, her brothers want her to make a good marriage, and so should you, Harald. If you allow the status of your acknowledged cousin to be lowered, then your own is lowered with it. We are her nearest kin, after her brothers, and we have our ancestors to answer to in the next world for our care of her and her interests. In any case, Gytha is not a bundle of trade goods, to be bickered and bargained over! It is for her to decide. If she would rather remain in Denmark and marry beneath her, I dare say we can reconcile ourselves to the idea, so be she's happy. If she chooses to take her chance and marry the prince in Rusland who has offered for her, then the least we can do is send her to him in a manner which can bring neither shame nor reproach on us. My kingdom is not too poor to manage that without undue hardship, or encroaching on your *possible* inheritance, Harald. What do you wish to do, Gytha? Think well before you answer.'

Gytha thought. Denmark was safe, but she had never been really happy here. For all Svein's kindness, she had always felt like a poor relation, under a burden of obligation to him, and obviously his generosity had aroused some resentment in Harald, and probably in his brothers as well. The jarls and housecarls were a set of rowdy, hard-drinking, uncultured men, not much better than their Viking ancestors, or else little more than farmers. On the other hand, Elisev was a literate cultured woman who presumably had not acquired her education in Norway.

'I should like to know a little more about Prince Waldemar,' she said.

Elisev put her braid-loom down on the floor beside her, as if to show that she was giving Gytha her full attention. 'My nephew is twenty years old,' she said in very precise tones. 'He is the son of my brother Vsevolod and a Greek princess of the Imperial House of Constantinople – I don't recall her name. His father is a literate man who speaks and reads five languages, and I should be very surprised if he has not made sure that his eldest son is equally well educated. Waldemar has led an army in the defence of Rusland since he was thirteen years old and is accounted a very able commander, an intelligent and wise ruler. He is also a devout Christian. I have, of course, never met him, as I left Rusland before he was born. All the members of my family are, without exception, to my knowledge, accounted handsome and personable.'

With that, she picked up her loom again and returned to her weaving with no sign of any interest in anything else. There was silence in the bower as the others awaited Gytha's reaction.

I could stay here, she thought, *and marry a prosperous farmer, forget all my high-flown ideas and be safe, or I can take the chance that Elisev is not lying and go to Rusland. Which? I must choose for myself, not let her or my brothers push or persuade me into doing as they wish . . .* She hesitated, making sure that her decision would be the one she really wanted, and closed her eyes for a few seconds, praying for guidance. The insistent voice of memory answered her: *Eastwards, beyond the sunrise. Take the hard path.* 'Everyone here in Denmark has been very kind to me,' she said firmly, looking at each of her hearers in turn, 'but, without wishing to appear ungrateful, I would like to go to Rusland and marry Prince Waldemar.' Again, the echo of Turkill's prophecy echoed in the back of her mind.

'You don't think it too far?' Elisev asked casually.

'It wasn't too far for you to come from there to Norway, and then to Denmark, so it can't be too far for me to go the other way,' Gytha replied, and, to her surprise, Elisev suddenly smiled at her in a manner which transformed her face with a warmth which she had always lacked before.

'That settles the matter, then,' Svein said briskly, silencing any possible protests from Gytha's brothers or Harald with an uplifted hand. It was very much the King who spoke, but it was Gytha's kindly cousin who added, 'It's too early in the year for you to start now, even if you were ready. We'll inform Prince Waldemar that you accept his offer, and you'll set out to meet him in the early summer. That will give you, say, three months to gather the clothes and so forth you'll need, and prepare your mind for your new life.' He hesitated, frowning thoughtfully, for a few moments, then went on, 'I'll hire ships and men from Gotland for the journey. They've beaten off the pirates so often that their ships are seldom attacked, and they know the way.' There was another brief pause, and then he said slowly and thoughtfully, 'I think your decision is a wise one. There's really nothing for you here in Denmark. I shan't live much longer, and my sons never knew your father. I spent most of my childhood in England, as a hostage to my Uncle Cnut for my father's good behaviour. Your grandfather was always kind to me, and your father was once very kind indeed.' He smiled at the memory.

'He must have been younger than you,' Gytha said, wondering what he meant.

'Yes, indeed. He was only half my age at that time. The Lady Emma had given him a cake – a very fine, rare delicacy, filled with ginger and fat raisins, such as hardly ever came the way of a child – something so desirable that my mouth waters to think of it, even now. He saw me sitting alone, feeling sorry for myself, and broke it in two, then gave me the bigger part.'

Harald scuffed his feet in the rushes, and the look on his face showed quite clearly that he thought the old man was maundering. Edmund and Godwin looked puzzled and embarrassed, but Elisev gave her husband a look which was interested and softer than usual, and Gytha exchanged a smile with him, understanding exactly what he meant.

She went home in a turmoil of emotions, half-frightened at the thought of what she had committed herself to doing, and half-excited because at last there was something to which she could look forward and make plans.

She found Mildyth sewing in a desultory fashion, and it seemed that she had guessed that something was afoot, for she dropped her work and started up as soon as Gytha entered the house. 'What happened?' she asked eagerly then recollected herself and murmured, 'Not my business – I'm sorry.'

'They've found a husband for me!' Gytha tried not to sound unbecomingly elated and eager. 'A prince, and his mother was the daughter of the Emperor of Constantinople!'

Mildyth's eyes widened to circles of astonishment, but her good common sense led her unerringly on the scent of possible snags. 'Why does he want a penniless wife, then?'

'He wants someone healthy, able to bear him children and with royal blood.'

'Children! Sons, you mean. That's all men care about. A woman's no more than a toy for an idle hour, a body to bear sons,' Mildyth said bitterly. 'Being married isn't anything wonderful. It's a pain and shock at the start, and beatings when your man's angry, and being used for his pleasure whenever he feels like it, and more pain bearing his sons. It's always your fault if he can't get a child on you, or if it's a girl; and wholly to *his* credit if he gets a boy. You can't ever call your body your own any more – it's just something to satisfy his lust, to be filled with his seed, and bring forth his sons. You'd be better off in the cloister!'

Gytha had never heard such an outburst from Mildyth before. In fact Mildyth hardly ever mentioned her dead husband and children, and Gytha had thought that was because she still mourned for them.

'Oh, Mildyth, how can you say that? You know how much I want children! Weren't you ever happy with your man and your family?'

'Happy?' Mildyth considered the word. 'Yes, I was happy in the courting and going to church as a bride, but he knocked all that out of me the first night, and every night afterwards, except when I'd just given birth. The children would have been something to give me a little happiness, but they died so easily, and, in the end, I was glad when he died too.'

Gytha stared at her, dumbfounded. She had known Mildyth so long, and never guessed that she felt so bitter about her marriage. Her own parents had been so happy together that it had not occurred to her that a woman might actually hate her husband, and her ignorance made Mildyth's references incomprehensible. She knew how babies were made, of course, and had seen animals coupling, and assumed that humans did much the same, and that giving birth was a painful but worthwhile business.

'I'm sorry, Mildyth,' she said helplessly, wishing she could say something more constructive.

'Well, sometimes it's different, I dare say. Where does this prince live? When is he coming for you?'

'He lives a long way to the east, and he can't leave his country for any length of time, so I'm to go to him in early summer.'

Mildyth look aghast. 'There's nothing but heathens and wild men in the east! And what kind of a prince expects his bride to go to his land for the wedding?'

'That will do, Mildyth!' Gytha knew that she must guard against letting the woman get above herself, and already she felt a sense of loyalty to the man she was to marry. 'If you think it's to far, or too dangerous, you're not obliged to come, and as for there being only heathens in the east – where did the Three Kings come from when they journeyed to Bethlehem?'

'Oh, you won't leave me behind?' Mildyth cried, her face falling into deep lines of anxiety and distress. 'Don't leave me all alone in this foreign place!'

'Of course I won't leave you, if you want to come, but neither will I make you come against your will. If you prefer, I could ask the King to send you back to Waltham, but I'd rather have you with me, in a strange land where I don't know anyone.'

Mildyth burst into tears and protested that she would follow Gytha to the end of the earth and couldn't bear to be left behind. When Gytha had dried her tears and promised to take her, there were no more grumbles or criticisms from her.

A few days later, Elisev sent for Gytha to come to her bower. Gytha found her there with her sewing-women and several chests of fabrics – fine woollens, snowy linen and rich brocades and silks. She was measured, and the sewing-women draped various lengths of cloth on her while Elisev sat in her carved chair, watching and giving a firm *yes* or *no* to each piece. Gytha's opinion was not asked. For a long time she was wrapped and unwrapped like a doll, until her back ached with standing, and then Elisev yawned, and said, 'That will do for now,' and dismissed the women with an impatient wave of one graceful hand.

'Sit down, girl,' she said to Gytha, gesturing towards a stool. Gytha sat and waited while the fabrics were folded and taken away. She tried to thank Elisev, but was not allowed to finish her first sentence.

'Of course you must have a suitable wardrobe. Svein would dishonour himself if he sent you with less than he would give one of his own daughters.'

'It was kind of you to find me a husband.' Gytha tried another tack.

'You may not think so when you're married! I hope you

haven't any nonsensical ideas about love and so on!' Elisev replied in her usual cool, aloof manner. 'A man doesn't care whether his wife likes him or not, whether she's happy or unhappy, as long as she's presentable in looks, satisfies him in bed, and bears him sons. Don't expect any more than that, and if you fail in the last respect, learn to expect less. You may end up in the cloister yet if you prove unfruitful! I'm not doing you any good turn in this matter. My nephew needs a wife, and you will do admirably. Svein is dying, and I can foresee nothing but trouble when he's gone. Those bastards of his will fight among themselves for his crown, and I've no wish for them to make matters worse by fighting over you as well! As I told you when we first met, I'll brook no rival here. Harald's wife is a nobody, and he'll do as I advise him, but I'll not have him set her aside to put you in her place – as he would, given the chance, despite the forbidden degrees.'

Gytha stared at her, startled, and Elisev gave an odd, twisted little smile at her surprise.

'Haven't you noticed that Harald, Cnut and Olaf all have a mind to tumble you? I think Harald at least would have the sense to set aside his wife and marry you for preference, but one can't be sure of the sense of the other two when their lusts are on them. I hope and trust that neither's been between your legs yet? You'd better still be a virgin when my nephew takes you to his bed, or there'll be trouble, not least for you! I can see by your face that you're innocent of that foolishness, and just as well. The men of my family are very particular about their wives. Do you know how children are conceived?'

'I – I think so,' Gytha stammered.

'Think!' Elisev gave an exasperated sigh, and proceeded to give a detailed and coldly unemotional account of the process, which made it sound thoroughly unpleasant. 'You'll find the first time painful and frightening, unless your prince is more considerate than most men. You'll get used to it in time, and may even come to enjoy it – it can be quite pleasant. Don't expect too much from this marriage, Gytha. You'll have an honoured position as the wife of a Grand Prince, especially if

126

you bear sons, and more freedom in some ways than you have here, but less in others. Your husband will be away from you most of the time – you may be glad of that, of course – so don't expect patience, affection or companionship from him.'

'Why will he be away?' Gytha asked.

'Rusland is under constant attack from both east and west. It's really no more than a string of cities stretching from the far end of the East Sea to the Black Sea, with hordes of heathens forever attacking from the east, and the Latin Christians attacking from the west. My nephew has spent every summer fighting one or the other for the past eight years – since he was old enough to wield a sword. His forefathers did the same before him.'

'Fighting Christians? But you said that he's a Christian himself?'

'Greek Christian.' Seeing Gytha's puzzled look, she expanded, 'Christendom is divided in two – didn't you know? One half uses Latin, the other, Greek. The Latin half is ruled by the Pope in Rome, and the Greek half by the Patriach of Constantinople. My people follow the teachings and customs of the Greek Church, although our services are in the Slavonic language.'

'Slavonic,' Gytha echoed, not as a question, but merely because she had not heard the word before.

'My people are Slavs – an Asiatic nation. A hundred years ago, some of them in Holmgarth, which is where you are going, invited my ancestor, Rurik, to rule over them and help them fight their enemies. He was a Swedish adventurer, on his way to serve in the Emperor of Constantinople's Varangian Guard. His sons and grandsons gained control of more cities along or near the River Road, and that's why the Swedes call our land Garthariki, the Kingdom of Cities.'

'I see. Thank you,' Gytha replied. She would have liked to ask a great many more questions, but Elisev was obviously bored by the conversation. She yawned ostentatiously, and gave Gytha leave to go, which was tantamount to a command.

During the rest of the winter, Gytha was summoned to

Elisev's bower many times to be fitted with her new clothes, and each time Elisev delivered a monologue about some aspect or other of life in Rusland and other topics. She advised Gytha about personal cleanliness, the inadvisability of taking a lover, but also the best way of conducting herself if she did, the process of childbirth and how best to wean a baby, the management of a princely household, how to fit into someone else's household, as she would be expected to make lengthy visits to her husband's relatives, and how to make a long journey in reasonable comfort. She also mentioned some of the customs of Rusland in passing. Gytha was to remember many of her hints and scraps of information later, and found them very useful. She always spoke in the same cold, calm tones, and appeared so impatient of questions that Gytha was reluctant to ask any, although there were many things she wanted to know.

She usually left these interviews in a disturbed state of mind, overwhelmed by the picture of a wholly unfamiliar way of life which Elisev had so incompletely revealed to her, and she would take refuge in St Lucius' church to pray and think before she went home to pass on some parts of what she had heard to Mildyth.

As the time of her departure drew nearer, Gytha made up her mind to brave Elisev's possible displeasure and said firmly, 'May I ask you some questions? There are still things I need to know.'

'Ask, then.'

Gytha paused, considering, then said, 'You've told me a great deal, but could you please tell me what my ordinary daily life will be?'

Elisev's eyebrows rose a little. 'I can tell you only what my own daily life was when I was at home,' she replied. 'I had two rooms – one for myself and one for my maid. I was unmarried and had only one maid. Once you are wed, you'll have more, of course, and you must insist on having three rooms for yourself and your particular maid, and other accommodation for the rest.

'We began each morning by attending church, usually in the cathedral, which adjoins the palace in Kiev. After that, we broke our fast together as a family, and then each pursued his or her own interests. My sisters chose to spend their time mainly in the *terem*, the women's quarters, reading, sewing, talking, singing . . . I found such a life too dull. I usually sat with my father and brothers in the Prince's daily council, where my father held discussions with the boyars – the nobles – or sat in judgment. Sometimes I would visit the shops or the market. Most days, if it was fine, some of us – sisters and brothers – went hunting, or just rode out into the countryside. I liked to visit the villages which belonged to me – the nearer ones, that is, for some of them were too far away. The whole family took supper together in state, and we often attended church again before bed. I suppose it was not unlike your life here.'

'You sat in your father's council?' Gytha asked. 'Is that usual – for a woman, I mean?'

'In Rusland, a woman's place is what she makes it. The Rus are a mixture of eastern and northern people. Some women follow the eastern custom and live in the *terem*, rarely appearing in public, but others choose to live like Norse women. Some of them are traders owning their own businesses, if they're of the merchant or artisan classes. If they are of the princely or boyar families, they may take an interest in government, although only princesses may sit in the council. Some boyar wives are *terem*-bound, but others manage their husbands' estates, and their own, for a woman can own property in Rusland. If their husbands are at court, or in the army, then they are in charge of everything at home. You must choose the way you wish to follow, and do so with determination. I doubt if life will have changed much in the years I've been away from Kiev, and I don't know what your husband's attitude will be. You may have to insist on your right to live in the northern fashion, but always remember that it *is* your right, and you must find out for yourself how to reconcile your husband to it if he objects.'

Gytha left her that day feeling encouraged. It seemed that she would at least have some choice about the sort of life she would live, and it would not be unlike the life she was used to in Denmark. She found Godwin sitting on the bench against the wall of the side chapel near their mother's grave. He waited for her to finish her prayers, then beckoned her over to sit beside him so that he could talk to her.

'Are you sure about this marriage?' he asked. 'You'll be going into an unknown land, very far away, and we've only Elisev's word that this land even exists.'

'Naturally I'm apprehensive,' Gytha replied, speaking slowly, half to herself, and staring at the stone paving before her feet. 'Everyone has been kind to me, but I'm wasting my life here. I've always felt a stranger with no proper place. You and Edmund have slipped into the niches Cousin Svein made for you, but here I have no life or prospects. I've just drifted from day to day, waiting for a sign of what God wants of me, and I think that now I have the answer, the path for my feet.'

'If you simply want a husband and children, why not marry one of the jarls and stay here where you're safe, and Edmund and I can protect you?' Godwin said, looking puzzled.

'That isn't all I want,' she replied patiently, knowing that he was unlikely to understand. 'I want to do something for Father's memory. I need a husband who will give me a son to grow up and make us proud of him, to be a man worthy to be our father's grandson.'

'But you've no idea what this Prince Waldemar is like. He could be a monster!' Godwin was keeping to the aspects of the matter which were within the limitations of his imagining.

'I know, but equally he could be a good kind man, someone I can love. I *need* someone to love, Godwin, and I've no one since Father was killed and Mother died. You and Edmund went away before I was old enough to know you, and Magnus, Gunhild and Ulf are gone beyond my reach now. I need a husband and children. Father Turkill said I would go eastwards – remember? – and I think God has some purpose for me in Rusland. If I have a purpose, I can overcome whatever else there may be.'

Godwin sighed, still troubled and puzzled, but he made no further objection at the moment. Gytha left him, steeling herself against the doubts which she shared with him, and which would continue to creep up on her during the weeks of waiting.

A dozen gowns with overtunics were made for her, and carefully packed in stout, iron-bound chests, together with linen undergarments adorned with fine embroidery, and lawn and silk head-rails. Six pairs of soft leather shoes were packed and two heavy cloaks lined with coney-fur, for Elisev said that winters in Rusland were even colder than in Denmark. There were also suitable clothes for Mildyth, who would be an important figure as principal attendant on a Grand Princess.

Gytha had her mother's jewellery, but she gave that to the priest of St Lucius' to pay for Masses for the souls of Edith and Harold. That left her with her gold head-circlet, her amber necklace, and the cross and chain King Edward had given her. Svein gave her another amber necklace and a gold collar made up of small beasts gripping each other's tails and limbs in their jaws.

She had found a silver mirror, much dulled by age, among her mother's belongings, and when that returned from being re-polished by Svein's goldsmith, she had her first proper sight of her own face, for she had never had a mirror before. She saw a well-proportioned face, oval in shape, with a straight nose and smoothly-curving eyebrows above large cornflower-blue eyes, bearing, she was delighted to find, a strong likeness to her father, softened by her femininity. Her complexion was clear, but rather pale, and she could have wished that her mouth might have been more of a rosebud and less of a bow. It was Elisev who tactlessly likened it to the weapon which had wounded Harold in the battle against William of Normandy, which made Mildyth angry. This did not worry Gytha, as she had never been told about it, and only knew that her father had died from the strokes of many swords.

Godwin viewed all the preparations with doubt and apprehension, frequently repeating his warning to his sister not to trust Elisev. 'There's something I don't understand about all this,' he said. 'Why is she going to all this trouble? If only it were not so far away! What if you go there and find that he doesn't even exist, or that he's hideous and deformed, or mad? I wish we could find out more about him.'

'You could ask some of the shipmasters who sail to the other end of the East Sea,' Gytha suggested, thinking that, despite her outward show of confidence, she would be glad to know that someone else had at least heard of the man she was travelling so far to marry.

Godwin who had apparently accepted that his sister, despite being a mere woman, had sharper wits than he, went off to the harbour to talk to any seaman he could find who had heard of the River Road. He found a great many who had actually travelled on it, and were full of tales about the wonders they had seen. They all told him that the princes of the House of Rurik, the rulers of Rusland, were splendid, handsome fellows, although they could only name two or three of them. Some of them had heard of Prince Waldemar, whom they said was a great soldier, but he could not find anyone who had actually seen him. Nevertheless, he went back to Gytha feeling more confident, and she was heartened by what he had managed to glean.

By Pentecost she was ready, with all her possessions packed into four great chests, which were sewn into wrappings of tarred canvas to protect the contents from the sea. Her fears and moments of doubt were more or less overcome, and a feeling of excitement mingled with apprehension was growing in her every day.

'Time to go, then,' Elisev said one morning, arriving at her house with the news that the shipmaster was ready to set sail.

'I'm ready,' Gytha replied, stifling a desire to beg for more time. 'There's no reason to delay any longer. I must thank you again for all your trouble.'

'Thank me?' Elisev raised delicately arched eyebrows in surprise.

'I have no wish to remain unwed all my life, or to enter a convent, and I know that, without your help, I would not have found a prince willing to wed me, so I'm very grateful to you.'

Elisev smiled faintly. 'I've told you before that you may find you have nothing to be thankful about, although I hope all may turn out well for you. I wish simply for you to be gone, one way or another. As I have a liking for you, this is the least – er – distressing way for me. I have a small gift for you, before you go.'

'But you've already given me so much . . .'

'Those were Svein's gifts, not mine. This is all I shall give you.' She held out a long rope of little freshwater pearls with the iridescence of the rainbow. 'They're of no great value, but will serve as a keepsake.' She cut short Gytha's attempts to thank her by walking away, and Gytha did not see her again.

The day of departure dawned cold and wet. Gytha and Mildyth were escorted across the island of Sjaelland from Roskilde to the east coast by her brothers and Svein's two elder sons, Harald and Cnut, on horseback. Svein himself travelled in a horse-litter, for he had suddenly aged and become very lame in the past few weeks.

Svein had made the arrangements for Gytha's journey with great care and in good time, sending to Gotland for three of the ships which the Gotlanders built to carry goods safely from one end of the East Sea to the other, fighting off pirates when necessary. The three ships he had specified were the property of the shipmaster of the largest, who was well known to Svein. He was a tall, lean man with sharp grey eyes and a face seamed with hard weathering and two or three sword-cuts. He was typically Scandinavian in height and colouring, but unusually silent in comparison with the garrulous Danes of Svein's court.

His name was Sigurth Tovisson and the largest of his ships was called, naturally enough, *Sea-Fafnir*, after the dragon slain by the legendary Sigurth. She was more than thirty strides long and five strides across the middle, a beamy, high-sided vessel, half-decked for carrying cargo, with holes cut in her sides for twenty long sweeps, but depending more on her great wadmal sail. Unusually for a cargo ship, her prow reared high above the water and was carved into a fierce dragon-head, with a smaller and lower head on the sternpost, poking out its tongue in a very cheeky fashion at all the ships which were too slow to keep up with her. A large and fairly comfortable cabin was built into the afterpart of the ship, partly lowered into the hold to give it more headroom without rising too high above the deck. The escorting ships, which had waited offshore while *Sea-Fafnir* went in to take the passengers on board, were smaller and narrower un-decked fighting vessels, each carrying thirty oars, and were called *Mew* and *Tern*. Their sole purpose was to guard *Sea-Fafnir* from the pirates which were the plague of the East Sea, and they were built of heavier timbers than usual, even for fighting ships.

The whole party went aboard *Sea-Fafnir* to inspect the cabin in which Gytha and Mildyth were to travel, and Svein pre-sented Sigurth with something of a flourish. 'The best ship-master in Gotland, and that probably means in the world!' he announced with unaccustomed enthusiasm. 'Sets his own con-ditions, mind you! Won't carry a gaggle of screeching females, so that's why you've only one maid to go with you, but nothing to fear – you'll be perfectly safe in this ship, my dear. Sigurth's reputation as a wholly reliable man means more to him than a little pleasure with a female passenger, eh?' He dug Sigurth in the ribs with a salacious grin, but the shipmaster's face re-mained expressionless, save that he raised one eyebrow a frac-tion, and inclined his head to Gytha in what she felt was a private signal affirming what Svein had said.

'Well, I suppose he can't be blamed for not wanting unneces-sary females in his ship,' Edmund said grudgingly, 'but I do feel that our sister should have an escort, you know. Half a dozen housecarls, at least . . .'

'I gave you both the chance of going with her yourselves but you declined,' Svein pointed out. 'What use would housecarls be? She's going the whole way to Holmgarth in a ship, with the two best Gotland fighting ships to escort her. Good God, man, have you any idea what it costs to hire Gotlanders? Besides, Sigurth wouldn't take housecarls – they'd get in the way of his men.'

'We never carry more than two passengers. No room for

more,' Sigurth confirmed briefly, and gave Edmund a look which effectively silenced him.

'You'll be wanting to catch the tide,' Svein said abruptly. 'Goodbye, my dear girl. I've enjoyed having you at my Court, and I'm sure you'll be very happy in your new home, with your quick wits and your good sense. God bless you.'

He kissed her cheek, patted her shoulder, and turned away to busy himself with the problem of getting off the ship with his lame leg. Harald gave her a formal blessing and a wintry smile. Cnut wished her good luck in a doubtful tone, and they both hurried after their father.

'Be happy, little sister!' Edmund said with unusual emotion, hugged her, and pressed a purse of money into her hand. Godwin hung a gold chain round her neck, bade her remember England, their parents and himself, embraced and blessed her, then carried away by the emotion of the occasion, embraced and blessed Mildyth as well, which quite ruffled her feathers and made her cry.

Edmund was already ashore, and Godwin turned to follow him, then checked a moment to say, 'If you're not happy, write to me and I'll try to come to you.' It was kindly meant, but Gytha thought it unrealistic. If he was really concerned about her, why had he not offered to escort her? She doubted if either of her brothers would really miss her for very long.

In a few minutes the ship began to glide away from the shore, the five men standing on the shore to wave, watched at a discreet distance by Svein's escort, and then a curtain of sleet swept across the cove and they were lost from view.

Gytha watched the Sjaelland coast recede, as she had once watched England fade away into the distance, and thought to herself that here was another chapter of her life ending, another beginning. Turkill had told her that she would travel far beyond the sunrise, and now his words were coming true. What would she find there?

The East Sea

Chapter Eight

The weather was dreadful. Although it was now May, the wind blew from the north and was bitterly cold, and the ships, with sails brailed round and reefed, sailed across-wind, rolling wildly in the rough sea. Gytha and Mildyth huddled together in the cabin with cloaks and sheepskins round them, shivering. The wind found every crack in the cabin walls and roof and forced eddies of sleet in on them, and there was nothing to do except talk, for the cabin had no windows, and the only light came from a little oil-lamp, floating in water for safety.

After a long time, there was a knock at the cabin door. Mildyth had to be pushed into going to see who was there, and seemed to expect a horde of pirates to burst in when she opened it, but it was only one of the seamen with the women's supper of hard bread, cheese, dried fish and ale. It was unpalatable, but they both knew from their earlier voyage from England to Denmark that it was impossible to cook food at sea, so they ate what they could without complaint.

The motion of the ship grew worse, and soon Mildyth was sick, and then lay on her plank bed moaning and incessantly reciting poetry for hours. Gytha stuffed her fingers in her ears and fought a long battle with her own squeamish stomach and her fear of the grey, wild sea outside the frail walls of the cabin.

The little chinks of daylight between the planking faded into darkness, the lamp burned out, and still the ship tossed and rolled, seeming as if she must overturn, yet always reaching a point where she hung suspended for a moment, then rolled back just as violently the other way. Mildyth was flung on the wet floor once, and howled like a frightened child until Gytha found her in the dark and helped her to wedge herself more securely into the low bed.

'Make them go back!' she begged. 'We'll be drowned and battered to pieces. Svein Estrithsson's a murderer, sending us out in this terrible storm!'

'Oh, hush, Mildyth!' Gytha begged her. 'Don't make such a fuss! What's the use of turning back? We'd only have this part of the journey to do all over again. I'm sure Sigurth knows what he's about, and he wouldn't have sailed if there was any danger.'

Mildyth returned to moaning, praying and reciting – she seemed to know the whole of *Beowulf* and *The Wanderer* off by heart – and Gytha made her way back towards her own bed, which was not easy in the dark, with the deck heaving and swaying under her feet. Before she reached it, there was a thunderous knock at the door, and she turned towards it, arriving with a rush as the ship gave a tortuous wriggle and pitched her in the right direction.

'It's me, Lady – Sigurth the shipmaster,' a voice said loudly in her ear as she opened the door a crack. 'What was all the screaming?'

'Mildyth fell out of bed.'

'Is she hurt?'

'Only frightened. Is it always as rough as this in the East Sea?'

Sigurth laughed, the sound mingling with the shrilling of the wind. 'Not always! This isn't much, compared with the Ocean. It's rough because we're going across the wind, but when we get into the lee of Svealand, you'll feel the difference. You're not afraid?'

'A little,' Gytha admitted.

'No need to be. There's no danger, only discomfort. This is safer than a flat calm, because it keeps the pirates away. Are you cold?'

'Yes.' Gytha was shivering.

'Have a swallow of this.'

She felt something brush against her face, cold and hard, put up a hand, and found a pottery flask, from which she took a good mouthful, thinking it was mead.

It wasn't. Liquid fire ran down her throat and exploded in her stomach, sending a warm glow through her veins in seconds.

'Oh!' she gasped. 'Whatever is it?'

'The Scots call it *the Water of Life*,' Sigurth replied, laughing. 'Wrap yourself in your sheepskins, Lady, before it wears off!'

Gytha thanked him, shut the door after a struggle against the wind, and found her way back to her bed, where she managed presently to drift into a restless, anxiety-ridden sleep. When she woke, the ship was rolling far less, for the wind had dropped and a watery sun was struggling through the clouds.

It was still very cold, and during the next seven days Mildyth did nothing but shiver, grumble and pray under her sheepskins. Gytha wrapped herself in one of her fur-lined cloaks and walked briskly up and down the small afterdeck, sometimes across the ship, sometimes along the bulwarks, looking at the grey wilderness all around. Sky and sea were the same depressing leaden colour, the only difference being the wrinkled and foam-flecked look of the water.

Sea-Fafnir cut through the swell, her great sail pulling well, until they took a more northerly course towards Gotland, and then the sweeps were put out and the crew took turns to pull them, singing to keep time. It was hard, warm work, and most of them stripped off their long woollen gowns and worked in their baggy, cross-gaitered breeches and linen shirts. Those who were not rowing kept up the incessant baling out of the hold, using a chain of leather buckets, for the ship had taken in a great deal of water during the storm. *Mew* and *Tern* kept station on either side, close enough for the exchange of friendly insults and banter between the men manning the great steering-paddles.

The days were interminable. Everything was damp, if not actually wet, all the time, and it was impossible to sit comfortably without holding on to something to steady oneself, so Gytha could not even sew to pass the time. Eventually a darker shadow appeared on the skyline to break the monotony of greyness, and gradually drew near enough to resolve itself into a long coastline with black cliffs and patches of yellow sand. It was Gotland.

After more than a week at sea, Gytha was thankful for two nights and the intervening day of rest in the small harbour at Vlatergarn on the north-western shore of the island. Sigurth had cargo from Sjaelland to unload and sell in the busy market, and even Mildyth was sufficiently roused from her misery to go ashore with Gytha and walk amid the bustle of merchants and housewives, although she did complain at first that the ground wouldn't keep still under her feet.

Gytha was amazed at the variety of goods for sale. Gotlanders sailed all over the East Sea, and far beyond, travelling east for silk, spices and carpets from Sirkland and Constantinople, and up the rivers that opened on the south coast of the East Sea for wine, glass and metal goods. Some went north up the Norway coast for walrus ivory and sealskins, or westwards over the Ocean to Greenland and Iceland for wool and soapstone. She was tempted by many beautiful and unusual things, but she had only the small purse of coins Edmund had given her, and she was afraid to spend any in case she needed them later. She did, however, expend a quarter of a silver penny on the hire of riding ponies and a groom for a couple of hours' gallop through the miniature forests of pine and spruce and across the pastures of the island. When they returned to Vlatergarn, it was natural to go into the handsome church to give thanks for having come thus far in safety, despite the weather, and to ask the Lord's protection for the rest of the journey.

As they were walking back to the ship they met Sigurth, who greeted them with a beaming smile, pulling off his woollen cap and making a little bow to Gytha. 'A good day's bargaining, Lady!' he said. 'King Svein's goods sold well, so there's a pleasant little bag of silver for you.' He handed Gytha a weighty leather money-bag.

'For me?' she asked, surprised.

'Yes. The King gave me cheeses and bales of cloth to sell for you.'

Gytha, who had been worried about her small supply of money, was delighted. When Sigurth had gone, she peered into the bag, and found an interesting assortment of coins. Some were French, some English – one with her father's head on it, which she decided to keep for a talisman – and many with inscriptions in strange lettering, or with swirls and dashes which seemed to have no meaning at all.

'That Sigurth!' Mildyth burst out suddenly, as if she could no longer hold back a comment which she hadn't wished to make before. 'Did you see what was hanging round his neck?'

'Not particularly,' Gytha replied, trying to remember. 'A silver cross, wasn't it?'

'No, it was not!' Mildyth cried indignantly. 'It was a hammer! The man's a wicked heathen!'

Gytha knew that many Scandinavians followed the Old Gods, but, as far as she knew, she had never met one of them before. She was so used to seeing a cross worn as an amulet that she had only half-seen what Sigurth wore, and had mistaken it. He was on deck when she and Mildyth returned to the ship after another look round the market, and a covert glance showed her that he was indeed wearing an image of Thor's hammer, which was an alarming sight for anyone brought up on tales of the ferocity of the wild heathens of the Northlands.

'My father-in-law is giving a feast tonight, Lady,' he said to her. 'He'd be honoured if you and Lady Mildyth would join us.'

Gytha involuntarily looked at Mildyth for guidance. The woman's face was a study, half delighted at being called a lady, and half horrified at the thought of entering the house of a heathen. Gytha came to a swift decision in favour of accepting the invitation. She must keep on the right side of the man on whom she depended for her safe arrival in Holmgarth, and could not risk offending him by refusing, so she said that they would both be delighted to attend the feast.

In the comparative privacy of the cabin, Mildyth tried to persuade her to change her mind, but Gytha explained why she had accepted, and that was sufficient to silence Mildyth for several minutes, but she soon thought of another problem. All the chests containing Gytha's new clothes were packed away in the hold, but she recollected that the smallest of them contained two almost new gowns which would be fine enough for the feast, so she asked Sigurth if she might have it out.

'I've no wish to cause your men extra work,' she said, 'but neither do I wish to insult your father-in-law by appearing in my salt-stained travelling gown.'

Sigurth smiled a little, and brought the chest up himself, saying that it was no trouble. Gytha unpacked the two gowns, one blue and the other dark green, shook them well, then hung them on a rope across the cabin for the creases to drop out.

'I think the green will fit you,' she told Mildyth. 'I'll not put Sigurth to the trouble of searching out your chest as well, as it's a big one, and sure to be at the bottom. I think we can manage with these.'

Mildyth's seasickness had slimmed her enough to enable her to get into the green gown without difficulty, and she made no protest, obviously enjoying the feel of the fine woollen cloth as she smoothed it over her hips, for her own clothes, although suitable for a royal servant, were not of this quality. The gowns were not among the best of Gytha's clothes, but they were richly trimmed with some of Elisev's woven braid, and looked very well when Gytha had put on her collar of gripping beasts, and given Mildyth Godwin's gold chain to wear.

Early in the evening, Sigurth came to escort his guests to his father-in-law's hall. He was resplendent in a fine green woollen tunic, braided heavily about the neck and cuffs, with cross-gaitered breeches to match and soft leather boots. Two great gold and enamel brooches as big as his fists fastened his darker green cloak to his shoulders. He looked more like a prince than a shipmaster, and Gytha was glad that she had thought at the last moment to add a girdle of fine gold mesh to her own ornaments.

Sigurth's father-in-law, Thorvald Grimsson, was an old white-haired man, but his back was still straight and his light blue eyes still undimmed despite nearly sixty years of gazing over the bright sea. He was two ells tall, with a jutting, arrogant, aquiline nose and a weathered face that looked as if it had been carved out of oak. He greeted Gytha and Mildyth with courtesy, but not even a pretence of humility, no doubt feeling that the owner of many ships, cattle, sheep and horses had no need to consider himself in any way inferior to a woman, even if she were a king's daughter.

The hall was large and well built, with the luxury of a stone-flagged floor under the rushes, and the walls were made of upright tree-trunks, each one larger than any tree Gytha had seen in Gotland during her ride across the island. When the first greetings were over and a brief pause signalled the time to start general conversation, she complimented Thorvald on his fine hall, and he told her, in a gruff, pleased voice, that his father had built it, bringing the wood from the mainland.

The body of the hall was set with long trestles and benches for the household and farm-workers, whose food was served on wooden trenchers, but the high table was a massive affair of solid oak, and there were high-backed chairs for the guests and for Sigurth and his wife, as well as for Thorvald. Sigurth's wife was a thin, pallid creature with no life in her at all. She hardly said a word all the evening, and, from the shapelessness of her body, Gytha thought, with a flicker of apprehension, she was probably worn out with over-frequent childbearing.

The plain but ample food was served on silver platters, and the horns of ale and mead were silver-rimmed. For Gytha's use, there was a beautiful silver cup which, she thought with misgiving, looked remarkably like a chalice. By unobtrusively turning it round a little, she saw that the wide borders of ornament engraved round the rim and the foot were made up of vine-leaves, grapes and ears of corn, which confirmed her fears and made her reluctant to drink from it.

'Isn't the mead to your liking?' Thorvald asked her suddently. 'I've some Rhenish wine, if you prefer it.'

Gytha hesitated for a moment, perplexed. If she explained why she could not drink from the chalice, she might give serious offence to her host, but her conscience told her that she must make a stand for her own faith. She wondered fleetingly what her father would have done in her place. *Honours and titles bring responsibilities*, her memory prompted.

'I've no wish to offend you,' she began cautiously, 'but I would prefer to drink from a horn like everyone else, if you'll forgive me. This cup is – is . . .'

Thorvald's puzzled expression suddenly cleared, and he exclaimed, 'Oh, I see – you're a follower of the White Christ! We're not.'

'I realise that,' Gytha said as calmly as she could manage. 'You see, in my Faith this cup is a sacred thing, set aside for the use of a priest. I know you intend to do me honour by serving my drink in it, but . . .'

'But I'm asking you to commit – what do you call it? – sacrilege? You're right – it came from one of your temples. My father got it when he went to England with Svein Forkbeard. Did you not know that we're not of your Faith before you came?'

'Yes. I've seen that Sigurth wears Thor's hammer.'

'Yet you still came. I take that very kindly!' Thorvald exclaimed. He summoned a servant with a snap of his fingers and gave a few crisp orders. Within minutes, Gytha was given a silver-mounted horn like the others, filled with mead. The chalice was emptied and wiped, and then carefully wrapped in a large piece of fine red silk.

'A small marriage-gift,' Thorvald said in an offhand manner, and presented the bundle to Gytha with a pleasant smile and a bow, waving aside both her protests and her thanks, and firmly changing the topic of conversation to what he could recollect of Rusland and the River Road to Constantinople, which he had travelled several times in his youth.

Gytha listened eagerly, asking questions when he paused, to prompt him to go on. Her interest in the strange land which would be her home gave her usually pale cheeks an unaccustomed touch of colour, and her blue eyes sparkled. Sigurth, watching, remarked to Mildyth, who was sitting next to him, that her mistress was very beautiful, which set Mildyth in a flutter between pleasure at hearing her nursling praised, and alarm that the praise came from a wicked heathen, which made her

146

reply more than a little incoherent.

'I don't expect you'll ever travel as far as Constantinople if you're to live in Holmgarth,' Thorvald was saying. 'There's a great city – Constantinople, that is. It has a fine harbour – they call it the Golden Horn – and the biggest temple to your Christ that you can imagine! Holy Wisdom, they call that – Hagia Sophia in the Greekish tongue. The Emperor lives in the city, in a palace all coloured stones and gold, and all his court is dressed in silk. For all his wealth, he has to depend on us northerners for his guards. The Varangians, they're called – the companions. Swedes, Danes, Norwegians, Gotlanders, English . . . You've heard of Harald Sigurthsson of Norway, who was called Hardrada?'

'Yes,' Gytha replied. 'My father killed him. In battle,' she added hastily.

Thorvald looked at her in a curiously blank fashion for a moment, and then said, 'Oh, yes, I remember. Offered him seven feet of English ground – a good jest, that! Well, Hardrada was captain of the Varangian Guard in Constantinople before he was King of Norway. Yes, a great city.'

'Is Holmgarth very big?' Gytha asked.

'Holmgarth? No, not very big. Busy, though. Full of people. Plenty of trade. It's built on both sides of the river, with the burgh on one side and the Prince's palace and the market on the other . . . ' Thorvald was silent for a moment, remembering, and then he suddenly said, 'Kiev, now – that's quite a size. It's built on a cliff, and you can look east from there, across the river, and see for miles, almost to the end of the world, I should think! It's as flat as the sea, and covered with trees. The chief Grand Prince rules there, the one all the Rus princes obey. In my day it was Yaroslav – they called him the Wise – and a fine man he was, shrewd and just and very clever. A good soldier, too, for all he was as lame as Old Brock. One of his sons rules there now, but none of them is a man like old Yaroslav!'

'You wouldn't know Prince Waldemar, I suppose?' Gytha ventured, but without much hope, for it was clearly a long time since Thorvald was in Rusland.

'Waldemar? That's not a Rus name. You must have it wrong, Lady. That's a German name, and none of the Rus would have it. They all have Slav names, you see, as they rule over Slavs. No, it can't be Waldemar,' which left Gytha puzzled and uneasy.

This was the second time that someone who knew Rusland had denied any knowledge of Prince Waldemar. It seemed very strange. Surely all the members of the ruling family would be well known, unless . . . Could there be some reason why he was never mentioned? Perhaps he was an invalid, or mad . . . ? Hastily she stifled the thought, and tried to pay attention to what Thorvald was saying.

Sea-Fafnir, *Mew* and *Tern* sailed again in the morning, creeping north-eastwards along the coast of Gotland, and then turning east before a light breeze. Gytha watched the island fade into the misty horizon with a feeling of sadness, for it seemed to her to be the final disappearance of her old life. The next land she saw would be completely foreign, outside the loosely related group of northern lands where the Norse language was understood. This was a greater change for her than going from England to Denmark, for many Danes knew England, had kin there, and the language was not very different, but now she was going to a land where possibly nobody would know where England was and where everything – language, customs, even religion – would be different.

The sea was very calm and there was nothing to look at but the other ships. Even the horizon seemed almost invisible, and she realised that it was shrouded in mist. Even as she watched, the grey sky seemed to close in until all that remained was a small disc of silver-grey water, just big enough to contain *Sea-Fafnir* and her two escorts, surrounded and tented by a wall of fog which reached out clammy fingers and made her shiver. There was only the faintest breath of air, just enough to keep the ships moving, and that, too, was cold.

'Fog,' said Sigurth, coming up behind her. 'There's still ice about, for all it's mid-May.'

'Ice? You mean the sea is frozen?' Gytha asked.

'Not completely, but further north there are floes drifting about. They won't melt until the weather is really warm. The ship won't be troubled with them – my fine lady can cut through them – but the ice brings fog, and that's a nuisance.'

He went on along the deck to see to something in the hold, and Mildyth came to join Gytha.

'You don't like Sigurth, do you?' she asked.

'He seems a pleasant man, and he must be honest and trustworthy, or King Svein wouldn't employ him,' Gytha replied.

'That's not what I meant,' Mildyth said irritably. 'You know it isn't!'

Gytha looked at her steadily for a few moments, thinking that Mildyth, for all her good qualities, could be perverse, mulish, prejudiced and presumptuous at times. On the other hand, she had willingly left her home in England to flee to Denmark, she had been devoted in her care for Edith, and now she had even come on this long and dangerous journey without hesitation. Moreover, she was Gytha's only link with the old, happy life which was now slipping away into greater remoteness of time and place.

'If I choose to like a man, should it be your concern?' she asked with an odd mixture of aloofness and gentleness.

'Oh, well, you'll do as you please, of course!' Mildyth said huffily. 'You're not a child any more, but you don't know much about men!'

'Perhaps not, but I know whose daughter I am, and what is due to my birth and my Faith. I also know my duty to my God, my family and my husband,' Gytha replied quietly. 'Sigurth is a kindly man, and one to be trusted, I believe, for all that he wears Thor's hammer.'

'He prays to Niord as well.' Mildyth was diverted from Sigurth's potential as a seducer to his undoubted heathenness.

'Niord?' Gytha queried. Her knowledge of the Old Gods was limited to the better-known ones – Odin, Thor, Frey, Baldur.

'God of the Sea,' Mildyth involuntarily lowered her voice and glanced at that element, which lay placid and glassy all about

149

them. 'One of the *oldest* gods!' she almost whispered, and hastily crossed herself.

Gytha also looked at the sea, her eyes wandering idly across the limited area within the wall of fog, which was only a few hundred paces beyond *Mew* on the steerboard side of *Sea-Fafnir*. If one could measure distances at sea in paces, that is. Christ could, and St Peter . . . *What was that?*

Something – a dark shape – had appeared momentarily in the edge of the fog, but it was gone again almost before she had seen it. Had the sun been shining, it might have been *Mew*'s shadow. Without stopping for any conscious consideration of what it might have been, she called, 'Sigurth! There's something over there!'

Sigurth's head appeared over the edge of the deck, rapidly followed by the rest of him as he ran up the steps between the two levels, looking towards where Gytha was pointing.

'Well done, Lady!' he exclaimed, his face breaking into a beaming smile, then he cupped his hands about his mouth and bellowed to the master of *Mew*, who raised a hand in reply and jumped up on to the steerman's platform, staring into the fog. Even as he did so, he was calling orders to his men, who ran to ship their long oars.

Within seconds, *Mew*'s sail was down and she leaped forward as the sweeps bit water, swinging away from *Sea-Fafnir* and heading straight into the fog. The effect was extraordinary, for the forward part of the ship seemed to vanish, and then the whole craft stopped dead with a fearful jarring crash, hung still for a moment, then shot smartly backwards as the oarsmen reversed their stroke. A hoarse babble of screams and shouts came out of the fog, and *Mew*'s crew replied with a short bark of a cheer.

Suddenly the fog swirled and retreated like a curtain lifting. Gytha saw three ships, smaller than *Mew*, bunched in confusion, as though they were moving one behind the other when disaster struck. In front of them, the dragon-prow of a fourth vessel stuck up out of the water, with a *mélange* of broken planks and oars floating amid a number of splashing, struggling swimmers.

Mew was already swinging towards the next ship in the line and gathering forward speed as she headed in to ram, and *Tern* was coming rapidly across *Sea-Fafnir*'s stern to join the attack.

'What's happening? Who are they?' Mildyth gasped.

'Niord's sent us four little pirates!' Sigurth said joyfully. 'Oh, the foolishness of them! To attack Gotlanders, and hardly out of sight of our own island! The insolence! The sheer, stupid insolence!' and he flung his head back with a shout of laughter.

Mingled with the sound came another great crash and outbreak of screams and shouting, and then another, as *Mew* and *Tern* smashed the oars and frail sides of two more of the pirate craft, and then both ships, having backed clear of the wreckage, leaped forward again, their crews screaming encouragement to themselves and insults to each other as they raced for the fourth pirate.

'What happened?' asked Gytha. 'It looked as if *Mew* and *Tern* crashed into the sides of them.'

'Yes. Both the ships are strengthened in the bows with timber and iron sheathing, and have a ram sticking out in front under the water. It's a trick we learned from the Greeks. You don't wait for the enemy to come alongside and fight hand to hand, but you go for him as hard as you can, using your whole ship as a weapon, and hit him in the side, where his ship is the weakest. If you're going fast enough, you can turn him over, or cut him in half!' Sigurth was still shaking with laughter as he explained.

He stopped speaking as another tremendous crashing, splitting noise signalled the sinking of the fourth pirate. It sounded as if *Mew* and *Tern* had struck her together, but the fog had come down again on the scene and nothing was visible. The crew of the *Sea-Fafnir* peered into the white murk, straining their ears as they tried to guess what was happening by the sounds of shouting, screaming and rending, and it was lucky for them that their own lookout at the masthead remembered his duty. It was his shout of alarm which alerted them to their own danger as the fifth and largest pirate vessel shot out of the fog on their other beam and was grappling alongside them even as they ran to grab their weapons from the barrels which were lashed to the bulwarks, and turned to defend their ship.

Mildyth took one look at the wild men swarming over the ship's side, screeched 'Vikings!' and scuttled down the steps into the hold. Gytha heard the door of the cabin slam behind her, but stayed where she was, against the opposite side of the deck.

For a few moments she watched in shocked horror as a fierce battle spread along the length of the vessel, then fought down her own terror and seized one of the few swords remaining in the weapons barrels. Only a few days before she had looked at them and thought how sensible it was of Sigurth to keep them ready to hand, in case . . .

The sword she had was short and light, and when she drew it from its scabbard, the blade glimmered with the subtle patterns, like flowing water, of the strip-welding which she had often watched the blacksmith at Waltham working for similar blades. This was no time to admire the workmanship, however, so she gripped the hilt, tried to remember the sword-drill she had watched Godwin carrying out with his company of house-carls at Roskilde, and held it across her body, waiting, and wondering if she would find the courage to use it.

Suddenly the confused struggle on the decks shook itself into an orderly pattern as Sigurth's men began to work to the plan that had served them well in the past, fighting shoulder to shoulder and pressing steadily against the pirates, who were more used to fighting as individuals, without discipline or organisation. Steadily they were driven back until the fighting was against the bulwarks. The quiet lad who brought the ladies their food, now fighting like a berserker, seized an opportunity to slash one of the grappling ropes, and, within seconds, the others were cut and the pirate ship began to drift away, her crew scrambling to get back on board before they were left behind.

Another ship suddenly came out of the fog, charging at full tilt for the pirate, and there was a terrible rending crash as she struck the enemy amidships. She was *Tern*, having circled round silently in the fog, coming to the rescue of the mother-ship. *Mew* came only seconds behind, but was too late. The pirate, smashed and overturned, had already sunk.

'I'm sorry about that,' said Sigurth, sounding more than a little pleased with himself as he wiped the blade of his battle-axe on the tattered shirt of one of his victims and returned it to its place in a barrel. 'Let me put your sword away for you, Lady. I'm glad you had no need to use it!' He did not sound at all surprised to find her armed, and seemed to assume that she would have been capable of defending herself with it, had it been necessary. 'I see you've inherited more than your looks from your father,' he added with a grin.

Mew and *Tern* were already returning to their places on either side of *Sea-Fafnir*, and, within minutes, both were sailing along demurely, looking innocently peaceful, like a pair of baby dragons out for a swim with mother. *Mew* had a large sheet of wadmal wrapped round her dragon-head, and four of her crew were engaged in freeing it without tearing it – the stout woollen sailcloth was worth its weight in silver. The dead and wounded pirates who remained on board *Sea-Fafnir* were thrown overboard, the decks washed, the wounded bandaged and, in minutes, no sign remained of the battle.

Gytha stood in bewildered silence while all this was happening, listening to cries for help fading away behind them, and then said hesitantly, 'But you've left men in the sea back there! They'll drown!'

'Most of them were wearing ringmail, so perhaps Niord will think they died in battle and will persuade Father Odin to let them into Valhalla,' Sigurth replied, then, seeing the shock in Gytha's face, added, 'They're pirates, Lady! If we hadn't struck first, they'd have killed us all, sooner or later. Those who died in the fighting would have been the lucky ones, and the rest would have begged for death in the end – you and your maid more than any! My men and I have spent years sailing the seas, from Greenland to Constantinople, by the Ocean and the Middle Sea, or by the River Road. We've seen North Cape and the Golden Horn. Gorm, who commands *Tern*, has been across the Ocean to Vinland, on the world's edge. Nowhere, in all those days of ploughing the grey gull's path, nowhere have we met any peril worse than the Wendish pirates of the East Sea! Be glad they're drowning, and thank your White Christ for saving you from them. I mustn't forget, too, that we must all thank your bright, sharp eyes that gave us those extra seconds of warning.'

Gytha shook her head wordlessly, and turned away from him, shaken and sickened. She suddenly found herself at the ship's side, for she had walked blindly up to it, and stood for a few minutes looking down into the curve of green water that sloped away from the hull as *Sea-Fafnir* glided on her way. She could imagine drowned faces staring sightlessly up at her from the depths, and when a large fish suddenly appeared for a second, she gave a gasping cry of shock before she realised what it was.

She had often heard people in Denmark complain about the pirates and blame Svein for not acting more vigorously against them, but she had never thought much about them, even when she learned that her journey would take her along the length of the East Sea, for would she not be travelling in a Gotlander ship, and everyone said that the Gotlanders were a match for the pirates? It was only now that she was afraid of them, of the possibility of being captured, and of the unimaginable things they would do to her . . .

At the same time, those pirates left struggling and dying in the sea were men, and if Sigurth meant what he had said about her sharp eyes, some of the responsibility for their deaths lay on her own soul. She closed her eyes and prayed for the souls of the dead and dying, and for a safe voyage for the rest of the way. As she prayed, she became aware of a pleasant warmth on her back, opened her eyes to find the fog almost gone and the sun shining on a sparkling, almost blue sea. She pulled herself together and went to find and comfort Mildyth.

The good weather continued for several days, with a fresh breeze keeping the three ships cutting smartly through the waves, heading steadily eastwards. Hour after hour passed, each day a long, long interval between dawn and dusk, with nothing to do but sit with Mildyth in the shelter of the high stern, sewing or weaving braid, and talking. Even meals were not much of a break in the monotony, for the food was cold and unpalatable; bread and smoked or dried fish or meat.

One day Mildyth asked, 'What made King Svein choose a husband for you so far away?'

'He said it would be impossible to find a prince for me in the west, but Prince Waldemar lives so far away that he probably hasn't heard anything about what Duke William said about my father. He only knows that I'm the daughter of a king, which is true.'

'How did King Svein come to hear about the Prince?'

'I thought you knew – did I never tell you?' Gytha exclaimed, recalling now that Mildyth had not been present at the conference about her marriage. 'The Lady Elisev came from Rusland. Prince Waldemar is her nephew, and she arranged the marriage.'

'The Lady Elisev!' Mildyth looked at Gytha with round eyes and open mouth. 'That black-eyed witch! Oh, we must turn back! You can't marry a man *she's* found for you. He'll be mad, or maimed, or so ugly you can't bear to look at him.'

'Don't be silly, Mildyth!' Gytha exclaimed, trying to speak sharply, but her heart misgave her, for Elisev's kindness had been unexpected. Perhaps Mildyth was right – perhaps it wasn't kindness at all!

She suddenly remembered Elisev's first words to her – *So this is the daughter of Harold Godwinsson* – and the story that Mildyth had heard from one of Elisev's waiting-women; that her mistress had loved Harald Sigurthsson and had married him in spite of her father's disapproval. What if all this – the whole plan to send her to Rusland to marry Elisev's nephew – what if it was some sort of revenge on her father for killing Harald Sigurthsson?

Perhaps there was something dreadful about Prince Waldemar, or perhaps he didn't even exist! What if she reached Holmgarth and found no prince, no husband, perhaps even nobody expecting her? What could she do?

Mildyth was watching her with growing concern as she sat quite still, staring into space, her lower lip caught between her teeth as she tried to think coherently about this abyss of doubt which had suddenly opened before her.

'Hadn't you thought that the Lady might be spiting you?' Mildyth asked anxiously. 'Oh, my pet, you never trusted her, did you? I never dreamed it was she who arranged all this. Lord have mercy on us! Whatever can we do?'

'Do?' Gytha echoed. 'What can we do but go on, and make the best of whatever we find in Holmgarth.'

'We could go back . . .'

'Go back to what? King Svein hasn't long to live, and Harald Sveinsson would hardly welcome the expense of keeping me, and the Lady would find some other way of . . .' Gytha shook her head.

'There's your brothers.'

'They can't help me. They depend on Harald Sveinsson. He'll keep them, because they're good men and earn their keep. If we go back, it will have to be right back – to England, and the nunnery at Wilton, if Duke William's offer to dower me there still stands.'

'Well, a nunnery might be better than . . .' Mildyth said dubiously.

'There must be nunneries in Rusland.' Gytha lifted her chin in a resolute fashion, looking so much like her father that Mildyth's spirits unaccountably rose a little. 'We'll go to Holmgarth and see what happens. It may all turn out for the best, and if it doesn't, it won't make much difference whether I'm a nun in England or in Rusland, for I'll see nothing outside the walls of my nunnery!' Her voice cracked a little on the last hated word, but she bit her lip again and firmly applied herself to her sewing. Mildyth, about to say something more, hesitated, changed her mind, and carefully avoided any mention of the future for the rest of the journey.

The damage was done, however. In the long hours of uneventful sailing there was far too much time for thinking, and however hard Gytha tried to stop them, her thoughts would keep turning towards the question of Elisev's motives and the various possibilities of what she might find waiting for her in Holmgarth. Once, she had an idea which lifted her heart for a few hours, remembering that she had never asked Sigurth if he had met Prince Waldemar, but when she took the first opportunity to do so, he shook his head and looked puzzled.

'I don't know. There are so many Rus princes, all with strange names. I know two of them quite well, but they're called Svyatoslav and Gleb. They're all fine-looking men.'

After that, she could do nothing but pray as every crawling hour carried her nearer to the end of her journey, which would, at least, bring the end of speculation.

During all this time they saw few other ships, and only the most distant glimpses of land, so she was both surprised and relieved when one evening Sigurth said to her, 'Tomorrow, at some time during the day, you'll see land ahead of us. That will be Domesnes. Just off there is an island called Osel, where we'll stop to trade and take in fresh water. You'll be able to stretch your legs and eat hot food for a change.'

He sounded so confident that Gytha woke in the morning with a feeling of anticipation, and found herself looking past the mast and sail every little while towards the horizon. There was nothing to see but sparkling water and little white foam-caps on the waves.

During the afternoon, she looked ahead for perhaps the twentieth time, and saw a faint shadow breaking the smooth circle of the horizon directly ahead. It rose higher and higher and came steadily closer for the next hour or two, and by evening the ships were passing north of a great headland and heading towards the island which was now in sight across the strait. In the long twilight of a northern summer night, they rounded a tree-clad point and anchored in a sheltered bay, *Sea-Fafnir* close inshore, with her escorts further out and ready to defend her from attack from the sea.

There was a village beside the bay, quite small, with twenty or so stout little wooden houses clustered in front of a modest hall. A dozen fishing-boats were pulled up on the beach, and wooden frames supported a mass of drying nets, giving out an all-pervading smell of fish, which made Mildyth hold her nose and wish aloud that the wind would blow the smell away instead of towards them.

Most of the inhabitants came down to the shore to welcome Sigurth and his men, and an impromptu market was set up on the beach, the half-light being augmented by flaring torches, which shed a smoky glow over the chattering, gesticulating little groups chaffering over iron-work, cloth, pottery, morse ivory, made from walrus tusks, and glass beads.

Mildyth went to bed, but Gytha accepted Sigurth's offer of a walk on the land, and went ashore in one of the ship's small boats. The village was dirty, and the aroma of fish was mingled at close quarters with even worse smells, so she walked along the beach, looking for amber, and did, in fact, find a dozen small pieces, which she put in her purse. It was a rare pleasure to walk about completely alone, as she had been used to do at Waltham, in her childhood, and even sometimes at Roskilde. She supposed that she would always be attended by someone in Rusland, so this might be her last chance to walk by herself.

When she came to the end of the bay, a steep cliff barred her way, so she turned inland and walked among the pine trees, enjoying the peace, the feel of firm ground beneath her feet and the smell of the trees.

She found herself thinking about Sigurth, whom she considered a fine-looking man, and wondered if the unknown Prince Waldemar – if he existed – would look anything like him. Quite possibly he would, if the Rus princes were descended from a Swedish chieftain. She hoped that her future husband would be tall and fair like Sigurth – like her father . . .

Somehow she wandered further from the beach than she had intended, and found herself coming out from among the trees behind the village, close to the back of the hall. She was about to go round it and down through the village, when she heard Sigurth's voice.

'We're bound for Holmgarth on an errand for King Svein, this time,' he said. 'I might go on to Kiev, or even Miklagarth, if the River Road is peaceful this year.'

'What cargo are you carrying?' asked a gruff, deep voice, speaking in Norse, but with a thick accent.

Gytha realised that the two men were inside the hall, or, rather in a small room opening off at this end of it, and she could hear them through the chinks in the log wall.

'The usual things,' Sigurth replied. 'Is there anything you need?'

'I saw two women on the deck when you came in, and the younger one came ashore. How much are you asking for her?'

'What, are you tired of all your wives already?' Sigurth asked lightly, and Gytha felt a tremor of fear. Was he about to bargain over her?

'Wives grow fat after a few babies, and there's no excitement in them any more. Come on, Sigurth – name your price! I've some gold, if our fish or carved wood don't interest you.'

'Have you found a dragon's hoard back there in your pine-woods?' Sigurth asked. 'It would cost you that much at least to buy this one, I assure you!'

'Be sensible, Sigurth! No woman's worth that sort of money. Not like a horse, or a ship, that'll last for years! A woman's worn out after a few months' use. Stop joking and name your price!'

Sigurth laughed. 'I don't deal in slaves. She's not for sale; she's a passenger, and the other is her waiting-woman.'

'I admit she's unusually pretty, and I'll give you a good price for her,' the other persisted. Gytha thought he must be the village chief.

'Pretty! She's a real beauty, and you know it, with your eye for a woman! No, old friend – she's really not for sale, and if she were, she's not mine, more's the pity! She's Svein Estrithsson's favourite daughter, and I'm taking her to Holmgarth to marry one of the Rus princes.'

'Old Svein's marrying her to one of those damned Slavs? What a waste! They wouldn't appreciate a beautiful woman if they saw one! Their own are flat-faced and shapeless as old sows.'

159

'The princes are no more than half-Slav. The other half's as Swedish as you are,' Sigurth replied, laughing again.

'I'll tell you what I'll do. Sell her to me, tell the Prince that she died on the way, and I'll give you the use of her every time you come here!'

Gytha felt quite sick at the thought of being the slave of this man, of being left in this stinking cesspit of a village, and waited, hardly breathing, for Sigurth's reply.

'Do you think the Prince would believe me? He'd have the truth out of me with red-hot pincers, at least! What would I say to him then? *I'm sorry, my lord, but I sold your bride to an old goat in Osel.* And Svein Estrithsson? *I'm sorry, Lord King, but a man in Osel wanted her for his bed, so I sold her, and got a good price.* He'd make the blood-eagle of me to start with, and ruin my trade with Denmark into the bargain. No, Olaf Valdernarsson, my princess goes to Holmgarth, and you make do with the wives you have! Why don't you buy yourself another in Kurland? They have pretty girls there, and sell willingly. It's not worth having your village burned about your ears for trying to take Svein's favourite daughter.'

Gytha realised that the last sentence was a threat, and was grateful to Sigurth for it, as well as his refusal to consider selling her. She thought it would not do, nevertheless, to be found by Olaf so close to his hall, so she hastened away, through the village and down to the beach, thanking God as she went that Sigurth was worthy of the trust Svein had placed in him, even if it was really only to safeguard his trade in Denmark. She wondered why he had said she was Svein's daughter, but thought it was probably because it sounded more impressive. Svein could certainly be expected to take revenge on anyone who carried off his favourite daughter, but he might not bother overmuch about a distant cousin!

Down on the beach, the trading had almost finished and the torches were burnt out. The young master of *Tern* hastened across the shingle and asked anxiously if she was ready to return on board. 'I was just coming to look for you – Sigurth Tovisson would have my ears off if he knew I'd let you out of my sight!'

'I'm sorry – I didn't think you'd be anxious. Yes, I'm ready to go back to the ship, thank you.'

Mildyth stirred and sat up as Gytha slipped into the cabin and began to prepare for bed in the faint light of the little oil-lamp.

'What did you see on land?' she asked.

'Just a dirty little village and a great many trees. The villagers were busy buying things, and Sigurth was talking to the thane, I think. He wanted to buy me!'

'He what?' Mildyth exclaimed, scandalised. 'The insolence!'

'He offered a good price.'

'I should hope so! What did Sigurth say?'

'He told him that I'm King Svein's favourite daughter, going to Holmgarth to be married, and I'm not for sale, so you'd best remember that if anyone asks you tomorrow!'

'I shan't go ashore here, not for anything! I don't like this talk of buying women,' Mildyth said disgustedly. 'You mind what you're about, and don't go near that thane!'

Gytha did mind. She went ashore again in the morning, while the seamen were filling their water-casks and loading them, together with the furs and dried fish which the villagers had bartered for their purchases, but she avoided the village, and walked along the beach only a short distance, keeping well in sight of the ships. When she returned, she encountered the thane, whom she recognised by his voice when he spoke to her. He was very polite and called her 'Lady', snatching off his woollen cap and bowing, but his merry blue eyes looked her over admiringly in a surprisingly youthful manner, considering his grizzled hair and beard and his heavy body. She was as gracious and regal to him as she could be, and he seemed a little awestruck by the time he had walked down to the boat with her. He handed her into it as if she were made of eggshells, and stood bareheaded, watching, until she was safely back aboard *Sea-Fafnir*.

'Was that him?' asked Mildyth, who had been watching from the deck.

'Yes.' Gytha turned and waved her hand to him in a very

regal fashion before she went down to the cabin.

They set sail again in the afternoon, gliding under oars along the coast of the island, and Gytha saw that the pine-wood covered only a small part of the island, forming a protection for the village from the bitter north wind. The rest of the island was ploughland and pasture.

By morning, the ships were once more sailing on an easterly course, with the mainland still visible on the right. Several small craft came in sight during the day, but they were all busy fishing, and only one ventured within hail, slipping past on the opposite course, with a cheerful wave from her steersman and a shouted greeting from her lookout that Gytha did not catch, but it made the crew of *Sea-Fafnir* laugh.

Halfway through the seventh day out from Osel, the coast was still near on their right. There was nothing much to see – just a strip of beach, rising ground of no great height behind, and clumps of trees. They were not very tall, and their trunks shone silver where the light caught them, so Gytha thought they must be birches.

When she went out on deck on the eighth morning, there was land ahead. At least it wasn't sea, but it was very low and hardly rose out of the water. Sigurth pointed to it and told her it was salt-marsh, and they were entering the mouth of the River Neva.

'It's not unlike the estuary of your River Thames in England,' he said, 'but much more narrow. We're leaving the sea now, and the rest of your journey will be by river and lake. This is the beginning of Rusland and the River Road.'

Novgorod

Chapter Nine

Gytha contemplated her new country with no great enthusiasm as the ships slowly entered the river mouth and fought their way up under oars against the strong current. On either side, the marshland stretched as far as she could see, threaded by bright channels of water. It was a desolate prospect, with no sign of life apart from myriads of sea-birds. The powerful river wound between marshy islands, splitting into smaller channels and coming together again, turning north-eastwards, then gradually making a great curve towards the south.

All day long the oarsmen strained at the long sweeps, cursing the heavy cargo-ship and the strong current, and making slow progress. Early in the evening, they pulled into a small creek and anchored, *Mew* and *Tern* on either side of *Sea-Fafnir*. The heavy smell of rotting weed and mud rose in the mists from the marshes, and frogs croaked incessantly all night.

The heavy toil continued all the next day, the river curving to and fro like a great silver snake, not becoming much narrower, but gradually tending more northeasterly. The marshes continued, flat and unprepossessing, until late in the afternoon, when the ground began to rise a little on either side. Then, quite suddenly, they rounded a bend, and the banks fell away as they entered a great expanse of water, which stretched into the distance.

'Lake Ladoga,' Sigurth said, with a comprehensive sweep of one arm. 'We'll anchor now, for the men need a rest before we go on.'

That night, once more, everyone remained on board, for the shore of the lake was still marshy, but two days later they swung southwards into the mouth of another river, plunging into a dense forest of pine and birch, and, after a couple of hours, reached a small town and tied up by a long wooden quay for the night.

'This is Aldejuborg,' Sigurth told his passengers. 'The Rus sometimes call it Staraya Ladoga. It used to be a great trading-place where the Northerners met the Slavs, but Holmgarth has taken nearly all the trade now. There are all sorts of folk here still – Finns, Swedes, Lapps, Danes, Gotlanders, and Slavs, of course. Would you like to come ashore and take a cooked meal with us?'

Gytha accepted for both of them with alacrity, for they had been cooped up in the ship for so long with only cold, barely edible, food and, in any case, she was longing to look about the first town she had seen in her new country.

Sigurth and the masters of *Mew* and *Tern* escorted them ashore. The quay was a broad, well-built wooden construction, lined with large wooden storehouses. Beyond these were narrow streets paved with logs, difficult to walk on, for they were slip-pery. The houses were log-built too, but, unlike the houses in the Norse lands, the logs were laid horizontally, with notched ends interlocking to make strong corners, and the roofs were covered with wooden shingles. They passed a church, also wooden, with a very strangely shaped roof, all double-curved gables, with a curious helmet-shaped cap on the top of its stubby tower. Mildyth nudged Gytha and pointed to the top of it, where a gilded cross gleamed in the evening sun. The sight of it removed one of Gytha's worries, for it confirmed Elisev's statement that Rusland was Christian, although she thought it an odd cross, for it had a second small cross-piece above the main one, and a third, set slantwise, half-way down the upright.

There were people about, all seeming very busy and purpose-ful. Many of them Northerners – tall, fair-haired, blue-eyed – but the rest were shorter, squarely-built people with black hair and high, prominent cheekbones which gave their faces a cat-like cast. The men wore long fur-trimmed gowns to their ankles, and the women were bundled up in heavy shapeless clothes, with head-dresses which echoed the double curve of the gables of the church roof. Their round faces were doll-like, all looking much the same with those almond-shaped eyes, which glanced sidelong and curiously at the two Englishwomen as they passed.

News of their arrival must have flown through the town, for as soon as they entered an inn which Sigurth seemed to know, the innkeeper barely waited for them to be seated before enquiring the prices of iron cooking-pots and Rhenish wine. Sigurth answered in a business-like manner, adding that a hot and tasty meal might well reduce the figures a little. The innkeeper took the hint, and they were soon served with a thick meat and vegetable broth, followed by meat and worts, and slabs of moist and sticky dark brown bread and goats-milk cheese.

'This is peasants' bread!' Mildyth said contemptuously.

'Not in Rusland,' Sigurth replied. 'The summers are short here, and not much wheat and barley can be grown so far north. Even the Prince's household eat rye bread, and I think you'll find it good – better than the black bread of the west.'

'It's fresh, and you won't have to soak it in ale to make it edible,' Gytha pointed out slily, for Mildyth had found that the only way to make the bricklike ship's bread chewable, her teeth being unreliable.

'That's the first time I've heard you complain about the dreadful food we eat in the ship, Lady!' Sigurth exclaimed, smiling. 'I'll admit I'm ashamed that's all we had to offer you, and that's why I don't like carrying passengers. They usually grumble all the time, and with good reason, for they suffer cold, damp, boredom, lack of exercise and inedible food! I admire the way you two ladies have endured it all without complaint.'

'But it's the same for the seamen,' Gytha pointed out.

'We're used to it, and we have work to keep us busy and give us appetite enough to eat anything, even weevily bricks and green, slimy meat. Most of us have hardly known any other life, but you've lived in palaces, in comfort, with good food,' *Mew*'s master replied.

The walk back to the ships was pleasant in the half-light of the northern summer night. Gytha was impressed by the solid, comfortable look of the houses, and the size of the town, which was bigger than Roskilde, and seemed to have none of the ramshackle one-roomed hovels which made up the greater part of towns in England or Denmark. They took a different route, and walked between the houses and a stout rampart composed of a high earthen bank topped by a palisade of thick tree-trunks, with watch-towers at intervals. At Sigurth's suggestion, they climbed the wooden steps to the walkway near the top of the palisade, and looked over.

There was a clear area about two hundred paces wide all round outside the rampart, and beyond that stood the dark forest, seemingly poised to surge forward and reoccupy the site of the town at the first opportunity. Tall, straight pines crowded together, with the occasional gleam of a silver birch and the white blossoms of rowan shining between the dark trunks. Close to, the square watch-towers looked strong and well built, with whole skins of leather covering their wooden shingles.

'They seem ready to be attacked here,' Gytha commented. 'I heard that there's much fighting in Rusland. Is this town often besieged?'

'The warfare seldom comes so far north, Lady,' Sigurth answered. 'The forests are dense, almost impenetrable. Further south, there's much flat and open grassland, and tribes from the east come invading, seeking plunder and slaves in the towns of Rusland; sometimes the folk to the west invade, trying to seize the trade-route and the rich farmland. The rivers form the backbone of the land, but there are no natural frontiers to defend to east or west, so it's a continual struggle to keep out the Polovtsy, the Pechenegs and the Bulgars from the east, and the Poles and the Germans from the west. Aldejuborg and Holmgarth are by far the safest places in Rusland, being in the northern forests.'

This was quite a long speech for the taciturn shipmaster, and Gytha, comparing its content with what she had heard earlier, was comforted to find that Elisev had told the truth about this, as well as about the religion of the Rus.

Most of the crew remained ashore for the night, but a strong anchor watch remained on board the three ships. Gytha assumed they were there to guard the cargo, but when, waking in the night and feeling restless, she opened the cabin door and looked out, she found a burly seaman sitting on a barrel only a few feet away with a naked sword across his knees and a cowbell by his feet, obviously guarding Mildyth and herself. She kept the discovery to herself, thinking there was no sense in alarming Mildyth unnecessarily.

She was anxious, having reached Rusland, to get to Holmgarth and find out what was really going to happen to her there, but the days seemed to pass more slowly than ever as the ships toiled on up the river, for this – Sigurth said it was called the Volkhov – flowed into Lake Ladoga, not out of it, so they were still going upstream.

At least there was something other than unending sea or marsh to look at, for the forest linked the banks on either side. Most of the trees were pine, with some birch and rowan. Honeysuckle and eglantine wreathed about the lower branches of the deciduous trees. Squirrels chattered at the ships from high branches, and reminded Gytha of the Forest at Waltham, save that these squirrels seemed to have a black sheen over their russet coats. Sometimes she caught sight of deer, disturbed by the approach of the ships as they were drinking from the river. Once, in the long twilight, she saw a great furry creature, as tall as but more bulky than a man, walking upright between the tree-trunks. One of the seaman who was off-watch shot an arrow at the bear, and Gytha was unaccountably glad when he missed. There were also insects, and they were the least welcome of all, for they bit!

Several times during the nights she and Mildyth heard dogs howling. She asked Sigurth why the villages hereabouts were set back out of sight of the river.

'There are no villages,' he replied. 'People are thinly scattered in this part of Rusland.'

'But we heard dogs howling in the night, baying the moon!' she protested.

Sigurth laughed. 'They weren't dogs, Lady! Haven't you

169

heard wolves howling before? You wait until winter – if it's a hard one, you'll see wolves in the streets of Holmgarth.'

Gytha shivered at the thought, and that was another discovery which she did not mention to Mildyth.

After four days out from Aldejuborg, they reached a small clearing where some strong wooden cabins had been built, and a thick rope stretched across the river. Here they stopped, the rowers just holding them still with an occasional stroke, *Mew* and *Tern* closing up in position between *Sea-Fafnir* and the settlement.

A man in ringmail and a conical iron-bound leather cap came out of the nearest cabin and swaggered out on a wooden jetty, standing arms akimbo, looking carefully at the ships. More men, similarly dressed, appeared and stood watching as the first man's eyes travelled rapidly over the lines of the ships, the faces of the seamen, Gytha and Mildyth, and finally came to rest on Sigurth.

'I know you,' he said in strangely-accented, foreign-sounding Norse.

'Sigurth Tovisson,' the shipmaster replied. 'And you're Stepan Igorovich.'

'Of course. I see you've brought the Princess. Is she well?'

'Perfectly well, apart from being eaten alive by mosquitoes and gnats,' Sigurth replied. 'How are things in Holmgarth?'

'Quiet.' The man sounded as if he meant too quiet. 'Prince Gleb still rules, and Fedor is still bishop, although he's very old now. There's nothing new in the New Town.'

Gytha listened, wondering what he meant by the 'New Town', but most of her attention was taken by the name of Prince Gleb, who must be her intended husband, although the name bore no resemblance to Waldemar. Why had Elisev called him that – unless he had two names, one for public use, and the other, more private, for his family?

'We're expected then?' Sigurth was saying, having deduced this from Stepan Igorovich's reference to the Princess. Stepan Igorovich – did that mean Stepan Igorsson?

'Yes, but not yet,' he replied. 'The tale was that she would come in the winter – that's why I didn't recognise you at first, because I wasn't expecting you much before Christmas. (Christmas! thought Gytha. Then they really are Christian!) You'll be pleased to hear that the Prince has instructed that we're not to charge you any toll. I'll send fast riders to the city to tell them you're coming, and you'd best go on now. You can stop for a good gossip on the way back.'

'I might go on to Miklagarth and go home by way of the Middle Sea.'

'Miklagarth? Oh – you mean Constantinople. We usually call it Tsargrad. Have you any good swords for sale? I don't trust mine – we haven't the secret of making them, or perhaps we don't use the right enchantments.'

Sigurth laughed, and clattered down the steps to the hold, returning with a long, cloth-wrapped bundle. 'Look at this!' he said, drawing out a fine sword. Its blade was rippled with different shades of metal, like water, and its hilt was plainly but serviceably made by the bodies of two intertwining dragons, their tails curving to form the guards. 'A gift!' he added, wrapping it again and tossing it over the two smaller ships and the intervening water to Stepan, who caught it deftly, unwrapped it, and looked it over approvingly.

'Just what I wanted!' he exclaimed. 'Thank you!' and he called to his men to lower the rope barrier. *Mew* was across almost as it splashed down into the water, the other two ships following close behind.

Looking back, Gytha saw one of the men mounting a horse. She said to Sigurth, 'Was he a Slav?'

'Yes. You saw his high cheekbones and black beard.'

'Why did you give him a sword? Wasn't he asking to buy one?'

'He collects toll from ships going up to Holmgarth for the Prince, Lady, and he's entitled to keep some for himself, and to pay his men. As the Prince told him not to take toll from us, he'd lose money. In any case, I've known him a long time, and a soldier needs a good sword.'

'Was it a good one?'

'Of course. A man's life depends on his sword. If I gave him a poor one, I'd be a murderer!' Sigurth looked angry at the suggestion, so Gytha apologised, which he accepted with a jerky bow, his frown dissolving into a grin. 'We'll arrive in Holmgarth in the morning,' he said. 'You'd better have the chest which holds your finest gown up from the hold, or say your prayers. Maybe both! I don't know anything much about the man you're going to marry.'

Gytha did both, but did not, in fact, select her finest gown, wishing to have that in reserve to be married in. However, she chose one almost as grand, a fine woollen with a silk overtunic, both in the rich sapphire blue which enhanced the colour of her eyes and the clarity of her complexion. The tunic was trimmed with a wide band of embroidered braid round the hem and the wide sleeves, which made it hang straight instead of clinging to the wool 'like a wet dishclout', as Mildyth had said before they thought to add the braid. It and the gown were creased, but the creases might drop out before morning. She felt nervous now and even less confident about Elisev's good faith, although she had clearly told the truth about some things. At least she was expected, to judge by Stepan Igorovich's remarks. Before she went to bed that night, she took a last walk along the deck, and found Sigurth fishing the evening rise with a line over the side.

'Fresh fish to break your fast in the morning, if I'm lucky,' he said.

'What did you mean when you said you didn't know much about the man I'm to marry?' Gytha asked.

'That I'm not sure which one he is,' he replied. 'There are at least a dozen princes in Rusland, each ruling a town for the Grand Prince of Kiev. They're all his sons or his nephews or his brothers . . . I'm never sure which is which.'

'I'm to marry Prince Waldemar.'

'Well, as my old father-in-law told you, Lady, Waldemar's not a Slav name, so that's the puzzle. All the princes have Slav names, so I don't know which he can be, unless Waldemar is his private family name – some of them have those too, I believe.'

'The Lady Elisev said that he's the son of the Grand Prince of

Kiev,' Gytha said, then added, 'I think,' for she was suddenly uncertain whether Elisev had actually said that. She had certainly said that he was the son of her brother, but she might have more than one brother . . .

'The present ruler in Kiev has six sons, I think. I wonder which one is yours. They're all fine, handsome fellows, but I haven't seen all of them, only Gleb, David and Oleg. Anyway, you'll know tomorrow.'

She slept badly that night, and was out on deck early in the morning. The forest still hemmed in the river on either side, and everything seemed very dark and dismal, for the sky was heavily overcast and it was raining. She felt too nervous to eat when the quiet lad brought bread, freshly-cooked fish and ale, but she managed to force some of it down, then wished she had not, for it lay in her stomach like lead and made her feel sick.

About an hour later, the forest suddenly came to an end, as if it had been cut off. Judging by the mass of tree-stumps and piles of logs along the banks, that was exactly what had happened, but this orderly devastation soon gave way to a flat plain, stretching as far as she could see. They passed a group of buildings on the left bank which looked like a monastery. The river wound across the plain, isolated log-houses appearing here and there, and great areas of pasture with herds of animals – cattle, sheep, goats and horses – with their attendant herdsmen.

The horizon was shrouded in mist, but something loomed through it in the distance, directly ahead. It looked like a great jagged crag, a huge mass of rocks rising in irregular pinnacles, suddenly leaping skywards out of the flat plain.

'Holmgarth!' said Sigurth. Gytha had to look at him and follow the direction of his outflung arm and pointing hand before it dawned on her that she had been looking at her new home.

The rain slackened and stopped, and the clouds began to break up. When the sun emerged, it picked out the strange shapes of several church towers above the huddled houses of the town, and the pinnacles she had first seen resolved themselves into a cluster of five helmet-shaped domes on the top of a high and massive building which shone pinkish-white in the sun.

'Are all those domes churches?' she asked Sigurth.

'Yes, Lady. Most of the people follow your Christ, including the Prince and the important men and the rich merchants. The others worship Thor, but they call him Perun.' Sigurth's hand unconsciously grasped his hammer amulet as he said the name of his god. 'That great building with the five domes is the Bishop's church. Saint Sophia, they call it. My father-in-law told me what it means once, but I've forgotten.'

'It means Holy Wisdom, the wisdom of God,' Gytha explained. 'Is all the rest of the city made of wood?'

'Why not? There's no shortage of trees!' Sigurth grinned.

She stood watching Holmgarth drawing nearer and nearer, her thoughts and feelings in a turmoil of excitement, hope, fear, apprehension, doubt. Mildyth, who had come up from the cabin to stand beside her, suddenly took hold of her hand and whispered, 'What will it be like?'

'I don't know,' Gytha whispered back. 'Oh, Mildyth, we mustn't be afraid!'

'Your head-rail is crooked,' Mildyth replied, 'and you're still wearing your old gown.' She pulled her mistress towards the cabin. Gytha went with her, but reluctantly, half-unwilling to leave the sight of Holmgarth.

In the cabin, she took off the crooked veil, changed into the new gown which she had got out ready and let Mildyth brush and replait her long hair, then put the head-rail on properly. The creased gown could not be smoothed, but the gold collar of gripping beasts, the two strings of amber and the gold circlet distracted attention from it. In the cramped cabin, personal washing had been far from easy, but the silver mirror showed Gytha that at least her face was clean, and her cheeks had a becoming touch of colour.

She turned her attention to Mildyth, who had put on a drab but clean gown. A bright silken girdle and a pair of silver brooches with a string of glass beads between them made an improvement, and then, with unspoken agreement, they both knelt in prayer for a few minutes before returning on deck.

Mew had fallen astern, alongside *Tern*, leaving *Sea-Fafnir* to lead the way to Holmgarth. A large silk banner had appeared from somewhere and was flying from the top of the mast. When the wind caught it, Gytha saw with surprise that the golden dragon of Wessex blazed across its folds.

'King Svein gave me it to fly for you,' Sigurth explained when he saw her looking at it.

'How kind of him to think of it,' she replied absently, for her mind was filled with a picture of the last time she had seen the banner of Wessex – the last time she had seen her father. He had kissed her and said, 'Always remember that King Svein of Denmark is your cousin. He will help you if – if you have need . . . Look after your mother.' Then he had mounted his horse and ridden away. His friend Ansgar had been at his side, carrying his banner – just such a banner, with that golden dragon shining in the October sun. He had looked so fine and kingly, with his golden hair and his blue cloak flying in the wind. She had watched him ride away across the causeway over the marshes, leading his escort, until he was out of sight, and the very last thing she had seen was a bright flash, as if someone had flourished a sword . . . She had not known then that she would never see him again. Her eyes brimmed with tears, but she rubbed them away quickly, before anyone should see.

Directly ahead, a stout wooden bridge spanned the river, and the right-hand side of it seemed to emerge directly from the middle of a long wall of creamy-white stone rising nearly three times the height of a tall man, with large wooden towers set at intervals along its top. Above the wall soared the five grey domes of St Sophia's cathedral.

On the left-hand side, the bridge ran straight into a very large market-place open to the river all along one side, and swarming with people among the orderly rows of stalls. In the middle rose a stubby wooden bell-tower, and beyond, closing off the south side and facing St Sophia's across the river, was a great rambling wooden building, two floors high in some parts, three in others, with a profusion of carved and curved gables amid its wood-shingled roofs. Two or three more churches and some large houses enclosed the other two sides of the market-place, and beyond lay more streets of houses.

'That's the Market Side,' Sigurth said. 'We have to tie up there, as they don't allow foreign ships on Sophia Side.'

Sea-Fafnir and her escorts glided under the bridge, their masts dropping back in some clever way to allow them to go under, and then rising again as they came neatly alongside the quay and tied up.

The next few minutes seemed to Gytha to be something of an anticlimax, because nothing happened. The bustling crowds in the market took no notice of the new arrivals, nobody appeared so much as to glance in their direction, and she stood on the deck, wondering what to do next.

Suddenly the great bell began to chime in the bell-tower, and everything changed. The people seemed suddenly to become aware that something unusual was happening. Heads turned towards the ship and necks craned as the crowd began to converge and form two parallel lines, running diagonally across the market-place from *Sea-Fafnir* to the great rambling building on the south side. There was a little sporadic shouting, which grew to actual cheering as a group of people emerged from the building, descending an imposing flight of steps from a large covered porch on the upper floor, and walked in stately procession between the watching crowds towards the quay.

'Here they come!' said Sigurth. 'The big man with the fur edge to his gold cap is Prince Gleb, and the old man with the golden bee-skip on his head is Bishop Fedor. Are you ready, Lady?'

'Yes,' Gytha replied in a voice which seemed to belong to someone else.

Sigurth took her hand and led her across the broad plank which had been set from *Sea-Fafnir*'s bulwark to the quay, with Mildyth following. Then he stepped back and left Gytha standing alone, facing the approaching group of men.

They were all bearded. Most of them were dark-haired, but the two who walked side by side in front were not, the younger having a crisp, curly golden beard, and the older – much older – a long white one. All but the old man were dressed in long robes of rich fabrics, trimmed and banded with fur, which reached to

176

their ankles, and all wore pointed caps. The golden-bearded man's cap was made of a gleaming gold fabric sewn with jewels and edged with black fur, and his robe seemed even more gorgeous than the others. The old man was dressed differently, in black, with a gold and blue cape, similar to a western bishop's cope. The bee-skip-shaped mitre was jewelled, and the old bishop carried a long staff topped by a silver cross of the same odd shape as those which crowned the domes of his cathedral. He had dark eyes, which looked benignly at Gytha, and his beard did not conceal a kindly smile. Gytha gave him a grateful look, then turned her attention to the Prince.

He was older than she had expected, looking nearer thirty than twenty, but very handsome with his golden hair, bright blue twinkling eyes and shapely red lips. He must have been nearly two ells tall, and looked a typical Norseman, reminding Gytha that Elisev had said that her ancestors had come from Sweden. As he neared Gytha, he smiled and extended a hand gloved in fine leather and gleaming with jewelled rings.

'You are welcome to Novgorod the Great! We are happy to see you, and wish you a long and contented life in the Land of the Rus! I am Gleb, Grand Prince of Novgorod, and this is Bishop Fedor.'

Gytha took his hand and sank into a low reverence, murmuring 'My Lord Prince,' then made another reverence to the bishop, kissing his ring, and he pronounced what was obviously a blessing in a sonorous voice, but, while Prince Gleb had spoken in fairly fluent Norse, the bishop used a totally strange language, which was certainly not Latin and did not sound like Greek, although she could not be sure for she had heard Master Athelard read Greek aloud only a few times.

Prince Gleb had gone to greet Mildyth, who goggled open-mouthed at him, but managed to whisper something in response and make her reverence, and Sigurth, who seemed impressed, but not awe-stricken, and then Gytha found herself walking towards the great building, which was apparently Gleb's palace, with the Prince holding her hand in a formal fashion and leading her.

She felt less frightened now, for he was certainly not repulsive, and seemed both kind and friendly. The crowds of people pushed and jostled each other to have a look at her, and she nodded and smiled to left and right in response to their words of greeting, which sounded friendly, even if she could not understand the language. The big bell in the market-tower was ringing erratically, and the bells in the church towers joined in, clashing and clanging in a disorderly fashion which sounded joyous, but might equally well be warning of invasion, fire or disaster.

When they reached the palace, Prince Gleb led her up the steps to a raised ceremonial entrance, where they paused to wave to the people before going through the door into a small hall. Two maidservants came forward and offered the new arrivals bread and salt in welcome, and Gleb quietly prompted Gytha to take a morsel of bread, dip it in the salt, and eat it, and Mildyth followed her example. It was only then that Gytha realised that Sigurth had been left behind on the quay, and she had neither thanked him nor bidden him farewell.

'This is the palace,' said the Prince. 'My grandfather built it when he was Prince of Novgorod, and we live here. There's another palace across the river in the kremlin, but it's very plain, poky and uncomfortable.'

'Kremlin?' queried Gytha.

'Fortress. Stronghold,' he clarified. 'Come and meet my wife.'

Gytha stopped dead. 'Your *wife!*' she exclaimed. 'But I thought . . . Aren't you . . . ?'

Gleb had gone on a couple of steps, but he turned back to her with a puzzled frown, then suddenly realised and started to laugh. 'Oh, you thought . . . No, my dear! I'm sorry – I didn't realise! It's my cousin you're to marry, not me!'

'Prince Waldemar?' Gytha queried, feeling nervous and worried again.

'No, not Waldemar. Vladimir.'

Gytha essayed the name, and came out with '*Val*dimir.'

'Vladimir,' Gleb corrected with a broad smile.

This time she got it right, and Gleb went on, 'He's Vladimir

Vsevolodovich – son of Vsevolod, you see, and I'm Gleb Svyatoslavovich. My father, Svyatoslav, is Grand Prince of Kiev and overlord of all the Rus – that is, all the people of the River Road south of here, all the way to the Black Sea.'

'I don't understand,' Gytha said. 'I thought I was to marry the Prince of Holmgarth, and Sigurth said that this is Holmgarth, but you called it something else . . .'

Gleb made a little smiling gesture with both hands, and said, 'I'll explain it all later. Come and meet my wife.' He took her hand again in a ceremonious style and led her for a considerable distance through a succession of small halls or large rooms, each divided from the next by a lobby. The walls of all the rooms were covered by colourful hangings, painted or embroidered, and there was plenty of furniture – heavy tables, scissor-legged chairs and stools, and great carved chests. Every room had a large stove in one corner or in the middle of one wall, and windows with ornately carved frames and panes of mica. The floors were covered by large mats of woven rushes. It all seemed very comfortable and opulent, far grander than Svein's simple hall and assortment of built-on rooms, or even King Edward's palaces at Winchester or Westminster.

Eventually they arrived at the door of the women's quarter, which Gleb called the *terem*, and all the men except Gleb and the bishop stopped, remaining in a particularly large room outside the door while Gytha and Mildyth were taken in to meet Gleb's wife Anastasia.

She was a small, plump, dark-eyed woman, very Slavonic in appearance, and seemed to Gytha to be more like a doll than a human, for she was dressed in an elaborately embroidered gown so stiff that it stood away from her body as if it could have stood on its own, without support. Her hair was hidden by an embroidered silk veil under a crown-shaped head-dress and her cheeks and lips were painted an unnaturally bright red. She smiled shyly at Gytha, but it soon became clear that she knew very few words of the Norse tongue.

'Now, let us sit down quietly and talk,' Gleb said, seating himself on a carved chair and gesturing towards two similar chairs for Gytha and the bishop. Anastasia sat on a padded bench along the wall and busied herself with threading some beads, making no apparent effort to follow the conversation.

'First of all,' Gleb began, 'the name of the city. The trouble is that nearly all our cities have two names – one Slavonic, the other Varang, or Norse – here we call the Norsemen the Varangs. This city is Holmgarth in Varang, but we call it Novgorod – Lord Novgorod the Great, when we're speaking formally, for it's an independent, self-governing city. Kiev is called Koenigarth by the Varangs, and they sometimes call our land Garthariki, but we call it Rusland. Is that clear?'

'I – I think so,' Gytha replied doubtfully.

'Now my father is Svyatoslav, Grand Prince of Kiev. He has a brother called Vsevolod, and Vsevolod's eldest son is called Vladimir. Vladimir is the one you are going to marry. He's Grand Prince of a town called Suzdal. His father, Vsevolod, is Grand Prince of Pereislavl. When my father dies, he'll become Grand Prince of Kiev, and Vladimir will probably take Novgorod from me and be Grand Prince here.'

'Why?' asked Gytha, who thought it sounded a very strange arrangement.

Gleb hesitated, then said, 'It's complicated, but perhaps it's best if I try to explain it to you now, because it causes an immense amount of trouble in our family. My grandfather, Yaroslav, decided that each of his sons in turn should rule Kiev. Novgorod is the next most important city, and the eldest son of the Grand Prince of Kiev rules here, so when my father dies and Vladimir's father inherits Kiev, Vladimir will expect to have Novgorod. I think that's enough to be going on with! You'll find out soon enough about our family complications and feuds.'

Gytha thought privately that she would probably never fathom it all – it sounded remarkably involved. 'Is Prince Vladimir not here, then?' she asked.

'No. He doesn't come here very often, and never in the summer. He usually spends the summer fighting our various enemies, but my father has sent him to Poland now, to make a peace treaty with King Boleslaw. We weren't expecting you until winter, you see. Travelling's easier then, on the ice, and we thought King Svein would send you then. How is my Aunt Elisev, by the way?'

'She was quite well when I left,' Gytha replied, thinking that Waldemar – Vladimir – could not be sick or mad if he could be sent to do something as important as making a peace treaty. How strange to live in a country where travelling was easier in winter than in summer!

'And Uncle Svein?'

'He grows very old.' It slipped out unbidden, and Gytha felt a momentary panic, wondering if she had been foolish to tell him that her powerful cousin might soon no longer be there to protect her interests.

'I'm sorry,' Gleb said politely. 'I've never met him, of course, and I don't remember Aunt Elisev, to tell the truth. It must be twenty years since she left Kiev. You look tired and bewildered. I'll leave you now with Anastasia. She'll show you your rooms. Vladimir asked that we give you your own apartment, as we understand that Varangian ladies don't shut themselves away in a *terem* like some of ours.'

'When do you expect Prince Vladimir to come?' she asked quickly, before he could leave without telling her this important information.

'Oh, not until midwinter at the earliest.' Gleb did not seem to be at all apologetic about it. 'He's usually busy fighting all summer. This is the first interval of peace that we've had for years, and he has to make that treaty to protect our western borders so that he can concentrate on fighting the Polovtsy, the Cumans and the Pechenegs when they start attacking us again from the east. Then there's his own city to be governed in between, of course.'

'Shouldn't I go there to wait for him?'

'What, to Suzdal?' Gleb looked astonished. 'Good heavens, no! It's not safe there – it's a little place right on our eastern border. No, you'll stay here. That's the arrangement we've made.'

'Here? Not in Kiev, if Suzdal's too dangerous?'

'No. Here.' Gleb frowned. 'It's not only your safety. You're a pledge as well.'

'A pledge?'

Gleb hesitated, then gave a sharp exhalation and said, 'Best if you know the worst, I suppose. Vladimir's promised that he'll never try to take Novgorod from me. You're to be his pledge on that.'

'You mean, I'm a hostage.'

'Well, I suppose so, but you'll not be a prisoner – nothing like that. You'll be as comfortable and safe here as I can make you, and Vladimir will come here as often as he can – you wouldn't see even as much of him if you lived in Kiev, because he avoids going there, whereas he likes coming here. You wouldn't like Kiev, anyway. There's a great deal of bickering and unpleasantness goes on there, and my mother's not a friendly woman . . .'

Gytha gave a wry smile, and said, 'My Uncle Wulfnoth, my sister Gunhild and my brothers Magnus and Ulf are all hostages to William of Normandy – my grandmother too, for all I know. It seems to be a family occupation.'

'You'll be happy here – one of the family,' Gleb said reassuringly. 'You'll never be treated as a prisoner.'

'But I may not leave.'

'I wouldn't say that.'

'But you and my husband would quarrel if I did?'

Gleb made a smiling gesture of acknowledgment that she had grasped the situation, and rose to go. The bishop, who had not spoken since his first blessing, also rose, and said in Norse, 'Have no fear, my daughter. If you stand surety to the Prince for your husband, I stand surety to God for you.' He gave her another blessing, and went away with Gleb.

Gytha looked about her hopelessly, wondering how she was to communicate with Anastasia, or with the dozen or so other women who stood or sat about the room, staring at her. Mildyth looked close to tears with the strangeness of it all. Anastasia smiled and nodded whenever Gytha caught her eye, but not a word did anyone say for quite five minutes.

'May I speak, Princess?' a voice asked in Norse.

Gytha turned to see who had spoken, and found that it was one of Anastasia's ladies, a pleasant-faced, pretty woman of about her own age.

'Oh, please do!' she said eagerly.

'My name is Yevpraksia. I speak your tongue a little. If you and your lady will come, I will show you the rooms which the Prince has chosen for you.'

Gytha made a smiling but small bow to Anastasia, deciding that, as the wife and future wife, respectively, of Grand Princes, they must be equal in rank, and followed Yevpraksia, Mildyth crowding close behind as if she feared she might get lost.

The rooms to which they were taken were near the *terem*, but did not seem to be a part of it. They were on the upper floor of the palace, and occupied a corner, some windows looking out across the market-place and others over the shingled roofs of the town, past a rampart like that of Aldejuborg, and, beyond that, across some strips of ploughland and pasture which stretched to the distant horizon.

There were five rooms. The first from the *terem* side was fairly small, and Yevpraksia said it was for Mildyth, who was delighted with the idea of having a room to herself. The next was Gytha's bedchamber, then came the biggest room, which occupied the corner of the building, with windows looking in both directions. The lobby between this and the other two rooms had a door which opened on to an outside landing, which looked on to an internal courtyard, with a flight of steps, under their own shingled roof, leading down to the ground. Beyond the lobby were two small rooms, each plainly furnished with a bed, a table and some chairs and storage chests.

Yevpraksia said she would leave them to rest, and return later to show them how to find their way about the palace, and that food and Gytha's boxes would soon arrive.

Mildyth turned her attention to their two bedrooms first, but Gytha was more interested in the big corner room. Its wall-hangings showed a hunting scene, carefully painted on stiff cloth, and there were cushions embroidered with similar pictures on the wide window-sill, suggesting that it was a good place to sit and look out on the market.

She opened one of the carved chests, and found that it contained no fewer than fourteen books, each bound in wooden boards covered with leather, and carefully wrapped in linen. To her disappointment, not only were they written in a strange language but even in a different alphabet, with only a few letters looking familiar, the others looking completely unlike any she had seen before.

'You've a fine big bed!' Mildyth exclaimed, coming into the room. 'Come and see!'

Gytha went to look. The bedchamber had embroidered hangings depicting an enchanted forest of flowering trees, with gaily coloured birds among the branches, and animals and flowers between the tree-trunks. The bed had a carved wooden frame, and the palliasse was supported by strips of woven leather, only it was not a palliasse, but a thick mattress with a linen cover, stuffed with something firm but soft, perhaps wool or feathers. The covers were fine linen, with a woollen coverlet woven in patterns like fir-cones in soft blues, reds and yellows on a green ground.

There were four carved chests of very large size ranged against the walls. They were all locked, with three heavy locks a piece and Gytha wondered why they had been left there. Perhaps their owner had forgotten about them.

A loud knocking sent Mildyth hurrying to the corner room to see who was there, and then a great deal of puffing and panting followed as Gytha's chests of clothes and Mildyth's modest box were brought up from the courtyard by a squad of servants, all broad-shouldered, stocky fellows with cheerful grins on their Slav faces, dressed alike in blue tunics and breeches, with soft leather boots, each with a bronze trident-shaped brooch pinned on his left shoulder, which Gytha thought must be Gleb's badge or sign. They were followed by three more servants bringing warm water to wash with, white bread, fruit, cheese and wine.

When they had eaten, Mildyth began to unpack their belongings, while Gytha went to look more closely at the two rooms beyond the landing.

The first was clearly a man's room. The bed was narrow and hard, and the chests contained male clothing, some of it in rich fabrics, but the rest well worn, plain and practical. A hauberk of ringmail on a stand occupied one corner, while a conical helmet lined with padded leather and edged with fur balanced on the top of the stand, with a bow and full quiver hanging on the wall above it. Gytha sat on the bed and thought to herself that this room must belong to Prince Vladimir, and she looked at the various things, wishing they could tell her something about the stranger who was to be her husband.

Then she realised that they could. The hauberk showed that he owned at least two, for he must have another with him. It was of very good quality, the rings silvery and unmarked by rust, although some repairs showed that it was far from new. The repairs also showed that the wearer had been wounded in the side and left shoulder at some time. It looked as if it would fit a slimly-built man with broad shoulders, but gave no clue to his height – at least, none that Gytha could read.

A candlestick with eight branches stood on the table under the window, and another book lay beside it, so it would seem that he was literate, and liked books enough to own a remarkably large collection of the precious things. Surely he must have even more, if he could leave so many in a place which he seldom visited?

The wall-hangings were rather old and shabby, and it was only by looking at them carefully that she could see that they were painted with birds, animals and plants, which made her think that he must like such things. A pair of jesses and a hawking-glove lay on one of the chests, so he hunted. There was a little shelf set across one corner, fairly high, above her head when she stood up to look at it. She wondered what it was for, recollecting that there was a similar one in each of the other rooms. Puzzled, she stood on tiptoe and ran her hand along it, but it was empty. There was not even any dust on it.

She had a sudden feeling that she was prying into things

which were none of her business, so, instead of giving way to the temptation to explore those chests and search about for more clues to Prince Vladimir's character, she looked into the fifth and last room, and found that it was very much like Mildyth's, so it was probably meant for the Prince's attendant. She then returned to her own room to help Mildyth sort out the contents of her chests of clothes.

Later on, Yevpraksia returned and asked if they would like to visit the bath-house. She explained on the way that there were several in the palace, one for the men of the princely family, one for the *druzhiniki*, which appeared to be the Slav name for house-carls, and others for the servants. The one to which they now went was in the *terem*, and was reserved for the ladies of the household. It was a steam bath, of the sort which Gytha had heard were used in Sweden, and she found it surprisingly pleasant.

After the bath, there was just time for Gytha to put on one of the new gowns she had brought with her, and most of her jewellery, and for Mildyth to change her gown, before Yevpraksia came again to take them to join Anastasia and her ladies in a formal procession to a very large hall, where Gleb and his family took supper in state with the *druzhiniki* and many richly-clothed nobles, who were called boyars.

During the meal, Gleb explained something of the peculiarities of the government of Novgorod to Gytha, who was seated on his right. It appeared that the people of Novgorod considered their city a sovereign state and not part of Rusland, although it acknowledged the eldest son of the Grand Prince of Kiev as its Prince.

'But I'm really only the commander of the army, as was Rurik – you've heard of Rurik? – my ancestor, who came from Norway to Rusland,' he explained. 'When I took office, I was elected by the people and, in theory at least, they could have chosen someone else.'

'There's something similar in England,' Gytha said. 'The Witan, the council of the most important men in the kingdom, choose the new king when the old one dies.'

'Are the members of the Witan elected by the people?' Gleb asked.

'No. They're appointed by the king.'

'In Novgorod, the heads of the chief families of the city do most of the governing – what the Greeks call an oligarchy. They elect a *posadnik*, a chief citizen or mayor, and he calls meetings of the heads of all the households of freemen to discuss anything of importance – it's called the town meeting, or *veche*. You'll hear the bell in the market-place toll when it's called. It goes on for hours sometimes, for everyone there is entitled to give an opinion, and sometimes they come to blows! If they reach complete deadlock, they ask me, or the bishop, or both, to advise them, and they usually take our advice. I can summon the *veche* myself if it's a military matter.'

'It seems strange that your palace is here, by the market-place, and not over the river in the fortress,' Gytha remarked.

'There's a small palace there, but my grandfather, Yaroslav the Wise, built this one when he was Prince here. Rurik and his immediate successors had a place further up the river, between here and the lake, and later the Prince lived in the kremlin. For the last thirty or forty years we've had this palace, and the bishop lives in the kremlin. He even has a small farm within its walls – cows and goats and chickens, mostly – and what with that and his palace and the cathedral, and living quarters for the cathedral clergy, it's rather cramped. The richer merchants live on Market Side, and the craftsmen and the poor folk live on Sophia Side.'

'I didn't see any ploughland as we came to the city,' Gytha said, 'although I can see a little from my windows. It doesn't seem enough to provide food for a town this size?'

'No. Nearly all the land near the city is pasture. Most of our crops are grown further away, around the subject villages and towns. The *smerdi* – the peasants – pay taxes in food, and lend horses when the army needs them. The boyars draw their food supplies for their households from the large estates which they own, but my household is supported by the city out of taxes. By the way, Sigurth, your shipmaster, is going on to Kiev the day after tomorrow. I thought we might go in state to the Gotlanders' Yard tomorrow to thank him. I'll give arm-rings to all his men on Vladimir's behalf, and a specially fine pair for Sigurth. I expect you'll want to give him some little reward yourself, but it need only be small, for King Svein paid him well to bring you.'

Gytha, of course, agreed, but she lay awake for a long time in her big comfortable bed, wondering what she could give Sigurth. She had only the money which Edmund had given her, and the proceeds of Svein's trading venture on her behalf, and she was afraid to spend any of it, for she had no idea when or how she could replace it. On the other hand, she was very grateful to Sigurth for his kindness and for bringing her safely to Holmgarth-Novgorod. Eventually she decided to give him her collar of gripping beasts, which was as suitable for a man as for a woman. It would be hard to part with it, for it was a reminder of her old life, of Svein's kindness, of the decorations of the books and carved stones of England and Denmark, of all that was now lost to her for ever.

'No use clinging to the past,' she told herself. 'Everything is different now, so look ahead and learn, and don't think about the past at all.' They were brave words and good advice, but they did not prevent her from weeping over the collar before she wrapped it ready for presentation.

The visit to the Gotlanders' Yard was certainly a very impressive demonstration of Gleb's idea of 'going in state'. To her surprise, they went in sledges, gliding quite smoothly over the corduroy street surface. Yevpraksia, who travelled with Gytha and Mildyth, explained that wheeled vehicles were not allowed in the city because they damaged the log roadways too much. The sledges were gaily painted, and drawn by matched trios of small, sturdy black horses wearing coloured leather harness decorated with bells, and plumes on their heads. Gleb travelled alone in the first sledge, as Anastasia had not accompanied him, and wore a robe of even greater magnificence than that in which he had first greeted Gytha on the quayside. The small procession was preceded, accompanied and followed by *druzhiniki* in fur-trimmed blue tunics and breeches of a finer material than that worn by the servants, and their trident shoulder-brooches were made of silver instead of bronze. They were mounted on black horses, rather larger in size than those which drew the sledges, but with similar coloured leather harness and bells.

Sigurth had obviously been notified of the visit, and was waiting on the quay beside *Sea-Fafnir*'s gangplank with his crew lined up along her bulwark, all in their best clothes. *Mew* and *Tern* were also moored at the quay, one at each end of their bigger sister, and their captains waited with Sigurth, but a pace or two to one side.

Gleb made a formal speech of greeting, to which Sigurth replied equally formally, and then he invited Gleb, Gytha and Mildyth to come aboard. Gytha found it oddly reassuring that Gleb, who went before her, hesitated briefly before entrusting his not inconsiderable weight and fine robes to the narrow, springy plank, although the two young captains had stationed themselves on either side to give the visitors a steadying hand if one was needed.

When they were safely on the deck, Gleb made another speech, thanking Sigurth and his men on behalf of himself, Prince Vladimir of Suzdal and King Svein of Denmark for bringing Princess Gytha safely to Novgorod. Then he snapped his fingers in a peremptory fashion, for the *druzhinik* carrying the gifts was still standing on the quay, gazing with interest at the rigging of the mast. He jumped to attention and scurried up the gangplank to give Gleb several heavy leather pouches, which he presented to Sigurth, one for each of the two young captains, one for each crew, and a larger one for Sigurth himself, saying that they were gifts from Prince Vladimir.

Sigurth accepted the gifts in a gracious manner which combined a sufficiency of gratitude with a total lack of obsequiousness, as was proper for a free and independent Gotlander shipmaster.

Gytha then presented her collar to him. She had wrapped it in a piece of cloth, which he removed with one swift movement, and then looked from the collar to her face with an expression of mingled surprise and anxiety, and she knew that he realised that it was the only thing of any great value which she possessed.

'I would like you to have it,' she said quietly. 'You've been a very good friend to me.'

He bowed and said 'Thank you' equally quietly, and then raised a finger to the cabin boy, who was waiting close at hand with Sigurth's gifts for his guests piled on a cask beside him. There was a bolt of best woollen cloth for Gleb, another for Vladimir, and, for Gytha, a small heavy cloth-wrapped parcel. She thanked him, but did not open it until later, when she found that, inside an outer layer of linen, the wrapping was a piece of blue silk containing a fine torc in heavy silver, fashioned in the form of dragons and ornamented with coloured enamel. It was much more beautiful than her gold collar, and looked very magnificent on a plain gown.

Vladimir

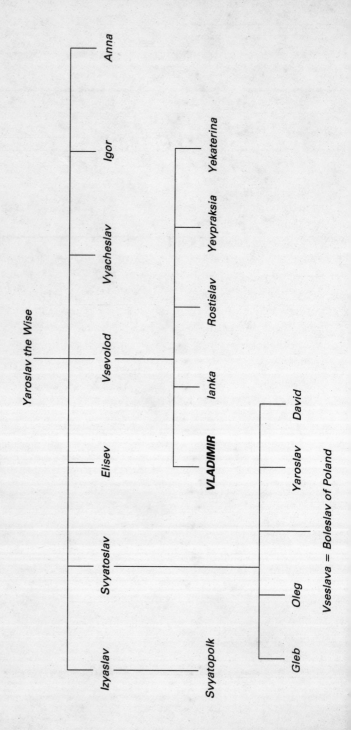

VLADIMIR'S FAMILY

Chapter Ten

During the next few weeks, Gytha gradually became accustomed to her new life. Anastasia made no attempt to speak to her, but greeted her friendly overtures with a frosty smile. Yevpraksia, who seemed to be the only one of her ladies who spoke Norse at all fluently, seemed willing enough to be helpful, but answered most of Gytha's questions with an anxious, 'I'm very sorry, but I don't know.' Because of this, the four great chests in Gytha's bedchamber remained a mystery, and her attempts to find out more about Prince Vladimir were unsuccessful.

Another thing which puzzled her was the difficulty everyone seemed to have in pronouncing her name. Even Gleb hesitated slightly before saying it, and everyone else called her either 'Princess' or 'Gita Garoldovna'. Eventually she asked Gleb about it, and he, smiling ruefully, said that the problem arose because the Slavonic language did not contain the sounds 'th' or even 'h'.

Each day followed more or less the same pattern, starting early in the morning with a ceremonial attendance at a church service with the Prince and Princess and their attendants. This was in one or other of the churches on Market Side on ordinary days, but in the cathedral of St Sophia on Sundays, fasts and feasts. The women of the household stood together on the north side of the ordinary churches, with the men in the central area, but there was a gallery for the Prince's household in the cathedral, where they all stood together.

The church buildings seemed strange at first, being of a different and much heavier construction than Gytha was used to. Instead of a long, open building with columns like tree-trunks supporting the roof, they were made up of square, boxlike structures, each capped by a rounded vault, with the intervening walls pierced by arches, often leaving a surprisingly small area of wall to support the vault. The same construction had been used for wooden churches as for stone ones, despite the different possibilities of the material. The Sanctuary was hidden by a high wooden barrier covered with holy pictures, and in the larger churches, and, particularly, the cathedral, figures of saints were painted on the walls, as in western churches, but, somehow, they seemed different, as did the service itself, perhaps because they used a different language of symbols and words. The cutting-off of the altar by the screen worried her at first until she became accustomed to it, and then she appreciated the revelation which came when the central doors of the screen were flung open at the Eucharist and light blazed out from the Sanctuary into the dark body of the church. A detail which also caused her some anxiety was the way in which she was now expected to cross herself, as her hand seemed to move of its own accord from left to right in the western manner, and she had difficulty in checking it and making it go the opposite way as the others did.

After church, there was a brief gathering in the *terem* with the other women for a light meal, and then Brother Isak came from the bishop to the corner room to instruct Gytha and Mildyth in the eastern form of Christianity and the Slavonic language for two or three hours. This was followed by another light meal, and an hour or two of rest, when everyone apparently went to bed. Gytha and Mildyth used the time to go over what they had learned in the morning, and, eventually, Gytha began to try to read the books she had found in the corner room, while Mildyth sewed and listened, and occasionally offered a possible meaning for the words which were unfamiliar.

The later afternoon was occupied by excursions about the city with Yevpraksia, or, more often, hunting with Gleb and his attendants, either hawking over the meadows, or following the hounds in pursuit of deer or boar. Sometimes they went on the lake in boats to shoot wildfowl with bows and arrows. Gleb was pleased that she and Mildyth were competent horsewomen, and that Gytha was a fairly good archer, for Anastasia took no interest or pleasure in these pursuits, and rarely accompanied them. When she did, she rode in a little carriage, and, as she particularly disliked boar-hunting, refused to come if they were to be the quarry. Gytha thought no more of hunting those ferocious creatures than any other beast, even when, as often happened, a boar charged a man, who barely had time to position his spear to take the charge and kill the animal.

In the evening, the household dined in state, and after there was conversation, during which Gytha learned much of the history and customs of Novgorod and Kiev. Finally, there were evening prayers in the palace chapel, after which everyone retired to bed.

It soon became apparent that Anastasia and her ladies led a suffocatingly dull life in the *terem*. They did not appear to have any books, or to do any form of handwork other than a little bead-weaving and simple sewing. Most of their time was passed in playing childish games and gossiping. A few of the ladies went out to the market, usually to buy sweetmeats, and some asked, through Yevpraksia, if they might go with Gytha when she joined Gleb's hunting expeditions, seeming glad of a chance to ride out. Anastasia was clearly a remarkably lazy woman, with little interest in anything but her clothes and her face-paint, and hardly stirred out of the *terem* at all, except for church-going and meals.

Recalling what Elisev had told her – that although many high-born Rus women lived in the *terem*, some chose a more active life – Gytha took the first opportunity that she could find to broach the matter with Gleb. 'Am I expected to live in the *terem*, as Anastasia does?' she asked, trying not to sound truculent.

Gleb looked surprised, thought for a moment, and then replied, 'I don't see why you should be. I believe that ladies of your rank live fairly active lives in the western countries.'

'Indeed,' said Gytha firmly. 'In Denmark, I attended King Svein's councils, and also when he sat in judgment. My aunt, who was King Edward's wife in England, always attended his councils, and was busy on her own account about schools for noble children, and some of the larger nunneries.'

'And you wish to do much the same here?' Gleb's voice was markedly without expression.

'If I were living in my husband's city, I would expect to do so, in order that I might help him and take his place, in some respects, in his absence, as my aunt did.'

'You don't mean that she actually ruled the country?' Gleb sounded shocked.

'No, but she sat in the council which carried on the government during his illness, and she knew how he wanted things to be carried on. The important thing was that she knew his opinions and his plans.'

Gleb bit his lip. 'Your situation is different. You're living here, so you can do nothing in Suzdal. You may attend my councils, if you wish. I don't mind, as long as – to put it bluntly – you don't interfere. You're not my wife – although I'd be pleased if Anastasia took more interest . . . You'll have to work hard with Brother Isak, though, or you'll not understand a word!'

'You don't think Anastasia will mind?'

'Mind? No – why should she? She knows very well that she can attend councils, if she wants to, but she never shows the slightest interest.'

'Then I'll accept your invitation, and thank you very much,' Gytha said with enthusiasm. 'I'll keep working at my lessons – I'm already making progress!'

The morning lessons with Brother Isak went well, for he was a good teacher, and they progressed rapidly in their knowledge of Slavonic. The monk was a lean, melancholy-looking young man with thick, curly brown hair and beard, a long nose and sad brown eyes, who seemed at first to dislike his role as a teacher, but when he found that his pupils were eager to learn, he became a little more cheerful. He arrived punctually, with a spring in his step as he came up the stairs from the courtyard, a small boy following his black-clad figure, carrying his books.

On his first visit, he looked at the odd little shelf across the corner of the room, and said in fluent Norse, 'Where is your icon? Do you keep it in your private room?'

'Icon?' queried Gytha. 'I'm sorry – what is that?'

'Your holy picture.'

'I haven't one.'

'No icon! You do pray, I trust?'

'Yes.'

'Then to whom do you address your prayers? Which saint intercedes for you?'

'The Holy Cross,' she replied.

'Don't you have a picture of It, to help you collect and concentrate your thoughts?'

'No. At least – at home in England there was a – a representation of It in the church, but I've never had one of my own.'

Brother Isak gave a sharp exhalation down his long nose, which sounded remarkably like a snort, and explained about icons, which he said were like windows into heaven, through which the person praying could address the saint represented, or even Christ or the Holy Virgin, and also be seen by those in Heaven. Gytha found it very interesting, and carefully studied the icons in the churches she attended, and soon grew to think of them as windows. She found that many of them seemed to portray the saints in an oddly distorted manner, but there were others which showed a particular type of face – usually a young saint, such as St John, St Demetrius, St George or the Archangel Michael, with large, impenetrable dark eyes, close-trimmed black hair and beard, and a remote, inscrutable expression, which had the strange effect of making her shiver, not with fear or cold, but with a feeling which she could not understand. Brother Isak was pleased with her questions about icons, and explained that this particular type was Greek in origin, as were, he said, all the best things about the Church in Rusland and Novgorod.

A few days after his question about Gytha's lack of an icon, he brought her one as a gift from Bishop Fedor. It was a very beautiful Adoration of the Cross, painted in smooth, pale colours and gold on a thick piece of wood, and Gytha found it a particular comfort as it showed two angels kneeling, one on either side of the Cross, and was very much like the seal her father had given his college at Waltham. She did not altogether understand Brother Isak's explanation about why an icon was particularly holy, but she put it on the little shelf across the corner of her bedroom, and it was certainly a great help to her in concentrating her thoughts when she prayed. Brother Isak brought another for Mildyth, of the Holy Mother, and Mildyth was so moved when she received it that she dissolved into tears.

As Gytha learned more of the language, she found that the liturgy was not so very different from the familiar Latin services, and tried to discuss what differences there were in an intelligent fashion with Brother Isak. Apparently he was pleasantly impressed, for, just before Christmas, she was invited to visit Bishop Fedor several times, and by then had a good enough grasp of the language to talk with him about the differences, with Brother Isak interpreting where necessary. She gave the bishop the chalice which Thorvald Grimsson had presented to her in Gotland, explaining where it had come from and how and why she had been given it. He was pleased, and said he would put it in the cathedral treasury, to be used in services, and gave her a book of prayers when he found that she could read. It took her a little time to puzzle out the writing, as she found Slavonic handwriting harder than capital letters, but then she discovered that it contained a prayer for almost every occasion, from rising in the morning to going to rest at night, and observation showed her that people did actually use these prayers, so she did so herself, and found it spiritually helpful.

The time seemed to pass quite quickly. Gradually, she learned her way about the palace and the city. She became familiar with the surrounding countryside, and ventured out into the market with Mildyth to make a few modest purchases and watch the mountebanks, who tumbled, juggled, danced or showed performing animals. She was often embarrassed when the merchants insisted on showing her fine fabrics or jewels, or rarities from foreign lands. She would admire them and praise their beauty, value or strangeness, but was unable to buy, for her store of money was dwindling steadily. She was expected to give money at church every morning, and there were always beggars outside the churches and the palace. She could not pass them without giving the more obviously needy a small coin. The situation became steadily more embarrassing, for the more she gave in alms, the more beggars gathered, and the more she refused the merchants' goods, the more eager they seemed to show them.

One fellow seemed particularly persistent, although it was not clear what he was trying to sell. He was a fat little man with a round, red face, freckled nose and short-cut hair which gave him a distinct resemblance to a hedgehog. He frequently way-laid Mildyth and tried to talk to her, but her natural suspicion of strangers and her initial incomprehension of the language made her gesture sharply to him to go away, and she would whisk past him as quickly as she could. Before long, he tried to approach Gytha directly, but Mildyth would block his way and stamp her foot at him until he shrugged and gave up, only to re-appear the next day.

'Wasn't that the little hedgehog man again?' Gytha said one day, when the summer had abruptly ended and given way to winter almost overnight. 'What does he want?'

'He keeps on about *dengi* or some such thing,' Mildyth replied indignantly. '*Dengi* means money, doesn't it? He must be a beggar. I think you should ask Prince Gleb to do something about him.'

In fact, it was Gleb who raised the subject, and from an unexpected direction, for he drew Gytha aside one evening and said hesitantly, 'Forgive me for mentioning it, but I wonder if there's some misunderstanding. Some of the merchants have been to me to complain that you never buy from them, and the boyars have commented that you always dress in the Varangian fashion, never in our style. Also, your *ognishchanin* is very worried because your waiting-woman won't let him speak to you.'

'My *ognish* . . .' Gytha queried. 'I'm sorry – I don't understand. Who is my *og* . . . What you said?'

'*Ognishchanin.*' Gleb considered for a moment, then translated, 'Bailiff. He looks like a *yosh* – a little animal with spikes all over it.'

'A hedgehog!' Gytha exclaimed, realising whom he meant.

'As Vladimir's wife, or promised wife, you're entitled to a certain income, you see, and the poor fellow can't get near you to pay it. He's afraid Vladimir will come and be angry with him, or suspect him of keeping the money. Didn't Anastasia tell you about him?'

Gytha was nonplussed, not liking to say that Anastasia, although quite friendly in an offhand way, usually seemed to be either asleep or busy when Gytha went to the *terem*, and left it to her ladies to entertain her, saying very little herself, although she did nod and smile when Gytha caught her eye.

'Doesn't she speak to you in Norse?' Gleb asked sharply, and when Gytha, anxious and embarrassed, shook her head, 'Little minx! She told me that she can speak Norse, and often chats with you! She's so lazy ...! I suppose that explains why you haven't worn any of the clothes Vladimir sent for you, or the jewels! What's become of them, then? There should be four great carved chests of them somewhere in your rooms.'

'Oh!' she exclaimed, recalling the mysterious chests, apparently full of someone's belongings. 'Are they for me? We thought someone had left them there and forgotten about them!'

Gleb looked at her blankly for a moment, then began to laugh. 'A fine family you must think us!' he said. 'Didn't you wonder why we gave you no income, and your bridegroom sent you no presents?'

'I didn't know what the customs are here,' Gytha tried to explain. 'No one said anything, so I supposed that I was expected to live on what I brought with me until the wedding.'

'I'm sorry!' Gleb sobered and apologised. 'I should have realised that my silly wife is too idle to do anything properly!' He gave Gytha an uncertain, sidelong glance, and added, 'I expect you've gathered that it's not much of a marriage. I suppose I was unwise to let my father persuade me into marrying the daughter of a Cuman chieftain for the sake of a possible peace, which didn't last long in any case! I tried, to start with, but she didn't have any children, and we have no interests in common, so we each go our own way, and meet only on formal occasions. I should really send her to a nunnery and marry again . . . I hope you and Vladimir have better fortune.'

Gytha was embarrassed by his frankness, particularly as it was accompanied by a look which made her feel that he was envying Vladimir rather more than was proper. She made an excuse, and hurried off to tell Mildyth who the little hedgehog man was, and explain about the four great chests of clothes. They spent some time delving into them before they went to bed, and found that one of them contained summer garments of fine silk and linen, and the other three, heavy sarafans and kaftans of thick winter fabrics, furs, jewelled head-dresses of the open crown shape, and *kokoshniks*, which were head-dresses shaped like the triple-curved gables of the churches.

There was a small chest buried at the bottom of one of the big ones. This was full of gold brooches and neck-chains, a rope of pearls in a soft leather bag, rings set with sparkling stones, and several arm-rings. In among these treasures was a small scroll of birchbark, which was used here for writing on instead of parchment. Gytha broke the seal and opened it, and found a brief letter, written in Norse in a small, very neat hand.

'My dear wife-to-be. I bid you welcome to Novgorod, and hope with all my heart that you will be happy in Rusland. I am more sorry than I can tell you that I cannot be in the city to welcome you when you come, but my duty calls me away from personal pleasures and desires, as you, a king's daughter, will understand. I send these few gifts to tell you I care about your welfare, and beg you to rely on my cousin Gleb for whatever help or advice you may need. Do not doubt that I am eager to be with you as soon as God wills. His blessing rest on you. Your husband-to-be, Vladimir.'

'What's that?' asked Mildyth.
'A letter from Prince Vladimir.'
'Letter! Hm! He'd do better to be here himself. A fine bride-

groom, who doesn't come to wed his bride until she's been kept waiting for months!'

Gytha was about to remind her that the Prince was not expected to arrive until midwinter, but thought better of it and said firmly, 'That will do, Mildyth. You may go to bed now.'

Mildyth looked as if there was a great deal more she could have said, but she knew roughly how far she could go before her mistress put her in her place, so she made her formal reverence and withdrew to her own room. Gytha sat on her bed, drew the candles nearer, and read her letter through again, trying to find out more about Prince Vladimir from it, assuming that he had written it himself, for it bore no indication that it was the work of an amanuensis. It confirmed her belief that he was literate, which she had already deduced from the presence of his books, and showed that he had a good understanding of Norse, which would help them to converse better than if they had to rely on her still limited grasp of Slavonic. Otherwise, she was left with a thwarted feeling that the man behind the neatly-written words was as shadowy and unknown as ever.

In the morning, she made a determined effort to talk to Anastasia, and persisted in addressing her remarks to the Princess, rather than allowing the waiting-women to monopolise her. To her surprise, Anastasia began to respond after a few minutes, perhaps because Gytha spoke entirely in Slavonic, albeit with plenty of errors. To begin with, she corrected the mistakes, but presently began to talk herself, saying that she was bored to distraction by the chatter of her servants and it was good to talk to a sensible woman of her own rank. She even made an attempt to use a few Norse words. Presently she dismissed her women, and began to talk of more personal matters.

'I told my husband that you probably didn't understand about the clothes, or your income,' she said smugly. 'I thought he'd told you, but you didn't care to wear the things. After all, you have your own rather peculiar garments to wear, and one expects a king's daughter to come to her husband with a great deal of money and clothes. I've heard that you don't patronise our merchants, but I assumed that you didn't think their goods

were fine enough for a *king's daughter*. I find them all very satisfactory myself, but, of course, my father is only a Cuman chieftain, not a king, and I told Gleb that he shouldn't blame me –
it's not *my* place to tell a *king's daughter* how she should dress or
what to spend her money on, is it? It was no use him coming
last night to shout at me about it. It was his business to tell you,
not mine! He blames me for everything, and I can't think why,
for it's nearly always his fault. Men are all the same, you know!
Prince Vladimir is just as bad. He's not the slightest bit interested in anything we women have to say, but talks only about
fighting, hunting, making treaties and dealing justice. I do hope
you haven't any foolish ideas about love and such nonsense,
dear Cousin – all princesses are cousins, aren't they? Unless
they're more closely related, of course. If you think Prince Vladimir will love you for your golden hair and blue eyes, I assure
you that he won't. All he wants is a healthy wife to bear him
legitimate sons, and his interest in you will begin and end with
that! When he wants a woman for *pleasure*, he'll go elsewhere, as
Gleb does. Oh, and be careful, my dear! Gleb sometimes thinks
that, as I haven't given him any sons, he might as well be rid of
me and try again with another wife. He could be thinking even
now of sending me to a nunnery and marrying you, before Vladimir comes to claim you, and that would cause *problems*, I can
tell you!'

'But . . .' Gytha tried to interpose, in vain.

'I wouldn't give way to you meekly, I assure you, and you
needn't think I couldn't put a stop to it. My father may be only
a Cuman chieftain, but he's not far away and he has a very
large army. Your father's dead, isn't he, and your uncle's far
distant? Besides, Vladimir is very anxious to have the daughter
of a real king for his wife, not a mere chieftain's daughter like
me, and Heaven knows there's more than enough quarrelling
between members of the family without Gleb and Vladimir falling out. I sometimes think they're the only really sane ones.
Why, even Gleb's own brother's tried several times to take Novgorod away from him, and Gleb's father took Kiev from his
elder brother, who should have had it, and Vladimir's father

constantly makes mischief between all of them ... Imagine, princes fighting over single cities, when your father ruled over a whole kingdom!'

'But I ...' Gytha began again, but Anastasia had only paused for breath, and went rattling on heedlessly, telling Gytha about all the family scandals and quarrels that she could remember. Much of it went back many years, before Anastasia herself had come into Rusland to marry Gleb, and Gytha was thankful when one of Anastasia's ladies came to tell them that it was time to leave for church. She went with the others to the service, her head spinning with a jumble of strange names, and a conviction that the family she was soon to marry into was so viciously quarrelsome that even Svein's turbulent sons were angels of peace in comparison.

As for Anastasia – she assumed that Gleb must have reprimanded her for not talking to their guest and she had gone to the other extreme. It was clear to her now that Anastasia was a gossip, and Gytha determined to be careful in future not to confide anything to her which she did not wish to become common knowledge. Her sarcastic harping on 'king's daughter' was understandable, particularly if she really thought that Gleb might set her aside in order to marry the newcomer, but there was certainly some spite mixed with the jealousy and fear, and it would not be wise to ignore it.

She had dressed that morning in Novgorod fashion, in a heavily-embroidered and braided sarafan, but the garment was so stiff and heavy that she decided to wear such things only for going to church, appearing in public and dining in state. During the more active part of the day she continued to wear her Varangian garb, which was much more comfortable and convenient, particularly for hunting. She no longer wondered why Anastasia preferred to ride in a carriage!

During the mid-day period of rest, she started to write a letter to Prince Vladimir, printing the newly-learned Slavonic letters neatly in black ink on a piece of birchbark with a well-sharpened writing-stick. It took her two afternoons to marshal her knowledge of the language into a dozen lines of rather formal thanks for his generosity, and then, in an attempt to reach out to him over distance and strangeness, she added a short account of her journey in Norse, adding a brief explanation, without ascribing blame to anyone, of why she had only just found his letter. It took another day to make up her mind to send the letter, for she thought it inadequate, but could not see how to improve it. When she asked Gleb how she could send it, he took the scroll with a casual, 'It can go with my monthly letter to him,' which was the first time he had mentioned that he was in such regular communication with his cousin.

By then, she had made contact with her *ognishchanin*, although she still had some difficulty in pronouncing the word. The little hedgehog man was called Maksim Nestorovich, and he seemed almost unable at first to believe his good fortune when Gytha sent Yevpraksia to find him and bring him to her. He wasted much time in bowing and stammering apologies until Gytha explained the misunderstanding, deciding to tell him that it had arisen because Prince Gleb and his wife had each thought that the other had told her about him, and in no way was it his fault. He then turned into a very understanding, tactful, sensible person, explaining how Gytha's income was arranged in terms of food and money, where it was drawn from, and how she should deal with it, which was easy, as her estates were administered by Prince Vladimir's servants, and she had only to look through and check the accounts Maksim brought her. These were written clearly on birchbark, which seemed to be used for a variety of purposes in Novgorod, being much cheaper than parchment, but almost as durable.

Maksim explained that, as Prince Vladimir's wife, she was entitled to a sizeable part of his whole income, and he had ordered that it be paid to her from the moment of her arrival in Novgorod, without waiting for the actual marriage, which she thought a kind and generous gesture. ('Hm! The least he could do!' was Mildyth's tart comment, albeit under her breath, from the corner where she was sitting sewing and listening.) She was entitled to keep everything she had brought with her, any gifts made to her by the Prince or anyone else, and anything bought with her own income, or made by her own hands. This last clause, Maksim said apologetically, applied more to the wife of a *smerd* than to a princess, of course.

'If by any sad chance, which Heaven in Its mercy forbid, you are left a widow, you would be head of your family and keep all that you have, and your children must give you a part of whatever they inherit from their father,' he finished.

Gytha raised her eyebrows even further than they had already risen, thinking of the far less generous provision made for wives and widows in England and Denmark. Maksim surprised her still more when he went on to give her some idea of what she might expect to be able to spend. It was a startlingly large amount to someone who had never really had any money of her own before, for, while her father was alive, the only time when she might have been accounted rich, she had been a child, with only the occasional silver penny to spend. She resolved to be careful not to let this sudden change in her fortunes tempt her into extravagance.

'Where does it all come from?' she asked.

'Ah. Well.' Maksim produced another sheet of birchbark and spread it out on the table between them. 'This is a list of all the villages Prince Vladimir has given to you. You own land in each one, which is let out to the villagers for rent. In some places, individuals are your tenants, and in others the village council rents the land and allocates it between the village families. The rents can be paid in either money or produce. As all the estates are either around Suzdal or near Kiev, rents in produce are sent to market, and the money realised comes to you. You have a steward in each village, and he has a piece of your land as payment for his work. Some of your bigger villages have markets, and everyone who sells at a market pays your steward a small fee for his pitch, which comes to you.'

'It all sounds very much like the way things are managed in England,' Gytha commented.

Maksim seemed to find that particularly pleasing, as he beamed with delight and exclaimed, 'How interesting! So far away! Why, right away where the sun sets into the Great Ocean they do things much as we do them here! How wonderful!'

He now came regularly every week, and Gytha enjoyed learning from him about her estates and the lives of the people who lived on them, and she found great pleasure in being able to give generously to beggars in the streets and the alms-boxes in the churches. She liked to be able to buy some of the interesting goods for sale in the market, and, with the help and approval of Brother Isak, acquired a small library of beautifully written books from the scribes at the monastery of the Transfiguration, which was the group of buildings she had passed a few miles to the north on her way to Novgorod.

She had thought that the weather was cold in October, but in November the real winter began. The temperature dropped sharply and snow fell unceasingly for several days. Frames with a double layer of mica had already been fitted to all the windows in the palace, and she marvelled that it was still possible to see out through them, albeit in a somewhat distorted fashion, and daylight could still penetrate into the rooms, and yet every stove-heated room was comfortably warm and there were hardly any draughts.

Out of doors was a different matter. One short journey across the market-place to church with only a fur-lined cloak over her gown taught her to dress herself very thoroughly before venturing out in future. This was a lengthy business, with thick felt boots to pull over the soft leather ones which were so comfortable to wear indoors, and layers of woollen garments to put on, topped by a magnificent cloak of soft fur which covered her from ears to ankles, with a hood to pull up over her head. The most remarkable thing about it was that it was completely reversible, with sable fur on one side and white ermine on the other. It had been in one of the chests that Prince Vladimir had sent for her.

Once the snow stopped falling, the sun came out on a transformed city. Everywhere was sparkling white, and it was so cold that even in the market the snow remained crisp between the carefully cleared pathways. The air was crisp and exhilaratingly dry, so that the scent of pine, which always pervaded the

207

city from the logs with which most of it was built, seemed stronger and fresher than ever. Perhaps, as Mildyth remarked, that was only because the snow had covered the animal dung which filled the yard of every house and, in warmer weather, produced an aroma which fought a winning battle with the pine!

The river froze over, and dozens of horse-drawn sledges glided about on the ice, crossing from one side to the other, the bridge having been dismantled for the winter, or going up and down, all of them hung with little bells which kept up a merry jingling all day long.

There were skaters, too, gliding about with bone skates strapped to their feet, as they had sometimes seen in Denmark, and wooden scaffolds were put up in many of the open spaces in the streets to make sliding hills – carefully built-up slopes of hard, polished snow – and everyone seemed to find time to swoop down them on little sledges. Gytha tried it, and found it very exciting, safely gripped between Gleb's knees and with his strong hands holding her waist. Mildyth tried it once, screeched all the way down, and refused to go again, despite the persuasions of her partner, a burly and not unhandsome member of Gleb's *druzhina*.

There were always pedlars about the market, but they seemed to acquire an entirely new range of goods in the winter. There were people selling hot pies and roasted chestnuts, and all sorts of gaily painted wooden toys as Christmas approached. Advent, however, was kept as a strict fast, and all the jugglers and acrobats disappeared as soon as it began.

Christmas was not very different from the feast Gytha and Mildyth had known in England and Denmark, and gifts were exchanged at New Year in Rusland too. Gytha enjoyed choosing them for others and receiving them herself. Vladimir sent her a fine saddle and a set of harness with silver ornaments which jingled musically with the horse's movements, and she guessed that Gleb must have reported that she was a good rider. She sent him a shirt which she had stitched herself, judging his measurements by the hauberk and other garments in his room.

She had hoped that he might arrive in time for Christmas, but nobody even mentioned it as a possibility.

Disappointed, she tried to console herself by asking Anastasia and her ladies to tell her more about him, and wished afterwards that she had not done so, for Anastasia told her that he was very proud and cold, and had no patience with women.

'You'll have to accept that you'll matter to him at all only because you're a real princess, a king's daughter, and marrying you will reflect glory on him, because his cousins have only chieftains' daughters, like me, for their wives. He won't care what you look like, as long as you bear him sons, and, because you're royal, he'll be able to marry them to kings' daughters and make his family more important in the world.'

This speech filled Gytha with dismay. She felt her stomach churning with anxiety. What if he found out the truth about her? Would he refuse to marry her – or, worse still, if he found out afterwards, would he repudiate her?

At that point, she looked up and saw one of Anastasia's ladies looking at her with obvious amusement. She was a very beautiful woman called Ekaterina, and Gytha knew that she was a widow with a young child, who was boarded out somewhere in the city. She had come to Novgorod a few weeks before from somewhere in the south, with a letter to Anastasia from the wife of Gleb's brother Oleg, saying that she had been recently widowed and wished to move away and make a fresh start in a new life. Anastasia had taken her into her household as a matter of course, as Oleg's wife had probably intended that she should.

Now she was smiling in a way which made Gytha feel even more uneasy. She had glossy dark hair, black eyes, a creamy complexion, and red lips which curved in a catlike smile, revealing small white teeth; something about her expression made Gytha feel that she *knew* something, understood Gytha's fears, and was amused by them.

'It must be obvious to you that he doesn't think your feelings matter much, or he wouldn't keep you waiting like this,' Anastasia added. 'He knows very well that you've been here for months, but he's not trying very hard to come here himself, is he?'

Gleb said that he thought Vladimir might come in time for the New Year festivities, but the only newcomer then was Oleg, Gleb's brother, the Grand Prince of Tmutorakan. Like Gleb, he was big and fair, but where Gleb was quiet and thoughtful, Oleg was brash, noisy, tactless and arrogant. He reminded Gytha of Svein's rowdier sons, and, although she did not exactly dislike him, she found his manner very irritating and he certainly did not seem to like her at all.

'Oh, so this is Vladimir's princess that we've all heard so much about, is it?' he said when they met. 'Well, I suppose he'll be pleased enough to find that she's quite pretty as well as royal. Can't think why he has to bring in someone from so far away, and a Varang at that – as if you're not plagued enough with damned Varangs in Novgorod! He'd do better to make peace with some of our enemies by marrying some important chieftain's ugly daughter, as you and I had to do, Gleb.'

Anastasia bridled visibly at this, and Gleb looked annoyed, but said nothing.

'All this fuss about royal blood,' Oleg went on. 'Can't forget that his mother was born in the purple, I suppose! An emperor's daughter she might have been, but little use to a man – it only took one baby to kill her off. You watch this one, Gleb, or she'll be prodding at Vladimir to get himself a more important city than Suzdal, something more befitting her royalty.'

'Like Novgorod?' Gleb asked in the expressionless voice Gytha had heard him use at council meetings when he wished to withhold any clue to his own opinions.

'Yes, like Novgorod,' Oleg affirmed. 'I've warned you before, Gleb, and I'll warn you again – don't trust any man's promise, particularly a Ruriki's, when it concerns cities, not even our saintly Vladimir's. Half the folk here have Varangian blood, and if it came to a choice between you and Vladimir, I've no doubt your wives would be taken into account!'

'Rubbish,' Gleb said dismissively, and changed the subject, but it was one which seemed to obsess Oleg, and he returned to it at least a dozen times during the week he spent in Novgorod, making Gytha feel that he was determined to stir up trouble between Gleb and Vladimir, and she remembered Anastasia's long catalogue of the many feuds in this turbulent family. Gleb merely looked blank when Oleg harangued him, but did not stop him.

On the night before he left Novgorod, Oleg was particularly irritating, continually harping on Vladimir's obvious lack of any sense of urgency about their marriage, and about the effect of ambition on a man's trustworthiness. After supper that night she went to Vladimir's room and tried to comfort herself by reading his letter yet again, telling herself that he did not sound in it at all like a man who was eaten up with ambition, or indifferent to her feelings.

Feeling a little comforted, she was about to cross the landing to her own side of the apartment when an impulse made her step out on to the top of the stair down to the courtyard for a breath of fresh air. Lamps had been hung at intervals round the walls to light the way of anyone who needed to cross the yard to any one of the stairs or doors opening out from it, and the reflections on the snow filled the area with a surprising brightness.

Over by the door to the *terem*, two people were standing close together, talking in whispers. Gytha could hear the sibilants, but not what they were saying. The height of one, and the fair hair and beard gleaming in the soft light, showed that it was Oleg, and the other she could recognise by the distinctive cloak draped about her shoulders – a dark fur with a long inverted triangle of white fur let into the back. It was Ekaterina.

Gytha watched for a moment, puzzled, for they were not behaving like the trysting lovers she had thought them to be at first. They seemed to be arguing, and that was confirmed when Ekaterina suddenly said aloud, 'You'll have to leave it to me to find the way and judge the time. Your way is too clumsy and obvious – you're simply making Gleb feel sorry for her! Leave it to me – I'll not fail you!'

'You'd better not, or you'll regret it!' Oleg replied sharply, and strode away across the courtyard. Ekaterina watched him go, then gave an ugly little laugh and disappeared in through the doorway.

Gytha, who had stood too long in the cold, shivered and hurried in to warm herself by the stove, aware of a sense of menace, for she thought that the 'her' Ekaterina had referred to might be herself. Clearly Oleg did not want Vladimir to marry her, but what had Ekaterina to do with him, and what could either of them do to prevent the marriage?

Oleg left the next morning, and Gytha, apart from regarding Ekaterina with distrust, thought no more about the incident, for she had enough to worry about, what with Vladimir's continuing absence and Anastasia's strange mixture of friendliness and jealousy. On the credit side of the balance, however, she now had a good command of the language, thanks to Brother Isak, and she seemed to be making some progress with the members of Gleb's council.

To begin with, they had looked askance when she entered the council chamber, and Gleb had offered them no explanation of her presence. For several weeks she had simply listened and said nothing, biding her time, and that came eventually when the subject under discussion was the necessity for checking the quality of goods offered for sale in the market.

'It's important for the city that the traders who come here find all as it should be,' the *posadnik* (or mayor) explained. 'If cloth is too narrow, or poor quality, for example, the traders will feel cheated, and they'll spread the word that our market should be avoided. How can we see that all goods are as they should be?'

There was a thoughtful silence, and Gytha took the opportunity offered. She stirred in her chair and cleared her throat. Gleb looked at her, and she treated his glance as permission to speak.

'Who does the shopping for your household?' she asked the *posadnik*.

'My wife, and our cook,' he replied frowning.

Gytha smiled comprehensively at all these grave men with

their rich robes and bearded faces, and said, 'And I dare say you would all give much the same answer. If you want a length of good cloth, or a basket of fresh vegetables, you send a woman to buy it. Why don't you find two sensible widows, used to marketing for a family, and appoint them to go round the market to inspect the quality of the goods at random. They need not check every trader's goods every day, but select a dozen or so at a time. No trader would know when his turn would come, so he could not guard against being found out if his goods were poor. If your inspectors found poor goods, the trader could be fined, and the money used to help pay the women for their work. You would have to pay them quite well, or they might be tempted to take bribes.'

She sat back and looked gravely at their solemn faces. She could see that some of them were on the point of speaking against the idea, simply because they could not imagine that a woman was capable of solving their problem, but she smiled a little, thinking that no doubt those same men were unconsciously following the advice of their wives every day of their lives.

'That would solve the problem,' Gleb said, giving her a nod of approval. 'Does anyone know of any suitable women?'

Several names were suggested, and the *posadnik* undertook to consult his wife for further advice. The idea was adopted without any argument, and after that, Gytha's presence at councils was accepted, and her occasional remarks were treated with courtesy, if not always with enthusiasm.

The snow and bitter cold intensified in the New Year and were worse than anything Gytha and Mildyth had known before. It appeared, however, to be quite normal to the people of Novgorod, who carried on their lives as if snow as deep as a man's height and cold that could freeze a bird in flight were quite ordinary and acceptable. Indeed, buildings and clothing were well suited to it, so that it was still possible to live quite comfortably.

Between Christmas and Epiphany, Bishop Fedor against invited Gytha and Mildyth to visit him. He received them in a kindly fashion, and questioned them closely about their religious beliefs in a more formal fashion than in his earlier conversations with Gytha. He seemed particularly concerned about their baptisms, asking when they had taken place, which was apparently a point of some importance. In Mildyth's case, it soon appeared that there was no problem, but there had to be a certain amount of counting up of years where Gytha was concerned, complicated by the different method of computing dates in the Eastern Church. The difficulty, it emerged, arose from the excommunication of the Pope by the Patriarch of Constantinople in the year of Gytha's birth, but all was well when it was established that she had been baptised quite four months before that happened.

'And have you been anointed?' Fedor then enquired.

'Anointed? No,' Gytha answered for both of them.

Brother Isak murmured something about different customs in the west, and, after a lengthy meditation, during which Gytha and Mildyth sat like petrified mice, Fedor pronounced very formally that he would anoint Gytha and Mildyth at Epiphany, and they might then take the Eucharist as full members of the Church.

This proved to be very similar to the western confirmation ceremony, apart from the chrismation. The Eucharist, too, was much as they had been used to in the past, and had, in any case, become familiar during the months that they had been in Novgorod, although it emerged during Brother Isak's instructions to them before the anointing ceremony that they should have left the church before the Eucharist when they had not been anointed. However, it was too late to do anything about it by then, so he did not pursue the matter. They were surprised to find, at their first Eucharist, that the bread really was bread, not a wafer, and the laity received wine as well, mixed with the bread and given on a spoon.

Lent began in mid-February, and Gytha found the approach of this sad season particularly irksome this year. She had to check herself constantly from being irritated over trifles, and from a tendency to sit about doing nothing and feeling miserable, which Mildyth blamed on the cold and greyness of the long winter, but Gytha knew that it was really due to the non-appearance of Prince Vladimir. If only he would come and resolve all the doubts and fears which were now increasing and building up into an unbearable tension. Time had passed and was passing, and still he did not come, or even send word when she might expect him. Even Gleb, who had talked confidently of a midwinter wedding, now rarely mentioned it at all, even when he received his regular letters from Vladimir. On those occasions he would tell her that his cousin was well, and that his visit to Poland seemed to be successful, so she assumed that he was still there. Only once did Gleb say anything about his coming, and that was when he noticed that Gytha looked sad, and tried to cheer her by saying, 'I expect he'll come by Easter, but if he doesn't, I've a good mind to pack Anastasia off to a convent and marry you myself!' He said it in a jocular fashion, but it made Gytha uneasy, and she avoided being alone with him after that.

On the first day of Lent, they went across to St Sophia's for the morning service, travelling under piles of fur on bell-less sledges, such levity as bells being unsuitable at such a season. They were attended by servants carrying flaring torches, for the days were still very short and the overcast sky made it even darker. Inside the cathedral, the Sanctuary was a blaze of light from hundreds of candles, but the rest of the building was full of shadows and it was difficult to see anyone in the congregation as more than a dark figure, what with the poor light and the all-enveloping winter clothing which everyone wore, for the great building was very cold, despite the charcoal braziers. Gytha could tell which was Gleb only by his height, his golden beard and the jewels on his golden cap, which caught the light from the Sanctuary. He usually stood alone, a little in front of his attendants, when they all descended from the gallery to take the Eucharist, but soon after they went down on this occasion, another man slipped through the ranks of boyars and *druzhiniki* and stood beside him. Gleb gave him a swift embrace, but then both gave their full attention to the service, and went up to receive the wine-soaked bread together, shoulder to shoulder, save that the newcomer was nearly a head shorter than Gleb. Gytha wondered who he was, but was distracted by Anastasia saying that she felt faint.

'What is it?' Gytha whispered. 'Are you ill? Do you wish to go home?'

'Yes,' Anastasia whispered back, 'but I can't yet – I must stay for the Eucharist. Pass me the aromatic vinegar, Marya, quickly!'

A small smelling-flask was produced by one of the ladies in attendance after some fumbling with gloved fingers in her purse, and held under Anastasia's nose.

'Prop me up,' she instructed with surprising briskness for someone in danger of fainting. Her ladies gathered round and supported her as if they were used to the manoeuvre, and Gytha turned her attention back to the service, casting only an occasional glance at Anastasia to see how she did, although it was hard to tell as her face was so heavily masked with paint.

After the Eucharist, Anastasia tapped Gytha on the arm and beckoned, and they, with their attendants, crept out of the building instead of returning to the gallery, and went back to the palace.

'That's better,' Anastasia said cheerfully as she entered the *terem*, casting off articles of clothing as she went, each being neatly caught by one of her ladies. 'Now, come and sit down, Gita, and we'll have some hot soup and mulled wine to make us feel better.'

'Shouldn't you lie down for a while if you feel faint?' Gytha suggested.

'Faint? I never faint!' Anastasia gave a gurgle of laughter. 'It's only that sometimes when I'm cold and bored I think I *might* faint.'

Gytha tried not to look disapproving, and also hid the fact that she had been worried, for faintness was often the precursor of illness. She was glad of the warming soup, for it had been bitterly cold in the church, and settled down to listen to Anastasia's chatter, which flowed unceasingly. Three times one of her attendants tried to tell her that a message had come from Prince Gleb, but she waved the woman away impatiently without interrupting her flow of conversation.

Eventually Gytha made an excuse and left her, for it was past time for her lesson with Brother Isak. She hurried back to her own rooms, rehearsing an apology for her lateness in her best Slavonic, and not waiting for Mildyth, who was deep in conversation with Yevpraksia.

She had a dislike of unpunctuality, so she broke into a run, regardless of dignity, darting through Mildyth's bedroom and her own, and arrived in the corner room a little out of breath, her lips parted for an apology, to find that Brother Isak was not there. Instead, a strange man was sitting on the wide sill of the window which looked out on the market, his back propped against the side the embrasure and one booted foot on the sill, the other swinging loosely.

As Gytha stopped and stared, he turned his head and looked at her, and she caught her breath in a gasp of surprise, for he looked exactly like those strange Greek icons which gave her such an odd sensation. His hair and beard were black and close-cut, his eyes had that same dark, piercing look, and his rather thin, clear-skinned face the same remote, unfathomable expression. The only difference was that his firm, well-shaped mouth was curved in a faint smile as she stood looking at him, and there was a slight softening of the piercing quality of his gaze.

'Princess Gytha?' he enquired, pronouncing her name correctly. He swung his feet down to the floor and stood up in one lithe, flowing movement. He was quite tall and his body was lean and agile, unlike Gleb's heavy muscular bulk. He was dressed in plain dark grey breeches and tunic with a plain leather belt and long boots, and wore no ornament but a ring set with a red stone on one long-fingered hand, and a massy gold chain about his neck. He crossed the room in surprisingly few strides, gripped Gytha's shoulders with firm but gentle hands, and kissed her cheek. His beard was soft against her skin, not wiry, as her father's had been.

'Who – Who are you?' she asked in a breathless croak, although she had already guessed.

'Vladimir Vsevolodovich, Grand Prince of Suzdal,' he replied, with a disarming flicker of amusement at the grandiose title. 'Your husband, come at last! Has it been so long that you'd forgotten I was coming?'

Gytha felt a great surge of relief. He *did* actually exist, he was certainly not repulsive, and he sounded pleasant, good-humoured and kind. After all her fears and doubts, she was so relieved that her knees almost gave way under her. She wondered inconsequentially if the stiffness of her kaftan would hold her up, but apparently it did not, for Vladimir suddenly transferred his gentle grip on her shoulders to her elbows, saying, 'No! The daughter of a king does not kneel to the son of a prince!' and then, realising that she had turned pale, 'Sit down here, Princess. I'm sorry – I didn't mean to frighten you! Did you not receive Gleb's message that I'd arrived?'

'No.' Gytha recollected the persistent messenger who had been sent away unheard by Anastasia, as she sat down rather suddenly on the chair which he had somehow pulled into position behind her. 'I'm sorry ... I've been expecting you, of course, but I thought you'd send ahead to say you were coming ... I'm very glad to see you, my lord.' Her tone sounded strange in her own ears, varying from a breathy outpouring of nonsense to a cold formality.

'I could get here myself as quickly as any messenger, and I've kept you waiting for me too long already. I'm sorry. I wanted to come much earlier, but ...' He shrugged.

There was a moment's silence, and she heard herself saying in a very stiff manner, 'I hope you are quite well, and had not too unpleasant a journey?' How should she address a total stranger who would soon be her husband? She added 'My lord', which sounded even more formal.

'I don't bite women during Lent,' he said solemnly. She looked up, startled, and met his dark, intense gaze. There was a smile lurking somewhere in his eyes, but he seemed to be searching deeply into her mind. It was a disconcerting sensation, and she could bear no more than a moment of it before letting her eyes drop away from his, passing down as far as the front of his tunic, where she suddenly saw a glimpse of a white shirt embroidered at the neck with a band of blue and yellow which looked familiar.

'Did the shirt fit you?' she asked in something more like her natural voice.

'It's the best shirt I've ever had!' he replied seriously, then made an odd sound between a sigh and a laugh. 'I can't believe this! Aunt Elisev said you were passably attractive and intelligent, and Gleb went so far as to say you were pretty, but now I find you're beautiful! Your eyes are so blue, and your skin . . . I wish I could see your hair!'

Gytha felt a shivery sensation at the base of her throat, not so much at his words but at the tone in which they were spoken. She put her hands up to the elaborate *kokoshnik* and veil that concealed her hair and swiftly removed the pins fastening them to her plaits, then laid them on the table, smoothing the veil with nervous, clumsy fingers. One of the plaits fell down over her shoulder, and she pulled off the scrap of ribbon that secured its end and shook it out, then loosened the other, running her fingers through her hair until it cascaded in a heavy golden shower down her back to her waist and fell forward to cover her face, as she looked down at her hands, lying loosely clasped in her lap.

Vladimir was silent for what seemed a long time, then he gave a deep sigh and took a step nearer, lifted one tress in his long fingers, and raised it to his lips. 'Thank you. You are very lovely, my Princess!'

She thought that he sounded as if he meant it, and was not simply paying an empty compliment. She gathered her hair together and tied it at the nape of her neck with one of the pieces of ribbon, and said shyly, 'I'm glad I please you, my lord.'

'Oh, you do! More than I dared hope! Do I please you?'

Again she looked up to encounter that searching gaze, and again found it too much, but she sustained it long enough to reply, 'Yes, very much. You're like the icon of St George in the cathedral.'

219

'That's a suitable likeness for a soldier!' he replied, looking a little puzzled. 'In what way am I like him?'

'It's the dark eyes, and the way your hair curls, and its colour.' She took a breath and made herself continue, 'And the way you look through and beyond things.'

'I'm half Greek,' he replied to the first half of her statement, and left the second half without comment. 'My mother was the daughter of the Emperor of Constantinople – Miklagarth – Tsargrad – Byzantium – whichever you care to call it.'

'It's very confusing that so many places in Rusland seem to have at least two names,' she commented. 'In the west, Rome is Rome, and not two or three other things as well!'

'Don't let Bishop Fedor hear you say that!' Vladimir suddenly smiled, revealing even, white teeth, and a glint of amusement in his eyes. 'To him, Rome is Wrong! Do you find our worship very different?' suddenly becoming serious again.

'No, my lord. I did at first, but now I've learned the language and can follow the service, I find it much the same.'

'Do the differences in belief worry you?'

'No. Brother Isak explained them, and satisfied any doubts I had.'

'You've no icon in here.' He looked at the empty shelf in the corner. 'Shall we ask the bishop's painters to make a new one, with both our saints on it, yours and mine together? Would you like that?'

'Yes, but I have no patron saint.'

Vladimir looked at her, and again her eyes dropped after a second or so. 'What is your baptismal name, then?'

'Gytha,' she replied, puzzled.

'Don't you have the name of a saint for your font-name, apart from the name by which you're known?' Then, seeing she did not understand, he went on, 'People here who are Christian are always baptised in the name of a saint, but often have a familiar name as well. In the House of Rurik, we all have a font-name and a Slavonic name with a meaning. My font-name is Vassily, after St Basil the Great, and my Slavonic name, Vladimir, means the Power of the World. You don't have that custom in

England?'

'No, my lord. At least – anyone who is born heathen and then becomes a Christian takes a new name at baptism, but not otherwise. I ask the intercession of the Holy Cross when I pray, because my father built a church at home in Its honour.'

'I hope you will tell me all about your father.' Vladimir's voice had a warmth in it which was gradually overcoming Gytha's embarrassment at this unprepared meeting. When he turned away to look at the books she had bought, which were lying on a shelf by the door, she studied him carefully, admiring his slim, lithe body and the set of his head above his broad shoulders. It seemed a miracle that, after all her fears, he should turn out to be so ... She could not think of an appropriate word, but that hardly mattered. The most important thing was that Elisev had not lied after all. He existed, he was not ugly, or deformed, or mad, and she thought she could learn to like him.

She had thought that, once he actually arrived, all her doubts and worries would be settled, but she found that some of them still remained, and new ones appeared. Even Mildyth's irritating criticism of a bridegroom who failed to appear did not stop, but changed to complaints about a bridegroom who chose to arrive on the first day of Lent, when he must know perfectly well that they could not now be married until after Easter.

'Why couldn't he have managed to come just a week, just a few days, earlier?' she moaned. 'Another forty days at least, and probably longer, for we can't even make plans during Lent!'

Gytha smiled wryly, reluctant to admit that Mildyth was right, for Lent was kept so strictly that even talking about a wedding was forbidden.

'At least it will give me time to learn to know him,' she said.

Before the week had passed, the learning had been accomplished. She did like him, very much, but with a curious blend of awe with the liking. When she was not with him, she thought about him a great deal, and wondered how she could understand him. When she was with him, she felt tongue-tied and inadequate. She looked forward to being his wife without misgiving, yet she was not as happy as she should have been. He

221

was courteous, kind, attentive, and seemed pleased with her, but she felt that it would be very hard to know him thoroughly. Often he wore that remote, unreadable look which so much heightened his resemblance to the icons, as if one part of his mind were present, but the other part elsewhere, where she could not reach him. On the other hand, when she had his full attention, the intensity of his gaze was too much for her to bear for long at a time.

They were together a great deal, for Brother Isak no longer came to give her lessons, and she spent that time with Prince Vladimir instead so that, as he said, they would learn to know one another. Certainly he seemed to know her better every day, but she still felt that the innermost, private part of him was not open to her.

Superficially she learned much about his life, for he talked freely about his childhood, his ideas and beliefs, his work, his adventures, telling stories against himself at times, and recounting hair-raising escapades which had Mildyth, unobtrusively playing chaperon in the corner, agog with excitement, her mouth dropping open in amazement, and her sewing lying unnoticed in her lap.

There was nothing vainglorious about him, however; no bragging in his stories. He was a modest man, yet not falsely so, deeply religious, yet tolerant, certain of himself, his faith, his purpose in life, which was to bring peace and good government to Rusland, but aware that this could not be achieved in his lifetime, if ever, although still prepared to devote his life to it. Gytha soon knew him to be a fine, honest man, and that should have been enough, yet that deep-seated core of reserve in him, a barrier round his inmost personality, puzzled and even frightened her. She suspected that he might be a saint, and felt more and more certain that she could never attain the heights in which his spirit moved, never mean as much to him as he already meant to her.

The worst time came when he led the conversation to her own past life. She could tell him of her childhood, of her life in Denmark, or her journey to Novgorod, easily enough. Gradually she began to talk more freely about her beliefs, her hopes and fears, her loneliness, even that most dear of subjects, her father. In all those things she could trust and confide in him, but underneath she was becoming conscious that her whole relationship with him was based on lies.

This became evident in little things at first, beginning at that first meeting when he had called her the daughter of a king, which was true up to a point, and yet not the whole truth. Once, after they had ridden side by side in a mad chase across the plain after a herd of deer, outstripping Gleb and his household, he remarked smilingly that he had heard that the kings of England were mighty hunters, so the love of the chase must be in her blood. She felt a spasm of guilt because it was not true. Her veins contained not a drop of the blood of English kings.

By mid-Lent, she began to wonder if he knew that he had not been told the whole truth about her, and the suspicion hardened when one day he asked her about her father's military activities. She had related some of the stories she had heard about the Welsh campaigns, when Prince Vladimir remarked on how quickly Harold had been able to move his armies, so she told him about the amazing forced march from London to York before the battle at Stamford Bridge against Harald Sigurthsson and his Norwegians. 'But I shouldn't boast about that!' she said, breaking off. 'Harald Sigurthsson was married to your Aunt Elisev.'

'That battle was fought in the year of the Star, I believe,' he said, his face very still and his attention fixed on her with even more intensity than usual.

'Yes, my lord. Did the Star appear here, too?'

'I think it was seen all over the world, but that was nine years ago.'

'It seems much longer. Everyone in England was so frightened about it, but Master Athelard said it might portend something good, like the Star of Bethlehem. Master Athelard was . . .'

Vladimir interrupted. 'Nine years ago. You seem to remember it very well.'

'It's a year I'm not likely to forget,' Gytha said sadly. 'It brought so much sorrow for England, and for me. My father . . .' She bit back a sob at the memory.

Vladimir took her hand in a warm clasp and held it for a few moments, until he judged that she had recovered from the wave of emotion which had engulfed her. Then he said, 'You remember it remarkably well for a child of eight.'

'Eight?' Gytha was startled. 'I was twelve!'

His face had that remote look again, and after a weighty silence, he said, 'According to Aunt Elisev, you are now seventeen.'

'I'm twenty-one,' she half-whispered, a wave of guilt sweeping through her as she recoiled from the thought of all the other lies Elisev might have told about her.

'Yes, I thought you must be older than my aunt said. Not that it matters, for I'd rather wed a woman than a child – though a girl of seventeen is not considered a child these days, when females are sold off to husbands as soon as they're capable of bearing children. It truly doesn't matter, my dear!' he added, when she made no reply and kept her face turned away.

'It does matter, my lord. It was untrue.'

'Yes, but it wasn't your lie. It was unnecessary, in any case – I don't mind your being an old lady of twenty-one, for she didn't tell the truth about something else – your beauty!'

She turned to face him, her eyes wide and troubled, her lips parted to pour out all the other lies and half-truths which she suspected Elisev had told him about her, but before she could speak, the Prince leaned forward and kissed her lips for the first time, and the unexpected storm of excitement which swept through her then put everything else out of her mind. The kiss lasted a long time, and after it, the Prince was silent for nearly as long, then began to talk of other things, and the chance to confess to him had passed, and her courage with it. It would be very hard for her to make another such opportunity.

Chapter Eleven

'What do you think?' Gleb asked. 'You've spent four weeks with her now, and not said a word to me about her. Are you disappointed?'

Vladimir smiled and shook his head. 'How could I be disappointed? I'd schooled myself to hope for someone with a modicum of sense who wasn't physically repulsive, but I find that she's more intelligent than many men and very near to my ideal of beauty. I'm still stunned by my good fortune!'

The cousins were alone together in Gleb's private cabinet and had been discussing the past summer's campaigning and Vladimir's visit to Poland, but now business had been disposed of, and Gleb was interested in more personal matters.

'Yes,' he said reflectively, 'I could find it in me to envy you. Vladimir, take care of her. Don't let Oleg steal her from you.'

Vladimir frowned. 'I doubt if he'd do that. He's not a complete fool, and a wife is hardly in the same class as a horse or a saddle.'

'Or a mistress? Oleg calls himself your best friend, but he seems to use that as an excuse to acquire things which rightly belong to you. He might not know where to draw the line.'

'He believes that friends should share their belongings. I'll admit that the arrangement seems to be rather one-sided, but I've never felt any great longing for anything Oleg owns. He always returns his borrowings eventually – at once, if I ask – and I know why he does it. He's grown up in an atmosphere of mistrust, as you know, thanks to the constant plotting among our fathers' generation of the family, and he can't feel secure in our friendship unless he's forever testing its limits. It's not worth forfeiting his trust over trivialities when the whole future of Rusland could depend on the pair of us working together.'

'In my opinion, my brother's an unprincipled scoundrel with one saving grace – he can fight well,' Gleb replied. 'He's forever warning me against you, you know. Sometimes he almost convinces me that he's right, that even you will be unable to resist the temptation to take Novgorod when my father dies. God knows, I've no reason to wish father a long life after all the treachery and lying he's perpetrated, but I dread his dying all the same, because of the consequences.'

'The consequences will be simple,' Vladimir said confidently. 'My father will have Kiev, I'll be content with Pereislavl, Uncle Vyacheslav will have Chernigov, which may even please him, and you'll still have Novgorod.'

Gleb did not look entirely convinced, but his only comment was, 'It would take a miracle to please Vyacheslav! Is he still afraid of you? I take it that you called at Smolensk on your way here.'

'He isn't really afraid of me,' Vladimir protested. 'Why should he be? He jumps every time I speak to him, I'll admit, and he doesn't exert himself to be agreeable. I think he's just a very reluctant host to all the other descendants of Rurik because he doesn't trust any of us. How did Oleg behave towards Gytha when he was here?'

Gleb grimaced. 'He was constantly making references to her royal blood, and the fact that she's a Varang. It sounds as if he resents your father's insistence on a royal bride for you, when our father used our marriages to make peace of a sort with some of our enemies. He says that your marriage will be of advantage only to you, and none at all to the Rus.'

'True enough,' Vladimir replied equably. 'England and Denmark are too far away to be of any help to us. It's only because my mother's father was the Emperor of Constantinople. Father believes that being born in the purple transmits some peculiar glory to a person, and that person's descendants. Your own and Oleg's mother is an emperor's daughter – doesn't he remember that?'

'Only the Holy Roman Emperor – a mere upstart compared

226

with Constantinople!' Gleb replied, grinning. 'Reverting to Oleg's borrowings, though. Was what's-her-name – Katya something – they say she's very beautiful – was she a triviality?'

'Comparatively,' Vladimir replied, his face expressionless.

'Where is she now? Did he give her back to you?'

Vladimir shrugged. 'I've no idea where she is. I assume she's in Tmutorakan with Oleg, unless he paid her off when he married. I'm sorry if I sound hard-hearted, but you know how it was.'

'I do indeed.' Gleb sighed. 'I wish I could have married a woman I could talk to, like your princess. Mine thinks of nothing but food and clothes, and doesn't want to understand a word about anything more important. Talking of food – the household will be waiting for its dinner. We'd better join them before hunger drives the *druzhina* to rebellion!'

Prince Gleb was in the habit of inviting a variety of interesting people to dine with him, even during Lent, when the only differences were that more priests and monks were asked, and no meat was served. There were always the boyars, of course, who expected to be asked. Gytha thought of them as thanes, but they differed from English thanes in two respects – they owned far more land, because there was more available to be owned here, and they lived in the city almost permanently, rarely visiting their estates, which were run by their stewards. They were a stout, red-faced group, all much alike in appearance with their long beards, stiff robes and fur-edged caps, and their interminable talk of hunting, hawking, horses and the threat of war.

More interesting were the merchants. Sometimes they were foreigners – tall, fair Varangians, earnest Germans, lean, brown-faced black-eyed Sirks, voluble, gesticulating Greeks – but more often they were wealthy citizens of Novgorod, easy and relaxed in their manner, not much impressed by Gleb's princely state, and ready to put forward their own views and argue a point with the Prince or anyone else.

The most frequent guest from the latter group was said to be the richest and luckiest man in Rusland. His name was Sadko, and he was old – past sixty. His beard was white and wispy, his face a network of lines, yet his dark eyes were sharp, his mind as clear and his speech as direct as those of a man half his age. Gytha was always pleased to see him, for he was friendly, much travelled and full of interesting tales.

On that particular evening she sat next to him at dinner, and he remarked to her during the meal, 'You've found your happiness in Novgorod, I see, as I did myself.'

'Yes,' she admitted, 'but I travelled far to find it, whereas you were here already!'

He laughed, showing that he still had most of his own teeth. 'I travelled even further than you,' he said. 'Fool that I was! In my youth, I decided to travel the world and look for happiness, so I set out with what little money I had turned into goods to trade, and my gusli to keep me company.'

'Gusli?' queried Gytha.

'That little stringed instrument a minstrel carries to accompany himself. I could play and sing with the best of them in those days! I set off, and sought happiness most diligently all down the River Road to Tsargrad and far across Sirkland, by way of Antioch and Jerusalem, and along the banks of the Nile, then across the Middle Sea, to Rome and Iberia, through Franconia and Germany, into the Northlands, even to Iceland and the Frozen Sea.'

'And you didn't find it?' she asked, noting that she now knew roughly where Sirkland lay, for she had not asked, as she did not wish to appear ignorant.

'No. I made a great deal of money, but I was still as lonely and unfulfilled as ever, and homesick into the bargain. So I came home, and found myself the richest man in Novgorod, with all that money could buy, and still with a great emptiness in my life. I built a church – the one behind the Germans' Yard – and tried to do all the things a man should do to be blessed, but without avail. Then, one day, I saw my neighbour's daughter looking sad and careworn, and I asked her what was the matter. She said, "My father tells me that you are thinking of going on your travels again, although you've not long returned from your last journey." I asked why that made her sad, and she blushed and said, "I missed you while you were away." So I made her happy, and thereby found happiness myself, living next door to me all the time.'

'You married her?' Gytha asked, smiling.

'Indeed, and very happy she made me! That's the way of it, I suppose – we become happy ourselves by making someone else content. Prince Vladimir is a good man.'

'Yes, a very good man,' Gytha replied, smiling, but she wondered privately if Vladimir's goodness would extend to forgiving the lies and half-truths he had been told about her.

At that point, one of the boyars rose to propose a toast. Because it was Lent, the wine had been watered, but he had drunk a good deal of it and had managed to become expansive in both word and gesture. It was several minutes before it became clear that the object of his toast was Gytha, and he was particularly praising her royal blood and her descent from a line of great warrior-kings who were also renowned for their wisdom and justice.

He had just reached his peroration, and paused a moment before proclaiming the actual toast, when Anastasia suddenly interrupted. She always attended formal meals, of course, and sat beside Gleb at the high table, but usually she concentrated on eating and drinking and hardly spoke unless spoken to directly. Her sudden intervention now was all the more surprising, and her shrill, nervous voice immediately caught and held everyone's attention.

'Wisdom and justice?' she exclaimed. 'Nonsense! And the royal blood's nonsense, too.'

'Be silent, Anastasia!' Gleb ordered in a rumbling whisper. 'Have you taken leave of your senses?'

'I will speak!' Anastasia insisted. 'I'm tired of all this nonsense about royal blood, and making out that she's somebody very special because of it, and being made to feel an insignificant nobody beside her. I have it on good authority that her father was no king, and hadn't a drop of royal blood in his veins! He was just a boyar who usurped the crown for himself, and the Pope in Rome had to send an army to kill him and give the crown to the rightful king. It must be true, because he was killed, wasn't he? And the man who killed him became king and still rules!'

'Who told you this nonsense?' Gleb demanded, scowling.

Gytha stole a glance at Vladimir. He had turned his head to look at her, and their eyes met. His lean face looked set, the skin stretched tightly over the bones, and he was frowning slightly. She had no idea what her own eyes and face were conveying to him, but his seemed to be asking her, 'Is this true?'

'It is not nonsense!' Anastasia snapped defiantly. 'One of my ladies told me, and she had it from a merchant who'd been to the island Gytha comes from – I can't remember the name . . .'

'England,' Gleb supplied.

Anastasia shrugged. 'It doesn't matter – he'd been there, and he told her all about it, and she told me, and I'm telling you, because Vladimir ought to know the truth before he marries a fraud and a liar.'

'And because you're a silly, spiteful, jealous woman!' said Gleb in what was intended to be a private aside to his wife, but his exasperation made him speak more loudly than he intended, and the words carried clearly in the silent hall. 'Idle gossip! Send for this woman of yours, and let's hear what she has to say.'

'I can't. Her little daughter's very ill, and she's gone to nurse her. I don't know whereabouts in the city the child's foster-parents live, and I wouldn't call her back now if I did, when her child may be dying. You can question her when she comes back, but I've told you exactly what she told me.'

Ekaterina, Gytha thought. Why does she hate me? Is it something to do with Oleg? Is this what they were talking about that night in the courtyard?

Gleb lifted his hands and let them drop in a gesture of helplessness. 'I'm sorry, Princess Gytha, Prince Vladimir,' he said formally, even in this situation remembering that this was a state occasion, and there were comparative strangers present. 'Until we can question the woman – and the merchant, if we can find him – there's nothing I can do to put an end to their lies.'

'There are two sides to every story,' Gytha heard herself saying calmly. 'I think I can clarify the matter here and now, and show how the truth has been distorted; probably by my father's enemy.'

Vladimir made a sudden movement, which Gytha saw out of the corner of her eye. She made a little gesture towards him with her left hand, trying to indicate that he should let her speak, and he sat back in his chair in response.

'As you wish,' Gleb said, bowing slightly towards her.

She looked out at the faces of the merchants and boyars. They were all turned towards her, and their expressions showed curiosity, interest, but no apparent hostility. She could not see the faces of those on either side of her at the high table, and it was no use trying to guess what they were thinking, so she put them out of her mind and concentrated on what she had to say.

'King Edward, who ruled England before my father, was a wise and gentle man who spent his time in prayer and hunting,' she began. 'He married my father's sister, but he remained celibate, so there were no children. His only heir was a little boy, his great-nephew. The country was difficult to rule, because the earls – the boyars – quarrelled among themselves, and England does not occupy all the island of Britain. Wales to the west and Scotland to the north are separate kingdoms, and they often make war on the English. My father, who was a fine soldier, commanded the army for King Edward, who trusted him and relied on his advice and his great ability as a leader. As the King grew old, people became concerned about who was to be king after him. The King of Norway, who was married to Prince Gleb's and Prince Vladimir's aunt, Princess Elisev, claimed the crown, and so did King Svein of Denmark, and also Duke William of Normandy. They were all three related to former kings of England, but had no really strong claim to be Edward's heir.'

It was obvious to Gytha that the audience before her was listening closely, even enjoying the story about a strange foreign land and the quarrels of kings.

231

'Now, the crown of England is not inherited as a right by the next in blood, but is given by election,' she continued. 'The Witan, the great council of the boyars, the bishops and the abbots, elects a new king when the old one dies. They consider the late king's family, and also any wishes he may have expressed, and choose the most suitable man. When King Edward died, the Witan considered the foreign rulers and the little boy, and they also knew that King Edward had entrusted the kingdom to my father on his deathbed. They elected my father, and he was crowned. The King of Norway did not accept their decision. He invaded the north of England, and my father fought and killed him. Then the Duke of Normandy invaded in the south. My father took his men, many of them wounded and all of them tired by the first battle, and marched them two hundred miles to fight the Norman. My father was killed in the battle, and most of his men with him. This left no one to lead the English against the invader, and the Duke took the kingdom. The Witan then elected him king.'

There was silence for a few moments, and Gytha sensed that her audience had absorbed her story and accepted it, but the silence was broken by Anastasia's sharp voice saying, 'But your father had no royal blood!'

'Yes, he did!' Gytha replied, raising her chin in the reflected mannerism of her father. 'His mother, my grandmother and namesake, was the great-grand-daughter of both King Olaf of Norway and King Harald Blaatand of Denmark. Her brother married the daughter of King Cnut the Great of Denmark and fathered King Svein, my cousin. My father had as much royal blood as King Edward's great-nephew, and infinitely more than Duke William of Normandy, whose mother was a tanner's daughter and not even his father's wife! Of course Duke William, having killed him and taken his crown without right, called my father a usurper, and I suppose that is where Princess Anastasia's attendant's informant got his story.'

'Obviously,' said Gleb, frowning at his wife. 'That little matter being cleared up, perhaps Mikhail Sergeyevich would like to complete his toast?'

The boyar, who had sat down meanwhile, rose to his feet, collected his wits, and said, 'As I was about to say, I give you the health of Prince Vladimir's bride-to-be, the royal princess and king's daughter of the isles of the sunset, Gita Garoldovna!'

The toast was drunk with enthusiasm, and Gytha smiled and nodded her thanks, relieved that they appeared to have accepted her explanation, but she wished very much that she could know what Vladimir was thinking.

'Well done!' his voice said close beside her, under cover of the outburst of chatter which followed the toast.

'I only know what I was told,' Anastasia remarked loudly. 'Of course I can quite see how the story could have been twisted by Duke what-was-his-name. After all, people listen to the winner, don't they, and the loser isn't there to tell his version if he's dead.'

'Yes, Anastasia,' Gleb said heavily. 'Now we know the truth, and we can forget all about it, can't we?'

Anastasia shrugged and resumed eating, and Gytha wondered if anyone, especially Vladimir, would ever forget about it. How long would it be before Oleg, or whoever was making use of Ekaterina, sniffed out the matter of her own legitimacy. Best to tell Vladimir herself and risk his rejection, rather than be found out later; even, perhaps, be accused in public again.

She spent a sleepless night, rehearsing what she would say, and went as usual to the corner room after church. She found him waiting for her, standing by the table. He smiled at her as she entered, and looked past her to give his usual courteous greeting to Mildyth and Yevpraksia, but found that they were not there.

'Have your dragons decided to trust me with you at last?' Vladimir asked jokingly.

'They're helping Anastasia's ladies to paint the Paschal eggs,' she replied, twisting her hands together nervously. 'They have hundreds to do, and only two weeks left before Easter.'

'That's lucky. I'd rather speak to you alone. May I kiss you?'

She raised her face in silent assent, and he took her in his arms and kissed her. Being on edge and afraid that she would lose him in the next few minutes, she responded more than she had ever done before. He gave her a searching look as he released her and then led her to the table, where he had set two chairs on adjacent sides. He held one for her, then sat down himself on the other and looked at her with a serious expression.

'I was very proud of you last night,' he said. 'You spoke up so bravely, and told your story so clearly. I'm sorry you were put to the necessity, though. It's a pity that woman of Anastasia's got hold of such a garbled tale.'

'It's the version put about by Duke William's followers,' Gytha replied. 'I think there may have been more to it than just a woman hearing the story and passing it on to her mistress. She seems to dislike me for some reason, and I once saw her speaking privately to your cousin Oleg. I suppose you know that Oleg was here at the turn of the year? He kept on making jibes about my royal blood.'

'Gleb told me. Oleg's a curious fellow – very confused in his thinking. We work together extremely well on campaign, but he seems to be incapable of trusting anyone off the battlefield. He thinks I'll take Novgorod from Gleb when their father dies, which would be in accordance with our grandfather's will, but I've repeatedly said that I'll be content with Pereislavl. Of course he doesn't trust my father – or his own, for that matter. The pair of them conspired to oust their elder brother, Izyaslav, from the princedom of Kiev and drive him into exile. My family's not a happy or harmonious one, I fear. However, that's not what I wanted to talk to you about.'

He paused, assembled his thoughts, and then said, 'I know it's not proper even to think of marriage during Lent, but I have to know if you would be willing to marry me immediately after Easter. As you said, it's only a little over two weeks, and Gleb will want to make the preparations.'

He looked at her questioningly when she did not reply at once, and she stammered, 'Yes – I suppose so, my lord . . .'

'My father's written that he wants me to join him before Pentecost. It will give us a little time together before I have to leave

234

if we're married as soon after Easter as Bishop Fedor will allow.'

'Yes. If you still want to marry me . . .' She got it out somehow.

'If I . . . What do you mean? You don't imagine that Anastasia's outburst last night would turn me against you? In any case, you told us the truth – that was perfectly obvious.'

'There's something more,' she said wretchedly.

'Tell me, then.'

She gave a nervous gasp, and fixed her eyes on her clasped hands, which lay on the table before her.

'My parents were not married in church. My mother was just an ordinary woman – her father was steward of one of my father's estates. My grandfather wouldn't allow them to marry in church, but they lived as husband and wife, having taken each other as such before witnesses. It's called a Danish marriage in England, and the relationship is recognised in law. My mother and their children had almost the same rights as if their marriage had been in church, except that it could be set aside as it had been made – by mutual consent before witnesses. However, the Church didn't recognise it, so, in the eyes of the Church, she was only his concubine, and I'm his – his . . . bastard.'

There was a long silence, so long that Gytha cast a despairing glance at his face, and found that he was watching her and apparently waiting for her to go on. 'That's all,' she whispered.

'You said "children" – how many?'

'Godwin, Edmund, Magnus, myself, Gunhild and Ulf. Six.'

'How old was Godwin when your father was killed?'

'Oh – past twenty.'

'And Ulf?'

'Three.'

'This – relationship – it lasted for more than twenty years, then?'

'Yes. My father had to marry someone else when he became king, for political reasons. I think his new wife had a son, who would have been his heir. Otherwise Godwin would have been, but the child of a church marriage comes before the child of a – a Danish marriage. Father and Mother were unhappy about parting, but she told us that it had to be so, and we were to accept it as she did.'

'I heard that it was your mother who identified his body on the battlefield.'

Gytha wondered what else he had heard, and whether he had really known all that she had just found the courage to tell him, but she said nothing about that, and simply replied, 'Yes. She knew him by a birthmark that only . . .'

'. . . his wife would know,' he finished for her. 'She must have loved him very much to face such an ordeal to find him.'

'It broke her mind,' Gytha said tremulously. 'She never got over it.'

'No.' He was silent for a time, biting his lip pensively. 'Is there anything else?' he asked presently.

'No, I don't think so. At least, I don't know what Elisev told you, but I've guessed that she didn't tell you the truth about those things.'

'She wrote to my uncle Svyatoslav originally. She asked if he had a son or a nephew in need of a wife, who would marry the daughter of a king killed in battle by an invader who had seized his kingdom and driven his children into penniless exile. She said you were younger than, in fact, you really were at the time, of royal blood, from fruitful stock, healthy, and sufficiently attractive in appearance, intelligent, literate, brave enough to face the journey here. My father favoured the match for me, for, having given me the daughter of an emperor for a mother, he thought my wife should at least be the daughter of a king! Also, he wants numerous grandchildren, so the mention of fruitful stock attracted him.'

'And you, my lord?' Gytha wondered when he would come to the point of telling her that he no longer wanted to marry her.

'I? Oh, I was attracted by the magic of the story – of the beautiful princess who had lost everything, and I wanted a healthy, intelligent wife with a good education – not an easy combination to find in this outpost of civilisation!'

236

'I'm sorry,' she murmured.

'Sorry? For what?'

'That I've turned out to be the bastard of a man with only a trace of royal blood,' she replied bitterly.

'What do you wish to do?'

'I don't know. I don't think I could face going back to Denmark, and I'm not wanted there, in any case. That's why Elisev made me sound better than I am, I suppose. She wanted to be rid of me.'

'You wish to stay here, then?'

'If I may, but what do you want me to do?'

'I'd like you to marry me in two weeks, on the Wednesday after Easter. Unless there's something else you'd rather do instead?'

'No.' The one word found its way past her lips, and she was too surprised to say anything else for what seemed a long time. Then she managed, 'I didn't think you'd want me after I'd told you . . .'

'I'm glad you told me, but it makes no difference to me. You're all I wanted – beautiful, healthy, intelligent, brave, educated, and of fruitful stock and a king's daughter, which was what my father wants – no need to tell him that all the details were not quite correct until we've made him a grandfather. He won't care then!'

'What if I don't?' she blurted, remembering what Elisev had said on the subject, and her own fears.

'That's as God wills. Will you marry me, two weeks today, if possible?'

'Yes, my lord.'

'Then stop calling me *my lord*! You know my name.'

'Yes, my – Vladimir.'

'As a matter of interest, what did Elisev tell you about me?'

Gytha thought back, hearing Elisev's cold, incisive tones again. 'That you were strong, healthy, and sound in your wits.'

'And you came all this way for no more than that?' He sounded puzzled.

'It was better than staying in Denmark. King Svein was kind, but to everyone else I was just a nuisance, an object of charity or lust. After my mother died, nobody needed me and there was no purpose in my life. I thought that here, if I was lucky, someone might want me. As a wife, I'd have a place and a purpose, and children to care for.'

'And if you were unlucky?'

She shrugged. 'I suppose a nunnery is much the same in Novgorod as it is in England or Denmark.'

'You don't wish to be a nun?'

'No. I've no calling for the cloister. In fact, the idea of being shut up frightens me.' She shivered.

'These – accusations against your father,' he said, changing the subject abruptly, shifting in his chair, his black brows frowning and one hand making a quick flick of a gesticulation as he hesitated over the word 'accusations'. 'They seem to worry you. You loved your father . . . It distresses you that people think ill of him?'

'I loved him very much. He was a good, kind man, brave and religious. I know he was ambitious, but he was very intelligent and capable, and active. He couldn't idle his time away doing nothing when there were so many things needing to be done which he could do better than – than most people. It's unfair that Duke William and his friends say things about him now, when he can't answer them, and they tarnish all he did – the things he cared about and fought for. He loved England, and he didn't want it to be torn and spoiled by war or trampled and plundered by foreigners. When a man dies, all he leaves in the world is his claim to glory, his reputation. When someone tries to destroy that, or sully it, they damage all that remains of the man in this world. My father has been robbed of his glory, and I think that's wrong. They even try to claim that his soul would be denied salvation because of what they say about him! Duke William wouldn't even give him Christian burial at first.'

'These lies and distortions harm you and his other children as well.'

'Yes, but we're still here to speak and act for ourselves in the world, to show what good there is in us. He isn't. His enemies

harm him, and he has no means of avenging himself, except . . .'
She broke off, the word *avenging* making an echo in her memory.

'Except?' Vladimir prompted.

'I've just remembered. The night I left home – England – there was a priest of our church there who had the gift of fore-knowing. He said I would go eastwards, beyond the sunrise, because there was something for me in the east, and my father's glory would be avenged through me. I don't know what he meant.'

'That's the trouble with prophets and oracles – what they say is often so difficult to understand that you're no better off! Well, so far, in the east, you've found a husband. Is there anything more you wish to tell me?'

Gytha had noticed that he had a trick in conversation of sud-denly turning from one subject to another, as though his mind pursued one line of thought while he was speaking about another. 'Only that I'm surprised that you still wish to marry me.'

'Why?'

'I don't think I'm good enough for you.'

'Too much modesty is as great a fault as too little. Do you lead a wicked and sinful life? If so, I'm surprised that no one's thought to tell me about it! I hear nothing but praise of your vir-tue, your kindness, your good sense, your ability to learn, your diligence. Brother Isak, who has a poor opinion of women in general, has even praised you to me of his own volition. I could just as easily say that I'm not good enough for you!'

'You couldn't!' she exclaimed. 'That's impossible!'

'How do you know?'

She floundered. 'I just – I just *know*! I feel it – it's in all you do or say, your manner, the way you look. When I'm with you, I feel that I'm in the presence of someone good and – and . . .'

'Wholesome?' he offered.

'Yes, in a way. Right, and as you should be.'

'As I feel when I'm with you,' he smiled wryly. 'If I'm so right and as I should be, can I be wrong about you?'

She could find no answer to that. He waited, but she could

only shake her head, so he took her hand and said, 'So you will marry me, then?'

'Yes, and I'll try to be all you want.'

'I know, and I too . . . I'm not perfect, Gytha. I've lived as a soldier, not a monk. You understand?'

This time she met his gaze with confidence, and said, 'Yes, I understand. I know that it's different for men.'

'If you mean that men have more opportunity, less self-control and less to lose . . . You don't find that hard to accept?'

'No. That's in the past.' She hoped privately that it would remain so.

He nodded, satisfied. 'Shall we pray together, and then seek an interview with Bishop Fedor?' he asked.

They went together during that afternoon to the bishop, who spared them a little time in a very busy day, listened sympathetically to what they had to say, and agreed to conduct their marriage service on the Wednesday after Easter. Gleb was delighted with the news and flung himself into a great orgy of planning, sending his various servants dashing all over the place to organise the food, entertainment and guests he considered necessary for a modest royal wedding with only five days of festivities. Anastasia bestirred herself to call Yevpraksia away from the Easter preparations to explain the marriage customs of Rusland to Gytha, and Mildyth, predictably, turned from her criticisms of a bridegroom who kept his bride waiting nine months to a fresh tale of moaning about a bridegroom who gave his bride only a few days to prepare.

'But he's only been here four weeks,' Gytha replied, smiling. 'If he'd set the day earlier, you would have said that he was indecently precipitate!'

Mildyth sniffed, went to turn out all Gytha's clothes-chests, and announced that there was nothing in them fit for a royal bride to wear at her wedding.

A few minutes after this loud-voiced declaration, while Gytha was trying to point out that there were more than a dozen unworn gowns, after a knock at the door between Gytha's bedroom and the corner room, Vladimir appeared with what looked like a rainbow spread across his outstretched arms.

'I bought this last time I was among the Silver Bulgars,' he said. 'I think it came from somewhere far to the east.' He slid the fabric into Mildyth's arms and backed out, half-smiling, and closed the door before Gytha could thank him.

'Well!' exclaimed Mildyth, holding the garment against herself. 'Did you ever see anything like it? And who on earth are the Silver Bulgars?'

Gytha could not answer the second question, and had no need to answer the first. The gown was cut like a kaftan, flaring out from narrow shoulders, and fastened down the front with little gold clasps set on a broad band of blue silk braid. The sleeves were very wide, and trimmed at the hems with the same braid. The fabric was silk that shone with a silvery sheen one way, but turned to blue shading to pink as it moved in the light. It was embroidered all round the bottom with plants and flowers in silk threads of soft colour, the plants climbing naturally upwards, and interspersed with exotic birds and butterflies.

'I don't think there's any problem about what I should wear!' Gytha said after looking at it in silence for a long time.

There were other complications, but they were solved with equal ease. Custom required that the groom's friends should fetch the bride from her father's house the night before the wedding, so the old palace in the kremlin was opened up, aired, and a few rooms refurnished to serve as Gytha's home for a few hours on Tuesday. Vladimir, feeling that Gleb's plans were too extravagant, requested in a tactful manner that the amount of food to be served to the guests during the festivities should be halved, and the other half given to the poor, which Gleb seemed to find an acceptable suggestion, but he simplified the implementation of it by doubling the amounts already ordered.

Everything to do with the wedding came to a halt for the Easter celebrations. On Thursday, most of the morning was spent in St Sophia's while Fedor and the other clergy, Gleb and Vladimir washed the feet of poor men and women and gave alms. Everyone in the palace made confession during the afternoon, and spent Friday and Saturday at the penitential services, retiring to bed early on the Saturday evening, rising in time to go fasting to St Sophia's again before midnight.

The cathedral was full of people when the Princes' party arrived, but very quiet and dark. Gytha went with the other women to the southern gallery, where they looked out into the great central area. Only a few candles burned, casting strange shadows, and occasionally catching the watchful eyes of one or other of the saints painted on the walls, or a face among the ever-shifting, murmuring mass of people standing waiting.

Presently the clergy, led by Bishop Fedor, appeared with candles and censers, and began Matins. As soon as the service ended, candles were passed among the people, and everyone joined in a procession, which went out of the church and completely round it on the outside, symbolising the search for Christ after the finding of the empty tomb. It ended with everyone back inside the building, and then Fedor cried out 'He is risen!' in a clear, joyful voice which resounded and echoed among the domes and arches of the cathedral.

Everyone answered 'He is risen indeed!' and there was a hubbub of greetings as people embraced their neighbours. Gytha was clasped in Anastasia's perfumed embrace, and then turned to Mildyth. As she did so, she caught sight of Vladimir over by the icon-screen. He was looking up at her, and raised a hand in greeting, and kissed it to her as she responded.

The Great Liturgy of St Basil followed, which lasted for more than three hours as almost everyone present took the Eucharist. Afterwards, they returned to the palace for a hurried breakfast, and then Gytha, Anastasia, Gleb and Vladimir, with half a dozen attendants each and a score of *druzhiniki*, half Gleb's and half Vladimir's, gathered in the entrance hall.

The great baskets of painted eggs had been lined up along the walls in readiness. There were hundreds of eggs, and Gytha marvelled, not having realised until now just how much work Anastasia's ladies and the female servants must have done to prepare them. She had assumed that each egg would have been simply dipped into a colouring liquid, but a quick glance showed her that each had also been decorated with a pattern.

'Are we ready?' Gleb asked, marshalling his small force. 'Do you know what to do, Gytha? You give each person an egg and the greeting. If anyone asks for an extra one for someone ill or incapacitated, use your discretion. For Heaven's sake, don't miss a single child. Ready, everyone? Open the doors!'

The doors were flung open, and Gleb advanced to the top of the steps, magnificent in his heavy gold-embroidered robe and fur-edged crown-cap. The *druzhiniki* marched out in two files to line the steps, and the two princes descended slowly, Gytha and Anastasia behind them, followed by the attendants and servants carrying some of the baskets.

'I hate this!' Anastasia whispered confidentially. 'Most of them will smell abominably, although they'll nearly all have been to a bath-house. They never wash their clothes, you see.'

Gytha could think of no suitable reply, so murmured something about its not taking very long. Anastasia had been a little more friendly towards her since the night of her announcement about Gytha's father, but had never once mentioned the incident, let alone offered an apology. Ekaterina had not reappeared, and Gleb had not mentioned her, so Gytha assumed that it had been tacitly agreed that the matter should be forgotten.

The procession advanced across the market-place to a raised platform which had been set up beside the bell-cote. The crowds pressed back to allow them free passage, and the *druzhiniki*, advancing on either side, had no need to push anyone aside.

When they reached the platform, each prince handed his lady up the few steps, and the attendants followed, arranging their baskets in the middle. The *druzhiniki* formed a hollow square on the ground round the platform, allowing a passage-way along each side of it, and the town marshals pushed and pulled the nearer members of the great crowd into some sort of a queue, which began to move slowly along inside the line of *druzhiniki*.

Gytha looked out over the crowd, and realised with a sense of shock that these were not all those who were coming for eggs –

243

more were streaming in from the side streets and over from
Sophia Side, pouring across the bridge, which had been replaced now that the ice was breaking up on the river.

And I said it wouldn't take long! she thought as she took her
first basket of eggs from Mildyth, set it down beside her, and
bent to begin handing them out, giving each recipient a smiling
Christos voskresye (Christ is risen), to which they replied *Vo istinu
voskresye* (He is risen indeed). Many of them added a wish for
her future happiness, which she found very touching.

People of all ages came – old men and women, hardly able to
totter along with two sticks, holding out a gnarled hand for the
precious egg and glad of a helping hand from a neighbour or a
town marshal, to babes in arms swaddled against the bitter
cold, only their eyes visible among the swathing shawls, from
which the mother pulled out a starfish-like hand to receive an
egg. Gytha tried to give the little ones the prettiest eggs, and
smiled down into many bright-eyed, solemn faces of children
who gazed in wonder at the fairytale figures of real princes and
princesses – two of each, no less!

She made a point of looking at the face of each person as she
gave him or her an egg, because she remembered from her
childhood that it was somehow hurtful to be given something by
someone who could not be bothered to look one in the face.
After a time, she became aware that she was unconsciously
looking for one particular face – that of Ekaterina.

She had asked Yevpraksia if Anastasia had heard anything
from the woman, who had now been absent for six weeks, but
Yevpraksia replied that, as far as she knew, Anastasia had not
heard, and did not expect to do so until either the child recovered, or died, and it occurred to Gytha that Ekaterina might
bring the child to receive an egg, if she were not too ill. Then she
thought ruefully that it was a foolish expectation – how could
she possibly pick out one face in all this crowd?

As if to give her the lie, she then greeted a succession of
people whom she knew, most of them market traders, some of
them boyars' wives, for people of every rank had come. Even
the palace servants came, bringing more baskets of eggs, and

stopping to receive one, and the rest of the *druzhina*, some of them changing places with those who were on guard, so that they, too, could join the queue.

Sadko's shrewd, lined face smiled up at her, and Brother Isak's grave, placid features, the *posadnik*'s wife – her husband, Gytha saw out of the corner of her eye, went to Gleb – and, at the other end of the scale, some wretched, ragged beggars came, and were not turned away, but received an egg and a little money from one of the town marshals, who had been standing by the steps doing nothing in particular until then.

At last the queue dwindled and came to an end, and Gytha straightened her aching back and pushed away a stray lock of hair with a paint-streaked hand as she turned to give the last few eggs remaining in her thirtieth basket to her attendants.

'And one for you,' Vladimir said, smiling down at her as he gave her a bright red egg painted with a fir-tree pattern.

She gave him her very last one – it was blue, decorated with little red and yellow flowers – and he bent to kiss her formally on the cheek. The hangers-on left in the square gave a jovial, ragged cheer. Vladimir turned to raise a hand to them in smiling acknowledgment, and Gytha caught her breath as a surge of affection for him ran through her. He looked very handsome and princely, dressed in a long, stiffly fur-bordered kaftan of heavy green damask, with patterned green leather boots and a jewelled cap like a low crown banded with a fur as black as his hair and beard.

Gytha returned to her room to rest, and scrubbed her hands in the warm water which Mildyth poured into the copper basin that stood on a table by the stove, but they were still streaked with faint marks of green, red, blue and yellow when she went to the great hall for the festival meal. Mildyth attended her and tried to look as if it was not *her* stomach which was protesting so loudly about the long hours of fasting.

Monday was a very busy day. When the household returned from church in the morning, they found that Oleg had just arrived and was being helped out of his fur-lined outer garments in the entrance hall. His left arm was in a sling, and he was clearly in a bad temper.

'Damned horse slipped on the ice and threw me!' he said after an exchange of greetings. 'I expected to be here for Easter, but this delayed me, and I spent it on the road instead.'

'Why are you here, in any case?' Gleb asked, sounding suspicious and not too pleased.

'Father sent me. In any case, I promised I'd be Vladimir's groomsman when he was mine.'

'Why did Father send you?' Gleb asked sharply.

'He didn't say.'

'Well, whatever the reason, it'll be something to his own advantage, and certainly not family affection,' Gleb said bitterly. 'Come and eat, and then you'd best go to bed. You look exhausted.'

Oleg recovered his temper over breakfast, and said to Vladimir, in what seemed to be intended for a joking manner, 'You're going through with this marriage, then?'

'Of course,' Vladimir replied evenly. 'Why should I not?'

'Oh, I thought royal blood was so important to you, and in fact she hasn't any, has she?'

Breakfast was taken privately by the family, with only two servants attending. They both discreetly went on with their work, but Vladimir, Gytha and Gleb seemed to freeze for a moment. Anastasia gave Oleg a startled glance, and then carried on eating as if he had not spoken.

'And where did you hear that rumour?' Vladimir asked quietly.

Oleg, who was not a good liar, looked uneasy, and said, 'Oh – er – someone – a merchant – told me. Said he'd been in Denmark, and knew all about Gytha's father . . .'

'He had been misinformed,' Vladimir said firmly. 'And if I ever come across him, I shall make a point of teaching him not to spread false information. If he exists, that is! In any case, it's my father, not I, who has this enthusiasm for royal blood. You've been in Kiev, I take it? How is your father?'

Oleg grimaced. 'As sour and corrupted as ever. That ulcer on his leg gets worse instead of better – I expect it's the evil in him trying to get out! I'm off to bed now, if you'll excuse me. I'm dog tired.'

'Interesting,' Gleb remarked after he had gone yawning from the room. 'The same merchant, do you think? Or do you suspect that no such merchant exists? You implied as much.'

'I don't know,' Vladimir said thoughtfully. 'It seems odd. Why should any merchant go out of his way to tell Oleg, and also, apparently, try to ensure that Anastasia heard the tale? What could it advantage a merchant to stir up trouble among the Ruriki?'

Gytha puzzled for a moment over the word *Ruriki*, then recollected that she had been told that all the princes were descended from a Varang called Rurik.

'Has Ekaterina returned yet, Anastasia?' she asked.

'No,' Anastasia replied, wiping her mouth with a napkin and being careful not to smudge her face-paint. 'I'm afraid her child must be very ill – perhaps dead.'

'I'd like to see her when she does return,' Vladimir said grimly, and changed the conversation to the more congenial topic of the wedding preparations.

Gytha tried on several gowns during the morning, to see which looked best under the beautiful silk robe, and eventually decided on a simple one of white wool, which Mildyth thought too plain. After some discussion, a compromise was reached, and they and Yevpraksia sat down to stitch yards of gold braid round the neck, sleeves and hems of it. All sorts of bumps and bangs and mutterings were coming from the stairs to the courtyard, for Vladimir had been sleeping somewhere else in the palace since he arrived, not thinking it right to occupy his usual room so near to Gytha's before they were married, and the rest of his belongings were now being moved into it.

When the gown was finished, Gytha went into the corner room to read through again the copy of the marriage service which Fedor had lent her. She found Vladimir on his knees under the window, packing some more books into a newly-arrived chest. He looked up and smiled as she entered.

'You have a great many books,' she observed, sitting down at the table and contemplating his bent head as he went on with his task.

'Knowledge is more precious than jewels,' he replied. 'Some men store their wealth in neck-chains and arm-rings – I buy books.'

'If only there were some way to copy them more quickly,' she said. 'Many more people would learn to read if books were not so expensive.'

'I expect someone will invent a way one day. If ever I have time, I shall try to think of something – perhaps when I'm too old to fight any longer, and we've half a dozen sons to lead the armies for me.'

'Will the fighting ever stop, do you think?' She preferred not to talk about the half-dozen sons, in case she failed to provide them.

'I doubt it.' He twisted round to face her and sat on the floor, his back against the chest. 'The trouble is, you see, that there's some reason that sets up a continual movement of tribes and people coming this way from the east. It's as if God keeps on creating more and more of them somewhere, over there beyond the horizon. My grandfather fought the Pechenegs until they were beaten, but then the Polovtsy came in their place, and already the Polovtsy complain that they are being pushed harder and harder from the east by other tribes. They come flooding across the great plains until they reach Rusland, and we have to fight them to stop them overrunning us. We've no natural frontiers to east or west. We've just a string of cities, a belt of land, with the River Road running down the middle, right across their path. Perhaps eventually we shall have to give up everything east of the River Road, but then they'd cross it and sweep on westwards. The lands to the west don't seem to understand that we're protecting them, as well as ourselves, and they keep attacking us as well. It's like owning a very long, narrow field, with people trying to break down the fences on both sides. I dash from one breach to another, backwards and forwards, from side to side or up and down the length, pushing and patching, and governing my city between battles. I should dearly love to live in one place, govern properly, hunt, read my books, spend my days and nights with my wife, as Gleb does, but God sends me a different life, and we must both make what we can of it.'

'Shall I go with you?' Gytha asked. She had not forgotten what Gleb had told her about her role as a hostage, but she thought that perhaps Vladimir might have made some other arrangement with his cousin. She would prefer to live further south, where he would not have so far to come to her, and wondered why he had not mentioned the matter before.

He looked at her for a moment, then said, 'I'd live in a constant state of fear and worry for you if you did, with only half my mind on my task. If you're here, I'll know you're in the safest place that Rusland has to offer, and this is where I want you to stay.'

'Yes, I see, but could I not go to Suzdal, or Kiev?'

He said slowly, 'I thought Gleb had explained that we've arranged for you to live here, and the reason. Apart from placating Gleb and Oleg, which is important, I'd not have a moment's peace if you were in Suzdal or Kiev. Novgorod is the safest city Rusland has to offer, and here you can live much as you were used to do in Denmark. The people here, including Gleb, accept that women have a right to go about freely, to voice opinions, even to manage their own businesses. Suzdal is a frontier outpost, likely to be surrounded and overrun at any time. As for Kiev ... Yes, you'd be safe from outside enemies there, but Uncle Svyatoslav believes that a woman's place is in the *terem*, and his wife accepts that. You'd not be allowed to go about as freely as you do here, and you'd certainly not be allowed to attend Svyatoslav's council. I gather that Gleb finds you a useful member of his.'

'Anastasia lives in the *terem*, and seldom leaves it,' she pointed out, 'but that doesn't prevent me from going about as I please.'

'That's from choice, and sheer laziness! Gleb would prefer her to go about, to shop in the market, and take an interest in charitable work. He'd even like her to attend his council, despite the fact that her only interests appear to be food and clothes. Novgorod is really more of a Varang city than a Rus one, and the people like to see the Prince's wife taking an interest in them. Apart from all that, Gleb is really the only pleasant member of our family – you'd not like the others! Oleg can be pleasant when he tries, but he prefers to be difficult.'

Gytha was silent for a few moments, considering his words. To be compelled to live in a *terem* and go out only in the midst of full court ceremonial would be intolerable, and she did not much like what she had heard of Svyatoslav and his ways. When she did speak, it was to give tacit assent to staying in Novgorod by saying, 'Aren't you afraid, fighting all the time?'

'Afraid of what?'

'Being killed . . .'

'I'm sometimes afraid that I may lose, and see everything I've loved and fought for go down under the heathens, but dying . . . ? No. God knows the time and place of my death, and I'm in His hands. When He sends for me, nothing and no one can hinder it, but it's nothing to fear. I fight hard, and as skilfully as I can, to stay alive, but ultimately it rests with God. A battlefield is no more dangerous than anywhere else, once you learn to accept that. If He chooses, I shall live to be old, and die in my bed, or fall down the stairs tonight and break my neck. Either way, it's nothing to fear. Hallo – what's to do?'

He was on his feet in one easy, smooth movement, for the great bell in the market-place had begun to clang in urgent summons, with other bells joining in from the churches in a ragged clanging. Gytha joined him at the window, and helped him to unfasten the catches which secured the frame of mica that covered it. It swung free at last, and he leaned out, shouting to someone below.

'Fire in the Neryevsky End!' a voice shouted back. 'A bad one – the whole street's ablaze already!'

Vladimir drew in his head, picked up the window frame, and fitted it back into place, frowning with concentration.

'Neryevsky End – that's on Sophia Side, north of the kremlin, isn't it?'

'Yes. Between the kremlin wall and Leatherworkers' End. There was a fire there just before Christmas.'

'There's a fire somewhere in a wooden city almost every week!' he said grimly. 'I shall have to go over and help.'

'Yes.' Gytha tried to keep her voice steady. 'You'll take care, won't you?'

Vladimir smiled and kissed her cheek, then turned to go. He was out of the door in what seemed one movement, and his voice came back to her as he ran lightly down the stairs to the courtyard, 'Pray for the people!'

A few minutes later she saw him, with Gleb and many of their combined *druzhiniki* who were off duty, clattering out of the palace on horseback for speed, across the market-place and over the bridge, a man on a particularly fleet pony racing ahead, shouting for people to clear the way. Gytha ran to a balcony which jutted out on the river side of the palace to watch them go, and saw one horse come down as its rider pulled it round too sharply on the approach to the bridge. She was surprised to see that the wooden roadway was wet – puddled, even, in places, and water was dripping from the eaves of the palace. Over the river, well to the right of the grey domes of St Sophia's, a great black cloud shot with vermilion and crimson towered into the sky, and seemed to grow rather than diminish.

Remembering Vladimir's words, she prayed, for him and his safety as well as for the poor people of the Neryevsky End, and presently saw some refugees coming across the bridge, carrying bundles or dragging sledges piled with their belongings. They looked tired and frightened, their faces smoke-blackened, as they trudged across the market-place and were shepherded by some of the *druzhiniki* and the town militia towards one of Gleb's big warehouses along the quay, where they were apparently going to shelter.

Feeling that she ought to be doing more for them than stand watching and praying, she went to the steward's room to ask what she could do to help. There she found Gleb's harassed head steward, whose name was Avvakum Perkh. He seemed surprised, then pleased, when she asked what she could do to help the refugees from the fire, and suggested that she might visit them in the warehouse and speak kindly to them. She thought that an odd suggestion, but he seemed so certain about it that she conscripted one of the young women from the household, who happened to be passing, and two of Vladimir's *druzhiniki* for escort, and went across to the warehouse where she discovered that Avvakum was right – the presence of one of the Prince's family offering sympathy and listening to their stories obviously comforted the poor distraught workmen and their wives, and the emotional support was underpinned by the arrival, close behind Gytha, of servitors from the palace kitchens with bread, hot soup and ale, and stablemen with bales of straw for bedding.

She heard many tales of narrow escapes. A large number of the refugees boasted that they had been rescued personally by one or other of the Princes at great risk to life and limb, and consequently she was very relieved when Gleb's tall, broad figure appeared, towering over the townsfolk around him, with Vladimir's neat, dark head and calm, compassionate face behind him.

She politely disengaged herself from the family with whom she had been talking and made her way towards Vladimir, trying to hurry in a dignified manner, but finding herself balked by the sad little bundles of personal possessions and piles of furniture which stood about everywhere. He saw her when she was still some way from him, and moved towards her, showing surprise at her presence, but smiling as if he was pleased to see her there.

'Are you . . . ?' she began as soon as she was near enough for him to hear, but broke off as she took in his appearance. His face was smeared with ash, his eyes inflamed and red-rimmed, and his hair and beard were singed on one side. His clothes were torn, and one sleeve of his kaftan hung in charred tatters.

Her eyes widened, and returned to his face with a look of frightened concern which turned his smile to one of his searching looks as he replied to her unfinished question with, 'Several narrow escapes, but nothing serious. Gleb's hand is a little burned, but it'll heal.'

She felt a wave of nausea at the smell of burnt cloth which seemed to fill the warehouse, and leaned thankfully against him as his arm went round her waist. In a very short time she found herself entering the little courtyard below her apartment, and there Vladimir dismissed the maid and the *druzhiniki* who had been with her all the time.

'I was glad to see you there with the poor folk,' he said. 'I know that sometimes we can offer them nothing but sympathy, but it's important that they should know that we care about them.'

'Yes, that's why I went. Were many people hurt or . . .?'

'One woman killed, God rest her soul. A few were hurt, but the good brothers at the Zverin monastery have taken them in. Are you feeling better? Your colour has come back.'

'Yes, thank you. I must go back to Mildyth. She'll wonder where I am.'

He kissed her, then hurried away across the courtyard. She watched him go, and then went upstairs and through to her bedroom, savouring his words of approval. She still found him very formidable, and longed to be able to penetrate his reserve and draw closer to him. It seemed strange that she could touch the minds of so many people, yet Vladimir, who was so much more important to her, still remained a closed book beyond the shallow depth to which he allowed her access. His deeper feelings and reactions were still hidden from her, and she felt that she was only admitted to them as far as he wished, and no further. She would have to try hard to guard against becoming resentful of the shutter he kept over his inmost thoughts.

Mildyth was not there, so she sat on her bed and thought about Vladimir. In two days he would be her husband, and she felt no uncertainty or fear about that. She was very lucky to have a husband she could love and admire and trust, yet she wanted so much to earn his love, or at least keep the respect which he had already shown her. Her greatest fear was possible

253

childlessness. What if she failed to give him the sons he needed to take over his work as he grew old? As he said himself, that was for God to decide, but she wanted so much to please him, not to fail him.

There was a light tap at the door between her room and Mildyth's, and Anastasia wandered in, looking languid and bored as usual. Gytha met her in the middle of the room, and they exchanged a kiss of greeting, then Anastasia subsided on to the bed and looked about her.

'This is your bedroom, isn't it? Vladimir will come to you here, then, on Wednesday night.'

'Yes.' Gytha had no wish to discuss that with her, and wished she had not mentioned it.

'I thought I should make sure that you know what to expect, Gita. Do you know what passes between a man and a woman at that time?'

'Yes. I was told before I left Denmark,' Gytha replied a little stiffly.

'Oh, well – there's no need for me to bore you with the unpleasant details, then. I expect you're apprehensive, but I should think Vladimir will be patient with you, not rough, as some men would be. After the first few times it's not too bad, and you may even come to enjoy it. Where have you been, by the way? I came earlier, and couldn't find you, and your Englishwoman didn't seem to know where you were.'

'I went to the warehouse where the people from the fire are taking shelter. I thought I might be able to help them.'

'Fire? Oh, the fire over the river. Thank God it wasn't anywhere near the palace! You needn't have bothered – I'm sure that odd little fat man – Avvakum something or other – will have seen that they're fed. You might catch something unpleasant if you go too close to poor folk. You'd better go to the bath-house and wash the smell of them away before you go to dinner. Are you going to show me your wedding-gifts?'

Gytha was happy to do that. A surprisingly large number of people had given her a wide variety of things, which ranged from a beautiful book of Gospels from Bishop Fedor, the

254

stringed instrument called a gusli made of carved and polished wood with ivory pegs from Sadko, silks and linen from various merchants, and an assortment of jewels from the boyar families, to a simple piece of embroidered linen for a shift from two market-women who sold eggs, a little wood-carving of a bear stealing honey from a hollow tree from one of the palace doorkeepers, and a tiny icon of the Mother of God in enamel on copper from Brother Isak, the last three having been made by their donors.

She took Anastasia to the corner room to see them, but the Princess soon lost interest and wandered about the room, picking things up and putting them down again, remarking on the number of books – 'I can't be bothered with reading – all those silly little marks on a page! It takes a dozen just to say one word!' – and before long, she said that she must go. 'There are any number of things I must attend to, you understand.' Nevertheless, Gytha was grateful to her, knowing what an effort it was for her to stir herself to make a visit, and appreciating her offhand kindness and total lack of jealousy or spite.

Presently Vladimir joined her. He had been to the bathhouse to rid himself of the smell of smoke, and to have his burns anointed, his hair and beard trimmed and to put on fresh clothes. Even his eyes looked less sore. 'I thought we might spend a little time together before dinner, if you're agreeable.'

'Of course. Are your burns sore?'

'Not so bad. My man Efrem has a good salve.' He moved restlessly about the room, putting more wood on the stove, picking up Mildyth's sewing and putting it down again, and then took Gytha's hand and drew her over to sit by him on the window-sill.

'I must try to make something clear to you,' he said. 'I had to go today to help put out the fire because it was part of my – my duty as a prince and a man.'

'Yes of course.' She wondered why he thought it necessary to tell her such an obvious fact.

He appeared to consider her reply, then went on, 'There'll be many, many times when I shall have to go away from you, to fight, to travel abroad, to govern my lands . . . You'll often feel, I expect, that I should stay with you instead of going away, and you'll probably think that I don't – don't care about you, that everyone and everything else in the world is more important to me than you are.'

She suddenly realised that he was trying to open the door into that inner part of himself which she had found so inaccessible, and that he was finding it very difficult, and it dawned on her that he had not shut her out because he wanted to do so, but because he did not know how to let her in.

'It was so with my father,' she said. 'Always he wanted to be at home with us, but always he had to go away because it was his duty. The needs of his country and his people ever had to come before his own longing for those he . . .' She broke off, realising that in drawing her parallel she was giving the misleading impression that she thought Vladimir loved her.

'Loved,' he finished for her. 'Yes, of course. Your father was such a man as I would wish to be. I believe that a man should love his wife, but not be ruled by his love for her. I was born to a high position, with all its advantages of wealth and power, but my good fortune entails duties, obligations. I hope you understand. Indeed, from what you've said about your father, I think you do, but I want you to be certain that I shall never leave you because I don't want to be with you. I'll come whenever I can, but the intervals will seem very long to you, and I promise that they'll be long for me too. I shall never leave you or stay away by choice, nor will anyone else ever take your rightful place in my heart or life as long as you shall live.'

Gytha's heart was too full for words, but she replied by taking the initiative for the first time in their relationship, leaning forward to put her hands on his shoulders and kiss him full on the lips. He had not actually said that he loved her, but what he had said was enough to give her hope that one day even that miracle might happen. He held her close and said, in a tone of great relief, 'You do understand! The Lord be thanked for that!'

Chapter Twelve

Gytha rose very early, well before dawn, the next morning, and slipped out of the palace with only Mildyth for company to go to a small church nearby for an hour or so by herself, to pray and to prepare herself for what was to come.

'I'd like to be alone for a while,' she said as they entered the west porch. 'You wait here. If you feel cold, walk about, for I shall be some time.'

Mildyth opened her mouth to protest, then shut it again and sat down to wait, wrapping her thick cloak about her and giving an exaggerated shiver, which Gytha did not notice. The porch was enclosed, with an outer door which closed, and it was no colder than the church, as Gytha discovered when she pushed open the inner door and went in.

It was very dark inside, with only a few candles burning before the icons, and a single hanging lamp casting a dim glow on the Holy Doors. Gytha prayed before the icon of Our Lady, Mother of God for a while, looking into the gentle, sympathetic painted face and asking silently for a blessing on her marriage, that she might find happiness and bear children who would be worthy of her husband and her father. The thought crossed her mind that Vladimir's grandmother might have prayed in much the same words, but, if so, her prayer had not been answered, to judge by what she had heard of Vladimir's father and uncles.

The cold gradually crept into her bones, but she still had some thoughts to pursue and prayers to offer, so she withdrew to the end wall of the southern arm of the church, and sat on the stone bench against it, which was provided for the old and infirm. The silence and the shadows gathered round her like protecting wings and she relaxed, letting her mind open to what-

257

ever thoughts and messages might enter it.

'Why are you not attending to your duties?' an angry little voice said abruptly, just behind her right ear. It was a man's voice, sounding small and distant, yet perfectly clear. It startled her considerably, but before she could spring to her feet, it went on, 'What use are you to me, if you're not in attendance?'

He was answered by another voice, speaking in the same place and in the same distant way, but this time, it was a woman's.

'You know perfectly well why. He mustn't see me yet. I know what's happening – I have my contacts to keep me informed.'

'You lied to me – you said you would prevent the marriage!' The man again.

'I said no such thing! I'll see that it's spoiled, and that's more important. Set them against one another, even if it's only by destroying her faith in him. That will be enough. What use would it be to prevent the marriage? He'd only find someone else! Better to tie him irrevocably to a woman who mistrusts him.'

'Yes I suppose so,' the man answered grudgingly.

'You see that she stays in Novgorod. I'll do the rest. I know what I'm doing.'

'The revelation about her origins wasn't a great success! She had an answer ready.'

'I know. I told you that it wouldn't work. Why don't you stop interfering and let me carry out my own ideas? They'll work, I assure you. I've plenty more weapons to use against them. You'll be very surprised at what I shall accomplish.'

'Oh, very well.' The man sounded only partly convinced. 'I must go now, before I'm missed.'

'Good. Now, don't summon me again before he's left the city. I don't want to be seen here until I return to my "duties".' Her voice took on a wryly sardonic tone as she said the word.

Quick footsteps crossed the stone flags of the floor, some-where on the other side of the building. A door opened and shut. Gytha realised that the two speakers must have been opposite to her, in the northern arm of the church, and she sud-

258

denly guessed why she could hear them. There must be a sound-jar in the wall!

Brother Isak had told her about the practice, learned from the Greeks who had built the earliest churches in Rusland, of setting empty jars on their sides in the walls, with their mouths pointing into the building. They picked up sounds from the area within imaginary lines projecting from the mouth to the far side of the building, somehow concentrating them within the body of the jar, for the benefit of people sitting on the bench, who, being mostly old, were often hard of hearing. She had not realised how effective they were until now, for she had heard every word of a very quiet conversation, and could even be almost sure of the identity of the speakers.

'Fool!' The woman's voice sounded again in her ear. 'You and your petty concerns! When my prince comes and my God rules here, you and yours will have no place in this world!' There was a rustle of cloth, the same door opened and closed, and Gytha sensed that she was alone in the church.

Her mood of thought and prayer broken, she sat still for a while, thinking about what she had heard. She was fairly sure that the speakers were Ekaterina and Oleg, but she could not be certain. What they had said seemed to apply to herself and Vladimir, but, even so, they had said nothing that she had not already suspected. Oleg wanted a breach between herself and Vladimir, having failed to prevent their marriage, and he was using Ekaterina as his agent. If she knew about the plan, was there any point in telling Vladimir or Gleb what she had heard? It would only cause more trouble between the cousins, and she knew that it was important that Vladimir and Oleg should be able to work together in reasonable amity to fight the enemies of Rusland. Best not to say anything, but to be on her guard against any attempt to make a breach between herself and Vladimir.

Having made up her mind, she prayed again that her decision might be the right one, then collected Mildyth from the porch and returned to the palace to join the daily expedition to morning Mass. After that, she had no more time to think about what she had overheard.

During the next afternoon, Gytha went with Gleb to the old palace in the kremlin, attended by Mildyth and Yevpraksia, who there dressed her in a stiff Slavonic dress of ceremony provided by Gleb, made of some strange, heavy figured material in a rich blue, banded with lighter blue and red embroidery. They painted her face, turning it into a doll-like mask which felt very odd and uncomfortable, and fastened a veil over her hair. It was so long that it reached the ground when she stood up, and it was held in position by an elaborate jewelled *kokoshnik* of solid gold, which was so heavy that it made her neck ache.

When she was ready she joined Gleb in the great hall, and they sat at the table on the dais at one end of it, talking, while Gleb's escort of *druzhiniki* stood or sat about, gossiping quietly or playing chess.

'Are you content to marry Vladimir?' Gleb asked her. 'Not worried about it, I mean?'

'Very content,' she replied. 'Only . . .'

'Only what?' as she hesitated.

'I worry about whether I shall be able to – to be all that he wants.'

'Children, you mean?' Gleb, having a barren wife himself, easily guessed what she meant. 'He won't set you aside if you don't bear any, I know. My father tried to make me send Nastya to a nunnery when she didn't. Vladimir supported me when I refused. I sometimes talk about it, of course, but that's just to make her try harder not to be so lazy! Vladimir said that no man has the right to spurn his wife and blame her for childlessness, when the gift of children is from God. If God doesn't choose to give us a son, Nastya shouldn't be punished for it.'

Gytha had never heard Gleb use a pet name for his wife before, and she thought that it showed that he must have some affection for her, even if she hadn't given him children. Nevertheless, 'I'd feel I'd failed him, though.'

'Have you any reason to think you might not?'

'No.'

'Why worry, then?'

Gleb continued to talk in the waiting-time, telling stories of the adventures of Vladimir and Oleg, until presently sounds of voices raised in uneven and somewhat raucous song were heard.

'They're coming!' Gleb said warningly. 'Don't be afraid – they won't hurt you, and don't struggle. It's only a simulated abduction!'

The doors of the hall were flung open, and Gleb's *druzhiniki* drew their swords and formed a line across the hall between the dais and the door. Some twenty or so boyars trooped in, beaming cheerfully and red-faced with enjoyment, and, Gytha suspected, some of Gleb's best wine. They were led by Oleg, in boisterous high spirits, and apparently delighted to be assisting at his cousin's marriage. Gytha, almost sure that it had been his voice she had heard in the church that morning, was amazed by his duplicity.

He raised a hand for silence, and, when the noise died down a little, shouted above it, 'Where is the father of Gita Garoldovna, promised bride of Vladimir Vsevolodovich, Grand Prince of Suzdal?'

'I stand in his place!' Gleb declared, standing up.

'We come to take her to her bridegroom!'

'She is too young, and the bride-price in unpaid!'

'Her bridegroom thinks her of sufficient age, and here is the bride-price!' Oleg marched up the hall, the *druzhiniki* parting to let him through, and drawing back to leave a wide space in the middle of the hall. Oleg banged down a large leather money-bag on the table in front of Gleb, who picked it up, weighed it in his hand, and said, 'It is sufficient.'

At that, the boyars crowded up to the dais, pushing and shoving one another, and Oleg pointed to Gytha and commanded, 'Take the bride and let us be gone!'

She stood up as the boyars swarmed round her, and felt a wave of panic as they jostled her and one another, then seized her. She received a few sly, salacious pinches, even through the stiff fabric of her robe, and one hand tried to insert itself into the front of the garment, but was slapped away by another. Then her wrists were taken and held, quite gently, and she was led from the hall and out into the courtyard in front of the palace, where a magnificent litter was waiting.

It was constructed like a tent on carrying poles, and panelled with blue leather, painted with patterns in gold leaf and hung with little bells. Even the carrying-poles were gilded. She was helped into it by enthusiastic hands, and Mildyth and Yevpraksia were bundled in after her. Then the whole contraption was lifted, lurching alarmingly, and began to move along, swaying and bumping, with the boyars closing round it, and lifting their voices again in untuneful song.

'I hope they're not all drunk!' Yevpraksia exclaimed, crossing herself. Gytha crossed herself too, once more forgetting and moving her hand the wrong way, but Yevpraksia caught it and corrected her.

The litter was well padded with furs and silk-covered cushions, but the swaying movement and frequent tips and lurches were decidedly unpleasant, and Mildyth soon began to murmur under her breath, her eyes tightly closed. Yevpraksia probably thought she was praying, but Gytha caught a few phrases, and knew that she was reciting *Beowulf* as a possible panacea for sickness, as she had once done on *Sea-Fafnir*. To make matters worse, the procession turned away from the bridge and Market Side, and bore the litter out of the kremlin and through the streets of Sophia Side, cheered by the shoemakers, the leather-workers, the potters and their families, who came out of their houses and workshops to see them go through the different quarters.

Eventually they returned to the kremlin and came to a halt before the bishop's palace, where Fedor came out to give Gytha his blessing. Then they went on, over the bridge and across the market-place, but not directly to the palace. First they went through all the quarters of Market Side – the wax-traders', the carpenters', the Gotlanders', the Germans', and those of the merchants of Pskov and Tver, and stopped again outside the house of the *posadnik*, who came out in his best robes and presented Gytha with wine in a gold cup set with four great red carbuncles in a band of chased decoration. She drank the wine, thankful that the cup was only half-full, and would have handed it back as she thanked him, but he clasped her hands round it and told her it was a gift from the *veche*.

It was growing dark as the procession caried her to the palace, some of the fatter boyars dragging their feet with weariness by now. The litter was carried up the ceremonial stairs and through the palace to the largest of the halls, which was crowded with guests, already seated at the long tables. They were all shouting or singing at the tops of their voices, red-faced, sweating and enjoying themselves immensely, to judge by the look and sound of them all.

The litter was put down without over-setting, and Gytha stood up. A number of willing hands reached out to help her out, but before she could set foot on the floor, two great bear-like boyars seized her and set her on their shoulders, then carried her, with more speed and enthusiasm than care, the whole length of the hall to the dais, where Vladimir was standing, tall, slim and straight, in a little oasis of stillness and quiet amid the hubbub. One of the boyars tripped on the edge of the dais, and she was literally thrown into Vladimir's arms, which closed round her and swung her safely down to stand beside him, the guests roaring with approval.

During the feast that followed, Gleb gave her the money-bag which Oleg had passed to him earlier, shouting above the uproar that she'd better have the bride-price herself as he wasn't going to send it all the way to Denmark. Gytha attempted to protest, but couldn't make him hear, so she passed the heavy bag to Mildyth, and smiled her thanks to him.

A great deal of food passed before her and she made a good meal, but before long her head ached with the racket and the weight of her head-dress. It was a great relief when the entertainment began and the noise died down so that the singers and musicians could be heard. They were followed by a juggler, then a dancing bear, which performed very well to the pipe and tabor played by its trainer.

At the end of its dance, the bear was near the dais, and it

lumbered closer, walking on its hind legs, its forepaws held out before it, until it was immediately opposite Gytha across the narrow table. She looked into the little red-rimmed eyes peering out of the furry mass of its face and thought it looked sad, so she stretched out a hand to a nearby dish of honey-cakes and gave the animal four of them.

It was only then that she realised that Vladimir had risen and was standing tensely close beside her, and the bear-leader was equally close and tense beside the bear, and almost everyone else in the hall was watching in silence.

'What a good bear!' she said calmly. 'It dances very well!'

The bear stuffed the cakes in its mouth and looked about hopefully, so she gave it another four, and handed the remainder, dish and all, to the trainer, who led the bear away to uproarious applause. It shuffled along, still on its hind legs, assiduously licking the last crumbs from its paws.

'You weren't afraid,' Vladimir said softly.

'No. I didn't think it would hurt me – it was only attracted by the food.'

Vladimir gave a rueful grin. 'The last hungry bear I met bit me on the kneecap! You wouldn't believe how painful it was!'

'Well, now,' Gleb said suddenly, 'don't you think your Princess might be allowed to retire? She's had a tiring day, and needs some sleep. I don't expect she'll get any tomorrow night!' He gave Vladimir a meaning wink and a nudge in the ribs to underline it. Unfortunately he had spoken loudly to be heard above the conversation of his guests, but happened to coincide with one of those unexpected silences which sometimes occur in even the noisiest assemblies. Most of the people at the high table heard what he said, and some of the boyars began shouting out comments and advice to Vladimir, obviously of a ribald nature. Gytha's Slavonic vocabulary did not include many of the words they used, but there were enough gestures and grins to convey their general meaning, and she felt the colour rising in her cheeks, and was thankful for the paint which covered them.

Vladimir stood up, and his firm, decisive tones cut through the noise.

'That will do, friends!' he said. 'Your advice is well meant, but I assure you that I'll know what to do when the time comes. My dear wife-to-be is a gently-nurtured princess, and I'll not have her made to blush by you! What kind of savages will she think you are? The Polovtsy may not respect their women or guard their tongues before them, but the Rus and the folk of Novgorod are all civilised people. I'm sure you don't wish her to think otherwise!'

There was some sheepish shifting about after that, and more than a few muttered apologies. Vladimir held out his hand to Gytha, who took it as she rose. He drew her close and gave her a formal kiss on each cheek, bidding her rest well, then conducted her to the door at the back of the dais that led to the *terem* area of the palace. Gytha made a reverence to the company and another to him, and then escaped thankfully through the rabbit-warren of rooms and staircases to the haven of her own apartment, closely followed by Mildyth and Yevpraksia.

She was tired, but lay awake for a long time, staring into the darkness and wondering what tomorrow night would be like. How would it be to share her bed with a husband? Would he stay all night, or only until the – the business was completed? What would it be like? Would she understand him any better after-wards? Was he nervous, too? She didn't think he would hurt her any more than was necessary, but she still remembered Elisev's coldly factual exposition of the sexual act, and how unpleasant she had made it sound, and everyone mentioned pain . . .

Making herself think calmly, she sought back in her memory for the worst pain she had ever experienced, and decided that it was when she had grown a worm in one of her great teeth, and the blacksmith at Waltham had pulled the tooth for her. She had stood that well enough, without screaming or fainting, although she was but about nine at the time, and had only cried a little afterwards, and that was more from relief than pain. Surely what happened tomorrow night wouldn't be much worse than that – would it?

In any case, all women who married had to go through it, and at least she had a man whom she loved, whereas so many

265

had to suffer being bedded by a stranger, or someone they disliked, so she had much to be thankful for. She turned over and sighed, and then was startled to find herself being shaken awake by Mildyth, who was warning her that she would be late for her wedding if she slept any longer.

Of course, there was really plenty of time. Mildyth was making a great fuss of spreading out the bridal clothes all over the bed, so Gytha slipped into a warm woollen bed-robe and went into the corner room to say her prayers. She was surprised to find that a new icon had appeared on the shelf, which had still been empty the previous day. It depicted St Basil the Great as a tall, lean man, with a bald head and those dark, inscrutable eyes which reminded her of Vladimir, in an attitude of adoration before the Holy Cross.

When she had prayed for Vladimir and herself and for their marriage, she went across to the window and looked out over the market-place, all distorted by the mica panes. The sun was shining, and, over the crowded roofs on the other side of the open space, she could see the town rampart, the plain beyond, and the dark forest in the distance. Large areas of the plain were showing green, and there were silver streaks and patches shining in the sunshine. It was a few seconds before she realised that they were not snow, but water. The winter was over at last!

It seemed a good omen, and she went back to her bedroom with a lighter heart, to find that Yevpraksia had arrived with jugs of hot water, so that she could wash thoroughly before dressing. Then the two women helped her to dress, putting on a new shift of fine white linen, low-necked and sleeveless, and linen stockings which laced up at the back and felt stiff and uncomfortable. Over these came the close-fitting wide-skirted white gown, which also laced at the back, and white shoes of soft leather embroidered with gold dragons, a gift from the leather-workers. Then the beautiful rainbow robe of soft silk was brought from Mildyth's room, where it had been hanging on a rail to save it from creasing. Gytha put it on, and Mildyth fastened the gold clasps, then stood back and looked at her nursling in awed silence.

'Do I look well enough?' Gytha asked uncertainly.

Mildyth burst into tears, much to Yevpraksia's disgust, and sat down on the bed to indulge in a good cry while Yevpraksia combed Gytha's hair until it shone, polished it with a piece of silk to make it shine even more, then spread it loose over her shoulders. Then she brought the silver mirror. Gytha took it to the window, and tried to see as much of herself as she could in it.

It was hopeless. She could gain no idea of her overall appearance, but a critical examination of her head and shoulders showed a pale oval face framed by her hair, which still kept its corn-gold colour. It was simply parted in the centre, and fell in ripples from being plaited. She bit her lips to make them more red, then tidied the smooth curve of her eyebrows with a licked finger, not noticing the clarity of her complexion or the beautiful blue of her eyes.

'We won't paint you,' said Yevpraksia. 'It would spoil you.'

'Shouldn't I wear something on my head?' Gytha asked.

'You will, when you go into church,' Yevpraksia replied. 'Best sit down quietly now. You'll only have a little time to wait.'

Gytha obediently sat on one of the chests while Yevpraksia and Mildyth, still sniffing, tidied the room. After about ten minutes, Brother Isak knocked at the door from the corner room and invited Gytha to come and speak to Bishop Fedor.

She was startled to find that the bishop was sitting at the table in the corner room. She thought he looked very old and tired, and was sorry that he had climbed up the stairs from the courtyard, when she could have gone down to him. He sat talking to her for a while about the religious aspects of marriage, then gave her his blessing and left to go on to the cathedral.

After a longer wait, Anastasia and some of her ladies arrived, and Gytha walked in the midst of them through the *terem*, down the main staircase, and through the halls and rooms of the palace to the great door, where Gleb was waiting, glittering and gorgeous in crimson brocade sewn with jewels, white fur and gold-crowned cap, three or four massy gold chains on his broad shoulders and a dozen rings on his gloved hands. His bright eyes twinkled at Gytha, and he whispered, 'Vladimir is a lucky fellow! I wish I'd spoken for you first!' as he handed her down the steps and into the big sledge, wedging her in securely with cushions before plonking himself down beside her.

Three grey horses, harnessed abreast, drew the sledge. They, like the sledge, were hung with little bells, coloured ribbons were plaited into their manes and tails, and tall coloured plumes nodded on their heads. They set up a great jingling as they started across the market-place, the iron runners of the sledge making a roaring sound on the wooden roadway. The market bell began to chime, and, church by church, the other bells of the city took up the joyful sound, crashing and clashing in a great jangle and setting the pigeons whirring up into the air until the sky seemed full of wings.

Most of the citizens were about, dressed in their best and in holiday mood, to cheer their Prince and Vladimir's bride on their way, lining the route right across the market-place, over the bridge and up to the doors of St Sophia's.

For Gytha, everything was a kaleidoscope of colour, faces and voices. Afterwards she could hardly remember what had happened, only a few incidents standing out clearly, like events in a dream. She could recall Vladimir turning to greet her as she moved towards him across the patterned floor of the cathedral, his hand outstretched to take hers and lead her towards the iconostasis. He wore white, with no more ornament than a white fur edging and a simple gold collar, and his eyes smiled at her. She remembered the bishop crowning them with heavy gold crowns, like a king and queen, and exchanging vows, her own voice sounding clear but nervous, and Vladimir's calm and confident, its tones making her tremble until his grip on her hand steadied her. After that, they were given lighted candles to hold, and Fedor led them round the central area of the cathedral in a circling movement.

Naturally Gytha wanted to capture every second of her wedding in her memory, but some small part of her mind was busily thinking, 'I'm safe now, Ekaterina and Oleg can't stop him from marrying me, and they can't hurt me. He's good and kind, and perhaps he'll even learn to love me a little. I already love him, and I won't let any of their lies make me distrust him. If I can only give him a son, all will be well, and I'll have the chance to do something for Father's memory. I'll bring up our son to be like him, and people will see what a fine man he is, and they'll say he's like his father and his English grandfather.' Her thoughts were brave and confident, but there was still a small shadow of apprehension lurking in the background. She closed her mind to it, and concentrated on the ceremony.

After the Eucharist they went hand in hand from the cathedral, still wearing their crowns, into a sea of sunlight, white doves, cheering people and clanging bells.

'Shall we walk?' Vladimir asked her in a low voice.

She nodded, and they walked together, her hand resting in his, across the courtyard and over the bridge, smiling and nodding acknowledgment of the greetings and good wishes shouted at them from every side, with the princely court following two by two behind, excepting, it turned out later, Oleg, whose arm was aching badly, and Anastasia, who was horrified at the mere idea of walking, and among common people at that. They returned together in the bell-festooned sledge.

By now, Gytha's stomach was protesting about the length of time since supper last night, for she had eaten nothing since, and she was feeling a little peculiar, what with the weight of the heavy crown and the emotion of the occasion. As soon as they entered the palace, Vladimir drew her into one of the side rooms, lifted the crown from her head and placed it with his own on a table, then kissed her gently on her lips.

'I've never seen anything more beautiful and moving in my life!' he said. Gytha thought he meant the happy, well-wishing crowd. She swayed slightly as he released her, and he quickly pushed her very gently down into a chair. 'Rest for a while,' he said. 'I was a fool to suggest walking. I'm sorry.'

'I wouldn't have missed the walk for the world!' she replied. 'Everyone was so kind. I think they liked it.'

'Oh, they did! They all love a wedding, particularly when the bride is a fairytale princess. You're probably the most beautiful sight they've ever seen in their lives!'

She raised startled eyes to his face, but he was already turning away to pour wine for her. A jug and two goblets and a plate of bread had been left ready for them on the table, and they were both glad to eat a slice or two and exchange a silent toast, for Vladimir had not broken his fast either. Gleb entered while they were doing this, and enquired if they were ready for the feast. He fidgeted from one foot to the other like a restless horse while Vladimir carefully set Gytha's crown on her head again, then put on his own, after which they followed him into the great hall for the wedding feast.

The guests were much quieter than they had been the night before, so conversation was easier. Gytha was seated between Vladimir and Oleg. She had hardly spoken to the latter since his arrival, partly from lack of opportunity, but more because the sight of him reminded her of the conversation she had overheard in the church. She knew that she had uncovered a disturbing link between Ekaterina's strange attitude to herself and Oleg's ambivalent attitude towards Vladimir, but she had not had time to think about it and decide what she should do. Surely it was not urgent, and could wait until this momentous occasion was past.

'How is your arm?' she asked him.

'Painful. At least it was a clean break,' he replied irritably. 'The arm's not long healed from an encounter with a Polovtsian spear – I think I prefer the present injury of the two.'

'You fight with Vladimir, don't you?'

'By his side, usually. We make a good team, despite the odds against it.'

She looked at him enquiringly, and he went on, 'We're a family of warriors, and fight among ourselves when there's no other enemy. I suppose you've heard about old Yaroslav's will?'

'Your grandfather? Yes, I think so. Did he not arrange for each of his sons to rule Kiev in turn?'

'That's it. Guaranteed to cause trouble! The second and third sons – my father and Vladimir's – have already connived the eldest's exile. That's Izyaslav. That meant that his son, Svyato-polk, lost Novgorod, and he wants it back. Gleb has it now, but when our father dies, Vladimir will claim it. You know that Novgorod always goes to the eldest son of the Grand Prince of Kiev?'

'But Vladimir's promised that Gleb shall keep Novgorod!' Gytha exclaimed. 'Surely you know that?'

'Yes, I know that's what he says, but the recent history of our family is a catalogue of broken promises and treachery,' Oleg said gloomily. 'I even trust Vladimir with my life on the battle-field, but with nothing at all anywhere else. I don't even trust myself!' He lapsed into a brooding silence, and Gytha thought that he was either drunk or very disturbed in his mind.

'Don't talk of family troubles today.' Vladimir either did not hear, or pretended that he did not. 'This is a day for happiness!'

Oleg pulled a face, but changed the subject and asked Gytha, 'How do you like living in Novgorod?' but he hardly gave any attention to her reply, seeming more interested in what every-one else was doing or talking about.

The feast lasted a very long time, with intervals for entertain-ment between the courses. After the first hour or so, Vladimir and Gytha thankfully took off their crowns, which were then placed in front of them on the table in the middle of a great wreath of flowers that Vladimir's father had sent by relays of fast horsemen from the south.

'He sent you this, as well,' Vladimir told Gytha, and from among the flowers he drew out a long chain of gold discs, each about two thumb-spans across, and each ornamented with a bird or an animal in bright enamels, with jewelled eyes. He put it over her head, and it hung to her waist, a truly princely gift. While Gytha was examining it, Vladimir slid a hand under her hair to ease it out from under the chain, and, to her surprise, he caressed her neck as he did so. It was the first time he had touched her in a lover-like fashion, apart from his occasional kisses, and she wondered if she had mistaken an accidental touch for a deliberate one, but he repeated it before he removed

271

his hand leaving her with a confused, excited feeling, half hope and half incredulity.

Four times during the interminable feast he suggested that they might walk together among the guests, and she was glad of a chance to move, for the high-backed chair on which she sat was high-seated as well and her feet hardly touched the floor, so she found that they kept pricking with pins-and-needles. Each time, Vladimir took her hand and led her slowly round the hall, and then around the half-dozen other halls where the lesser guests and townsfolk were feasting, stopping every now and then to greet someone and exchange a few words with them. Then they went out to the great porch of the main entrance to wave to the people in the market-place.

On the last of these occasions she saw, with some surprise, that the sun was already setting behind St Sophia's, and Vladimir murmured, 'Only a little while longer,' as he led her back to the great hall.

As soon as they resumed their seats, a minstrel struck a rippling chord on his gusli and began a new and very lively song about a beautiful golden-haired princess, the daughter of the King of the Sunset Isles, who travelled far over the seas on the back of a fiery dragon to wed the Prince of the Land of the Sunrise, a mighty warrior famed for his strength, his wisdom, courage and justice. It was very high-flown and poetic, and Gytha was astonished when she realised that Gleb's master-minstrel had made the song especially for her wedding. It made her wonder about the origin of some of the folk-tales she had heard.

When the last swinging chorus, in which everyone joined, had ended, Vladimir rose and pledged the minstrel in a gold cup of wine, which he then filled with gold coins and sent by a servant to the man in the extravagant fashion expected of princes on these occasions. It was an oddly-shaped cup, more like a scoop with two handles, one long, one short. By now, most of the guests were red-faced and sweating, and very drunk. Indeed, some of them had already retired under the tables, where those still able to keep their seats kicked them from time to time, either by accident or for amusement.

Vladimir said something to Gleb, then looked across to the nearest table to catch Mildyth's eye. She had been waiting for the signal and touched Yevpraksia's arm, and the two women slipped away from the hall by a side door. After a few minutes, Anastasia, Gleb, Oleg and Vladimir rose, the latter taking Gytha by the hand and signalling her with a lift of his eyebrows to go with them, and they all slipped unobtrusively away through the small door at the back of the dais.

'I thought we'd do without the ceremonial bedding,' Vladimir explained to Gytha. 'It's an ordeal we can well manage without, and I think they're all too drunk to care.

Gleb bolted the door behind them, and signalled the guard waiting by it to keep it bolted, and then he, Anastasia and Oleg escorted bride and groom to their apartment. They shared a last glass of wine with them in the corner room, and then both men claimed a kiss from the bride before bidding them goodnight, with meaningful grins and digs in the ribs for Vladimir. Then they clattered off down the stairs to the courtyard, and Vladimir barred the door after them.

'I told Efrem, my man, to bar the door beyond his room, but I'll check it myself, and you'd best see to the one from the *terem*. We don't want a drunken rabble coming in search of us!'

Gytha did so, and was standing uncertainly in the middle of the corner room when Vladimir returned, nervously aware that she was about to find out either the best or the worst about her new husband, and her apprehension must have shown on her face, for Vladimir took her gently in his arms and said, 'Don't be afraid!'

'N – No,' she said doubtfully.

'Shall we pray?'

She nodded, and together they knelt before the icon, and Vladimir asked God, in very simple, everyday language, to bless their marriage and grant them the ability to give one another happiness. Afterwards he led Gytha to the bedroom door, said, 'I'll not be long,' and gave her a little encouraging push.

Mildyth and Yevpraksia were waiting for her. They helped her off with her finery, exclaiming over Prince Vsevolod's hand-

273

some gift, and Yevpraksia poured warm water into the copper bowl for her to wash. Then the two women stood side by side, looking a little awkward.

'We've put the herbs under the pillows,' Mildyth said, meaning the traditional bunch of those plants which were thought to promote love, conception and good health that were usually added to the marriage-bed in far-away England.

'Thank you. You may go now,' Gytha replied.

'Don't you want . . .' Mildyth began, but Yevpraksia tugged her sleeve, and they both bobbed a little reverence and made for the door, replying 'Goodnight, Princess,' to Gytha's 'Goodnight.'

They were both to sleep in Mildyth's room that night, so Gytha made sure that the door was firmly shut, then returned to finish washing, wrapping her bed-gown closely round her afterwards, shivering and telling herself that it was because the spring evening was chilly, although the stove was burning well. Then she combed her hair, and started to plait it, until she remembered that first meeting with Vladimir, when he had run his fingers through her hair as if he enjoyed it. She combed it through again, and left it loose.

It was very quiet. Even the usual creaks of a wooden building seemed to have stopped. She stood looking at the big bed, nerving herself to get into it, and gave a startled gasp as the door opened and Vladimir came in.

He stood still for a moment, looking at her as she spun round to face him, his face as closed to her as ever, without even a trace of a smile to break the stern, sombre set of his mouth. He was wrapped in a dark bed-gown, with bare feet, and looked more like one of those Greek icons than ever in the candle-light.

'Are you afraid of me, or of what you've been told?' he asked quietly.

'Both, just a little,' she replied, trying to be honest.

'There's no need. I won't hurt you any more than I must.'

He slipped off his bed-gown and turned to lay it across one of the chests. Gytha could not help staring at him, seeing him naked for the first time. His body was hard and muscular,

274

broad-shouldered and narrow-hipped, and marked with more than a dozen scars. When she looked at his face, she realised that he was standing still, watching her and waiting for her to finish her inspection, and her cheeks flooded with colour.

'I'm sorry it's such a battered, skinny body,' he said.

'It's not skinny!' she said indignantly. 'I don't like fat men!'

He smiled then, and advanced on her, and within seconds her bed-gown was off and she found herself being picked up and deposited gently on the bed, all but one of the candles were pinched out, and a warm, lithe form was beside her, caressing hands drawing her close.

She supposed afterwards that there had been some pain – not very much, though – and what there was was completely drowned in unexpected pleasure, which had spiralled up to an unbearably dizzy height before it exploded into a great sense of fulfilment. It was quite a long time before she recovered her senses enough to give any coherent thought at all to what had happened, and then she found that Vladimir was on his own side of the bed, lying quite still and quiet. Perhaps he was asleep.

'Vladimir?' she whispered.

'My Princess?' he replied in a lazy, contented tone she had never heard in his voice before.

She hesitated, not sure what she wanted to say, but instinctively moving towards him. She felt his hands touch her, wait a moment for her reaction, then draw her into a close embrace.

He was silent for a time, and she snuggled against him, thoroughly happy for the first time for more years than she cared to remember, even forgetting that there were still problems ahead.

'Was it very terrible?' he asked eventually.

'Not terrible at all. Just the opposite.'

And so it continued. For nearly five blissful weeks she blossomed in the warmth of at last having someone to love, someone who was kind and cared about her. She loved Vladimir more each day, riding with him across the thaw-sodden pastures or in the pine-scented stillness of the forest, sitting with him at dinner in the great hall or alone with him in the corner room, learning how very pleasant it was to share her bed with a gentle, considerate husband.

There were little flaws in her happiness, or she supposed it would have been too much to sustain. Every day brought the time nearer when he would have to leave, and, although he made love to her every night and spent the greater part of each day with her and seemed content to do so, she felt no nearer to knowing him. She still found it difficult to meet his intense gaze for more than a few minutes, and the remote, closed look was still in his eyes, except when they were talking very seriously about some impersonal subject. She was forced to the sad conclusion that he was content with an arranged marriage which had turned out to be satisfactory, in spite of Elisev's half-truths, with the physical pleasure of coupling with a responsive woman, and the relief of having a partner who was sufficiently intelligent at least to grasp what he was talking about, but he did not love her. Considering what it might have been like, she was very lucky that only the crowning glory was missing from the marriage. At least, he had tried once to let her into his private thoughts.

'How are things between you and your bride?' Gleb asked Vladimir during one of their private discussions in the cabinet.

'Very well,' Vladimir replied briefly.

Gleb raised his eyebrows. 'Such enthusiasm! I take it that you mean it's as well as can be expected for an arranged marriage, but she can't compare with, say, Katya Andreyevna?'

'She's nothing like Katya,' Vladimir replied seriously, then added 'Thank God!', and his lips moved in a little private smile.

'Ah-ha!' Gleb also smiled, fingering his moustache. 'I used to wonder about Katya, and I thought you seemed singularly unmoved when she went off with Oleg. Have you warned Gytha about my dear brother?'

His cousin shrugged. 'I see no need. Oleg seldom comes to Novgorod, and Gytha will be living here, as we agreed.'

Gleb made no comment, but thought to himself that he would find an opportunity himself to warn Gytha about Oleg after Vladimir had left Novgorod.

Leave he must, and did, all too soon for Gytha, riding away with Oleg and their attendants early one morning, a week before Pentecost. He had been particularly tender and passionate in his lovemaking the night before, but their last conversation was more practical than romantic.

'Gytha, find yourself some useful things to do. Laziness is the mother of evil – I'd not wish you to fall into Anastasia's idle ways.'

'I will, Vladimir.'

'My grandfather founded a school here – perhaps you might visit it sometimes – and the cathedral needs more embroideries. There are no skilled nuns here to do the work, as there are in Kiev.'

'I shall keep myself well occupied,' she promised, 'and do you take care!'

'I always take care. My time of dying is with God, but that doesn't mean that I can afford to be careless!'

They prayed together, then he gave her rather a hurried kiss, and left. She watched from the window as he came out into the market-square where Oleg and the others were waiting, and rode off with them, and then she sat down and cried for a while. Presently she dried her tears, called Mildyth, and went out into the market to buy linen, silks and gold thread to make an altar cloth.

It was only on her return that she remembered that she had not told Vladimir about the conversation she had overheard in the church the day before their wedding, but if it had really been about herself and Vladimir, there was nothing he could do about it without quarrelling with Oleg, and he could not afford to do that at the beginning of a season's campaigning. Best to keep silence, but be watchful, especially if Ekaterina returned to the palace.

Chapter Thirteen

Ekaterina came back at Pentecost and resumed her duties as though she had not been away for more than two months. Gleb questioned her about the misinformation she had given to Anastasia about Gytha's father, but she said that she had received it from a merchant in the market, a stranger, who seemed to know what he was talking about, and she had been worried about it, so she had felt it her duty to tell Anastasia. When Gleb said that it had proved to be untrue, she smiled and said she was glad to hear it, with apparent sincerity, and he seemed satisfied. Gytha asked her if her child was better, and she replied demurely that she was quite recovered, having had several weeks in the country, and that she was very grateful to Anastasia for allowing her to be with the little girl for so long. Gytha kept her feelings to herself, but was now quite sure that it had been Ekaterina with Oleg in the church.

The weeks passed painfully slowly. Gytha learned to play the gusli Sadko had given her for a wedding present, read and re-read all the books in the corner room and bought more to go with them, rode out with Gleb and his household on hunting, hawking and fishing expeditions, and worked at her embroidery. She now had a small household of her own, including six *druzhiniki*, and four ladies under the charge of Mildyth, seconded by Yevpraksia, who had transferred to her service at her own request. Vladimir had given each of them one of his lion-mask brooch badges to wear, silver for the men and the new ladies, but gold for Mildyth and Yevpraksia, who were quite overcome with the honour.

Gytha was surprised to find that the well-born girls had no knowledge of embroidery, and explained to them that English ladies were famous throughout Christendom for their skill with the needle. She taught them the stitches she had learned as a child, and between them they made a very creditable altar cloth for St Sophia's, and were very pleased with their new skill.

She visited Yaroslav's school, where some of the sons of the Novgorod boyars received a sound basic education, and gave money to buy the materials for new books to replace those which had worn out with constant use. The boys themselves made the new copies, working in groups, for there were more than two hundred of them to share the task.

Every three or four weeks Vladimir sent a courier to Novgorod, carrying news of what was going on in the south to Gleb, and now there was always a brief letter for Gytha as well. It usually contained a short summary of what he had said at greater length in his letter to Gleb, an account of what he had been doing, and a few lines at the end which were only for her – perhaps a comment on something he had seen or read, or an idea which had occurred to him, and, once, an account of an odd dream which had amused him. Gytha gained the impression that he was trying to make some sort of personal contact over the long distance which lay between them, which must have been difficult for such a reserved man.

She wrote back to him at greater length, having more leisure, beginning each new letter as soon as the last had gone off with Gleb's returning messenger, and adding a little each day in diary form, telling him what she had been doing and setting down some of her thoughts, but she tried not to include much of her feelings, her anxiety about his safety, her longing for his return, thinking that he would find them tedious or embarrassing. To her sorrow, the first letter she sent him after he left had to tell him that she was not with child, and she waited very anxiously for his reply. It came in one brief sentence at the end of his next letter: *'God's will does not always coincide with our own, but we must trust Him, for He knows what is best.'*

She found it enigmatic, for it could be interpreted in so many different ways, and it left her with an unhappy feeling of failure, which remained in the back of her mind, emerging to worry her

279

when she was wakeful at night or unoccupied during the day. Sometimes she tried to mention the subject again in her letters in the hope of a more comforting reply, but never quite managed to find the right words.

Gleb usually read his letters (or part of them, at least) to the small group of family and friends who gathered after the evening meal in the room he used as a cabinet and private sitting-room, often adding his own comments. Gytha was, of course, included in these gatherings, and the conversations enabled her to learn more about what had been happening in the rest of Rusland and to gain a greater understanding of the internal troubles and quarrels of the princely family. Izyaslav, the exiled uncle, who had been driven out of Poland as a result of Vladimir's treaty with King Boleslaw, had gone to the German emperor for refuge. He remained a constant threat to Svyatoslav's control of Kiev and also, through his son Svyatopolk, to Gleb's of Novgorod. Gleb appeared to dislike and distrust all of them – Izyaslav, his own father, Vladimir's father, and two more uncles, one of whom ruled Smolensk, and the other a town far away in the south-west. He obviously respected and liked Vladimir but was not entirely convinced that he was to be trusted, and his own brothers, Oleg, Yaroslav and David exasperated him.

Gytha continued to attend Gleb's court as well, listening to the discussions of the various problems which were referred to him for action or advice by the town *veche* or the boyars. The Prince had no official jurisdiction over the civil authority or the government of the town, but Gleb had been careful to build up a good relationship with the *veche* and had a considerable influence over its decisions. Anastasia, who was invited to attend but rarely bothered to do so, seemed to find Gytha's interest both surprising and amusing, but was not in the least jealous when the English princess was asked for an opinion, while she was not. 'I have no thoughts on such tedious matters,' she said placidly.

One serious problem arose quite unexpectedly in that brief period between harvest and the onset of winter, which in this part of the world was too short to merit the title of autumn. A magician who had been in the city for some weeks was performing a variety of tricks in the market-place which attracted ever larger audiences. Gytha had seen him several times, and even stopped to watch occasionally, intrigued by his tricks and wondering how they were managed. She thought very little about him until one evening when Gleb remarked that he thought the fellow was becoming a danger to public order.

'He's beginning to make some outrageous claims, and far too many people believe him.'

'A trickster, no more, and easy enough to discredit,' one of the boyars said with a dismissive shrug.

'Maybe, but I think he needs to be watched,' Gleb replied. 'He could cause trouble.'

The trouble came less than a week after. The magician, who called himself the Wonderworker, began to boast that he was sent by the god Pirun to save the good folk of Novgorod from the greed and false teachings of the priests of 'that false god they call the Christ'. Gytha had not realised how thin a veneer of Christianity overlay the paganism of many of the Novgorodians, but it was evident now in the great numbers who gathered to hear the Wonderworker and cheer him on to greater claims and more ferocious condemnations, prophesying terrible calamities unless the people obeyed him, and growing daily wilder and more extravagant in his foretellings and claims.

Gleb kept a careful watch on proceedings, and called together his friends and advisers with some urgency one evening to discuss what should be done. 'I asked Bishop Fedor to join us,' he said, 'but this Wonderworker has challenged him to a confrontation tomorrow, and he sends word that he must spend this night in prayer and meditation. I think tomorrow will be the turning-point, one way or the other.'

The *posadnik*, resplendent in his best robe, his chain of office gleaming on the rich fabric, tentatively raised a hand, and Gleb nodded to him to speak. 'Lord Prince,' he began, standing up, then sitting down again as Gleb flapped a hand at him. 'Lord Prince, I fear for the bishop's life tomorrow, and for our beloved

St Sophia's. Indeed, I fear for all our churches and all our priests! The ignorant *smerdi* and the lower-class workers of the town are in a ferment of near-worship for this Wonderworker, to the extent that most of them have downed tools and refuse to go to work. They're planning a great riot tomorrow, when the Wonderworker claims that he's going to walk dryshod on the waters of the river as a sign that he's as great a god as Our Lord. My – er – my agents tell me that the people are talking openly of storming the kremlin afterwards, crucifying the bishop, and burning all the priests and monks in St Sophia's as an offering to their new god. They're saying also that you – that the princedom of Novgorod has been usurped, and that Pirun is angry and wants the true prince restored to his – er – proper place . . .'

'Meaning my dear cousin Svyatopolk, I suppose,' Gleb said. 'In other words, they're claiming that I've usurped Svyatopolk's princedom.'

'Um – er – yes,' the *posadnik* agreed reluctantly, looking apologetic. 'They mean to attack the palace after they've finished with the kremlin, and burn the – er – the usurper and the – the foreign witch . . .'

'Oh? Which one? The Cuman or the Varang?' Gleb asked with heavy irony.

'I'm not sure.' The *posadnik* gave Gytha a nervous little smile, as if to apologise to her for his townsfolk's unreasonableness. 'Our marshals can't hope to control them, and I don't know if we can rely on the militia, so I must beg for aid from your *druzhina* . . .'

'Impossible!' Gleb declared positively. 'The *druzhina* of the Prince of Novgorod exists to protect the people of Novgorod, not to fight and kill them, and that's what it would come to if we try to put down a riot by force. Come, everyone, think! This fellow prophesies that he'll walk on the water, and presumably he has some trick whereby he'll make it appear that he does, and that will be the signal for the destruction of our St Sophia's – the pride and glory of our city – not to mention the murder of our saintly bishop. How can we stop it?'

There were more than forty of the leading boyars and merchants present, some of the ablest minds in the city, but they looked at one another in doubt and growing despair, shaking their heads gloomily.

'Perhaps I could mix with the people in disguise, and get near enough to the Wonderworker to kill him . . .' Onesifor, the captain of the *druzhina*, offered tentatively.

'If you murder him, you make a martyr of him, and, no doubt, of yourself, and the people will thirst for revenge,' Gytha heard herself saying. 'You'd do better to discredit him.'

'You're right, but how?' Gleb chewed the edge of his moustache.

'Perhaps he'll discredit himself when he fails to walk on the water . . .' Onesifor began hopefully.

'And perhaps he won't!' Gleb replied sharply. 'He wouldn't be fool enough to say he can do it unless he's certain that his trick will work, and it'll be too late to think of something then!'

'There's a story in England,' Gytha began hesitantly in the silence which followed, drawing on a shadowy memory. 'It's about the time when our people were still pagan and the first missionaries came. One of them, called Paulinus, gained the ear of a king in the north of the country, and travelled about with his court. They started on a journey one day, and came on a crow sitting in a tree and cawing. The whole court stopped, and the king said they must turn back, for the crow was prophesying bad luck for them. Paulinus took a bow and arrow from one of the king's guards and shot the crow. "A poor prophet who can't foresee his own death!" he said, and they went on with the journey.' She stopped suddenly, having come to the end of the tale, and was aware that most of those present were frowning impatiently at this irrelevant folk-tale. 'I mean, you must discredit him in some way,' she repeated nervously.

Gleb was staring at her, the beginnings of a smile on his face. 'Well, I've often wondered why the Holy Wisdom was given feminine gender!' he exclaimed. 'Now I think I know why! Thank you, my friends, for your advice and your time. I know what to do about the Wonderworker. Now, what about the dispute over the repairs to the rampart in Potters' End?'

Gytha was as puzzled as everyone else, but Gleb seemed quite confident, and no more was said about the Wonderworker that night.

In the morning, it was hardly more than half-light when the crowds began to gather in the market-place. A messenger from Gleb summoned Gytha to the porch overlooking the square at the ceremonial entrance to the palace, where she found Anastasia, yawning and out of her usual good humour, and a representative selection of the Prince's household. Gleb himself, with no more than a dozen *druzhiniki* in attendance, was standing at the top of the steps which led down to the market-place.

As the sun rose, the Wonderworker appeared, dressed in a bizarre robe of purple patched with stars, and a tall crimson hat, and attended by a score of pretty girls in white gowns, who strewed flowers in front of him as he walked arrogantly across the square to a point midway between the palace and the bridge, where a platform had been built jutting out over the river.

'Well, the usurper Gleb! Have you come to join Pirun's worshippers?' he shouted in a jeering tone.

'I've come to see you make a fool of yourself!' Gleb shouted back. 'My men will fish you out before you drown!'

'You may laugh now! What will you do when I show my power and walk on the waters of the Volkhov as if they were dry land?'

'If I see you do it, I'll believe you told the truth,' Gleb replied, sounding remarkably sincere and reasonable, considering that the conversation was being bawled for the benefit of the great crowd in the square.

'Then come closer and see better!' the Wonderworker invited.

Gleb descended the steps and walked in his usual easy swinging stride across the few hundred yards to the platform, the people making way for him as they had always done, for his manner was as confident and regal as ever. The morning was chilly, and he was wearing his usual fur-edged cap, and a voluminous cloak with a fur border and collar, which flowed about him as he moved in a very princely manner. The handful of *druzhiniki* followed, two by two, a few yards behind, just as they always did.

As he reached the platform and stepped up on to it beside the Wonderworker, he looked towards the bridge, and there, as if on cue, a solitary figure appeared, moving slowly across from Sophia Side to stand at the bridgehead. It was Bishop Fedor, wearing his richest cope, his jewelled mitre flashing in the morning sun, and his white-gloved hand holding the shaft of his pastoral cross. As the attention of the crowd turned to him, he cried in a loud, clear voice, surprisingly powerful from so old a man, 'Whosoever has faith in the magician, let him follow him, but whosoever trusts in Christ, let him come to the Cross!'

A murmur which grew into a snarl ran through the crowd. The *posadnik* and the *veche* marched across to join the bishop, and some of the older merchants went with them. Most of Gleb's council of boyars had assembled near the palace, and they moved across to the bridge in a solid phalanx. Gleb signalled to his little bodyguard to go too, which they did, but with obvious reluctance to leave their Prince. Gleb remained where he was, but he crossed himself with a full, theatrical, sweep of his arm to show where his loyalty lay. Gytha, taking a deep breath to steady herself, stepped forward and swept down the steps and into the square, vaguely conscious that others were following her. She held her head high, thankful that she had dressed in a magnificent kaftan and jewelled *kokoshnik*, ready for church, so that she looked regal, and her painted face concealed whether or not she had turned pale. The townspeople drew aside out of habit as she swept through them and marched across to join the bishop. Fedor greeted her with a blessing and a gentle smile, just as if this was a normal encounter in the shadowed splendour of his cathedral.

'You say that you can foretell the future?' Gleb's voice rang out clearly, sounding interested, and drawing all eyes back to the platform at the river's edge.

285

'All things, past, present and future, are revealed to me!' the Wonderworker intoned.

'You mean you know what will happen tomorrow?' Gleb asked.

'I know all things!'

'You really know what will happen tomorrow?' Gleb asked, appearing to be deeply impressed.

'To you, and to all men!'

'And to you also?'

'Of course.'

'So you must know what will happen, say, in the next five minutes?' Gleb persisted, still at the top of his voice, everyone in the great crowd silent and listening intently, obviously thinking that their Prince was being converted to belief in the Wonderworker.

'I shall work miracles!' declaimed the magician, flinging his arms out in a great gesture of omnipotence, his robe swinging out like wings on either side of him. He had flung back his head, and his face, turned up to look over the heads of his worshippers, was alight with confidence and exultation.

Gleb put his hand to his own throat in a perfectly natural gesture, and tugged the strings of his cloak, which dropped to the ground, suddenly revealing that he was wearing a hauberk of glittering ringmail, and his left arm, previously hidden under the cloak, held a battle-axe against his side. In an unhurried, almost leisurely fashion he gripped the handle of the axe with both hands, swung it in an arc with all the strength of his powerful arms, and sent the Wonderworker's head spinning from his shoulders. A fountain of blood spurted from the severed neck for a second, and then the magician's body fell in a heap of purple, silver and running scarlet into the river, and drifted away on the current.

'False prophet!' Gleb roared triumphantly into the stunned silence of the crowd. 'He couldn't even foretell his own death!'

Fedor began to intone a psalm of thanksgiving in that clear, carrying voice like a silver trumpet, and the crowd round him joined in. Gradually the volume of sound grew as more and more of the townsfolk hastily dissociated themselves from the idiots who had been fooled, and tried to convince themselves and everyone else that they had sided with Bishop Fedor all along.

When the psalm ended, Fedor exhorted the people to pray for forgiveness in their own churches, and the crowd began to break up into shamefaced groups and disperse towards the many churches, whose bells began to clang their summons to prayer. Gleb stood watching them, leaning on his axe in the naturally graceful attitude of a warrior at rest, a slightly sardonic smile on his normally good-humoured face. He nodded gravely in acknowledgment as many of the people who had cheered for the magician paused to thank him for showing them the truth.

Gytha also stood watching, catching sight of many faces she knew, most of them looking anxious and guilty, and she marvelled at the gullibility of normally sensible tradesfolk and artisans to be taken in by the Wonderworker's tricks. Had it really been a resurgence of paganism, she wondered, or had the key to the man's success been his attack on Gleb's right to rule the city? If Vsevolod and Svyatoslav had conspired to drive Izyaslav out of Kiev, presumably their conspiracy had also resulted in Svyatopolk being driven out of Novgorod, but with or without the townsfolk's consent? Was that the reason . . .

Her thoughts were sharply broken off as she caught sight of Ekaterina, not in her court dress with her jewelled *kokoshnik* framing her lovely face, but in a plain black cloak and headshawl. For a moment, she thought herself mistaken – it was only an ordinary woman who happened to look like . . . No, it *was* Ekaterina, white-faced, with staring eyes and tears pouring down her cheeks. Even as Gytha made certain, the woman drew her shawl over her face and disappeared into the crowd, leaving Gytha with a vivid picture of a soul in despair.

When the square was almost empty, Fedor pronounced a blessing on the city and stalked back across the bridge, as straight-backed and vigorous as a man half his age. The boyars wandered off in chattering groups, and the *posadnik* and his companions made low bows to Gytha and hurried off to the *posadnik*'s house, no doubt to hasten their recovery from the anxieties of the morning with some good ale. Gytha found herself left with the half-dozen *druzhiniki*, Mildyth, Yevpraksia and her other ladies and, to her surprise, Anastasia and her attendants.

'What a dreadful morning! I shall go straight back to bed and rest!' Anastasia declared firmly, and set off for the palace forthwith, her ladies trailing behind her. Onesifor, who was one of the *druzhiniki* present, offered his arm to Gytha, and conducted her homeward with more ceremony, and they were joined by Gleb as they passed the platform on the quayside.

'An excellent idea of yours, Gytha!' he said. 'Not that you actually spelled out the method, but you told me how to discredit him, and, by God, it worked!'

Gytha, who had caught sight of the magician's head staring at her with sightless eyes, felt a little sick, but as she turned her face away from that, she found herself looking at Gleb's bloodstained battle-axe, and felt worse. She returned to her rooms and sat quietly until her stomach subsided, then summoned a sledge and went, with only Mildyth and Yevpraksia in attendance, to Sadko's 'little wooden church behind the Germans' Yard'. In fact it was a large and handsome building with five helmet-shaped domes covered with gilded wooden shingles like golden fir-cones, and a profusion of *kokoshnik*-shaped gables. Inside, it was furnished with some magnificent hangings, ornate copper candle-stands and a gilded iconostasis. The priest was a monk, and consequently better educated and a more effective preacher than the average parish priest. He preached an extempore sermon on false prophets, in which he unhesitantly praised Gleb's action, quoting a number of texts in support of it, and Gytha felt less shocked about it as a result. He also stressed that sinners who repented their evil or foolish actions were assured of God's mercy, through the intercession of Christ and the saints, provided that they made every endeavour not to be led astray again by the wiles of the Devil.

Gleb called a special meeting of his council that afternoon to discuss the events of the morning. Gytha attended reluctantly, feeling guilty that a man had died as the result of her suggestion, but Gleb was pleased with himself and everyone else, and made a point of thanking her for her good advice.

'Now, clearly there was something more to this than one madman attempting to destroy our religion and our government,' he went on. 'There were two points at issue. The first is the sudden upsurge of paganism, and the talk of Pirun, the so-called Thunder-god. Obviously there must be a sizeable nest of pagan vipers in the city, and Bishop Fedor means to hunt them down – or, as he puts it, discover the lost sheep and lead them gently back to the fold of the true Church. To judge by the massive attendances at all the churches this morning, most of the greyish sheep are already back in the fold, but there must be some really black ones somewhere. Bishop Fedor will need help from your militia and marshals to find them and lead them *gently* to the monasteries for thorough and intensive instruction.'

The *posadnik* looked at the other members of the *veche* who were present, and they all nodded agreement.

'The other point was the claim that I usurped Novgorod,' Gleb went on. 'Presumably, this refers to the fact that when Izyaslav abdicated the princedom of Kiev and my father inherited it as the next brother, Novgorod passed, as has always been the custom, to the new prince's eldest son, myself. This leads me to suspect that my cousin . . .'

He broke off as the door opened, and Onesifor came in, bowed, and hurried to Gleb's side.

'We found his lodging,' he said quietly. 'Nobody had dared to go near it – everything was undisturbed. We found this, hidden in the false lid of a wooden clothes-chest.' He handed Gleb a small scroll of parchment.

'Ha!' said Gleb, looking at before he unrolled it. 'Not written in Rusland – we don't waste good parchment on letters! Ah, yes!' hastily scanning the contents. 'As I was saying, I suspect that my cousin Svyatopolk had something to do with this, and here is a letter from my uncle Izyaslav to the Wonderworker, ordering him to take control of Novgorod in the name of Svyatopolk. Mm – this is interesting – listen – it says here, "Be sure to consult my agent, of whom I told you when we last met, concerning all your actions, and do nothing in the re-establishment of government in the city without that agent's full approval." Now, who the Devil is the agent?'

His eye ran from face to face in the room as he gave the letter to the *posadnik*, who read it and passed it on to his neighbour. It made its way round the room as Gleb considered the members of his council, but clearly could not see any one of them as Izyaslav's spy.

Gytha sat thinking, trying to remember, and then said diffidently, 'I think I know who it is!'

Gleb flung up a restraining hand and said sharply, 'Don't name anyone unless you have good reasons to support an accusation!'

'I do have good reason.' Gytha was confident now. 'It's Princess Anastasia's waiting-woman Ekaterina.'

'A woman?' the *posadnik* said doubtfully.

'Yes. I heard her talking to – to someone . . .' She explained how she had come to overhear the conversation in the church on the morning of the day before her wedding, by means of the sound-jar.

'I'd seen the same two people talking privately together before, and I'm sure the woman was Ekaterina. When the other had gone, she said he was a fool, and added, "When my prince comes and my god rules, you and yours will have no place in this life!" I think now that she must have been referring to Prince Svyatopolk and Pirun.'

'Did you tell your husband about it?' Gleb asked. 'You certainly didn't tell me.'

'I didn't think it was important. They'd been talking about spoiling my marriage,' Gytha replied, thinking that she must sound remarkably foolish. 'I thought that, as I was forewarned, there was little they could do, and I didn't want to cause any trouble between my husband and – and somebody else, particularly not just then . . . I kept it to myself, and, well, I've been alert to anything that might have arisen from it.'

Gleb gave her a shrewd look, then suddenly struck the arm of his chair with his fist – a habitual gesture which had sadly damaged the fine carved ivory which decorated it. 'Ekaterina! The black-haired woman who came from Tmutorakan! By God, I should have realised when she spread that tale about your father! Katya Andreyevna, or I'm a Silver Bulgar!'

Everyone else in the room looked completely blank, except Onesifor, whose position at court allowed him to know a great deal about the private business of the princely family, and he looked at Gytha, bit his lip, and appeared apprehensive.

'You know the woman, Onesifor,' Gleb said to him. 'Search her out. Start at the *terem*, but I doubt if she'll be there, probably fled the city by now.'

'She has a child – a little girl, I believe,' Gytha put in. 'At least she claims to have a child, fostered out in the city, but I've never seen her . . .'

'A girl-child. I've seen her,' Onesifor stated confidently.

'Well, now,' Gleb said when his captain had left, 'thank you all for your support this morning, and for coming here this afternoon. The court is dissolved until our next usual meeting.'

'Just a moment,' the *posadnik* said, standing on his right to have his say on behalf of the citizens – after all, Gleb had the right only to *advise* the *veche*, not direct it. 'The woman was talking to someone. Does Princess Gytha know who it was, and should we not know? He might be involved.'

'I know who it was, and I give you my word that he had nothing to do with today's capers,' Gleb said briskly. 'It's more your concern at the moment to search out the bishop's black sheep, and you can leave the mysterious stranger to me.'

Onesifor's men failed to find any trace of Ekaterina anywhere in the city, and it was assumed that she had fled. A score or so of pagans were rounded up and taken in small groups to the various monasteries to be taught the error of their beliefs. Bishop Fedor said he thought that there were probably more, but it was difficult in so crowded and large a city to find people who were determined to stay hidden. Life in Novgorod returned to normal . . .

During the following week Gytha made one of her regular

visits to the market seeking silk fabrics, and threads for her embroidery. She found that the events of the previous week seemed to have made her more popular than ever with the traders, which caused her a certain amount of wry amusement. She was, however, delighted when a little girl of three or four stopped her between the stalls to offer her a tight bunch of wild flowers. They were past their best, for the first frosts had begun, but the gesture was well meant.

'How very kind of you!' she exclaimed, crouching down to the child's level. 'They're almost as pretty as you are!'

The child was indeed very pretty, with great dark eyes set in a very fair-skinned plump face, rosebud lips, and a wealth of pale golden curls cascading over her shoulders. She smiled shyly at Gytha and confided, 'My mama says you're a real princess, and I should be one too.'

'Indeed, I'm sure that you're her little princess,' Gytha replied kindly. 'What are you called, dear?'

'Vassilia Vladimirovna,' the child replied, stumbling a little over the patronymic's five syllables.

'And where is your mama?'

The child gestured behind her, and Gytha stood up as a richly-dressed woman stepped forward. She was veiled, but this did not surprise Gytha, as many of the boyarinas wore veils when they went out.

'Your daughter is very pretty,' she said pleasantly. 'You and your husband must be very proud of her.'

'I have no husband,' the woman replied in a husky drawl which was only too familiar to Gytha.

'Ekaterina?' she said, and looked round for a *druzhinik*, or one of the town marshals, but none was visible.

'Don't attempt to have me arrested.' Ekaterina sounded amused. 'I'd have to tell them who fathered the child, wouldn't I? That would be very embarrassing for you – and for him!'

'What do you mean?' Gytha asked stiffly, but the woman's tone, allied with the child's name and patronymic, had already given her the answer.

Ekaterina confirmed this by saying, 'How difficult it would

be for your saintly husband to explain how his mistress, the mother of his child – his *only* child – came to be involved in a plot to overthrow Prince Gleb! Who would then believe his protestations of having no desire to rule Novgorod himself?'

'You claim that Prince Vladimir is the father of your daughter?' Gytha heard herself saying quite calmly. 'What if he is? We know that he had nothing to do with the machinations of the so-called Wonderworker. Prince Izyaslav was behind that.'

Ekaterina drew her veil aside with a graceful gesture and said smilingly, 'Perhaps the Wonderworker thought so, but did Prince Izyaslav write the letter, or was it a forgery?'

'What do you want?' Gytha asked bluntly.

'From you? Nothing. You have nothing in the world that I could possibly want.' Ekaterina's eyes travelled slowly from Gytha's face to the point below her waist where her skirts hung straight and did not cover a significant bulge. 'Nothing,' she repeated. 'Good day to you, Princess.' She gave a mocking half-curtsy, dropped the veil over her face, took the child's hand and walked away, disappearing suddenly between two stalls.

'Where is she?' gasped Yevpraksia's voice just behind Gytha. 'Go after her, you fools! Don't let her get away!'

Two of Gytha's own *druzhiniki* ran past her and began to search between the crowded market stalls, while Yevpraksia, clutching her ribs, tried to recover her breath.

'I ran for help as soon as I heard who she was,' she gasped. 'I didn't think it was any use asking the traders – they're all foreigners here.' This was true, as this part of the market was set aside for the Sirklanders and Bulgars.

'No matter,' Gytha said absently. 'Thank you for trying.' She was thinking of what Ekaterina had said about the child. The suggestion that Vladimir was behind the Wonderworker she dismissed without a second thought. 'That was why she was absent for so long, saying the child was ill,' she said aloud. 'She didn't want to encounter Vladimir.'

'What do you mean?' asked Yevpraksia, clearly puzzled. 'What had Prince Vladimir to do with that woman?'

'Precisely,' Gytha replied crisply. 'I think I have all I need for today. We'll go home now, Yevpraksia.'

She told herself, reasonably calmly, that Vladimir had told her that there had been other women, and at least he did not appear to have any connection now with this Katya. But he didn't tell me that there was a child, she thought. Surely he must see his daughter when he comes here … Naturally enough she could see a parallel between Vladimir's situation and that of her father. What if it was the same story again – a man who loved a woman who had borne his children, but was forced by the obligations of his rank to marry someone else … Perhaps Gleb would know, and she decided to seek an interview with him in the morning.

'You wanted to see me, I gather,' he said, when she joined him in his cabinet. 'Is this a formal matter?'

'No. It's just that I need some information on a subject which is best discussed in private,' she replied. 'The woman Ekaterina approached me in the market – yes, the *druzhiniki* know. Two of mine searched for her, but she disappeared again among the market stalls. She had a child with her – her daughter. She claims that Vladimir is her father.'

Gleb bit his lip. 'Katya Andreyevna – yes, it is the same woman, then. Damnation!' He hit the arm of his chair with his clenched fist even harder than usual, and a piece of ivory inlay fell off and clattered on the floor. 'I'd no idea, or I'd have done something about her long ago.' He sighed gustily and paused, sucking his fist and eyeing Gytha thoughtfully.

'You know of her, though?' Gytha asked. 'I mean, you know that Vladimir had a mistress called Katya, but you didn't connect her with your wife's attendant, Ekaterina?'

'You're a cool one!' Gleb exclaimed admiringly. 'I'd have expected hysterics and tears if you found out that your husband used to keep a mistress!'

'*Used* to,' Gytha echoed with some relief. 'I didn't expect to be the first woman in his life – or his bed – and he told me that there had been other women … Is she still in his employ?'

'Good heavens, no!' Gleb replied, shocked. 'He'd have told you if he had a mistress now. He's honest to a fault, you know, and he'd not have tried to hide anything like that from you. No, Katya Andreyevna's very much in his past. He paid her more than generously for her exclusive services, but she entertained another man behind his back and went off with the other – oh, about four years ago.'

'Was he very upset?' Gytha asked, relieved to hear her own voice speaking steadily despite the turmoil of feelings inside her. Some detached part of her mind noted that she was not angry with Vladimir or disappointed in him – he was, after all, a man, and it had all happened before he had even heard of her. Most of her feelings were jealousy of Katya's outstanding beauty and fear that her own much quieter looks could not compete. Did Vladimir compare her with his former mistress? If so, he must find her disappointing.

'Upset?' Gleb replied thoughtfully. 'I don't think so. I'd say he was more irritated, but he didn't say very much about it. It was a business arrangement, as far as I could make out. I don't think he cared very much for her.' He hesitated again, considering, then went on, 'I've been meaning to tell you about Oleg, and now seems as good a time as any.'

'Oleg?' Gytha was startled by the sudden change of subject. 'I thought we were discussing Katya?'

'It's part of the same tale,' he replied. 'As you know, Vladimir and Oleg work excellently well together, but Vladimir has to keep a very tight rein on himself to keep their friendship firm. Oleg has a habit of stealing things from him.'

'Stealing? What do you mean?'

'Oh, Oleg doesn't admit that it's stealing. He believes that friends should hold their property in common – what's mine is yours, you know. The result is that when he sees something of Vladimir's that he likes, he takes it. Anything – a horse, a sword, a cloak, a servant . . .'

'A mistress,' Gytha added, enlightened.

'Precisely. The other man was Oleg. He took her off to Tmut-orakan, his city, without a word to Vladimir, and mentioned the fact only months later, when they were on campaign and he had a message from her about something or other.'

295

'Wasn't Vladimir worried when she disappeared?'

'Her servants told him she'd gone with another lover – that's when he found out that she'd cheated him – but they didn't know who it was. Oleg claimed that he'd meant to tell him, but forgot in the press of more urgent business.'

'What an extraordinary way to behave!' Gytha exclaimed. 'Is he always so casual about his taking of Vladimir's property?'

'Yes. Don't worry about it. Vladimir can manage him, and he usually gets the things back after a few weeks. He says Oleg has a deep-rooted need to test their friendship, or something like that. The only thing that might concern you is if Oleg is fool enough to take a liking to you, if you follow me . . .'

Gytha nodded. 'Yes, I see. So if he comes here, I must be courteous but distant.'

'That's it. Don't give him any encouragement, and don't accept any invitations to go riding alone with him. And look here – don't worry about Katya Andreyevna. It was all over before you came here, and she was just someone who provided a service that he needed at times. He leads a hard life, you know, and it's difficult for him to relax after a long summer of constant riding and fighting.'

'Does he know about the child?' Gytha asked.

'Child? I don't know. It's the first I've heard of her, so it may well be that he doesn't. Does she look much like him?'

'No,' Gytha replied thoughtfully. 'Not at all. Thank you, Gleb.'

He made her a smiling bow as he rose to his feet, and watched her leave the room with relief written all over his face. He then shouted for Onesifor, and sent his *druzhina* out to search the city again for Ekaterina-Katya, but again with no success.

Gytha's altar cloth was finished, and she began on a cope, designing small panels to go in concentric rows across it, each depicting a saint, with St Theodore Stratilates, the brother saints Boris and Gleb, St Vladimir of Kiev, St Basil the Great, St George and St Nicholas prominent among them, representing the patrons of the bishop, Gleb, Vladimir and Rusland. For the centre of the back she drew a design of the Holy Cross wreathed in flowers, and gave all her drawings to Brother Isak for his approval and comments. He was pleased with them, particularly by her choice of saints, and, although he did not say anything about it, she noticed that he lingered a little over the small representation of the Patriarch Isaac which she had included in thanks for the help he had given her during her first months in Novgorod.

'Bishop Fedor approves them,' he added as he returned them to her a few days later. 'He says you should have been named Dorcas for your skill with a needle. You do much good in keeping your ladies occupied with work for God's church. Laziness is the mother of evil!'

Gytha smiled at this echo of Vladimir's words to her, and occupied several afternoons in transferring her designs to the fine fabric that Sadko had obtained for her especially for this project, and deciding on the colours and stitches to be used.

A few days later she was sitting with Mildyth and Yevpraksia in the corner room, each making a start on one of the panels. They had returned from church and broken their fast, and the other ladies had gone to the bath-house. Mildyth and Yevpraksia were gossiping about some mild little scandal or other, and Gytha was daydreaming, wondering where Vladimir was, what he was doing, whether, by any chance, he was thinking of her, when a knock at the outer door heralded one of Gleb's messengers, who requested the Princess to join his master in his office, as some good news had just arrived.

Gytha folded her work and laid it carefully on the table, smoothed her gown, and darted a questioning glance at Mildyth, who nodded, signifying that her head-rail was on straight, for she had changed into her more comfortable Varangian garb after church. The messenger sped ahead while Gytha followed at a more dignified pace – Gleb did not call his messengers *bye-guni* or runners for nothing – wondering what the news might be. Perhaps there was a letter from Vladimir, although Gleb usually sent her any note which came for her, and saved his own letter for reading aloud after dinner. When she reached the office door, the *druzhinik* on duty opened it, announced, 'Princess Gita, Lord Prince,' in a subdued roar, and stood aside to let her pass, then shut the door after her.

Gleb, who was lounging in his great chair, stood up as she entered, and gestured towards the window, but it was a dull, overcast day, threatening snow, so little light penetrated the double panes of mica, and it was a full second before she made out a dark figure standing there looking at her. It was Vladimir. The shock of joy was so great that she ran to him, her face lighting up with pleasure, crying his name with such spontaneous feeling that Gleb raised his eyebrows and gave a rueful little grin, perhaps thinking that he had nobody who was ever as pleased as that to see him.

Vladimir's arms closed round her, and he looked into her shining face with a faint frown, as if he was puzzled. 'Your eyes are full of Christmas candles!' he said softly. 'Are you so glad to see me?'

'Of course! I'm so happy you're here! I was just sitting upstairs, wondering where you might be, and here you are! How are you?'

'Tired, stiff, hungry, and glad to have arrived. Are you well?'

Gytha's little bubble of joy broke at the last three words, and her eyes dropped before the dark, unfathomable gaze which searched her face. 'I'm sorry,' she whispered. 'I prayed so hard, but . . .'

'You don't think I'm the sort of fool who blames his wife if he doesn't get her with child the first time he tries, do you?' he asked quietly. 'God will give us children when and if He thinks fit. We can't alter that, and it's nothing for you to worry about, let alone apologise for. Didn't you get my answer to the letter you sent me about it?'

'Yes, but . . .' Gytha looked up, and found he was half-smiling, half-anxious.

'Don't worry,' he repeated. 'You're important to me for your own sake, not just for your potential as a brood-mare.'

'Somewhat coarsely expressed!' Gleb commented. 'You two will have a great deal to say to one another, so I won't detain you, Cousin. Perhaps we can talk at greater length tomorrow?'

On the way to their apartment, Vladimir said, 'Gleb was telling me how much he values your good sense. He's mentioned it several times in his letters as well – particularly over the business of the magician. He says you were the only one with any sensible advice to offer.'

'I didn't mean that he should kill the man!' Gytha sounded as troubled as she felt.

Vladimir, who was striding along, apparently unaware that she was having difficulty in keeping up with him in her long skirts, suddenly stopped and gave her one of his searching looks. 'Gleb's quite ruthless under his pleasant manner. We all are, for that matter, or we'd not have survived so long. Rusland can't be held by a weak hand, and neither can Novgorod!'

'Nor can any kingdom,' Gytha returned. 'They all have enemies without, and ambitious men within.'

Vladimir made no reply, but took her hand in a firm grip and held on to it until they reached the corner room. Mildyth and Yevpraksia rose as they entered, spilling embroidery silks from their laps, took one startled look at Vladimir, and scuttled out of the room with only the minimum of greeting, which seemed to amuse Vladimir. Gytha automatically gathered up the precious silks from the floor and put them on the table with the abandoned work.

Vladimir picked up one of the panels and studied it with interest. 'Is this your work?' he asked.

She took a quick glance at it, and answered, 'Yes,' for it depicted St Basil.

'It's beautifully done!'

'Englishwomen are famed for their skill with the needle. I'm no more than fairly good by the standards of home.'

He put down the panel, and said in an expressionless voice, 'England is still *home* to you, then?'

Gytha considered the matter, her fingers busy winding up a spool of silk, seemingly of their own volition. 'Only as some dear, long-lost place where I was happy, but can never go again. This is home now.'

He seemed, in his turn, to be thinking, and then he asked abruptly, 'Were you really as pleased to see me as you seemed?'

'Yes.'

He gave a little sigh, and turned towards the icon in the corner, kneeling rather stiffly, and Gytha dropped the silk and joined him. He slid one arm round her waist and drew her close, and they prayed together in thanksgiving for his safe return, and then he drew up two chairs before the stove, opened the door of it, and prodded the logs inside to a cheerful blaze.

'I've thought about this moment so often!' he said, stretching his legs in front of him and tilting the chair back on its hind legs. 'I've spent the last seven months travelling in every direction except the right one until I began to wonder if I was doomed to ride for ever over unending plains. Novgorod turned into a fantastic dream of domes and towers, with my fairy princess hidden away in the midst of them! The trouble with riding for long distances is that it gives so much time for thinking. I have to discipline myself, and make sure that I pray first, make my plans and alternatives, and consider what I should do if something else happens, then go over all that I did yesterday, whether it was right, what's likely to arise from it, and so on and so on. Only after all that may I let myself think of coming home, and you . . .' He broke off, suddenly aware that he was making, for him, a very long speech, and that Gytha was looking at him with astonishment in her wide blue eyes.

'I – I didn't expect you would think very much about me!' she stammered, sternly suppressing a fleeting speculation about whether he had ever thought so about Katya in the past.

'You're never very far from my thoughts. Do you ever think about me?'

'All the time.'

He was silent, and appeared to be trying to adjust to something unexpected. After a while, he said hesitantly, 'I don't find it easy to speak of my inmost feelings – lack of practice, I suppose. My mother died when I was very young, and my father is uneasy about emotion. There are many things I want to say to you, but I don't know how to say them.'

Gytha was experiencing an extraordinary feeling, which started somewhere very deep inside her and was swelling rapidly until she could hardly breathe. Some of it seemed to escape in the form of an explosion which burst from her lips as 'I love you!' in a very shaky voice.

Vladimir's thin, anxious face broke into a smile. 'That's what I was trying to say! That's the gist of it, anyway!'

There was a lengthy period of silence between them, broken only by the sounds of Efrem bumping up the stairs with his master's baggage, then moving about in the room beyond the stairhead, the small sounds of the logs burning in the stove, and the distant babble of voices from the market.

'Why are we sitting here?' he asked eventually. 'I'm bone-weary, but I think I can summon the energy to stagger as far as your bed, if you'll help me. What do you say?'

Gytha said nothing, but smilingly gave him a solicitous arm and led him to her room, where he soon discovered that he was not quite as exhausted as he had thought. It was some time before he fell asleep in the middle of a sentence, and Gytha, very contented, leaned on one elbow, enjoying the pleasure of simply looking at him. After a while she slipped out of bed, dressed, and went to sit by the stove in the corner room, savouring her happiness and doing her embroidery.

It was late afternoon when he emerged, kissed her in passing, and went off to the bath-house. When he reappeared, he looked much refreshed. He said that, as it was so late, he would not eat now, but wait for dinner, and sat down again by the stove, apparently content to watch Gytha and her attendants at their sewing.

'Have you been out today?' he asked presently

'To church this morning, and for a walk about the market this afternoon,' she replied. 'It was snowing, so we didn't stay out long.'

'Are you well?' he asked after a few minutes' silence.

'Very well.'

'Well enough to go on a journey?'

Taken by surprise, she hesitated, for she had not yet grown

used to the idea of winter as a good time to travel. In England or Denmark, people stayed at home in the bad weather and travelled in the summer, when the roads were dry.

'Where to?' she asked.

'Kiev.'

'Kiev!' she echoed, her face lighting up. Everyone at Gleb's court spoke of Kiev as if it were the centre of the world, and she had often wished that she might go there.

'My uncle and my father would both like to meet you, and I thought you might like to see the city,' he went on. 'It's a long journey. I'd not ask you to undertake it in summer, what with the heat and the insects, and the long portage from the lake to Smolensk, but it's easy in winter, along the River Road.'

'Sigurth talked of the River Road,' she said reflectively. 'I couldn't think what he meant until he explained. Is it really possible to go all the way to Kiev on a river?'

'Rivers.' He stressed the plural. 'Almost. There are stretches overland, but they're only portages, and the ships are taken over them on rollers. Sigurth was the shipmaster who brought you from Denmark? He's been to Rusland many times, and I think I know him. He is the master with the dragon-head prow to his ship?'

'Yes. He calls her *Sea-Fafnir* because, in the legend of Sigurth, he slew a dragon called Fafnir.'

'He's taken her many times to Kiev, and even to Constantinople, I believe, which is much further. It takes a determined man to portage a ship like that past the seven great cataracts below Kiev. Will you come, then?'

'Of course! When shall we go?'

'After Christmas. Can you be ready?'

'Of course.'

Mildyth and Yevpraksia looked calculatingly at one another, their minds obviously busy with thoughts of new clothes and packing, and their faces showed a mixture of disappointment and relief when he said, 'Don't take very much with you. We can buy anything you need in Kiev, where there's a greater choice. It's an even bigger trade centre than Novgorod, and you'll find treasures from the south, from Constantinople and Sirkland there, as well as goods from the lands to the west – even from England, perhaps!'

'And nothing from the east?' Gytha asked, pretending surprise.

'There *is* nothing from the east, except horses and trouble!' he replied, sounding a little bitter. 'The Pechenegs live there, and the Polovtsy, and they produce nothing save destruction.' He looked very bleak and weary for a moment, then shifted in his chair, laughed, and said, 'Your ladies look apprehensive at the thought of the journey, but there's nothing to fear, my dears! A sledge runs fast and smoothly on ice, there are good inns where we may eat and sleep, and we shall have a strong escort – not that the Polovtsy or the Poles come raiding in winter.'

'Are we to go too?' Yevpraksia asked hopefully.

'Of course! How could I manage without you?' Gytha exclaimed. 'They may come, may they not?' turning to Vladimir.

'You must take all six,' he replied gravely. 'It's expected that a Grand Princess should have that number. There's more ceremony at the court in Kiev than here in Novgorod. I'll tell you all about it on the way.'

At dinner, he mentioned quite casually that Svyatoslav wished Gytha to go to Kiev, that they planned to go together after Christmas, and added a suggestion that Gleb might like to accompany them. 'Your father is not at all well,' he added. 'I'm sure he'd be pleased to see you.'

'I'd be as welcome as a plague of rats, no doubt,' Gleb replied, sounding quite disagreeable, 'and I'm sure it would suit your father very well to have me away from Novgorod while my father's ill. I suppose this was his idea?'

'He mentioned that he was looking forward to meeting his daughter-in-law, but said nothing about your going to Kiev,' Vladimir replied calmly. 'I'm not plotting against you, Gleb.'

'I didn't say you were,' Gleb replied. 'Are you ending our agreement?'

'Certainly not,' Vladimir replied firmly. 'I have a letter here for you from your father. I asked him to write it, to explain that it's *his* wish that Gytha visits Kiev, not mine or my father's. My father knows that she's . . .' He broke off and looked at Gytha, who quietly supplied 'A hostage.'

Gleb flung up his hands, and sighed. 'I think of you as a dear cousin, a charming and useful asset to my court, and a sensible adviser,' he said apologetically, 'but yes – the hard truth is that you are a hostage. I'm sorry.'

'I do understand,' Gytha said, smiling. 'I give you my word that I'll come back, and you already have Vladimir's. Perhaps Anastasia would like to come with us?' she ventured, for Gleb's wife had frequently complained that Novgorod was a boring place where nothing interesting happened.

'Go to Kiev!' Anastasia exclaimed, sounding quite horrified. 'No, thank you! I'm sure you mean to be kind in asking me, but I couldn't travel all that way, and I wouldn't feel safe away from my husband!'

Gleb gave a self-conscious smirk and patted her on the arm, in much the same way as he caressed his great deerhounds. 'There, there, nobody's going to make you go to Kiev – at least, not until I go there myself,' he said gruffly. 'I need you here!'

Vladimir made a little smiling gesture, as if waving away his own suggestion and Gytha's rider to it, and changed the subject. It was not mentioned again, except when Gleb, on at least four occasions in the next few days, stressed that he expected Gytha to return to Novgorod before the end of the winter. Gytha was surprised that he made no more fuss than that, but when she asked him if he minded very much, he replied, 'What can I do? My father orders it, and I don't want to quarrel with Vladimir. I do trust you both, despite Oleg's prophecies of doom!'

After dinner that night, she had expected that Vladimir would wish to be alone with her at once, but instead he attended Gleb's usual evening conference and, disappointed, she went too. After that, however, they were alone at last, and his lovemaking seemed all the better for the delay.

Afterwards he held her in his arms, and said, 'I suppose we should talk.'

'About what?' she asked sleepily.

'Gleb tells me that the woman involved in Izyaslav's plot to recover Novgorod turned out to be Katya Andreyevna, and she has a child which she claims is my get.' His voice was hard.

'Oh.' Gytha was wide awake now. 'Well – Gleb told me that she was your mistress, and then she went off with Oleg. Why do you let him take your things from you?'

He sighed. 'It probably sounds ridiculous, but he has a constant need to test our friendship, I think. You see, he's lived all his life in an atmosphere of distrust and betrayal, and he can't accept that I'll not let anything break our partnership.'

'Surely he knows that he can trust his own cousin?'

'That's the point – there's been no trust within the family these last ten years or more. Most of us can judge how far any particular member can be trusted, but Oleg can't. Consequently, because we have to work closely together, he's constantly testing me, and "borrowing" my belongings is a part of that. He returns them after a while. Kilikia, his mother, has never taken the slightest interest in any of her children except Gleb. Once he was born, she seems to have resented having any more children. Perhaps because of that, Oleg has little regard for women, so he thought Katya was a piece of my property, like a sword or a horse.'

'So he's returned her?'

'No. He told me that she left him a long time ago. There was some trouble between her and the bishop in his city, and she took a sledge and troika from Oleg's stables and went off without a word to anyone.'

'Later, she turned up here with a letter from Oleg's wife, and became one of Anastasia's attendants?'

'Yes, and from what Gleb tells me, she was plotting with Oleg against you and me, and with Izyaslav against Gleb.'

'I think she was using Oleg. He thought she was working for him, but she'd used that as a means of coming to Novgorod and gaining access to the palace,' Gytha said thoughtfully.

'Ah, yes – the conversation you overheard in the church. Why didn't you tell me about it at the time?'

'It was the day before our wedding. We had more important things to think and talk about. In any case, I thought it was just Oleg's and Ekat – Katya's spite against me, and I didn't want to cause a quarrel between you and Oleg just when you would have to go off to fight the enemy together. It was only after the trouble with the magician that I realised what her last sentence meant. Why did Oleg want to stop you from marrying me? Was it simply because I'm English?'

'To everyone in Novgorod you're a Varang, as are about two-thirds of the citizens, by descent at least. Anastasia's a Cuman, and nearly all the Cumans are our enemies. If the people of Novgorod had to choose between Gleb and me, the fact that I have a Varang wife would make a difference.'

'I remember that Oleg said something like that when I first met him, but I didn't think he could be serious.'

'You don't have Oleg's tortuous and suspicious mind! Are you very upset to find that I've had a mistress, and possibly a child that I didn't even know existed?'

'Not now. I was shocked when I first encountered her, but no longer. You told me there'd been women before. After all, I thought about marrying two or three men before I met you.'

'Did you now! Well, I suppose you were bound to have thought about it . . . I did more than think, though!'

'It's different for a man. You didn't marry any of them, nor did I, so neither of us has anything to be hurt or angry about.'

'You're very understanding.'

She gave a little shrug. 'Am I? I only know that what I have is too precious for me to risk losing it by senseless jealousy or quarrelling. We'd best say no more about it, but be happy together while we may.'

The relationship between them seemed to have been strengthened by this frank conversation, and they gladly spent long days together, talking, or walking in the palace galleries in snowy weather and riding out when it was fine. One day, a week or two before Christmas, they went hunting together with

306

part of Vladimir's *druzhina*, and shared an exhilarating chase after a pack of wolves which took them deep into the forest.

On the way back, riding easily a little ahead of their companions, they came upon a clearing, which was unexpected in this part of the forest far from human habitation. They checked their horses on the edge of it, both conscious that there was something odd about this circle of open ground.

'How strange!' Gytha exclaimed. 'There's no snow lying here. It's all been cleared away and piled under the trees – and what's that tall stone in the middle? It looks like a monument of some sort.' She thought vaguely of the stone crosses she had seen in Denmark, but there was no crosspiece on this stone, nor any carving on its shaft.

'It's a heathen temple,' Vladimir said, his voice hard and angry. 'That's an idol of Pirun, the so-called Thunder-god, and the flat slab is an altar for sacrifices.'

The *druzhiniki* had come up with them and sat silently on their horses, staring; several of them crossed themselves repeatedly.

'So near the city!' murmured Efrem, who always accompanied his master. 'And still in use.'

'I know that Christianity sits thinly on some folk, and the so-called Wonderworker proved that many of them can be perverted back to paganism, but I thought that his downfall and Bishop Fedor's priests would have brought them back to their senses. However, it appears that there are enough Pirun-worshippers in Novgorod to keep a temple of this size in use. Pull that idol down, and overturn the altar!'

The *druzhiniki* dismounted and ran eagerly to do Vladimir's bidding, all of them disgusted at finding this heathen scar on the land of Novgorod. With ropes and horses they pulled down the standing stone, and they levered the altar from its bed with branches, then lit a fire on it which shattered the frozen stone to pieces.

'Mark well where this is,' Vladimir said, surveying the result of their work with a grim face. 'Bishop Fedor will want to send priests to cleanse this place.'

When they reached home, Vladimir went straight to Gleb to

tell him of their discovery and Gytha went up to their rooms alone, feeling a strange uneasiness, almost a foreboding, about what had happened in the forest. She remembered the crisis of the Wonderworker's challenge, recalling how easily many of the townsfolk had been turned against the bishop and the Church by that one man's chicanery, and she shivered, wondering how many worshippers of Pirun there were in the city and what they would do when they found out what had happened to their temple. It was not long before she found out.

Once a week, Gleb held an open court to which anyone could come with complaints or suggestions. He sat on his chair of state with his advisers about him, and listened, offering advice, taking note of good ideas, and occasionally giving judgment. More often he appointed someone to look into the complaints, which were always followed up, and usually proved ill-founded. Vladimir was expected to assist in this princely task while he was in Novgorod, and Gytha usually accompanied him. She was sometimes asked for an opinion, particularly if the matter under consideration involved a woman.

At the court held a week or so after the discovery of the pagan temple, she was surprised to see Katya Andreyevna enter the hall with the other townsfolk, and shocked by the woman's appearance, for her clothes were torn and her hair hung in elf-locks about her face, which was bruised and swollen. Instead of taking her place with the other petitioners, she pushed to the front and pointed an accusing finger at Vladimir.

'It's your fault!' she shouted. 'Her blood is on your head! Pirun curse you for what you've done! You tried to destroy our god, and your blood's been taken and shed to cleanse our temple of your crime!'

Gytha closed her eyes for a moment, filled with frozen horror as she guessed what the accusations meant, but Vladimir stood up and took a few steps forward to stand before the woman, frowning and at a loss.

'What do you mean, Katya Andreyevna?' he asked sternly. 'Are you saying that you're an apostate – a pagan? Do you worship the false god Pirun?'

'Pirun is the true god!' Katya screeched. 'He'll punish you for what you've done! He'll strike you with his thunderbolts, and you'll burn! You'll burn!' She laughed hysterically, sounding quite insane.

'Calm yourself, woman!' Gleb commanded. 'How dare you come here threatening the Grand Prince with your nonsense! You're the one who stands accused! We know that you plotted with the exiled Prince Izyaslav to overthrow the good government of Novgorod and replace the rightful prince, myself, with the exiled Svyatopolk, Izyaslav's son. If that were not crime enough, you were in league with the false magician to bring about the murder of Bishop Fedor and all the Christian priests and monks, and enslave the citizens of Novgorod to your false god, endangering their mortal bodies and their immortal souls! By God, I don't know whether you should hang for treason or burn as a witch!'

'Izyaslav promised,' Katya said, suddenly calm. It seemed to Gytha to be an unnatural calmness, coming so suddenly after her hysteria. The woman's eyes glittered, and her face abruptly contorted in an ugly grimace. 'Izyaslav promised!' she hissed. 'He swore by Pirun to free us from your false Christ! He would give us back our freedom, and rid us of the black priests and their dead god! You destroyed our prophet – Pirun will destroy you!'

Her face twisted even further, and her voice rose to a wail as her accusing finger swung back to Vladimir. 'He only killed our prophet, but *you* destroyed our temple! You profaned Pirun's holy place! Only your blood could cleanse it again! Only your blood! Oh, my baby – my poor baby! The sins of the father – *you* profaned it, but your child – your child – my baby – my lovely Vassilia . . . !'

There was a shocked silence for a moment as her meaning dawned on her hearers, and then Gleb passed a hand over his face, shuddered, and said in a shaken voice, 'She's quite mad! This child she keeps raving about – it must be the one Gytha told me of – the one she claims is yours . . .' He looked at Vladimir.

309

'I destroyed the temple,' Vladimir said, his face white and sickened. 'Only my blood could cleanse it. She claimed the child was mine, so they took it from her and ... Merciful Heavens! A child! My men – to me! Fetch the horses! We must go and see ...'

He turned as he spoke to look at Gytha, his face twisted with horror. She read the look in his eyes and nodded gravely.

'Yes,' said Gleb weightily. 'It's clear what she meant, but you'd better go see if it's true. Oh God! I hope it isn't,' he added under his breath.

Vladimir looked at Gytha again, and she mouthed, 'Be careful.' He gave her a quick nod of reassurance, then hurried from the hall, following the dozen *druzhiniki* who had already gone to fetch horses. Efrem went after him, but returned almost at once and took up an unobtrusive stance just behind Gytha's right shoulder, fixing his eyes on Katya, who was swaying slightly and mumbling under her breath.

Gleb also watched her for a moment, and then said, 'Lift her on to a chair – fetch that one over.'

The chair he had indicated was brought from over by the wall and two of Gleb's *druzhiniki* lifted Katya into it, then stood one on either side of her as Gleb, pulling himself together, went on with his court as if nothing had happened.

'As I said,' he began,' the woman has several charges against her of plotting against Princess Gytha, against Bishop Fedor and against Lord Novgorod the Great, but she obviously is in no state to be tried, so we'll leave her to calm down until Prince Vladimir returns. The first case, please.'

The first scheduled case concerned a dispute between two citizens over the ownership of a narrow alley which ran between their respective workshops and yards. Each produced witnesses to support his case, and it soon became clear that nobody really knew who owned the alley. The arguments put forward by the two disputants became more and more complicated and heated, until everyone in the hall was following the to and fro of their exchanges with close attention.

Not quite all. Katya had been sitting slumped in her chair,

oblivious of her surroundings, but suddenly she lifted her head and stared at Gytha. Her face contorted again, and she hissed, 'It's your fault, you whey-faced Varang! It was your spying betrayed us, and it was you who told him to kill our prophet! You took my man – I'd have won him back, and made him believe my baby was his . . . My baby! My baby!' Her voice rose to a wailing shriek as the whole court sat or stood aghast, staring in horror at her. Then she put her hands on the arms of her chair and levered herself to her feet. It seemed to take an enormous effort, but she managed it, and stood swaying, still staring at Gytha.

Gytha remained seated, but tensed and braced herself for whatever the woman would do next. The guards, suddenly coming to their senses, both moved to seize Katya's arms, but they were just too late. She pulled a knife from among the folds of her gown, and lunged forward towards Gytha.

The guards dived after her, but she moved too fast for them. She had only a dozen feet to cover, and Gytha, rooted to the spot, had only time to think, 'But I haven't borne my son . . .'

Something flashed past her face, the wind of its passing chill against her cheek, and Katya suddenly jerked to a halt, staring blankly at Gytha. There was a puzzled look on her face as she dropped her knife, and clasped both hands about something which was projecting from her breast. Her eyes moved away from Gytha, then turned upwards as she slowly subsided into a crumpled heap at Gytha's feet.

There was silence in the hall, and Gleb rose to his feet, taking two cautious steps towards the body, a puzzled frown on his face. Then Efrem walked round Gytha, picked up Katya's knife, then dropped to one knee, turned her body over with an apparently casual movement, and plucked his own knife from her breast. Then he stood up, turned to Gleb, and said formally, 'Do you wish me to surrender to arrest by your men, Lord Prince?'

Gleb's eyebrows shot up, but he quickly recovered a properly grave expression, and said calmly, 'I think not. A clear case of a good servant defending the life of his master's wife, eh, citizens?'

Those citizens present who had realised what had happened voiced their agreement, and those who were slower of wit, or had not been able to see very well, followed suit as soon as the others had explained to them that Katya had tried to murder the Princess, and Efrem had stopped her by throwing his knife.

'An exceptionally good and accurate throw,' Gleb added coolly. 'Well done, Efrem!'

Efrem bowed and retired to his place behind Gytha, who had sunk back into her chair as her knees gave way under her. He smiled and shook his head when she tried to thank him.

To Gytha, the rest of the proceedings passed unheard and unseen as Katya's body was removed by the two men who were supposed to have been guarding her, their faces showing clearly enough that they did not assume that unpleasant task to be their only punishment, and Gleb continued with his court. She had been shocked by Katya's appearance and behaviour, and was only just beginning to realise how near the woman had come to killing her, but even that could not turn her mind from worrying about the poor, pretty child . . .

Vladimir returned after the court had ended and Gytha had at last been able to return to the corner room to pray, and then to sit quietly, waiting for him. She rose to her feet as he entered, still cloaked and booted, and stared questioningly at him.

'How are you?' he asked, taking her by the shoulders and gazing searchingly into her face. 'I heard what happened . . . What was Gleb thinking of, to leave her unguarded?'

'He didn't . . . It doesn't matter – Efrem was there. Thanks to him, she didn't come near me. I tried to thank him, but he wouldn't . . . What did you find?'

'Thank God for Efrem,' Vladimir replied, avoiding her eyes. 'Don't worry – I'll see to him. Come to the stove, sweetheart – I'm so cold!' He opened the stove doors and huddled over the fire for a few minutes, then unfastened his cloak and let it fall to the floor. 'It was as she said.' He looked at Gytha, his face drawn with the pain of what he had seen. 'They'd murdered the poor child – there was blood everywhere. I wouldn't have believed that there could be so much from one small body.' He shuddered.

Gytha put her arms round him and held him close, and somehow they sank together to the floor. 'Poor little thing,' she said. 'Perhaps it's better than growing up with that woman, though. She'd have taught her the same evil, turned her into a pagan witch . . .'

'Yes.' Vladimir sighed. 'I've seen so many bodies before, on the battlefield – you'd think that the sight of one more would hardly bother me . . . It's not knowing, I suppose. She might have been my daughter. If she was, I failed her. A father should care for his child, but my actions led to her death . . . her horrible death . . .'

'It wasn't your fault,' Gytha said firmly. 'Everyone who was there when we found the temple agreed that it should be destroyed. How could we know that the pagans would sacrifice a child? What will happen to them?'

'The *posadnik*'s men are out hunting them, with most of our combined *druzhiniki*. The news of what they did to the child has opened some mouths in the city, and I think there's a good chance that the leaders will be caught this time. I wanted to do something myself, but Gleb won't let me. He says that my personal involvement makes it unwise.' He gave a little twisted smile. 'I suppose he's right. The people mustn't see personal revenge mixed up with justice.'

'That's true,' Gytha reassured him. 'What will happen to them when they're caught?'

'They'll be tried. Gleb's all for hanging them, but Bishop Fedor insists that heresy outweighs murder and he's claiming them. I expect it will be lifelong imprisonment.'

'What will happen if Gleb insists that they're his responsibility?'

'He won't. The *posadnik* agreed with the bishop, and, don't forget, Gleb doesn't rule Novgorod – he can only advise and protect. I suppose it's as well – Gleb might be too incensed on our behalf to do them justice. Oh, God in heaven, Gytha! If only I knew whether she was really my child!'

'Would it help if you knew?' Gytha asked hesitantly.

'Yes, I think it would. I'd know how I should feel. As it is, I'm confused, and that makes it worse.'

'She couldn't have been yours,' Gytha stated flatly.

Vladimir looked into her face, startled. 'How do you know?'

'You're very dark haired and so, I suppose, was your mother. Is your father dark?'

'Yes, as was my grandfather. All the family are, excepting Svyatoslav's sons. Aunt Kilikia, their mother, is as fair as butter . . . What are you saying, Gytha?'

'That the woman was as dark as you, so how could the two of you have a golden-haired child?'

He stared at her for a moment, the strain slowly fading from his face, then, eventually, he said, 'Oleg,' and grimaced. 'Poor little thing. A father who would never care for her – a bastard girl, no use to him – and a mother who was a witch and a whore!'

'Perhaps Oleg didn't know about her . . .' Gytha ventured.

'Had Katya borne him a boy, he'd have recognised him, but not a girl. I suppose that's why she tried to foist her on me. I'll ask Bishop Fedor to have prayers said for her soul, poor child.'

'Did you love Katya very much?' she asked tentatively.

He pulled a face, and said, 'I was young and foolish. She dazzled me at first, until I found out how selfish and greedy she was.'

'We all fancy ourselves in love a few times when we're young,' she observed.

'You too?' he asked curiously.

'Of course. Nothing came of it, but I dreamed of marrying each of them in turn. I know now it was only infatuation, but it seemed very serious at the time.'

'Yes, it does seem so, until you find the real thing.' He looked at her with that piercing gaze which she had always found so intimidating, but this time she met and returned it with complete understanding.

Kiev

Chapter Fourteen

Despite Mildyth's head-shakings and anxious frowns, Gytha's best gowns and ornaments were packed in great wood and leather chests in good time, and the expedition set out for Kiev a few days after Christmas. Their baggage was tied firmly on a large sledge and covered with a sheet of wadmal, well lashed down. Gytha and her attendants travelled in three special sledges with padded seats, roomy enough for three people to sit abreast, well supplied with fur rugs and cloaks and pillows for comfort, and almost completely enclosed within a stout wooden framework covered with leather, with mica-covered windows to let in some light. The driver sat on a raised bench in front, and controlled his three cobby little horses by means of reins sewn with silver bells, which set up a fine cheerful jingling as they drew away from the palace, threading their way across the market and down on to the frozen river.

They had all attended church before setting out, but Bishop Fedor did them the honour of coming across from Sophia Side to stand on the quay with Gleb, ready to bless them as soon as their escort of Vladimir's *druzhina* had formed up round the sledges, their mounts breathing great clouds of steam in the frosty air.

'We'll be back before the thaw,' Vladimir said to Gleb, with a deliberation which made it a promise rather than just a remark.

Gleb's horse fidgeted, although its rider appeared at ease. He patted its neck and replied, 'Unless my father has some trick or other up his sleeve.'

'I'll take Gytha to Kiev at his command,' Vladimir said firmly, 'but nowhere else. I'm well aware of his liking for making trouble between members of the family, and Gytha returns to Novgorod before the thaw, whatever he says. I want to know that she's in the safest place before I return to Poland.'

'I'd rather you both stayed here until then,' Gleb said frankly. 'It's not that I don't believe that you mean to bring her back, but Oleg will make an inordinate fuss when he hears that she's gone to Kiev, and he'll come nagging me about it. I don't trust my father, either – there's more reason behind this than just a desire to meet your wife.'

'*Honour thy father and thy mother*,' Bishop Fedor quoted a trifle sententiously. 'A difficult commandment, in your case,' he added drily. 'The ladies appear to be ready, and your *druzhina* in position.'

Peering out from her sledge, Gytha thought that Novgorod looked like a fairytale city that morning. Clean, crisp snow capped the domes of St Sophia's and all the myriad other churches, crowned the walls, and decked the gables of the houses. The sky was a bright, clear blue, and everything sparkled with frost and sunlight.

'Madness to travel in winter!' Mildyth grumbled quietly. 'We'll freeze to death, and what if the ice breaks?'

'Why should it,' Gytha asked. 'Everyone in Rusland prefers to travel in winter, so why should we object? Look how many other folk in sledges are out on the river! Why should we fear the ice breaking when they don't?'

Bishop Fedor, who had been talking to Vladimir and Gleb on the quay, suddenly flung back his robe, lifted his hands in an attitude of prayer, and addressed Heaven in his clear, carrying voice, calling down blessings on Prince Vladimir, his wife and his companions on their long journey, and pronouncing anathema on anyone who sought to hinder or attack them.

'Attack!' Mildyth exclaimed, naturally singling out the one ominous word in the prayer. 'Those Cumans and Pechenegs and Poles will attack us, and we'll all be murdered and raped and robbed!'

'As long as it's in that order,' Gytha said mischievously, 'we've little cause to worry! You know very well, Mildyth, they don't raid in the winter, and look how strong an escort we have.'

'There must be danger, or we wouldn't need so many,' said Mildyth in her most gloomy tones.

Yevpraksia, who was sitting on the other side of Gytha, clicked her tongue reprovingly. 'Such nonsense!' she said. 'This is quite a *small* escort for a Grand Prince and his wife. When Prince Gleb travels, he has *twice* as many, and *three* times if Princess Anastasia goes with him!'

Vladimir, meanwhile, had taken his leave of Gleb and the bishop, mounted his horse and moved to the head of the escort, and the cavalcade set off, the sleigh-bells giving warning to skaters to clear the way.

Gytha had often travelled up the river to Lake Ilmen on hawking and fishing expeditions, but not in midwinter. It was difficult to see where the banks of the river were, for snow was lying several feet deep over everything, and the countryside stretched out to the horizon, flat and virtually featureless. Only an occasional clump of alders or willows indicated where land met ice, and Gytha, thinking that the Volkhov was a very great river, wider than the Thames at Barking, wondered if the other rivers on which they would travel would be as broad and powerful.

The ice was smooth, for the *veche* of Novgorod sent men to clear the river of obstacles during the summer, so there were no rocks or fallen trees, half-submerged, to snag a runner or overturn a sledge. As long as the daylight lasted, Gytha and her ladies could sew, tell stories and even read, for she had brought books with her, and the two of her other attendants who were literate travelled one in each of the other sledges.

The hours of darkness were the most trying. The days were so short at that time of year and in that latitude that it was necessary to start and finish each day's journey in the dark, with every horseman carrying a flickering horn lantern, and others tied to the arch over the middle horse of each troika. At first it was fascinating to glide along in the dark, the runners hissing over the ice, the horses' hooves muffled by the snow, the gleaming lanterns like glow-worms on either side, and the snow sparkling softly in the fitful moonlight, but the fascination soon gave way to tedium. There was nothing else to see, nothing to do but talk and suffer cold and cramped limbs for hours on end, until the night's stopping-place was reached and the ladies could stagger out into the more than welcome light and warm stuffiness of an inn or, on several occasions where no town was near, the doubtful shelter of leather pavilions.

Lake Ilmen was reached and crossed, and their route followed the River Lovat, which flowed into the lake on the other side. From its headwaters, there was a long overland stretch across to the Dnieper at the city of Smolensk, which Gytha thought must be a great problem for shipmasters in summer, but was easily traversed in winter, the sledges gliding smoothly over the frozen snow on the well-worn portage route.

'Do they really bring ships all this way?' asked Mildyth. 'However do they do it? It must be as far as it was from Lake Ladoga to Novgorod!'

'On rollers, with teams of horses,' Yevpraksia replied. 'Our little draught-horses may not look much, compared with the great creatures the soldiers ride, but they're very strong, and they pull the ships over here with no trouble. The cargoes are carried in wagons, or on sledges, of course. Once they're across and on the Dnieper they can sail all the way to Kiev, hundreds of miles, and on to the sea, with some more shorter portages, and all the way across the sea to Tsargrad, if they want!'

'Tsargrad,' Mildyth repeated. 'I can't get used to everywhere having so many different names! Why can't everyone call it Constantinople?'

When they reached Smolensk, Vladimir said that they would stay for a few days' rest at the palace of the Grand Prince of the city, his uncle Vyacheslav. He greeted them with due ceremony but a complete lack of enthusiasm, and sighed deeply as he watched them take the customary bread and salt.

'You won't be staying long, will you?' he asked mournfully.

'Only a couple of days, to allow Gytha and her ladies to uncramp their limbs and see a little of your city,' Vladimir replied.

Vyacheslav sighed again. 'There's not much to see,' he said.

'Everything's under snow, and none of the stoves will burn properly. The firewood's all either green or damp. You won't be at all comfortable.'

'We'll manage very well,' Vladimir replied soothingly. 'We've not come to cause you any trouble, Uncle – just to rest a little.'

'Why is your uncle so sad to see us?' Gytha asked as soon as she and Vladimir were alone together in the room they had been allocated.

'He's a little afraid of me, I think. Did you notice how he starts every time I speak to him!'

'Why should he be afraid of you?'

'It's not me, really, but my father. Vyacheslav is the fourth brother, and I think his elders teased and bullied him when he was a child. They – Izyaslav, Svyatoslav and Vsevolod – were always quarrelling among themselves, and I think poor Vyacheslav was caught up in it like a bone between the dogs – each of them demanding his support, when all he wanted was to be left in peace. He's a good man, but a timid one, compared with the rest of the family. I think he'd hate the others, if he could find the energy! He rules Smolensk well, but the effort leaves him too exhausted to do anything else.'

Gytha found this to be quite true. Vyacheslav certainly attended to the affairs of government well enough, but otherwise did nothing but sit by the stove in one room or another, either dozing or complaining mildly about the weather, the servants, the food or the firewood, the latter being his particular *bête noire*.

On one occasion, finding himself alone with Gytha, he said confidingly, 'You seem a good-hearted little thing, my dear. Don't let your husband bully you, will you? He's kind enough at present, but his father and his grandfather were bullies, and so are his uncles – well, apart from me and Igor, that is! I wouldn't trust the others the length of my little finger. I wouldn't go to Kiev, if I were you. Svyatoslav's the worst of the lot. You should go and live with Igor. He's my younger brother, you know, and he lives right away in the south-west and has nothing to do with the rest of us. He's quite honest and pleasant – at least, compared with the rest of the family . . . Oh dear, here comes Vladimir back again . . .' He closed his eyes firmly and appeared to fall asleep.

Gytha was glad to leave Smolensk. They were seen off by Vyacheslav with, if possible, even less enthusiasm than they had been welcomed. 'I shouldn't go on,' he said, shaking his head. 'It's a long way. You won't like it in Kiev. Well, God go with you, if you must. Goodbye.' He went back into his palace, huddling his robe about his ears, before Gytha's sledge had even started to move.

From Novgorod to Smolensk, Vladimir had ridden with his *druzhina*, and Gytha, disappointed, had exercised considerable self-control in not asking him to ride in the sledge with her. As they were about to leave Smolensk, however, he had asked very formally if he might sit with her, and she had gladly rearranged her ladies in the other sledges so that she might be alone with him.

'He seems so sad and disappointed in life,' she remarked as the sledge glided down the slipway on to the frozen Dnieper.

'He feels himself to be slighted and left out,' Vladimir observed. 'Smolensk is a rich and important city, but less so than Kiev and Pereislavl, and it's not the city he should be ruling, according to Yaroslav's plan. When Svyatoslav took Kiev, my father should have moved to Chernigov, and passed Pereislavl to Vyacheslav. For some reason – greed, probably – Svyatoslav kept Chernigov himself as well as Kiev. Vyacheslav, rather unfairly, blames my father for not giving him Pereislavl, even if it meant leaving himself without a city. But that's more than enough about my impossible uncles! Did you have any?'

'Yes, I had five uncles,' she replied. 'One more than you.'

Vladimir grinned ruefully. 'But not such villains as mine, I hope! Tell me about them.'

'Svein was the eldest,' she said, her face unconsciously taking on a sad expression as she remembered the six handsome, intelligent men who were Godwin's sons, all of them so full of life when she had known them, and now all dead, except, possibly, the youngest. 'He carried off an abbess and lived with her, but refused to marry her, and he killed his cousin. His father sent him on a pilgrimage to Jerusalem, and he died in Constantinople, on his way home.'

'Reasonably villainous,' Vladimir commented. 'And the next?'

'Tosti was next, after my father. He ruled the earldom of Northumbria, in the far north of England, and he made the people there hate him so much that they rebelled against him and begged King Edward to give them a better man. He was exiled. He blamed my father for it, for no reason, and when the King of Norway invaded England, Tosti joined him, and was killed in battle, fighting against my father.'

'Two villains!' Vladimir exclaimed. 'I feel encouraged! What of the rest?'

'Gyrth and Leofwin were good men. I loved them both very much. They were killed, fighting beside my father against the Normans. The youngest, Wulfnoth, was taken as a hostage by William of Normandy, many years ago. I hardly remember him. I hope he may still be alive.'

'I wish I could have known your father, and those two uncles whom you loved,' Vladimir said, slipping his arm round her waist. 'Your father must have been such a great man and a fine soldier. We need his like here in Rusland. I'd gladly exchange all my uncles, and my father, for one such man as your father!'

'Why must you go to Poland again?' she asked a few minutes later, her mind having followed the train of thought begun by his reference to her father as a soldier. 'I thought you were needed to fight the tribes from the east.'

'It's part of the treaty we've made with King Boleslaw. I'm to help him fight the Germans for one summer. Oleg and my father must manage our eastern borders. They're both very competent commanders, and manage to work together in battle, but nowhere else! I'll be fighting Izyaslav and his son as well, I expect – they've taken refuge with the German emperor.'

Gytha shuddered. 'How any Christian prince could plan to

give Novgorod to the pagans, just so that his son could rule it!' she exclaimed.

'Almost as bad – he's been trying to persuade the Pope to support him! An Orthodox Christian seeking favours from the heretic Bishop of Rome!' Vladimir sighed. 'I sometimes wish that I'd been born into a family of honest craftsmen – wood-carvers or stonemasons, for preference. Tell me about your childhood, Gytha. I want to know everything about you, and we have so little time to talk. We've been married nine months, and I still feel that we're almost strangers, although I love you so much!'

Nine months! Gytha thought. Oh, please God, give me a son! but she kept the thought to herself, and told him about her happy childhood at Waltham with her brothers and sister, about her lessons in Latin and French with Master Athelard, and about Father Turkill's mysterious visions.

'He said I would travel beyond the sunrise,' she said, frowning as she tried to recall the exact words, 'and that my father would be avenged through me.'

'I wonder what that means?' Vladimir mused. 'Perhaps he meant that you'll have a son who will be a great man, and everyone will remember his English grandfather because of him.'

Gytha was startled that his interpretation so exactly matched her own, and gladdened by it. 'I thought the same,' she said. 'But if that's what it means, he's very slow about making an appearance! My mother bore Godwin within a year of being married. Have you any brothers and sisters? You've never said . . .'

'Yes. At least, my mother died soon after I was born, but my father married again, some eight years ago. He's had four more children, but three of them are girls.'

'And girls are less desirable and useful than boys?' Gytha asked with a touch of bitterness.

'In some ways, but it's as God chooses, whether we have sons or daughters. I'd like some of each,' he replied equably.

Gytha was silent, thinking, for a while, and then, apparently

324

at a tangent, said, 'Prince Gleb doesn't help you with the fighting?'

'He does occasionally, if we're hard pressed. He's a brave fighter, but not a good commander of an army. His talents lie in the fields of government and trade. He loves Novgorod. It's his native city, and he understands and truly loves it. It would break his heart to leave, I'm sure, and that's why I have no wish to take the city from him if my father becomes Grand Prince of Kiev, although he still finds that hard to believe.'

'Is that why you wish me to live in Novgorod? As a hostage?'

Vladimir was quite still for a moment, his face assuming its old, shuttered, remote look.

'Gleb chooses to believe so,' he replied. 'It's more complex than that, however. I wish you to be in a safe place, and Novgorod is the safest we have. Also, there's better company for you there. I admit that Anastasia's not your equal in intellect, but at least she's civilised. Uncle Svyatoslav's *terem* is inhabited by females who are not suitable company for a king's daughter, and my father's household is not much better! Also, Gleb has no prejudice against women, and believes that an intelligent woman is every bit as good as an intelligent man. I expect you've noticed that he welcomes and listens to your opinion on important matters, not just the trivial ones. Most of the other men in the family think women are inferior and incapable of understanding important matters. Besides all that, at Suzdal you'd be very lonely. There are no ladies there, and all the women are brave, hardy creatures who fight alongside their menfolk when necessary, and have few womanly skills. I don't doubt you'd fight alongside me if the occasion arose, but I'd rather you had a better and a safer life than that. Gleb would never mistreat you, whatever he suspects about me and my ambitions.'

'Unless you try to take Novgorod away from him?'

'Which I shall never do, so the question doesn't arise.'

Gytha nodded. 'He's always very kind and considerate, and I like Bishop Fedor very much. Anastasia's an easy companion – she demands nothing but a little gossip!'

'So you have no objection to returning to Novgorod after our visit to Kiev?'

'None at all, unless you wish otherwise. I shall go wherever you choose, of course.'

'You don't find the thought of being a hostage disagreeable?'

Gytha give a crooked little smile, and replied, 'My uncle and my youngest brother are hostages to Duke William, and my aunt, my sister and my third brother, although under the protection of the Church, are almost equally in his grasp. My elder brothers are honoured members of King Svein's court, but I think they'd not find it easy to leave him! It would seem that I'm following a family tradition.'

'Tell me some more about your family – you've heard more than enough about mine!' he said, half-jokingly.

Despite these interesting conversations, which had made Gytha realise that her husband valued her mind quite as much as did his cousin Gleb, the books to read, the embroidery and the chatter of her ladies, the journey seemed interminably long and dull. There was little variety in the scenery to arouse interest. Gradually, larch, fir, spruce, birch and rowan gave way to oak, ash, chestnut, beech and hornbeam. The river became wider as one tributary after another joined it, and the right bank became perceptibly higher than the left bank. Eventually, the right bank became a high cliff, towering over the river, and the forest on the left gave way to open, rolling country, which stretched away to an infinitely far horizon.

'The steppes,' Vladimir said bleakly when Gytha asked him about the great plain. 'Two more great rivers flow through them, the Don and the Volga, and beyond that, for all I know, they go on to the edge of the world, although the Cumans say that the land where silk comes from lies on the far side of them.'

'I thought silk came from the Holy Land and the Sirkland round about it,' she remarked.

'Some of it does, but the best comes from the east. Do you remember the robe you wore for our wedding?'

'Of course! It's the most beautiful thing I've ever had!'

'The Silver Bulgars told me that it came from far in the east, from a country they call Kitai. I don't know how far that may be. I've only travelled to the Volga, and that's far enough for me.'

'Are the Cumans out there somewhere?' she asked, looking apprehensively to the east, where the rising sun made a blood-red pathway across the snow.

'And the Polovtsy and the Pechenegs and the Bulgars. They'll all be in their felt tents for the winter. They live by herding horses when they're not raiding our cities, and move from pasture to pasture. They have no towns or even permanent buildings. Look, do you see on the cliff there, in the distance before us?'

He pointed ahead and a little to his right, and Gytha saw that the sun had caught something which gleamed gold instead of the ubiquitous white of the snow.

'Is it a church?'

'It's the bell-tower of a monastery at Kiev. It's built on the rim of the cliff, and makes a fine landmark. It was the first monastery ever built in Rusland, and it's still the biggest and most important.'

'It's in Kiev? Then we're nearly there!' she exclaimed, and just managed to stop herself from adding 'Thank Heaven!'

Vladimir said it instead, and added, 'You must be as thankful as I am! It's very pleasant to travel with you, but it's an intolerably long journey to wish on you in midwinter. I had good reason to ask you to come, however. I'd better mount and ride now. The good citizens will think I'm crippled if I arrive in a sledge.'

The cavalcade halted at a little village on the left bank of the river, and the travellers prepared themselves for their arrival in Kiev, replacing the well-worn harness of the horses with fine trappings of coloured leather, decorated with silver bells, and richly embroidered saddle-cloths. Serviceable travelling dress was exchanged for rich robes, the *druzhiniki* all alike in costly black-dyed woollen over their ringmail, each with the lion badge of Suzdal on his left shoulder.

Gytha's ladies commandeered the hut of the headman of the

village for a dressing-room, and dressed Gytha and themselves in heavy court robes and *kokoshnik* head-dresses, painting their faces in the approved style for their rank. Gytha disliked this custom, and seldom wore face-paint in Novgorod, but Yevpraksia insisted that she must wear it, at least for her arrival in Kiev, so she submitted, but resolved not to conform more than she could help in this respect, for the paint was like a stiff mask and she hardly dared move her lips when she spoke for fear of cracking it.

When all were ready, the last short stage of the journey began, and the tall bell-tower with its golden dome came steadily nearer. Before long, Gytha could see other buildings around it on the cliff-top and running down towards the river, but all appeared to be part of the monastery. There was no sign of the city, except for a long wooden quay at the edge of the ice, a row of warehouses, and what looked like an extremely steep roadway running up through a crack in the cliff face.

'Where's the city?' asked Mildyth, puzzled. 'I thought Kiev was supposed to be a great city, bigger than Novgorod, but there's nothing but the quay, the warehouses, and that monastery!'

'It must be set back from the edge of the cliff,' said Yevpraksia, who had not been so far south before, and was very excited by the thought of seeing Kiev at last. 'There's a huge cathedral with *thirteen* domes, no less, bigger than our St Sophia's at home, and two palaces, and many other churches, and a stone wall with a great gate, and more houses than even Lord Novgorod the Great!' She was careful to give her home city its glorious title, even when expounding the riches of its rival and supplanter.

Vladimir was once more leading the cavalcade, and his standard-bearer was riding beside him, the great banner embroidered with an icon of St Basil blowing out in the wind as the horses trotted briskly along. Gytha saw him signal to the men behind him to wheel to the right, and the procession swung in towards the quay. As they did so, a squadron of horsemen debouched from the steep roadway and came trotting towards them. Every man in Vladimir's escort eased his sword in its scabbard in one well-drilled movement, but the leader of the advancing column called out a welcome as he approached. His men performed an elaborate manoeuvre which ended in half of them falling in on either side of Vladimir's escort, and the rest dropping into line behind as a rearguard.

'What do they want?' asked Mildyth nervously. 'Are they taking us prisoner?'

'No. I think it must be a guard of honour,' Gytha reassured her. 'See Prince Vladimir is talking to their leader, and the others are laughing and talking with our men. Prince Vladimir is the Grand Prince's nephew, and I expect they're particular about ceremony and rank in Kiev.'

'Oh, indeed!' Yevpraksia confirmed. 'Much more so than we are at home.'

And so it proved. The travellers were escorted up that extremely steep roadway, which was paved with rough granite cobbles to give the horses' hooves purchase, but meant a very rough ride for the passengers in the sledges. When Gytha saw how steep it was, she feared that even the strong little sledge-horses would not manage to drag their load up it, but men ran forward with more horses and harnessed them on to each sledge, six in front and two behind, in a few seconds, and the ascent resumed with hardly a check.

'They've put horses at the back!' exclaimed Mildyth. 'Why did they do that?' She had lived all her life in fairly flat country, in Essex, in Denmark and in Novgorod, and had never before seen a horse-drawn vehicle ascend a really steep hill.

'They must be to stop us slipping backwards,' Gytha said, and she was proved right, for the rear horses, which were much larger than the others, pushed from behind and steadied the sledge as the beasts in front strained to haul it up the incline.

When they reached the top, the full glory of Kiev was suddenly revealed to them. It was indeed a great city, greater than anything Gytha had ever seen before. A thick white stone wall surrounded it, buttressed by stout round towers and pierced by arched gateways, and above the wall rose a vast mass of elaborate wooden gables, crowning the hundreds of houses within. Gilded or green copper domes, set on tall, narrow drums and clustered in groups of three or five, marked the many churches. They were not the helmet-shaped domes of Novgorod, but were simpler, more like upturned acorn-cups. One group of no less than thirteen rose higher than all the rest, and Gytha realised that it must be the cathedral Yevpraksia had mentioned.

She was right, for after the cavalcade had skirted the city wall for some distance, it clattered through a great towered gateway, bigger than all those they had passed, which Yevpraksia said must be the famous Golden Gate of Kiev. Inside the city they traversed a broad street, at the far end of which was another wall, and, rising above that, the group of thirteen domes soared up from the roofs of the biggest stone building Gytha had ever seen.

'St Sophia's Cathedral of Kiev!' Yevpraksia announced with vicarious pride, crossing herself three times in its honour. 'See the domes? Our Lord Christ and His Apostles!'

'We seem to be going to it!' Gytha commented, thinking how small all the churches she had ever seen in England and Denmark would seem beside it. Even her father's minster at Waltham, or King Edward's at Westminster, which had once seemed so great and imposing, would fit easily inside this one with room to spare.

There was a gateway in the second wall, much smaller than the Golden Gate, but still wide enough for the cavalcade to pass through unimpeded, and Gytha assumed that this must be the kremlin of the city. An open stone-paved square lay before the cathedral's west front, which seemed amazingly long until she realised that two other buildings lay one on either side of the open arcade which sheltered the entrances to the cathedral. They were large and imposing, as befitted their situation, but much lower than the great edifice between them.

Before she could form any opinion about their use, Yevpraksia said in tones of awe, 'The buildings on either side are palaces, one for the bishop and one for the Grand Prince.

They're mostly built of *stone!*'

Gytha was impressed. In England and Denmark, only churches were stone-built, and not many of them, at that. It must be strange to live in a stone house ... Well, she would soon find out. Her sledge had passed the cathedral by now, and was coming to a halt before the grand carved stone entrance-staircase of the Prince's palace. She alighted with some relief, for she was both cold and cramped, and looked about her with interest, trying to behave as if she had often seen sights as impressive as this. She was conscious of a feeling of apprehension mixed with depression, for the early winter dusk was falling, and dark clouds were coming up from the east, robbing the scene of colour. The buildings and the kremlin wall were all stark black against the white snow, and the gilded domes of the cathedral, which must be catching the last of the sunset, were invisible, masked by the bulk of the building beneath them.

'The Grand Prince is waiting to receive us,' Vladimir said quietly in her ear. 'It's all very formal, I'm afraid. You may send your women to see your boxes to your rooms and start unpacking. They won't be expected to attend you to the hall of audience.'

Gytha's apprehension increased at the words *hall of audience*, and two fleeting visions passed through her mind from the past – King Edward, at ease in his pavilion, inspecting a loaf she had once baked for her father and not really knowing what to say to her, and King Svein, lolling in his great chair, sardonically amused by the formalities of receiving ambassadors ... The coming interview sounded very different!

The stairway to the entrance door on the first floor was similar to that at Novgorod, with soldiers of the Grand Prince's *druzhina* standing on each step, armed with tall spears and each wearing the trident badge of the senior line of the descendants of Rurik gleaming in gold amid the dark fur of his cloak. They reminded her of chessmen, for, their faces being obscured by the nasals and ringmail side-flaps of their helmets, they all looked alike.

The pillars of the canopy above the stairs were painted with wild animals, which seemed, in the flickering torchlight, to prowl in wait, ready to pounce. Within the doorway, the vestibule was similarly decorated, with the addition of huntsmen riding amid the beasts, as if to chase them out of the palace.

The vestibule opened into another, twice the size, and that into a third, even bigger. The atmosphere was chilly, despite the brick stoves in each corner, and she was reluctant to surrender her great hooded fur cloak to Mildyth, who was led away by a servant as soon as she had it safely in her keeping. A steward appeared to bid them welcome in the name of the Grand Prince, and the customary bread and salt were offered and eaten.

Vladimir, who had also removed his cloak and helm, turned to look at her, touched her *kokoshnik* as if to adjust it slightly, smiled, and murmured, 'They won't eat you, remember.'

She managed a faint smile in reply, but the silence and lack of bustle in the vestibules had further unnerved her, for it seemed strange that so many soldiers and servants should be standing still and silent, watching them. Heavy curtains of some glittering fabric were drawn aside at the end of the long room. Vladimir took her hand formally and led her forward, and they entered the hall of audience, the curtains swishing together behind them.

It was a very long hall, and seemed dark, despite the many torches burning in stands near the walls, for those walls were covered with dark hangings. Out of the corner of her eye she caught the occasional gleam of light on a hand or face, and realised that scenes were depicted on the hangings, but she could not tell what they were. A row of benches ran along either side, leaving a broad passage in the middle, and men sat on the benches. They were all dressed in rich, dark robes, ankle length and bulky with fur collars and bands, with gold chains and adornments gleaming, and great black fur caps on their heads, making them look inordinately tall. Every one was heavily bearded, and, as nearly all the beards were as dark as their clothing, they looked to Gytha like a double row of large bears, and she could not help smiling a little at the likeness. They rose to their feet, two by two, as the newcomers passed between

332

them, and bowed in a stately fashion.

Vladimir led her up the hall, neither too quickly nor too slowly, occasionally inclining his head to acknowledge an acquaintance. She turned her head a little from side to side, not wishing to appear to ignore them, for she had guessed that these were the important boyars of Kiev, and they were sure to be as easily offended as those of Novgorod.

There was a deep dais across the whole width of the far end of the hall, with a door in the wall at each corner. In the middle stood a large throne, ornamented with jewels and enamelled panels, and raised on three steps. Ranged on either side of it were ornate carved chairs, spaced out as if their occupants were not in the habit of speaking to one another. Only one was, in fact, occupied, but Gytha's attention went first to the man sitting on the central throne.

He did not seem to be particularly tall or stout, but was so swathed in robes that it was not easy to be sure of his size. He wore a jewelled dome-shaped cap, with a small cross-crowned ball on the top of it, and a rim of sable fur at its edge, a more elaborate version of the cap-crowns which she had seen Gleb and Vladimir wear on formal occasions. His face was expressionless, set in a slight frown, and his dark eyes, alert and watchful, seemed to be the only mobile part of his features. His right leg was propped up on a stool, and he held a walking-staff in his right hand, lightly tapping it on the floor, as if with impatience, as he watched Vladimir and Gytha walking towards him.

They stepped up on to the dais, and Vladimir bowed, not too deeply, and said formally, 'I bring you greetings from your eldest son, Gleb, Grand Prince of Novgorod.'

'You are welcome, Vladimir Vsevolodovich, Grand Prince of Suzdal, for your own sake as well as for the messages you bring us from our beloved and ever-dutiful son,' the Grand Prince of Kiev replied, his lack of expression unchanged.

'I bring my wife, Princess Gytha of England, to make your acquaintance,' Vladimir went on smoothly, turning towards Gytha as he spoke and drawing her forward a couple of steps.

'My uncle, Svyatoslav Yaroslavovich, Grand Prince of Kiev – and Chernigov.' He added the last two words with a distinct pause between them and what went before, as if they were an afterthought, but Gytha sensed that they were not, and the pause had been deliberate.

'The Princess is welcome to Kiev,' Svyatoslav replied, with no apparent enthusiasm. 'The Grand Prince of Pereislavl is also present.'

This was obviously intended to convey permission for Vladimir to greet his father, for he turned to the only other occupant of the dais, bowed, and said, 'Greetings, Father.'

Vsevolod nodded, said, 'Greetings, my son and my daughter,' formally, then stood up and walked forward to embrace Vladimir as if he were genuinely pleased to see him, and the two men hugged affectionately.

'My father, Vsevolod Yaroslavovich, Grand Prince of Pereislavl,' Vladimir said, bringing Gytha forward to be embraced in her turn.

Vsevolod was taller and more heavily built than his son, although still smaller and slighter than Gleb. His beard was short-trimmed like Vladimir's, but did not disguise a weak mouth and chin, and Gytha noted with misgiving that he did not quite manage to look her straight in the eyes as he made a suitable little speech of welcome.

'Yes, yes – all very touching!' Svyatoslav interrupted sourly. 'May I remind you that we have business to discuss? No doubt, Prince Vladimir, you and your companion will be glad to bathe and rest, and we'll see you again at dinner.' The sentiment was considerate, but the surly tone of his voice robbed it of anything but impatience to be rid of them. Nevertheless, Vladimir replied with suitably formal courtesy, and led Gytha towards one of the doors at the back of the dais.

It opened as if by magic as they reached it, a servant being posted on the far side, presumably with his ear to the keyhole, for this purpose. As Gytha passed through ahead of Vladimir, she heard Svyatoslav add, 'And Chernigov is none of your business!'

'I think my uncle's leg must be painful today,' Vladimir said quietly, sounding very slightly amused.

'Is he always like that?' Gytha murmured.

'Mostly. Sometimes he's quite friendly, and sometimes he's downright rude,' Vladimir replied lightly. 'In fact, he was exceptionally courteous to you, as he doesn't usually recognise the existence of females on formal occasions, except to require them to kneel when they're presented to him. I'm afraid that a woman's place is considered to be in the *terem* in Kiev – another reason why I prefer you to live in Novgorod. Our rooms should be along here somewhere . . .'

Presumably the accommodation allocated to them had always been used by Vladimir on his visits to Kiev, for there seemed to be more of his possessions about in them than could have been contained in the small amount of baggage he had brought with him. Gytha thought that the two rather bare rooms intended for her and her ladies must have been added on from someone else's suite, for there were marks on the walls and floors where furniture had been removed, and a locked door at the far end of the women's room cut off access from the rest of the palace. Mildyth complained that it wasn't proper for six women to have to go through Vladimir's rooms to get out of the apartment, but Yevpraksia and the others seemed to find it preferable to being lodged in the *terem*.

'It's very cold in there,' one of them said after a visit to her cousin, who was in the service of Svyatoslav's German wife, Kilikia. 'It really *is* a tower, and the rooms are so small that half of them don't have doors. The windows all have grilles over them, so they can only peer out through the small holes, and hardly see anything, and very little light gets in. We're much better off here!'

Gytha shuddered at the thought of being shut up in such a place, and was glad to find next morning, when the shutters were opened, that the windows of her room commanded a view northwards over the city to the forest beyond.

She and Vladimir dined with Svyatoslav and his household later that evening. It was a quiet meal, with no entertainment and little conversation. Svyatoslav, who seemed lost in his own thoughts, picked at his food, and the rows of boyars in their heavy dark furs talked very quietly among themselves, as if afraid to disturb him. They still reminded Gytha of bears, even in the better lighting of the dining-hall, and she wondered what would happen if she offered them honey-cakes, making herself smile at the memory of her wedding-feast.

'My new daughter finds us amusing, I think?' Vsevolod remarked in a questioning tone to Vladimir. 'She smiles to herself. I wonder why?'

'I was remembering our wedding-feast,' Gytha replied for herself, although the question had not been addressed to her. 'Do you remember the bear that wanted cakes, Vladimir?'

Vladimir laughed. 'It seems funny now, but I thought at the time that I might be entered in the chronicles as the prince whose bride was eaten by a bear before he had had time to bed her!'

'Very unfortunate,' said Vsevolod solemnly, then gave a sly grin which reminded Gytha of Svein, and made her wonder if that cunning old fox still lived, and, if not, which of his sons had succeeded in taking his crown – or were they still fighting over it? This led her to reflect that power seemed more important than family to men. She remembered how her own uncle had turned against her father, and how, in Rusland, Svyatoslav and Vsevolod had driven out their elder brother, and Vladimir's cousins, for all their friendship and the threats to their country which they could only hope to deal with by working together, were yet poised to fight each other for possession of one city or another . . .

'Now she looks sad and anxious,' Vsevolod remarked, as before, to Vladimir. 'Is she perhaps wishing the bear had preferred her to cakes? What can be troubling her, do you think?'

Vladimir frowned a little, caught Gytha's eye, and quirked his eyebrows questioningly. She felt obliged to answer again, and, being unable to think of a convincing lie, risked something near the truth.

'I was recalling the many happy family occasions I've known, like our marriage-feast,' she said, 'and thinking how sad it is when families and friends fall out over things which – which might be settled by discussion if everyone could be patient and reasonable . . .'

'And trusting,' Vsevolod added. 'Nobody trusts anyone else these days. I'll wager Gleb didn't want you to leave Novgorod, and he won't rest happy until you're back there. You're his guarantee that Vladimir won't attack him and take his city from him, you know!' His tongue flicked his lips and his eyes darted from Gytha to Vladimir to Svyatoslav.

'Gleb knows I've no designs on Novgorod, and he has my oath on it!' Vladimir said sternly. 'Don't try to make trouble, Father!'

'It's all he's good for,' Svyatoslav said suddenly, showing that, despite his apparent abstraction, he had been listening. 'Apart from fighting. He should confine himself to fighting, and leave government to those who understand it.'

'I should have Chernigov!' Vsevolod stated, scowling.

'You'd have the people in open revolt within a year!' Svyatoslav snapped. 'If ever I give Chernigov to anyone, it will be to Oleg or Vladimir, not you.'

Vladimir gave him a startled, alert look, and firmly turned the conversation with his father to the discussion of plans for the summer's campaigning.

Chapter Fifteen

Gytha felt that her visit to Kiev had not made a very auspicious start, and she hoped that things would improve, but they did not. She saw little of Vladimir, which was a great disappointment, for she had expected to spend most of her time with him, but she had several empty hours in which to consider the matter and came to the conclusion that, although he had said he loved her, he put his love some way down on his list of priorities. It was a bitter realisation but at least he had said it, and that was much more than she had ever dared hope for when she first met him. She wondered if there was some fundamental difference between men and women in their attitude to love. It seemed that it meant more than anything to a woman, but was only one among many things that a man cared about, and was not even head of the list!

Of course Vladimir could only rarely have time to spend in Kiev, and it was important that he should make the most of the opportunity to discuss matters of consequence with his uncle and father while he was here. It was some consolation that he did take the trouble to tell her about the discussions and the plans that were being made.

'Uncle Svyatoslav wants me to go to Poland again,' he said. 'They're planning a war, and I'm to help them with it, as part of the agreement made in our treaty. It's important that we try to make the treaty last as long as possible, for we have – Heaven knows! – more than enough to do with the Pechenegs and the Cumans to the east, without constantly looking behind us to see what the Poles are about! Uncle Izyaslav has left them and gone to Rome, so there might be a chance of a longer peace with them. I'm sorry I'm not with you very much, but perhaps you can find amusement in seeing the city, and maybe you could make friends with Svyatoslav's wife?'

She tried, but Kilikia was a German woman of vast size and virtually no conversation. She had fulfilled her duty in giving her husband five sons and a daughter, and now spent her time eating and praying. She spoke little Slavonic, and five minutes of platitudes exhausted her conversational abilities and patience. If Gytha tried to persist beyond that, she turned her back and waddled away to talk to her attendants in her own language, ignoring Gytha, who could do nothing but withdraw.

The city was larger than Novgorod, but seemed bleak. There were many trees, but they were deciduous, Kiev being so much further south than Novgorod, and their bare stark trunks and branches, black against the snow, were depressing. Gytha found herself longing for the soft dark greens of the northern trees, and the all-pervading scent of pine instead of the all-pervading smoke from the wood-burning stoves of hundreds of houses.

The shops and markets were interesting, as Vladimir had said they would be. She visited the various markets several times, seeking fine fabrics for her embroidery, and finding a great range from which to choose. The market stalls were permanent wooden huts, unlike the temporary booths in Novgorod, and were heated by braziers or even proper stoves. As in Novgorod, the traders grouped themselves by nationality rather than by the type of goods they had to offer, and Mildyth at last found out what a Silver Bulgar was, for there was a small group of them, trading in embroidered silk fabrics. These were remarkably fine and beautiful, and they came, not from Sirkland, but from a very far country on the very edge of the world.

'We come from far across the Volga river,' one of them told Gytha when, prompted by Mildyth, she asked about his tribe and the origin of his goods. 'They call us Silver Bulgars because we mine silver in the mountains, but we also travel far across the great desert to meet the merchants from Kitai, on the eastern edge of the world.'

'Are the Slavs like you?' Gytha asked.

'No. They're small-boned people, with yellow skins and slanting eyes, much like the Tatars. They bring this exquisite silk from their own land, which they call the Middle Kingdom, because they think it's the centre of the world.'

'But Jerusalem is the centre of the world!' Mildyth exclaimed indignantly.

The trader shrugged. 'To most people, their own home is the centre of their world. Probably they've never heard of Jerusalem. Their Middle Kingdom is many thousands of versts to the east, over mountains, through dense forests and great deserts. That is why the silk is so costly.'

'I can appreciate that,' Gytha replied. It was, indeed, very expensive, but she bought three lengths of the beautiful fabric, one to take back to Anastasia, one for Kilikia, and one to send to Vladimir's stepmother.

Kilikia accepted the gift ungraciously, commenting that the silk was thin and unsubstantial, which it was not. 'I suppose it's quite pretty, though,' she admitted grudgingly. 'I didn't know you'd summoned merchants to the palace. It would have been more courteous if you had informed me – I might have wished to make some purchases.'

'I bought it in the cloth-market,' Gytha replied a trifle sharply.

'You went out into a market?' Kilikia exclaimed. 'Well, I'd heard that Varangian women are careless of their dignity, and probably their virtue as well! I wonder your husband allows it!'

Gytha bit back an angry reply, and did not report the conversation to Vladimir, as she thought he might complain to Svyatoslav about it.

Vladimir was surprised that she had bought none of the lovely silk for herself, and insisted that she should buy cloth of one sort or another, including the most costly, for at least a dozen gowns. 'And some jewellery,' he added. 'There's some very fine gold and silver work to be had, and the traders expect us to encourage them. You've no need to be so frugal, sweetheart.'

She did as he wished, and filled her jewel-case with fine gold and silver collars, chains and brooches decorated with gem-stones and enamels, and filled a whole great chest with lengths of cloth, from soft woollens to the finest of the embroidered silks, and another with materials for gowns for her ladies, less costly, but still of very good quality.

The churches interested her, particularly the Desyatinnaya, the oldest surviving church in Kiev, which, strangely for Rus-land, had no domes, but seemed more like a western church. In fact it renewed faint memories in Gytha of the old church which had stood in Waltham before her father's minster replaced it.

Next to the Desyatinnaya stood the original palace of the Grand Princes, now used only to house the lesser officials of the household, and as a barracks for the *druzhiniki*. Gytha was im-pressed by it all the same, for it was stone-built, and she thought that Rusland must be a rich country to afford so much masonry-work, despite the constant attacks from her neigh-bours on either side.

St Sophia's, being only next door to Svyatoslav's palace, was the church to which the princely family went for the daily ser-vice. It was very large, and, internally, not unlike its namesake in Novgorod, with the same box-like compartments, intercon-nected by imposing arches cut through the internal walls. Every inch of wall-space was covered with frescos or mosaics in bright, glowing colours, and wherever she looked she found herself under the scrutiny of the painted dark eyes of saints, prophets, apostles and angels, all with the inscrutable faces and watchful-ness which made Vladimir seem so much like them. Sometimes during the day she went privately into the cathedral, with only one or two of her ladies, to pray for the souls of her parents and for her various other concerns, particularly her longing for a child.

One morning she went with only Yevpraksia attending her, Mildyth, who was to have come too, having a cold in her head. Yevpraksia had tutted a little at the idea of a Grand Princess going about with only one attendant, but her pride at taking first place for once led her to conclude that, as it was only to the cathedral and not outside, it might not occasion comment. She was given to stopping suddenly before any icon which caught her eye to say a prayer about some particular matter which might interest the saint it represented, and then had to scurry to catch up with Gytha, who seldom noticed that she was not immediately behind for several minutes at a time.

It happened that an icon of St Antony hung near the door by which the princely family entered and left the cathedral. Yevpraksia, who had a great liking for pork, but found it gave her indigestion, suddenly recalled that St Antony had some connection with pigs, and stopped to address him on the matter. Gytha, unaware, went on, passed through the vestibule and started up the stairs which led to a gallery of the palace.

She was thinking that, when she was a child, the idea of travelling beyond the sunrise had seemed very exciting and mysterious, but in fact her new life here in Rusland was much the same as it would have been if she had married an English nobleman. The country was very much larger and wilder, the buildings different, the language and the customs strange, but the life of a woman in a princely household was just as circumscribed and monotonous as it would have been anywhere else.

This morning I've walked about and prayed in the cathedral. Tonight there will be dinner in the Prince's hall. It was the same yesterday, and will be the same tomorrow, I suppose, and the rest of the time has to be filled with whatever occupations I can convince myself are worth doing. It's better in Novgorod, where at least the important people seem to believe I have a mind, and an opinion worth listening to . . .

The walls of the staircase were painted with a lively depiction of life in the Grand Prince's household, with hunting and battle scenes, processions, great men sitting in council, or being entertained by tumblers and mountebanks. Very few women were depicted.

A woman's place is in the *terem*, she thought, with a mixture of resignation and irritation.

At that moment, running footsteps clattered round the turn of the stairs above her, and a tall, fair-haired man in a fine sable cloak over riding-dress came running down. He stopped sud-

342

denly when he saw her, and exclaimed, 'Why, Princess! How are you?'

'Prince Oleg!' she exclaimed. 'I didn't know you were here in Kiev! How is your leg? I heard you'd been wounded, but it seems to be better, judging by the way you were running down the stairs.'

'I – er – I was coming to look for you,' he said rapidly, taking her arm, turning her about and leading her back down the stairs. 'Um – my cousin Vladimir has had a slight accident. His horse slipped on the ice and threw him. He's been taken to my house, and I came to fetch you to go to him.'

'Is he much hurt?' she asked, alarmed, and began to hurry downwards of her own accord.

'Not seriously, I think. He's bruised and sore, but doesn't seem to have any bones broken. He thought it best that you should be told before you hear any wild rumours, and he wants you to go to him. You know how tales grow with the telling! This way – my sledge is outside.'

He led the way across the vestibule that linked the foot of the stairs with the cathedral, towards the outer door to the square. As they reached it, Yevpraksia emerged from the inner door, heard Oleg's last sentence, and recognised both his voice and his fair hair, but his companion was hidden from her view by his tall, broad form in its bulky cloak. Her attention was on catching up with her mistress, for she had lingered longer than she had intended with St Antony. She set off up the stairs at the fastest pace consistent with her dignity as the (temporary) principal attendant on the Grand Princess of Suzdal.

Oleg's sledge was waiting nearby, and its driver, alert to his duty, brought it forward as soon as his master appeared in the arcade. It was snowing again, so it seemed sensible of Oleg to hurry Gytha into the sledge as soon as it stopped, get in beside her, and call to the driver to move off, even as he was spreading the fur rugs over her and himself.

'It's lucky that I ran into you!' he said. 'I've been asking for you all over the palace. One of your women told me where you'd gone when I explained why I wanted you.'

343

She accepted his statement without question, and turned her attention to where they were going. 'You said that Vladimir is at your house? You don't stay in the palace when you're in Kiev, then?'

'No. I'm here quite often in the winter, so I have my own place. The palace is often overcrowded when all my family gather together – or most of them, at least, for there are some who prefer to stay at home and avoid my father's bad temper.'

It was snowing heavily by now, so Gytha found it hard to tell where they were going. She thought they had gone round behind the palace, and they certainly left the kremlin by one of the minor entrances, not the main gate.

'Whereabouts is your house?' she asked.

'At the top of the hill down to the quays,' he replied. 'Vladimir's horse came down on the steep road, and they brought him to my house because it was so near.'

'But he is only bruised?' She sensed that there was something not quite right about his story. It sounded perfectly reasonable, yet there was something in his voice which roused a faint doubt in her mind. 'Are you sure you're not concealing something from me?'

He met her frowning gaze with serious blue eyes, and replied solemnly, 'He's not hurt, I give you my word.'

There was a ring of truth in the statement, so, accepting it, she turned her attention to trying to judge where they were in the city.

In a few minutes the sledge passed under a gateway in the city wall, and then, only a short distance further, turned sharply right under an arch and entered a courtyard, where there seemed to be a great bustle of arrival going on. Several wagons drawn upon the far side of the court were being unloaded by a small army of servants, while uniformed men of Oleg's *druzhina* were unsaddling horses and leading them off through another arch, presumably to the stable court beyond.

'Have you only just arrived in Kiev?' she asked. 'I wondered why I hadn't seen you about before.'

'I arrived early this morning. There was a bright moon, so I

344

rode on ahead of my baggage.'

She was helped out of the sledge and, as she was not dressed for the bitter outdoors, quickly ran up the steps and into the house, where, with proper ceremony, the *druzhiniki* on guard came smartly to attention, and Oleg's steward hurried to make his bow, two maidservants bringing bread and salt immediately behind him. All three were a little out of breath, having been caught unawares by the arrival of a guest, but performed their duty in the proper manner, despite their master's obvious impatience.

'If you'll just come in here a moment,' Oleg said, taking her arm and hustling her along into a small side room, 'I'll explain everything.'

The door closed behind them, and Gytha, who, being without her thick cloak and hood, was very cold, hastened to warm herself at the stove, but at the same time she demanded sharply, 'Explain? Explain what?'

'That Vladimir isn't here,' he replied calmly. 'He doesn't even know that I'm in Kiev.'

'Then what . . . Why have you brought me here?' she asked, bewildered.

'An impulse.' He shrugged. 'I came on you, alone, and took my chance! You've no business to be here at all. Your place is in Novgorod, as a pledge to my brother that your husband won't attempt to take his city from him.'

'Yes, I know about that, but I'm here with Gleb's consent, at your father's command, and I'm going back to Novgorod as soon as my visit is over. Vladimir has given Gleb his word about that, and about not taking Novgorod from him. Do you dare to doubt that Vladimir will keep his word? Or that I will, for he swore for both of us?'

'Let's just say that my father's health is – uncertain – and not improving. I, and all my brothers, prefer you to be safely in Novgorod. I trust Vladimir's word as much as that of any man, and more than most, but nevertheless . . . If anything happens to my father while you're away from Gleb's safe-keeping, who knows what temptation might assail your noble husband? As soon as my men are rested and ready and we've found you some suitable clothing, we'll leave for Novgorod.'

Quelling an upsurge of both temper and fear, Gytha looked deliberately round the room, selected the largest and grandest of the six seats in it, a carved chair of imposing appearance, and, as she soon discovered, minimum comfort, and sat down in it.

'I've eaten nothing but a little bread this morning, and I go nowhere before I've had a proper meal!' she said firmly.

Oleg looked a trifle taken aback, but soon recovered, considered the matter, nodded, and said, 'That's reasonable. I'll have something sent along to you while I organise matters for the journey. There'll be a guard on the door, and that window is barred and looks on to the courtyard, so you won't – er – be disturbed.'

He made her an ironic little bow, to which she responded with her most disdainful stare, and went out. She heard him speaking to someone outside – presumably the guard – and then there was silence.

A brief reconnaissance showed that the window did, indeed, look out on the busy courtyard and was barred, so she returned to her chair, pulled it nearer to the stove, opened the small doors to let out more heat, and thought over what Oleg had said.

If he really intended to take her back to Novgorod to ensure Vladimir's good faith, at least he would do her no harm. He said he had come on her alone, so had taken his chance. This was not planned, then – obviously not, for he had just arrived in Kiev, and had probably not even known she was here until he saw her.

Alone! Yes, where had Yevpraksia got to? Surely she was not in the plot – but there was no plot, if what Oleg had said was true! No doubt she had seen another icon requiring a prayer, and had lagged behind. As soon as she realised that Gytha had failed to return to the palace, she would raise the alarm. Surely she would have the sense to tell Vladimir, and he would guess that Oleg had something to do with it – or would he? Did he

346

know that Oleg was in Kiev?

There was a thump at the door, which was opened from outside by some unseen agency, and two servants entered with the food she had demanded. They brought warm water and a towel, a platter of bread, some butter, a dish of stewed meat and vegetables, a flagon of wine and a cup, and a bowl of sugar-plums. There was a spoon, but no knife, and when Gytha pointed out this omission, one of the servants said apologetically, 'My lord said particularly no knife. There's a small spoon with the butter. Perhaps my lady could manage with that?'

'Is this the best you have to offer a guest?' She eyed the food disparagingly, trying to think of anything which would cause a delay in Oleg's planned departure for Novgorod. 'I'm accustomed to more dainty fare! Have you no chicken? Why is there no white bread? This wine is red – (she had lifted the cover of the flagon to see) – I prefer white.'

The servants were obviously concerned and embarrassed, but they assured her that the food was exactly what had been prepared for Prince Oleg, and was truly all that was available, for the Prince had arrived a day earlier than they had expected.

She felt a little sorry for them and would never have behaved in this fashion under normal circumstances, but there must be some further delay, so she instructed them to go back to the kitchen and ask again that she might at least have white bread and white wine. They did so, but returned all too soon, looking quite frightened and stammering apologies that neither was available.

'Oh, very well – if this is the best you can offer. My husband's servants eat better than this in our household!'

The food was, of course, much the same as she would have been served in any Rus palace, and rather better than most of that she had eaten at Svyatoslav's table, for his kitchens were situated at a distance from his dining-hall. She ate it with good appetite, and was sipping some of the wine when Oleg returned.

'I would remind you,' she said coldly, before he could utter a word, 'that I am the daughter of one king, the niece of another and the cousin of a third, not the child of a mere Grand Prince. I am not accustomed to being served by a mere pair of hobble-dehoys, and with *black bread*!' She put all the scorn she could muster into the last two words. 'I've condescended to eat the poor stuff you sent me only for fear of being given nothing more this day. And where are my attendants? Surely you don't expect me to travel without them? You seem to have little idea of the proper way to treat a person of royal blood!'

'There will be two or three women to attend you,' Oleg replied, looking startled by her attack.

'I hope you've thought of the consequences of this lunatic scheme of yours,' she said reflectively, deliberately changing her tone. 'Do you really expect Vladimir to allow you to abduct me without doing something about it?' She looked up suddenly and caught a flicker of unease in his weatherbeaten face, and found herself almost enjoying baiting him. This surprised her, for she knew very well that Oleg was no fool, and had a violent streak in his nature, yet she felt no fear. Perhaps she would be wiser if she did!

'And what good will it be to Rusland,' she followed up, wise or not, 'if you and he fall to fighting one another instead of the Pechenegs and the Polovtsy? All those years of struggle to protect your country thrown away because of a foolish, impetuous action which was, in any case, totally unnecessary! Why don't you come to your senses and take me back to the palace? We could say that you met me in the cathedral and brought me to see your house.'

Oleg hesitated, and she could see that he was at least considering her words, but then he scowled and said sharply, 'I don't allow a woman to tell me what I should or should not do! What do you know about anything? Keep to your needlework and your prayers. Attend to your business, and leave me to attend to mine!'

'Isn't the safety and welfare of Rusland as much my business as yours?' she countered.

'Your business is to bear sons for your husband. It's a pity you don't get on with it instead of interfering in matters which

348

are beyond your understanding!' he snapped. 'Put this on – we're leaving at once.'

He dropped a capacious sable clock, furred both inside and outside, and a matching cap, at her feet, and waited impatiently, foot tapping, while she slowly put them on, his handsome face distorted by an angry scowl.

'You'll regret this!' she said warningly.

'Your husband should have left you in Novgorod,' he replied curtly. 'Come along. You can go with dignity, on your own feet, or put up with being tied and carried.'

'Is this how you stole Vladimir's mistress?' she asked coldly. 'Or perhaps you offered her more money? I can't imagine that she went with you for the charm of your manners! Of course, as you're so used to – er – borrowing his property, perhaps it hasn't occurred to you that a wife is hardly in the same category as a sword or a horse, or even a mistress? I can assure you that my husband won't treat this matter lightly. You'd be wise to think about his reaction when he hears that you've abducted and raped his wife!'

'For God's sake!' Oleg exclaimed, thumping the table with his fist in exasperation. 'I'm taking you back to Novgorod, that's all! Behave yourself in a seemly manner and hold your tongue and you'll come to no harm!'

'Why should I believe that?'

'Because I give you my word on it!' Oleg drew himself up to his full height, his blue eyes blazing, and looking every inch the outraged prince.

'Why should I believe your word when you won't believe mine or Vladimir's?' she flashed back at him.

For a moment he looked disconcerted, his mouth dropping slightly open, but he recovered quickly and roared, 'You don't know what you're talking about! Be silent, woman, and do as you're told, or I'll have you trussed and gagged!'

He obviously meant it, and she had no intention of losing her freedom of movement, so she swallowed her anger, raised her eyebrows in what she hoped was a look of cold disdain and rose to her feet with all the dignity she could muster.

349

'Don't complain afterwards that I didn't warn you!' she said, moving slowly towards the door.

Before she was halfway across the room, the door was abruptly opened from outside and Vladimir walked in, one of Oleg's servants uttering disjointed protests just behind him.

'Good morning, Oleg,' he said briskly, shutting the door on the servant, then turned to find himself face to face with his wife. He looked startled for a moment, then turned his head to look questioningly at his cousin.

Oleg scowled, flushed like a schoolboy, then burst out irritably, 'She has no business to be here!'

'Precisely,' Vladimir replied crisply. 'But in that case how does she come to be here?'

'I mean she should be in Novgorod, not in Kiev!' Oleg snapped. 'You promised Gleb that she'd stay in Novgorod, so why is she here in Kiev?'

'Because your father ordered me to bring her here,' Vladimir replied. 'However, I've not come here to discuss that. Do sit down, sweetheart. I'm glad you're here, in fact, as you really know more about the matter under discussion than I do, as I was not in Novgorod when it all started.'

'The matter under discussion is why you've broken your promise to Gleb!' Oleg snarled.

'No, it isn't, because I haven't. The matter I've come to discuss is your treasonable behaviour towards Gleb, and your plotting with Izyaslav and Svyatopolk to drive Gleb out of Novgorod and murder Bishop Fedor and his priests,' Vladimir replied coolly.

He tossed his cloak across a side-table, took the cloak and hat that Gytha had just taken off again, and piled them beside his own, and then looked enquiringly at Oleg.

His cousin's face was a picture of shocked amazement. His mouth had dropped open, and he seemed to have lost the ability to speak, so Vladimir turned away, gave Gytha a reassuring wink, and crossed the room to sit in the second most imposing chair, Gytha having subsided into the one she had occupied before, and they both stared expectantly at Oleg.

350

'Well?' Vladimir prompted. 'Katya Andreyevna – you do remember her, surely?'

'I – I thought you'd dismissed her,' Oleg stammered. 'What has she to do with this – this plot you're accusing me . . . Are you mad?'

'No, but I think you may be.' Vladimir replied in a very business-like fashion. 'You don't deny that you sent Katya to Novgorod with a letter from your wife, to gain admittance to Gleb's household and make trouble for Gytha?'

'Oh, that . . . I thought it would be better for Gleb if you didn't marry a Varang.'

'I'd guessed that. With Anastasia being a Cuman, and most of the Novgorodians having Varang connections, it's not difficult to work that out. You were seen and heard plotting with Katya in Novgorod twice, and your plotting has never been exactly subtle. This morning's fiasco appears to be a typical example!'

'What do you mean?' Oleg sounded injured.

'You were just about to abduct Gytha, weren't you?' Vladimir replied. 'Travelling-sledge in the yard, two female servants dressed for travel, *druzhina* saddling up, supply-sledge being loaded . . . A glance at your courtyard indicated to me that, having just arrived in Kiev, you were just about to depart again with a female companion. In here, I find my wife about to explode with fury, and you complaining about her not being in Novgorod. Obviously you're about to carry her off, and *I'll* give you credit for knowing the difference between my mistress and my wife, although I doubt if anyone else would!'

Oleg made a violent gesture, as if brushing aside a particularly annoying irrelevancy, and said, 'What are you talking about, me plotting against Gleb with Katya? It was nothing to do with Gleb. I was just trying to stop you marrying Gytha. I failed, and I've not done anything else against her. Why should I? The marriage took place, and I can't unmake it, so there's nothing more to be done, except make sure she stays in Novgorod as you promised. I don't bear grudges. If Katya's been up to further mischief, it's on her own account, and I know nothing about it!'

351

'So you deny that you were both working for Izyaslav?' Vladimir asked mildly.

'Why should I do anything for Izyaslav? He's my father's enemy, isn't he? I've not set eyes on him since the Kievans drove him out.'

'Since your father and mine drove him out,' Vladimir corrected quietly.

'Well, yes, I suppose so – but I've not seen or heard from him since then. I heard he was in Poland, but Boleslaw turned him out when you made that treaty with him, and that's all I know.'

'Then you haven't heard that Izyaslav sent a magician to Novgorod last autumn?' Gytha asked. 'He stirred up the people against Gleb and Bishop Fedor, and frightened a large number of them into reverting to the worship of Pirun, because they thought his god was more powerful than Christ. The plot would have succeeded if Gleb hadn't found a way to discredit and kill him.'

'Well, thank God for that!' Oleg exclaimed. 'But what has all that to do with me?'

'His accomplice, Izyaslav's agent in Novgorod, was your co-plotter, Katya Andreyevna,' Vladimir said. 'You sent her to Novgorod. You supplied her with a letter to Anastasia. You were seen and heard plotting with her . . . What are we to make of all that?'

'I knew she had some interest in paganism,' Oleg said slowly. 'She was in trouble with our bishop about it, and that's why she had to leave Tmutorakan. She offered to help me to stop your marriage in return for an introduction to Anastasia's household. She was no use at all . . . Completely failed . . . You mean . . . ' The full enormity of Katya's actions suddenly broke on him. 'You mean she *used* me? Why, that damned, lying, heathen bitch! How dare she! I was good to her, I took her on when you dismissed her, I gave her money for our child, and she *used* me against my own brother!'

'You should learn to distinguish which people are not to be trusted, and which people honour their promises,' Gytha put in with considerable satisfaction. 'Katya had already proved herself untrustworthy with Vladimir, as you well knew, yet you accepted her promise to help you. Vladimir had never failed you, by your own admission, but you won't accept his promise not to take Novgorod away from Gleb.'

'I . . . ' Oleg looked frantically about the room, as if seeking an answer among the furniture. 'Oh, damnation! I was only going to take you back to Novgorod – I wouldn't have done you any harm! Vladimir, you know I wouldn't make off with your wife!'

'You've just said that you were about to do precisely that,' Vladimir pointed out.

'No, I mean, I wouldn't have . . . Oh, for God's sake, man, you know damned well what I mean!'

Vladimir laughed. 'Luckily for you, yes, but I'm taking Gytha back to Novgorod myself at the beginning of next week. Have I ever broken my word to you, or to any one of your brothers?'

'Not that I know of,' Oleg admitted grudgingly.

'Where else would I take her, in any case?' Vladimir asked. 'Even Kiev isn't exactly safe these days. Your father's health's uncertain, and you know full well that, if anything happens to him, my own father will be hard put to it to hold the city, especially if Uncle Izyaslav or Cousin Svyatopolk tries to capture it. Novgorod's the safest place in Rusland, and it suits me quite as well as it suits you and your brothers that Gytha remains there. I only brought her here because your father commanded it.'

'I'd rather take her back myself, to make sure,' Oleg said ungraciously.

'If you don't trust me, why should I trust you?' Vladimir asked, leaning back in his chair. 'How do I know that this isn't just an excuse to make off with her for your own enjoyment? She's very beautiful. After all, you do have a habit of – er – borrowing my belongings, and there's the precedent of Katya Andreyevna . . .'

They both looked at Gytha, who had been listening to their conversation with some irritation at being allowed no say in the matter, mixed with considerable fear that the two cousins might quarrel beyond mending. Vladimir seemed to have his temper well under control, but Oleg was a volatile, arrogant man. If he insisted on having his own way, Vladimir must either give way or . . . what? Fight him? She wondered if he had come with an escort. Presumably others knew where he was, and would come looking for him if he did not return within a certain time.

'Nothing to do with it!' Oleg said indignantly.

Vladimir smiled. 'Try to see it from the point of view of a Kievan boyar, or, say, a Chernigov peasant! Oleg Svyatoslavovich abducts Vladimir Vsevolodovich's beautiful wife. They won't believe you did it simply because you couldn't trust me to take her back to safety after her visit here. You've often tried to find out the limits of my friendship, and now you've succeeded. Everything I have is yours, if you want it, excepting my wife and my honour, and those two things you may not touch. I'd have to protect my own honour by hunting you down, and hers by killing you, or you'd have to kill me, and poor Gytha would then be obliged to go into a nunnery. Meanwhile, the treaty with the Poles, which depends on my going to help them to fight the Czechs, collapses, and they go back to supporting Uncle Izyaslav, while the Pechenegs, Polovtsy and Cumans, hearing that we're busy fighting one another and laughing heartily at our foolishness, do as they please down the length of the River Road and sack our cities! Is that what you want? You've trusted me with your life often enough, yet you can't trust me to keep my sworn oath to Gleb, and you'd risk the whole future of our country over whether my wife returns to Novgorod today, or next week. Really, Oleg! Think!' He had leaned forward during the latter part of this speech, but he now sat back and regarded Oleg quizzically.

The big, fair man, who had remained standing all this while, opened his mouth, shut it again, scowled, shrugged, then suddenly gave a reluctant grin. 'It does sound a bit stupid, if you put it like that,' he admitted. 'Would you like some wine? I've brought some very good stuff with me. Bought it from a Greek merchant.'

Vladimir smiled. 'It would be very welcome. All this talking is thirsty work.'

Oleg summoned the wine by the simple method of opening the door and shouting for it, reminding Gytha of the lack of ceremony at Svein's court, which had contrasted with the more civilised customs of England, just as Oleg's did with those of his brother in Novgorod. She thought to herself that he was very much like the rough Viking leader that his ancestor, Rurik, had been.

The wine arrived, and was served, however, with proper ceremony by servants with white linen napkins draped over their arms, who presented fine golden goblets on bended knee. One of them even placed a dish of honey-cakes within Gytha's reach, presumably thinking that a lady would require something sweet to offset the dryness of the wine. She was reminded again of the bear at the wedding-feast, and was tempted to offer Oleg one, but refrained, as she was not sure whether or not the situation had been resolved.

'So,' said Vladimir, raising his goblet in a toast. 'To our journey next week to Novgorod! Would you care to come with us, Oleg? I'm sure Gleb would be delighted to see you.'

A succession of expressions crossed Oleg's face, starting with a frown, for he had not yet conceded that Gytha was to travel next week with Vladimir instead of today with him. That was followed by surprise, then thought, realisation, relief and, finally, amusement. 'That's a good idea!' he said. 'The hunting's better around Novgorod than it is here! Yes, I'll come, by all means!' After some thought, he continued, 'Vladimir, you didn't really think I was involved in Izyaslav's plot, did you?'

'No more than you really believe that I would break my promise to Gleb,' Vladimir replied ambiguously, then, leaving Oleg to puzzle that out, he turned to Gytha and raised his goblet in a silent toast to her, his eyes glowing in a manner which set her heart racing. 'How did you get her to come with you?' he asked Oleg conversationally.

'I told her you'd been hurt in an accident,' Oleg replied as if nothing untoward had happened.

Vladimir nodded. 'I thought it must have been something of the sort. I couldn't imagine that anything else would have persuaded her to go off with you!'

Gytha was amused to see that Oleg had not noticed that his last sentence was as much an insult to him as a compliment to her, and that both men were regarding her with undisguised approval.

'She turned into a regular termagant when she found out I'd tricked her,' Oleg said musingly, 'I'm glad she's your wife, not mine!' and Gytha thought wryly that honours appeared to be even.

A little later, Vladimir borrowed Oleg's sledge-carriage to take Gytha back to the palace. He travelled in it with her, leaving his horse to be led by one of his escorting *druzhiniki*.

'How did you know where I was?' she asked him as they set off.

'I didn't. I was as much surprised to find you there as you were to see me,' he replied.

'I'm sure he didn't mean me any harm,' she said tentatively.

'I know he didn't. He's a fool only in certain matters. He knows very well that too much depends on his working closely with me to risk anything like that. You saw how quickly he grasped the chance to abandon his plan, once I'd pointed out what could happen if he insisted on carrying it out. He'd obviously acted on impulse – he met you unexpectedly on the stairs, I gather? I think he was already regretting the impulse when I arrived. He won't give you any more trouble, sweetheart. He expected that you'd dissolve into tears or just do as you were told, like his own meek little wife, and found he'd caught a Tatar! I nearly laughed out loud when he said he was glad that you're my wife and not his – I've never agreed with him more about anything in all our lives! But don't let's waste time talking about Oleg. We've another ten minutes at least before we reach the palace – just time for a kiss!'

Gleb seemed more pleased than relieved to see them back when they reached Novgorod, although he had not expected them so soon. 'I thought you'd wait until after the thaw,' he said. 'Even though it's easier to travel so far while the rivers are still frozen, of course, you could have come back on one of the trading-ships. How did you like Kiev, Gytha?'

'Very much,' she replied. 'It's a beautiful city, with so many fine trees and buildings! I should like to go there again in summer one day, when all the trees are in leaf. St Sophia's is magnificent! I'm glad to be back, though. Your palace is so much more comfortable than your father's fine residence, and my friends are here.'

Gleb smiled, obviously pleased, but sounded anxious as he asked, 'Was my father reasonably polite to you? He's – er – a little irascible at times.'

'He was very kind, but I think his leg pains him a great deal. He doesn't talk much,' she replied tactfully.

Mildyth was also glad to be home, and said so, frequently and at length, once she and her mistress were alone in the bedroom. She complained about the length and discomfort of the journey, now it was over, and the cramped conditions in the room which she had shared in Kiev with Gytha's other ladies.

'No room to turn round without bumping into one another, and two of the others – naming no names, mind! – snored. And the stove! No use at all, always either almost out, or so hot that we were all like to suffocate, and the windows sealed up so there was no air, and smelling of smoke all the time. And we weren't accorded our proper places at meals, but pushed in anywhere, even lower than some servants *far* lower in rank than us. I didn't complain, of course, not wanting to make things difficult for you with that old grouch of a Grand Prince, and as for Prince Vladimir's father! Well, if he'd been anyone else's father, I'd have complained about him, I can tell you, with his pinches and his sly grins and his suggestions! Wanted us all in his bed, all six of us, and all at once, I reckon! Yevpraksia gave him a piece of her mind when he squeezed her breasts, and said she'd tell Prince Vladimir if he did it again. Old goat!'

'Mildyth!' Gytha exclaimed, cutting into the flow. 'Why on earth didn't you tell me?'

357

'How could I, with you doing your best to impress them all and win their liking? What could you have said that would do any good and not make them angry with you? There's troubles and quarrels enough in that family without the likes and dislikes of humble folks like me and the other women causing trouble between Prince Vladimir and his father and uncle. No, we put up with it, and I only tell you now so you won't think we're ungrateful if we don't spend the rest of the year saying what a wonderful time we had in Kiev.'

Gytha wondered whether to say anything to Vladimir about Mildyth's revelations concerning his father, but found it unnecessary, for when he joined her that night, he said, 'You must be glad to have that long journey behind you. I know things were difficult for you in Kiev, and I'm grateful to you for putting up with it all so cheerfully. You were so patient with my uncle and father.'

'They were quite kind . . . ' she temporised.

'Svyatoslav was downright rude, and my father's conduct towards your women was disgraceful! Why didn't you tell me what he was up to?'

'I didn't know until Mildyth told me this evening. They thought I had problems enough without being worried by that,' Gytha said ruefully. 'How did you know?'

'Efrem saw him with that pretty little girl with the black eyes – what's her name?'

'Anna?'

'Yes, that's the one. He told me, and I guessed there'd been other – incidents – of a like kind. I spoke to Father about it, but it was the day before we left – rather late. I wish I'd known sooner! Well, some good came of it – Efrem is courting her, and means to see her mother as soon as he can.'

'Her mother?'

'Yes. Mothers arrange their daughters' marriages in Rusland. Don't they in England?'

'Yes, but the hopeful man sees the father about it.'

'Ah, I see. As I was saying – I thought you were the soul of tact with him and my uncle, and the way you handled Oleg was

358

admirable. He told me about his – er – interview with you when he carried you off to his palace. You made quite an impression, for he's not used to being ordered about by an irate princess! I think he's learned to respect the female sex a little more – well, one of its members, at least. Ah, well – it's over, and you can settle down again here. At least you've no troubles of the sort my father causes with Gleb, I take it? He's always been a chaste man, and I think he would like to have been a monk, had he been born to another family.'

Gytha tried to imagine Gleb as a monk, and found it not impossible, for there was a certain air of patience and calm about him which reminded her of the canons at Waltham. On the other hand, his triumphant slaying of the Wonderworker had horrified her, and she knew that there was a ruthless and perhaps violent streak in his nature. Arising from that train of thought, a question which had long troubled the back of her mind rose to the surface, and she asked, 'Vladimir, do you enjoy fighting battles?'

'Enjoy? Gracious Heavens, no! I'm terrified half out of my mind before the fighting starts, desperate to get it over while it's happening, and sick afterwards! I'd much prefer a peaceful life, more like Gleb's.'

'You do remind me of my father,' Gytha murmured, contentedly snuggling against him.

'I'm flattered, but I'd rather be your husband,' he replied, and began to caress her in the way she longed for so much while he was away.

'He loved my mother very dearly,' she said, her mind still lingering on the likeness.

'If she was anything like you, I'm not surprised,' he said, and after that, there was no room in either of their minds for thoughts of anyone else but each other.

They had two brief weeks of happiness together in Novgorod, and then Vladimir set off for Poland, saying that he hoped he had not left it too late to get there before the thaw bogged him down in some wretched village miles from anywhere.

'I'll be back next winter,' he promised, holding Gytha closely

359

as they stood on the steps of the palace, his men waiting in the square. 'I'll write to you as often as I can, and you must write to me, as you did last year. Your letters were such a comfort and delight. You've no idea how much I valued them, and thanked God for a literate wife! I couldn't bear to be so far away from you for so long and have news of you only at second-hand. Write me all your news, your thoughts and feelings, and think of me every night, as I will of you.'

'Of course!' she assured him. 'God bless you, my dear, dear man, and bring you safe home.'

He held her at arm's length, and smiled into her eyes, the old, unreadable mask quite gone, and said, 'It's turned out well, hasn't it – this marriage made by my aunt at the other end of the world? Are you glad you came beyond the sunrise?'

'Very glad.'

'And I!' He kissed her, then turned to clasp Gleb's hand, to kiss the bishop's ring and receive his blessing, then mounted and rode away, without looking back.

Gytha watched him out of sight, then shivered and turned to go indoors, thinking, 'If only I might have been able to tell him that I'm with child before he left. Oh, will I ever be able to say that to him? Please, Lord, please – let me not be barren!'

'I expect he'll be back for Christmas,' Gleb said encouragingly, taking her arm. 'Come and drink some spiced wine – you look pinched with cold. Where's Anastasia? She should have come down with you. She grows more lazy and fat every day, I swear, but, we'll have her out hunting in the summer, shall we, and wear some of the fat off her on horseback, eh? Ah, here's the wine . . . Drink up, and get some colour back in your cheeks. We can't have you catching a chill, can we? Vladimir would never forgive me if I let you fall ill.'

But a few days later she thought she *had* fallen ill. She was perfectly well when she went to bed the night before, but when she got out of bed in the morning, the room swayed and lurched around her, and she sat down abruptly on the edge of the bed, put a hand to her head, and said, 'Oh dear! I think I feel faint!'

'What is it, my pet?' Mildyth, alarmed, hurried to her side. 'What's wrong? Lie down, and let me fetch you a draught of something soothing . . . Peppermint, maybe, or hyssop? Camomile? What would you like?'

'Nothing, thank you,' Gytha replied wretchedly. 'Oh, quick! Fetch a basin! I feel sick!'

Yevpraksia was nearest to the basin, and brought it in time, despite barely avoiding a collision with Mildyth on the way, and Gytha was, indeed, very sick.

'I do hope I haven't caught something!' she gasped between bouts. 'Perhaps I ate something which disagreed with me . . . Oh, dear!'

When her stomach had voided itself, she lay down in the rumpled bed and closed her eyes. Mildyth brought warm water and bathed her face, while Yevpraksia rubbed her feet, which felt cold. After a while she began to feel better, and presently sat up.

'It seems to have passed now,' she said, 'I feel quite well again, and hungry. Oh, I could just eat a whole plate of those little buckwheat cakes, with a great spoonful of soured cream on every one! How peculiar! I've just been so sick, and now I want cream! Whatever's the matter with me?'

Yevpraksia looked puzzled and concerned, but Mildyth began to laugh, and eventually sank down on the edge of the bed, wiping her eyes and hiccuping.

'You don't fancy an onion, or strawberries, do you?' she asked. 'Or both at once? They're the usual things!'

'What do you mean?' Gytha asked, mystified.

'Oh, my dear!' Mildyth sobered suddenly. 'And your man so far away. Pray God he comes home at the right time! When did you last have your courses?'

Startled, Gytha counted on her fingers, then gasped, 'Oh, Mildyth! Do you really think . . . ? Could it really be . . . ?'

Mildyth nodded. 'Early days yet, but I shouldn't be surprised!'

Gytha closed her eyes and prayed hard that it might be so, and this time her prayers were answered. The morning sickness

361

continued, and soon she was able to send a letter to Vladimir with the news that, God willing, she would bear their first child before Christmas.

Waltham

Almost exactly nine months later, a box of books for copying arrived at Waltham from Canterbury. It was two days before Christmas, and Master Athelard did not find time to open it and investigate the contents until Holy Innocents' Day. Turkill helped him, spreading the precious volumes on a cloth-covered table in the Sacristy and pausing to look into each one before lifting out the next.

'What's this?' Athelard had come upon a large roll of parchment in the bottom of the box.

Hastily Turkill cleared a space for it, piling the books carefully, and then the two canons unrolled the stiff sheepskin, taking care not to crack it.

'It's a map of the world!' Athelard exclaimed. 'I saw one, long ago, in Utrecht, but I didn't know that Canterbury Priory had such a treasure!'

Turkill moved a branch of candles a little closer and peered at the colourful drawing. 'A map?' he asked. 'Oh, I see – you mean a picture of the world. Yes, there's Jerusalem in the middle, and the four rivers going out from Eden . . . I've often wondered where Eden was. What a strange shape that is, look – like a leg with a foot – it says Italia . . . and there's Rome!'

'Here's England, right on the edge,' Athelard interrupted from the other side of the map. 'Yes, and somewhere here . . . there it is! Liège, my native city!'

'If Jerusalem's in the middle,' Turkill said thoughtfully, 'there must be many more countries further east. I've always thought of Jerusalem being nearly as far east as anyone can go, but of course there must be places even further, or I couldn't have told little Gytha . . .'

As he spoke, his eyes had travelled northwards across the map from Jerusalem, and now he suddenly drew a sharp, hissing breath, then stood transfixed, staring.

Athelard looked up, saw the expression on his face, and waited in re-

verent silence as the Sacristan's eyes focused on one particular spot, then seemed to follow a series of invisible lines running out from it.

'What do you see?' he whispered.

'A vine. The tendrils of a vine,' Turkill replied abstractedly. 'They have their root there,' pointing to the spot to which his eyes kept returning, 'and they're spreading and growing all over the picture . . . eastwards, westwards . . . Yes, to Francia, and rooting there, and now another branch comes down here . . . What does it say? Graecia, yes . . . Now . . . Oh, God be praised! They come to England! See?'

His finger traced a meandering line across Europe, and he looked up into Athelard's puzzled face.

'You can't see them?' he said, surprised. 'No, of course . . . I was forgetting. It must be to do with Gytha's son, I think. Perhaps it means that his descendants will spread all over Christendom, and one day come back to England. I feel very happy.'

Athelard looked at the map and wondered, but he knew Turkill's foreknowings too well to doubt their truth.

'Yes,' he said. 'Indeed, it would be a happy thing if King Harold's line returned to England one day through dear Gytha's children. A son, you say? Well, well. The Lord bless and keep him. I wonder if she's named him Harold.'

Gytha's and Vladimir's first child, a son, was born in Novgorod and was named by his father. His Slavonic name was Mstislav, meaning Avenger of Glory, and his Christian name was Harold, although no saint of that name appears in the Orthodox calendar. Gytha and Vladimir had six more sons – Izyaslav, Svyatoslav, Yaropolk, Vyacheslav, Roman, Yuri Dolgoruki (the founder of Moscow), and three girls – Evfemia, Agafiya and Marina. Gytha died in 1107. Vladimir later made a political marriage and had another son, Andrei. He died in 1125, having ruled, by popular demand, as Grand Prince of Kiev from 1113.

Mstislav-Harold married Christina of Sweden, and from that marriage are descended both Queen Elizabeth II and Prince Philip, Duke of Edinburgh.

Historical Note

The bare bones of this story can be found in the following:

England
  Florentii Wigorniensis Chronicon ex Chronicus (Florence of
  Worcester)
  Tractatus de Inventione Sancte Crucis Nostre (BM Harleian
  3766)
  Domesday Book
Denmark
  Historia Regus Danicae Compendiosa (Saxo Grammaticus)
Russia
  Lyetopsi Novgoroda (The Chronicle of Novgorod)
  Povest Vremmenikh Let (The Russian Primary Chronicle)
  Po-ucheniye Vladimira Monomakha (The Testament of Vla-
  dimir Monomakh)
  Secondary Sources include *Edward the Confessor,* by Frank Bar-
  low, and *Kievan Russia,* by George Vernadsky.

The quotations from *The Wanderer* are taken from the trans-
lation by Richard Hamer, with his kind permission.